DEMONS & ANGELS

WALKING BETWEEN WORLDS
- BOOK I -

Demons & Angels

Walking Between Worlds
- Book I -

J.K. Norry

Demons & Angels
Walking Between Worlds Book I

ISBN 978-0-9907280-2-3

Second Edition, Published Fall 2019

www.SuddenInsightPublishing.com
Indie publishing for the Indie Author

Acknowledgements

This book has been a culmination of many things coming together for me. I had to become the person that could write this book, and I also had to admit that I needed help with virtually every other aspect of it. A lot of work has gone into making this book a reality, and much of that work was not done by me.

Thanks go out to my dad, Larry Norry, for getting all this started in so many ways. From my actual physical beginning when you delivered me with your own hands, to the first books you let me read that may have been considered age-inappropriate to less evolved parents, to being a supportive and real friend to me in adulthood after I gave you such hell as a child.

Thanks to Bill Irwin, for wisely reminding me that it is better to make a pact with God than to make a deal with the Devil, and for lighting the way in the darkness. I miss your big hugs, Cousin...

Special thanks to my mom, Leslie Irwin, for passing on the writer gene and for your interest and support when it came to this book. Thank you for turning the first couple hundred pages of my chicken scratch into an electronic document, for the precious long hours you spent translating "Jayanese" to English and typing, typing, typing...

Thanks to all the authors who gave me license to listen to the strange and wonderful voices in my head and consider the possibility that these stories playing out in a dimension near me might deserve writing down: Richard Bach, Piers Anthony, Isaac Asimov, Ray Bradbury, J.R.R. Tolkien, George R.R. Martin, Stephen King, and Bill Ferguson, to name some favorites...

Thanks to my angels and lights, for whispering sweet love in my ear and guiding me always towards greater love...

Thanks to my devils and demons, for giving me a resistance worth overcoming, a thousand voices to keep me humble, and a complicated but beautiful dance worth learning.

And special thanks to Dawn...my "Awesome Girl", my best friend and my sweet love, for all the typing and editing and formatting, for the websites and the blog and an online presence that can actually be referred to as "social networking" in all seriousness. Thank you for making my story into a book and for making so many dreams come true...

Thank you, God, for making everything possible...

THIS ONE'S FOR YOU, DAD . . .

CHAPTER 1

The alarm clock was going off, a high-pitched grating pulse of sound echoing loudly off the walls. It had been going off for a while, but the shapeless form huddled under the covers made no move to silence it.

It was a small room, dirty and messy at the same time. There was an ashtray on every surface; the nightstand, the dresser, the mismatched speakers that cluttered every corner. Every ashtray was full, overflowing with cigarette butts and half-smoked joints. Posters and tapestries decorated the walls in a random rock theme that spanned the decades. The white walls were yellowed with age and smoke, cobwebs wisping where they met the ceiling.

Against one wall was an electric guitar on an upright stand, the only thing in the room that didn't look like junk, a dark blue Fender Stratocaster. A black cord trailed from its snug housing in the body of the guitar to a knee-high amplifier sitting nearby. Another ashtray sat on the amp, a dusting of ashes all around it. A small television was housed in a beat up oak entertainment center whose remaining shelves were dominated by long tangles of guitar pedals and extension cords, open empty compact disc cases and a haphazard teetering stack of old vinyl.

A steady rhythmic pounding joined the blare of the alarm clock, and a voice shouted muffled through the wall. The thin sheetrock shook with the force of the pounding.

The covers stirred, an arm reached out from beneath them and silenced the alarm. Mason threw the covers off and rolled out of bed, his feet clumsily finding the floor. He sat on the edge of the mattress for a long moment, elbows on his knees and his face buried in his hands. Heaving a sigh, he peeked a look at the digital face of the alarm clock. He cursed.

Then he was a flurry of action, dressing himself frantically in jeans and sweatshirt. One moment sitting still in boxers and a stained tank top, his mussed longish hair askew in every direction; the next he was up and moving, opening and closing dresser drawers and tripping through piles of soiled clothes on the floor. Two doorways cut the wall opposite the entrance into thirds, one a doorless passage into his small excuse for a kitchen and the other a door open to the cramped bathroom. Dashing in and out of the open door, he emerged first with his hair wet and flattened to his head, then with a toothbrush sticking from his mouth, then with a hand towel he held cautiously to his dripping face. He crinkled his nose in distaste and threw it to the floor. Wiping droplets of water from his skin with the sleeve of his sweatshirt, Mason worked his feet into his sneakers and bent to tie the darkened laces.

On his way out the door, he stopped at an ashtray and pulled two half-smoked joints from the ugly collection of twisted stained tan speckled filters. A smashed cigarette butt fell from the ashtray to roll onto the speaker and from there to the stiff carpet below. Mason didn't bother to pick it up. He put one joint in his pocket and one between his lips and walked out the front door.

CHAPTER 2

Paul pushed his way through the swinging steeled glass into the coffee shop. The jangle of the bell hanging over the door announced his arrival, and he stopped a moment just inside the entrance to gaze about the room. A wave of aroma greeted him, the warm welcome smell of fresh brewed coffee tickling his nostrils pleasantly.

The place was huge, especially considering how many customers frequented the spot. Longer than it was wide, the single room was wide enough yet for four tables, the coffee bar and aisles between all of them. A paneled wooden island on a sea of hardwood floor, the coffee bar was long and narrow, twin counters mirroring each other with matted work space between. Two people behind the bar would have trouble passing without touching, but the length of it would let three or four people move about freely. Stools were placed along the length of the bar for customers, steel and vinyl and old and currently unoccupied. The island was closed at one end by a cash register facing the entrance and a swinging waist-high door at the opposite end. A slab of counter on hinges served as horizontal barrier above the thin swinging door. Sturdy wooden tables were placed almost randomly about the open hardwood floor. There were less than twenty, though the space could have easily held twice that. Only three were occupied, less than half a dozen customers in the whole place.

Paul approached the register as the girl behind the counter turned to see who had come in. She smiled, a pretty sweet smile under pretty honeyed blonde hair and pretty bright blue eyes.

"Good morning, Paul," she said. "White mocha?"

"Morning, Jessica," Paul smiled back. "Yes, please."

"Brenna's here," Jessica inclined her head toward a table in the back while she rung up his order. "Anything to eat?"

"Yeah, a blueberry muffin," Paul answered, digging his wallet out of his back pocket. He dropped a dollar bill in the tip jar that sat next to the register and handed her a twenty. She counted out his change and reached across the counter.

As their hands touched, Paul heard an explosion. Loud and muffled at the same time, it was followed by a thin, shrill scream. He jerked his hand back, looking around the shop bewildered. No one stirred or looked up; no one did anything. His eyes met hers, his heart pounding.

"You okay?" Jessica asked him. She was still holding out his change, but her look had become one of concern.

Paul looked around again. "You didn't hear that?" he asked her quietly.

"Hear what?" She cocked her head to listen.

"Nothing." Paul shook his head. "I must be hearing things. Thanks, Jess." He took his change and walked the length of the bar. It wasn't until he was almost at Brenna's table that he noticed the big man huddled over another table in the corner furthest from the entrance.

"Morning, Roche." Paul called to him.

Surrounded by books and ledgers sprawled haphazardly across the table, the man seemed oblivious to his environment. A big round head sat atop his mountainous shoulders, bald and topped with a battered black fedora. A blue pocket tee tried to contain the bulk of his torso, and a pack of cigarettes strained the pocket on his left breast even further. He made a notation in the ledger before him, cursed, erased it, and glanced up.

"Paul," he nodded, then looked back down at the page before him.

Brenna had her laptop on the table and a tablet of hand-written notes beside it. They both sat neatly square with the edge of the tabletop, a cup of coffee just within reach on one side and an untouched slice of lemon poundcake on the other. She stopped typing as he approached and looked up at him.

Her hair was black and straight, parted down the middle to brush against her shoulders equally on both sides. The dark of her hair was in stark contrast to her smooth and milky white skin, and her face was a study in perfection. High cheekbones, full red lips and a small button of a nose all took a backseat to the beauty of her eyes, though. So brown they were almost black, Brenna's eyes seemed to swirl with depth and beauty and sensuality. She had a way of looking up at him without raising her head that he found adorably breathtaking. A little horizontal line appeared across her forehead, and her big dark eyes got bigger and somehow more beautiful. It was how she was looking at him now. A slow smile started on her lips as their eyes met, and Paul leaned over to cover it with his own smile. She tasted of coffee and mint and lipstick.

"Good morning, gorgeous," Paul sat next to her as she snapped shut the laptop. She took a moment to close the notebook and set it perfectly square on top of the computer, then slid them both to the center of the table.

When she was done, she turned sideways in her chair toward Paul and put her hand on his knee and her full attention on him. He saw the agate oval that hung always at her throat from a delicate silver chain, hovering over the modest cut of her light blouse.

"Good morning, my love." Her voice was soft and low, and her eyes lingered on his. "Are we still on for tonight?"

Paul nodded while Jessica approached the table with his order. "Absolutely," he told Brenna, then looked up at Jessica while she placed the coffee and muffin on the table. "Thanks, Jess."

He sipped his coffee and turned again to Brenna. "Where's your brother?"

She rolled her eyes and frowned a little. "He didn't come home last night." When she saw Paul's frown, she squeezed his knee gently. "Don't worry, he'll be here. Where's Kris?"

"Running late. As usual." A plain round clock hung on the wall above Roche, and Paul turned to glance at it. He reached across the table and slid Brenna's breakfast and fork in front of her. "Better eat while you have time," he said, and took a giant bite of his muffin. Crumbs littered the table while he reached to snatch a paper napkin from the small stack by her plate.

Her fingers, slim and delicate, moved from Paul's knee to pick up her fork. She cut a small perfect square from the corner of the cake and slid the fork underneath it gingerly. She chewed slowly and deliberately as she spread a paper napkin over her right knee. She swallowed, had a sip of coffee, and turned her gaze on Paul again.

"What time tonight?" she asked.

Paul shrugged. "I should be home about six or six thirty. I can be at your place by seven." He took another sip of his white mocha. It was cooling down, so he took a long drink.

"Okay," she nodded. She glanced at the clock, and her fingers strayed unconsciously to the amulet at her throat. "I should probably get going." Brenna was never late. For anything. Ever.

The door opened then, the bell clanging noisily as two young men entered arguing.

Tall, with dark hair cut short and styled to careless perfection, one man moved his hands excitedly as he spoke. "It's called a pre-emptive strike," he was saying loudly. "The best defense is a good offense."

His companion was shorter, with a slight build and more subtle gestures. He was shaking his head slowly. Blue jeans and tee shirt and a light jacket all hung loose on his frame, and his hands were stuffed into the pockets of his jacket. Light brown hair covered his head in disheveled clumps, constantly threatening to fall into his eyes.

"How can you be the one defending yourself if you are the asshole that strikes first?" He was still shaking his head. "How can you know what would happen if you didn't attack if you always open with an attack?"

"It's the nature of the beast," the dark-haired one answered with finality. "These savages will move in at the first sign of weakness." His smile came as easily as the other's frown, and he seemed to be clearly enjoying the banter.

His companion appeared visibly uncomfortable, on the other hand. "We're not talking about war, we're talking about women," he said icily. He pulled his hands from his pockets and pushed a lump of hair from his forehead, quickly sweeping the room with a shy stare. Sharp gray eyes took it all in and came to rest on the girl standing behind the register. His eyes widened a little, a shy smile lit his face for a moment; then he looked away and stuffed his hands back in his pockets.

"Good morning, Jessica," he said, staring at the floor. He pronounced her name carefully, like it was a sacred thing.

"Hey, Kris," she replied, glancing away from the taller man behind him for a moment and then back. With a voice lower and slower she said, "Good morning, Matt."

"Hey, Jess," Matt answered as he stepped between Kris and the counter. "Two cups of your finest house brew, please. My companion will surely need cream and sugar; he can only swallow life and coffee masked by false sweetness."

"I customize my coffee to my taste," Kris said defiantly. He threw a scornful look at Matt and a softer one at Jessica before returning his eyes to the floor. "I don't just drink any dark and bitter brew someone else serves up for me."

A bark of laughter, and Matt called out to the man at the back of the room. "Hey Roach, Kris thinks your coffee is dark and bitter."

"*Roche!*" The man called out without looking up, correcting the intentional mispronunciation with deliberate rudeness. He made a mark in the journal before him, closed it, and stood up. Glaring balefully at Matt, he grumbled, "He was talking about life, not coffee, jackass." Roche turned to Kris. "Good morning, young man," he said, almost smiling. "Still casting your pearls before swine?"

It was Kris' turn to laugh. By the time he returned the greeting, Roche had turned and gone through the door at the back wall that said 'OFFICE' on a black and white plastic plaque affixed firmly at eye level. It slammed shut behind him.

Kris walked to their table, doffing his jacket and hanging it on his chair as he sat, while Matt got their coffee and followed him over.

"Hey, guys," Matt said casually as he sat lightly on a chair across from Brenna, setting his companion's cup on the table as he took the adjacent seat.

"You're late," Brenna said. Her voice was forgiving and reproachful at the same time.

"The day doesn't start until I start the day," Matt grinned. "I'm always on time, little sister."

"Drink your coffee," she said, ignoring him. "Don't make Paul late for work."

He ignored her for a moment too, reaching across the table to seize the rest of her lemon pound cake. Picking it up with his fingers, he bit off half of what was left in one huge bite and raised an eyebrow at her across the table. He gulped loudly, took a long pull off his coffee, gasped at the heat, gulped again and asked, "You weren't going to eat that, were you?"

Brenna rolled her eyes and stood up. "I've got to go," she announced. She looked hard at Matt. "I believe we all do."

Matt gazed up at his sister, and Paul was struck anew at how alike they could look sometimes. The very expression that was adorable to him on Brenna he thought made Matt appear a helpless silly puppy dog. Matt's long string of lovers surely thought it the other way around.

They made for the door all at once, cutting the number of customers in the coffee shop by half in one fell swoop. When they reached the door, Paul opened it and stood back, holding it open for the rest of them. Brenna reached out and brushed her fingers lightly across his abdomen, passing by first. Matt made as if to punch him in the gut as he walked by, his good-natured feint ending inches from Paul's stomach. As Kris passed, he mumbled thanks to Paul and stole one last glance at Jessica over his shoulder as she waved goodbye to the group. A smile played on the corners of his mouth as his eyes met Paul's...

...And when their eyes met, Paul heard it again: a loud thunderous crash, followed by a blood-curdling scream. It was louder this time, and he blanched, letting go of the door. It swung shut, barely missing Kris as he stepped hastily outside. Hanging there above the swinging steel and glass, the little brass bell bumped and rolled over the top of the door, clanging noisily. It clanged again as Kris opened the door and poked his head in, a concerned look on his face.

"You look like you've seen a ghost," Kris said, stepping inside again. "Are you okay, man?"

Jessica had come up behind him, looking just as concerned. "Paul? Are you alright?" She touched his shoulder lightly.

"Yeah, I'm fine," Paul forced a smile. "You guys didn't hear that?"

"Hear what?" Jessica and Kris asked together.

"Nothing." Paul shook his head, as if to clear it, and reached for the door again. The brass bell danced across the swing of steel, its last frayed thread giving way a little bit, but not breaking. It clanged again as the door swung shut behind them; then it hung silent and still, just a little lower than it had before.

Gathered outside, Brenna couldn't decide who to fuss over. She turned to Matt, but her eyes kept coming back to Paul. Taking Paul's hand, she spoke stern to her brother. "You should take him home; let him call in to work for both of you."

Paul was shaking his head. "I'm fine, sweetie." Encircling his arm around her slim waist, he pulled her close. "Besides, it's his first day, if I do get him a job. He can't call in on his first day."

Dark pools of love looked up at him, but her eyes turned to black ice when she looked at Matt. "He'll find a way to screw it up anyway."

Paul nuzzled Brenna's hair, in part to breathe in the smell of her and in part to hide his smile. Looking over the top of her head, he noticed a man standing across the street watching them. His garb oddly both out of season and out of place, he stared at Paul intently with neither guile nor candor. The man wore a leather cowboy hat and matching leather overcoat hanging from broad shoulders nearly to the ground. Leather boots poked out from under the long duster.

His whole outfit seemed cut from the same bolt of thick leather. Surely striking when new, the ensemble now hung limp, battered and worn. A deep oiled brown on the armpits, the overcoat was faded to a dry blond in many places. Clumsy stitches held the coat together in three different places with three different colors. At its hem, the trench coat looked scorched, and the boots had the same beaten and battered and burnt color. Banded in what looked like dull red snakeskin, the leather cowboy hat was perhaps the most abused part of his whole outfit. Misshapen by a dent, it looked like a part of the brim had been sliced off clean. A pair of holes the size of marbles punctuated the planned hollows of the hat, a few inches forward from the unnatural grapefruit-sized concavity. Apparently there were matching holes on the other side, as Paul could see daylight through them when the man turned his head slightly. He could also see little black rings around the holes, like scorch marks.

Paul was overwhelmed by an otherworldly feeling as he looked at the strange man, and he swooned a bit as he brought himself back into his world of Matt and Kris. And Brenna. He breathed her in deep, glad she hadn't noticed him waver a moment earlier. Paul focused on their words as she argued with her brother.

"It's like you think I can't do anything right," Matt was complaining. The only time he was not the picture of strength and confidence was around his sister. All it took was a critical word from Brenna, and the man became a boy again.

"No, you're good at lots of things," Brenna responded blithely. "Short and shallow relationships, making promises you don't keep, pissing away money." Her body was stiff and rigid against Paul, only increasing the discomfort he always felt when the siblings went at it. Later, he knew, he could look forward to each of them seeking a private moment with him to complain at length about the other. He would validate both of them, feeling they were each wrong in their way but never saying so. She knew her weaknesses and her limits; it was his happy job to let her blow off steam without fear of criticism. And her brother…well, lecturing Matt was as useless and obvious as telling a tree it is made of wood.

Paul pulled Brenna close to him. "Sweetie," he said. He was going to say, "We have to get going", but the door opened behind them, swinging inward to the coffee shop.

After announcing countless arrivals and departures, hanging as silent sentinel in between, the brass bell clanged once as it climbed over the top of the door one last time. Rolling, it clanged again and then again and dropped to the length of the one last thread holding it suspended. The thread snapped soundlessly, and the bell fell just as silently through open space. It clanged again as it hit the floor and half-rolled, half-skittered between the four friends and to the edge of the sidewalk. One more roll and it would have been in the street. Instead, it sat at the curb; silent, still and unnoticed.

CHAPTER 3

Mason drove with one hand on the wheel and the other constantly busy with some other vitally important task. Crossing Third Avenue, his right hand flipped through the pages of a thick case full of compact discs. Bloodshot eyes dancing between the road before him and the choices on the seat beside him, pages turned past Led Zeppelin and Pink Floyd, Sheryl Crow and Jewel, Megadeth, Bob Dylan, Katy Perry, even a Garth Brooks CD. He turned rapidly until he had gone past two pages full of AC/DC discs. Turning back a page, stealing a quick glance at the road, he slid a disc from its plastic sleeve and smoothly into the player on the dash. As the first strains of *Hell's Bells* filled the car, a slight smile softened Mason's face for a moment.

The passenger seat was for more than just music. A pack of Camel Lights lay next to a powder blue Bic lighter right where he had tossed them when he got in the car. The half-burnt roach in his mouth became smoky breakfast as orange flame leapt from the lighter. The windshield was lost behind a cloud of white-blue smoke for a moment while he dropped the lighter onto the seat next to him again, grasped the wheel with his right hand and worked the window crank with his left.

Smoke swirled out the thumb's width opening, and the windshield cleared to reveal a green light on Seventh and a clear road ahead. There weren't even any pedestrians on the sidewalk.

Mason swung down the visor and met his own eyes in the mirror inset for a long moment, hazel on white shot with red. The joint left his mouth for the first time since he had left the apartment, as he flipped the visor back into place and gently stubbed the smoking tip into the ashtray.

There were pedestrians at Eighth Avenue, two slim asian girls in shorts and tank tops and running shoes. They pumped their legs up and down, waiting for the signal and chatting while their sneakers tattooed a light rhythm on the sidewalk. Mason rolled to a smooth stop as the signal changed and watched bobbing ponytails and small dancing breasts cross in front of his car. One girl, young and pretty and all in shades of blue, glanced over in the last moment before they cleared his car. By then, Mason had turned away to look in the center console for some eye drops.

By the time the light turned to his favor, Mason had carefully squirted a few drops in each eye, wiped a little remainder and a bit of sleep from each eye, and relit the joint.

Brian Johnson was singing the first few bars of *Back in Black* as Mason slipped his foot off the brake pedal and mashed the accelerator. The vehicle lurched forward, trailing cannabis smoke and guitar riffs and picking up speed.

CHAPTER 4

With her left foot in the coffee shop and her right in the street, Jessica propped the door open behind her with one hand. The other held Kris' jacket, folded neatly to hang evenly from either side of her hand as she proffered it to him. Her smile was pretty and shy, and her bright blue eyes widened as she spoke.

"You forgot your…" Jessica took in the faces of the other three in a glance and must have sensed that she was intruding on a tense moment, "…jacket," she finished quietly, looking back at Kris as he took it from her.

"Thanks, Jess." Kris had his own shy smile for her; and after reclaiming the jacket, he stepped back two quick steps and then a third, slower. As he placed his right foot, toe to heel, his instep came down on the little brass bell that lay there on the sidewalk. He pitched backward suddenly and when he shifted his other foot it came down on the edge of the curb, throwing him even further off balance. The expression on his face was a combination of momentary panic riddled with embarrassment as he looked to Jessica. They all stepped forward to help, instinctively; Paul, Brenna and Matt all moving at the same time. All a moment too late.

Jessica began to start forward with the others, eyes on Kris as he tilted precariously backwards in a slow motion, unstoppable fall. Her gaze went through him suddenly then, eyes widening as they went out of focus while her mouth hinged open to scream. Then came the sound of an explosion, a rapid report that ripped through the morning chill with a suddenness and a loudness that turned all their heads to the sound. All but Kris, who was busy falling awkwardly backward into the street and into the path of the blue van hurtling cock-eyed toward him on a blown out front tire. Behind the windshield the driver sat slumped over the steering wheel, lifeless, as the vehicle canted toward the curb and the helplessly falling young man.

A shrill scream split the air, and Paul had a moment to wonder if the blown tire or Jessica's scream had come first. He watched Kris windmill his arms as one foot held onto the edge of the curb, and Paul found himself thinking, absurdly, *this isn't happening*. Then he watched his friend fall backwards into the street; and before Kris could land or take another step, the van caught him up in its grill and launched him bodily out in front of it.

A rag doll in jeans and tee shirt, Kris flew sideways through the air. Blood streaked the right side of his face, and his lower left leg stretched forward at an unnatural angle. His limp body turned slowly, almost gracefully, until the slow spin brought his head into the path of a street mailbox. Tall and wide and blue and bolted to the ground, the metal box let out a dull thud as it ended Kris' macabre flight. But for that and a small smear of blood down its side, the unyielding blue box was unaffected by the encounter.

Then the van took it, metal meeting metal in a nasty shriek of sound that would leave them both changed forever. Its side struck the mailbox at the same odd angle it had caught Kris, the rear end swinging slowly with the impact to keep the objects locked together in a long screeching kiss as the front tires straddled Kris lying unmoving on the street in their passing. The blown tire made an unnatural rhythmic thumping sound as it rolled inches from his bloodied face. A hot exhaust pipe loomed suddenly, though his eyes were not open to see it, but his twisted leg was caught then by a rear tire. It spun him so he thumped first onto the street, around to strike the broad undercarriage of the vehicle, then again against the hard asphalt. His body was spit out behind the wild charge of the metallic beast to land unceremoniously in a twisted tangled bloody heap on the pavement.

Impossibly, he moaned.

Paul dashed into the street to help his friend. He knelt beside him, reaching out gingerly, afraid to touch him. Movement caught his vision peripherally, but it didn't register. All that mattered was Kris, his friend, his best friend, his bloody battered broken best friend. Trying to find a pulse, trying to find wrist or neck without shifting or moving his body and possibly hurting him more, Paul was clenching his jaw and blinking back tears; but his hands were gentle as they flew over his friend's inert huddled form.

It wasn't until the second scream started that he realized the first had ended. This time it was Brenna who saw it coming first, and started screaming. There was a long unreal moment before Paul added it up in his mind, the movement from the corner of his eye and Brenna screaming. She was not screaming from grief or shock at what had just happened to Kris. Hers was a scream of anguish, the same as Jessica's had been, seeing what was about to happen.

Paul looked up, suddenly acutely aware of his surroundings. Everything seemed to be happening so fast, too quickly to react, while at the same time the seconds felt like they were ticking by in exaggerated slow motion to his mind. When he looked up, his back was to his friends and he faced the street opposite the side they stood on. The last thing he saw before the car took him was the man in the strange leather ensemble, striding toward him brusquely and seeming to pay no mind to the oncoming vehicle.

He had a thick book in one hand, bound in the same bolt of brown leather as the man himself, and his other hand was worrying at something that seemed affixed to the front cover. Finally, it came loose and he held it in his hand tight, closing his fist around it. One hand stuffed the leather bound book into a wide pocket on the side of his flowing duster. The other held out the object to Paul insistently as the man halted before him. Standing up and reaching out at the same time, Paul's hand clasped the proffered object, round and flat and glinting gold. As his fingers closed around it, the front bumper of a forest green Chevy Malibu caught him by the shin and tossed him into the air. There came another forever moment then; and as he spun slowly in empty space he somehow saw everything happening all around him in that moment.

A strange bright orb of light formed around the man with the leather hat. His form blurred, then drowned in the light, which shrunk to a pinpoint and disappeared. A ripple started at the vanishing and spread outward rapidly like a wave, turning the air to a warped version of itself as it spread, like the air rippling above a scorching fire. It passed through Paul and he felt a calm come over him, the ridiculous feeling that everything was going to be okay.

Churning the air, the ripple of energy passed through Kris next, and his crumpled form seemed to shift in a relaxing sigh as it settled lower on the pavement.

Matt and Brenna were both advancing on Paul, in slow motion, and the curve of the ripple caught them both at the same time. They each seemed to wink out of existence for a split second as the wave passed through them, and when they winked back into existence they were no longer coming toward him. Matt was on his knees, kneeling with his hands in his lap as he stared slack-faced and unseeing at the pavement. Brenna stood rigid and still, no longer screaming. One hand covered the other and that hand clasped the gemstone at her throat. Though she looked right at him, Paul got the sense she wasn't seeing him at all.

He saw the ripple take Jessica last. She was thrown back violently by it, and as he watched she bounced off the wall of the coffee shop and slid slowly to the sidewalk, unconscious.

The moment somehow lasted long enough for Paul to wonder if he was going crazy or just pleasantly hallucinating away his final seconds before his face flattened against the windshield in a spatter of blood. Suddenly forever ended with a dull squishing thud, and his world went black.

CHAPTER 5

Pinching the end between thumb and forefinger, Mason took three quick puffs from the dwindling roach, then one long last pull. Just as his lungs reached capacity, a red fiery tendril crept suddenly along the paper to his finger and burned him.

Mason cursed, flinging it away instinctively, violently, then cursed again when he realized what he had done. He took a long look at the road, saw the green light ahead on Nineteenth Avenue, then dedicated his vision to scanning seats and dash and floorboards to find the burning roach.

One hand held the wheel straight while the other hovered, moving over floorboards and under his seat, scanning for heat. His eyes darted this way and that about the car, no longer sleepy but alert and narrowed as he looked for a tendril of smoke drifting from some hidden place. One darting glance looked at the road ahead, but he was leaning over and all he saw was the green light hanging above the street and the top of the speeding blue van he had been trying to keep up with for several blocks now.

Mason cocked his head to the side, mildly startled by a distant sound that was all but lost in the high volume soup of sound that filled the car. Was that boom an offbeat bass drum, did that scream belong to someone other than Brian Johnson? Before his mind could wonder, his questing hand felt heat, and warm fingers of smoke curled around his own.

He laid his hand down, upside down under his seat and felt the sharp bite of pain along with the shape of the roach. Turning his hand, leaning over enough to shove half his arm under the seat, he tracked his progress by watching the top of the rear end of the blue van. With deft movements he pinched the roach between thumb and forefinger, dragged his arm out from under the seat and sat up straight.

The first sound was quiet, a muffled thump as his bumper hit something. The next sound was louder, another dull thump that happened only inches from his face as something hit the windshield. No, not something; *someone.* Mason saw it clearly, a split second image that somehow burned itself into his brain forever without him quite having time to register it fully in the moment. It was a face, a face pressed up against the windshield with such force that it flattened against the glass more than it seemed it should have, skin and cheek and chin all puddling shapelessly in a bloody mass of flesh through a thin sheet of transparency a breath from Mason's widened eyes.

Then the face was gone, leaving a smear of blood on the windshield and a clear view of what lie ahead. After careening off the mailbox, the big blue van had drifted out into the street again, only to climb the sidewalk one last time as it leaned in the direction of its flat tire. It ended its wave of destruction with a flourish, crashing headlong into a metal and glass bus shelter with the explosive sound of metal on metal and several sheets of glass shattering all at once. Rear wheels turned in place uselessly, the crushed grill of the van nuzzling the twisted frame of the shelter repeatedly with earnest violence. One tire stained the sidewalk over and over, letting out a little stink of rubber with each chirp. The broad rear end of the van hung awkwardly into the street on the other side, and that tire chirped and spun in place on the asphalt.

Mason saw the twisted wreck, stomped the brake and turned the wheel hard to the left. The tires squealed in protest, but the car swung around the van somehow before the rear wheels started to slide sideways. Mason's foot flashed from brake pedal to gas pedal and stomped it to the floorboard as he cranked the wheel. The tires squealed again, but the rear end swung neatly into line and he was suddenly pointed in the right direction and moving fast. He let up on the accelerator, but not so much that he stopped picking up speed.

Through two green lights and one red he sped, heedless of traffic laws and blind to all but the road before him. At Twenty-third, he slowed and signaled, taking a right turn and creeping slowly along the curb three quarters of a block before coming to a stop. He realized that his music was still blaring, and he tore down the thick wall of sound with the push of a button. His heart pounded in the disturbing silence.

Idling, the car sat at the curb quietly for long minutes. In the driver's seat, Mason sat with both hands on the wheel and stared straight ahead, his eyes fixed on the smear of blood on the windshield. He should go back, he knew he should. There was a wrecked vehicle and a smashed bus shelter and maybe people needing help. There was also a guy with his face smashed in probably lying in the street dead or dying.

Mason shook his head. No matter how much time he might spend in a room with iron bars for walls, that guy's face was not going to be any less smashed for it. If he was dead, Mason couldn't bring him back to life by turning himself in. He fished in the back seat for a moment and came up with a red oil rag, stained with streaks of brown. Calmly, he freed himself from his seat belt, pushed open the door and stepped out of the car. He rubbed at the bloodstain on the windshield vigorously for half a minute, then leaned in the open driver's side window and pressed the end of the plastic arm protruding from the right side of the steering column. A mist of light blue liquid showered the windshield, the wipers following the spray automatically with three quick swipes.

He wiped one stubborn spot of blood away and leaned in close to inspect the now spotless glass. Next he walked to the front of the vehicle and leaned over, making sure bumper and hood were unblemished. Then he crossed the sidewalk, knelt in front of a nearby hedge, and vomited quietly. When he threw up, he closed his eyes; and when he closed his eyes he saw a flattened puddle of bloodied flesh. So he opened his eyes again, walked back to his car, got in and drove away.

CHAPTER 6

Dreams had always been times of fun and happy adventure for Paul, easily controlled and easily remembered in detail afterward. This was a dream, a grand and elaborate dream, and he knew it for sure because he had been here before. He had walked these hallways and heard the soft murmurings of voices from the far side of closed doors. He had explored windowless rooms here, full of books with intricately bound covers full of blank pages.

He had always had a room in this place, as far back as he had dreamed and remembered the dreaming. There was a time when he had come here often, but that time was long past. The room had changed over the years, time shifting reality and dreams alike in its passing. As a boy, he had found this room to be nearly identical to the room he called his own in the house his parents owned. A little bed, a dresser, a toy chest and a bookshelf, pieces of a sturdy stained oak set that his parents had bought, all shared identical places in both worlds.

The rest was similar, but similar was not the same, and small differences can make a thing infinitely more interesting. On the shelf in his parents' house, books were lined neatly along the bottom shelf and halfway across the next shelf where the line of books abruptly terminated at the bookend that held them upright. The piece was heavy, a pewter likeness of a tyrannosaurus rex posed forever on the verge of a vicious attack. Finely wrought, its eyes were thin slits above a maw full of sharp teeth, muscular legs coiled taut under it in a leap that would never come. Nearly all of his toys had been dinosaurs at one point, rubber and plastic creatures that had all died a thousand fantastic deaths at each others' hands in his child's imagination. In dreams, the creatures came to life, remaining on the upper shelves but writhing madly and gnashing their teeth. They would stay in place until Paul called them forth in his mind, then leap from the shelf to the carpet below. In his other room, he had to hold a dinosaur in each hand and clack them awkwardly against one another to simulate battle, or position one on the floor or a shelf to swoop in and attack with another in hand.

In this room, stiff plastic and molded rubber became moving, living flesh, and Paul could watch the creatures tear each other apart without producing and directing the scene. There was no gore or gruesomeness about it, blood wasn't spattered about walls and carpet even when leg or head were torn from a dinosaur's body. Blood and gore were not a part of his imaginings, or his ability to imagine at that age, and this room was limited only by what he could imagine. He was just a little boy who thought it would be pretty cool to see dinosaurs fight, and in his mind that was how they fought.

Toys come to life was not the only difference between the two rooms. The same door that opened onto the carpeted hallway leading to his parents' room at one end and the living room at another, in this world revealed dimly lit stone hallways reaching infinitely into the darkness in either direction. Exploring those hallways had been dream fun for him from time to time over the years. Some of the stout wooden and wrought iron doors were somehow always locked to him, but most opened at a touch or a thought or a word, and otherworldly adventure always beckoned from within.

What other people might call a nightmare sometimes stalked him through hallways or lurked behind a doorway, but Paul could always just think of his room and be there again in this world. Fear never haunted his dreamscape, danger was always flavored by the rich taste of adventure rather than an anxious bile. Gleefully, he fought battles and rescued maidens and sailed the seas and floated in space. Each adventure was a mission, undertaken and accomplished all in a night's sleep, and he always woke feeling both renewed and resolved.

A window opened up over toy box in one world turned treasure chest in the other looked out over the same backyard in both worlds. He could go out the window in his dreams, fly over the neighborhood or the prettier countryside nearby. Once he had gone out the window, turned around and come back in the living room window. His parents were side by side on the couch, his arm around her shoulders and her head leaning back into the cradle of his elbow. Paul couldn't understand what the people on the television were saying, nor could he understand his father's words when he turned his head and spoke quietly.

Paul had walked to stand between them and the lighted screen, and they had stared right through him. They started to kiss then, and Paul was both bored and mildly disgusted by the scene. He had gone off to other adventures more exciting.

In the room that he called his which actually belonged to his parents, the closet was just a closet. Clothes and shoes and old discarded toys were all it contained. Here, the closet was no closet at all but a magic door. He imagined it a portal to some other place or time and it was; thinking of long walls lined with weapons and charms to equip him for some grand astral adventure, he would open the door to an armory of swords and shields, daggers and crossbows, amulets and scrolls. The only things that might not lie beyond that door were the things he couldn't think of, and he couldn't think of anything he couldn't think of.

Both rooms had been left behind long ago in the slow forgetting that is growing up. Then the forgetting itself had been forgotten, and Paul's daytime pursuits of a place in the real world had found their way into his nightscape. His dreams had become disjointed whispering and ghostly images to be evaporated by morning light and forgotten. Perhaps he still came here in his dreams, but he could not recall when he had last come here deliberately or woke remembering having been here. In the other world, the house belonged to some other family now, the room to someone else.

Being here now brought back a flood of memories, and the wondering of how he could have left behind such a big part of his childhood so completely. Looking around the room, the only dinosaur left was the pewter bookend, and the books it held were the science fiction and fantasy novels Paul had taken to reading when in fourth or fifth grade. The few toys scattered about the room were action figures poised in mock battle against each other on bookshelf and windowsill. One hung from a black string affixed to a plastic grappling hook snug between the pages of a hardbound book, pointing a futuristic laser rifle at a tiny man dressed in khakis just beginning to raise his own weapon.

The state of the room marked the timeline clearly; he was ten or eleven years old when he stopped playing with action figures and starting reading books and playing Dungeons and Dragons with his dad and Kris. Most of the little fighting men had been put away or given away or broken, but a few favorites had been placed here and there locked in mortal combat together.

He was here now, though; and he didn't know why. This place of power from his childhood was a place of helplessness now, the window gone, the closet just a closet, the action figures lifeless, and the hallway outside dark and foreboding and completely uninviting.

He knew where he wanted to be, and sometimes if he lay still and quiet on his back he could hear Brenna's voice. It came through a thick fog, words garbled and twisted beyond understanding. It was Brenna, though, her voice full of concern and love, and he melted into tones and textures as he missed every word.

Time passed, but he didn't know how much, and he caught himself wondering as he lay there whether falling asleep in this world would cause him to wake in Brenna's. No matter the effort he put into it, he couldn't seem to drift off, and thus engaged almost didn't hear the doorknob turning. Almost.

No one had ever entered this room before, invited or unbidden. Paul sat up quickly to watch the door inch its way open, intruder hidden behind it. Scrambling to back up against the far wall, he kept a wary eye on the door.

A head appeared through the opening, and Paul felt a rush of relief at the sight of the mussed hair and gray eyes and shy smile.

"Kris?!" Paul launched forward to embrace his friend. "What are you doing here?"

Kris laughed and stepped back. "What am I doing here? What are you doing here? You're supposed to be in class. Come on. I'll explain on the way. Sometimes it's a long walk."

CHAPTER 7

"You should go home, Bren." Matt came up behind her and touched her shoulder. Brenna sat where she had sat since the accident, in a cushioned straight-backed chair next to Paul's hospital bed. Most of the time she spent leaning forward and talking softly to Paul, one hand holding his while the other fingered her necklace idly. Sometimes she pulled the chair up close and knelt on it, crossing her arms in front of her on the bed and resting her head on his chest to lose herself in the sound of his heartbeat.

"I'll go home when he goes home," she said firmly, moving her hand from her necklace to pat Matt's hand on her shoulder with reassurance. "The doctor says he could wake up any minute, and I'll be here when he does."

The room was small, designed for single occupancy. Brenna had been grateful for that. What little square footage it had was dominated by the bulky hospital bed, a clumsy rolling eating tray, and the chair Brenna sat in. The head of the bed was against the wall, flanked by a sink on one side and a tall nightstand on the other. Brenna would push the chair against the wall and stand next to the nightstand when an aide or a nurse came in to check on Paul or take tests or vitals. They seemed happy to bend the rules on visiting hours so long as she stayed out of the way.

Walking around Brenna to perch at the foot of Paul's bed, Matt looked down at his sister. She thought he looked older; maybe it was just that he wasn't smiling. Matt looked as tired as Brenna felt, and in its way this was harder on him.

"Anything new?" Matt glanced at Paul, then to his sister.

Brenna shook her head. "Same thing. He's fine, he's healthy. Somehow there's not a scratch on him. His brainwaves are all over the place sometimes, but that's better than no brainwaves at all. At this point they're just waiting for him to wake up, same as me." Slender fingers touched gemstone, and she sighed. "What about Kris?"

He had been watching Paul, looking so calm and peaceful in sleep. At her question, Matt turned his head and barked a bitter laugh. "He's stitched up, he's not bleeding inside any more. That's about all the good news." When Matt looked at Brenna, his eyes were bright with tears. "They don't expect him to get any better, though. Even if he wakes up, he'll be messed up for the rest of his life."

Letting go of Paul's hand, Brenna stood and embraced her brother. Even perched on the end of the bed, Matt had to slump forward to bury his face in her shoulder, him as tall as she was short. Brenna held him and mussed his hair gently, telling him it had only been three days, it could change, that she was here, that she loved him. All the while she watched Paul from the corner of her eye.

CHAPTER 8

Mason was not much for drinking. He had a beer or three every now and again, and he always had a twelve pack in the fridge to share with his buddies when they came over to play music. If he drank too much, he felt sloppy and silly and couldn't play his guitar for shit. Weed made him feel sharp and creative, beer just made him feel stupid.

That was then, another lifetime. Now there was a bloody smashed disfigured face lurking behind his eyelids, and beer was its only weakness.

Somehow he had made it through that first day at work, climbing onto a forklift right away and joining two others in unloading pallets of computer monitors from a long trailer butted against the loading dock. Another trailer was being backed in as they trundled back and forth to a back row up a long aisle, dropping the pallets on the warehouse floor in neat straight lines so they could be inventoried and placed in storage racks. The whole morning went like that, except when he slipped out the back door with the two other forklift drivers and puffed madly on a joint with them. It was lunchtime before he saw his boss approaching as he parked the forklift in one of the taped-off parking spaces and killed the engine. The smell of spent propane filled the air.

"Hey, Dan," Mason said, sliding from the seat to stand eye-level with his boss.

"Mason." Dan never smiled, at least not at Mason, but he seemed more serious than usual.

For a moment fear gripped him, and Mason's heart forgot how to beat. The single image slideshow in his mind flashed its smashed and bloody face, and he wondered, *Does he know? Am I caught? Should I run?* frantically before Dan spoke again.

"You forgot to punch in this morning." Dan's voice was dull from a thousand reproaches, but still reproachful.

"You're right, sorry." Mason breathed a sigh of relief as his heart took up beating again. "I was late." He didn't say it wouldn't happen again. It would.

Dan stood there a moment, possibly trying to look threatening. Thinning and fading short brown hair topped his clean-shaved but chubby face, and an extra chin combined with his bulbous eyes to make him look a bit like a bullfrog. Plaid shirt, the sleeves rolled up to his elbows, revealed thin slivers of white undershirt between buttons where his round belly strained to make an appearance. Denim carpenter pants refused to stay in place on the man, and no matter how many times he pulled them up you could still see the crack of his ass when he knelt down or bent over to pick something up. His brown leather work boots were scuffed and worn, and he shifted them back and forth whenever he pulled his pants up.

"Was it the accident?" Dan raised an eyebrow. "The one I heard about, down on Nineteenth?"

Mason nodded slowly. Somehow his heart had climbed into his throat and started pounding furiously. He swallowed and looked away. "Yeah. I sat there waiting for ten minutes before they started re-routing traffic." He looked back at Dan. *I hit some guy and then drove around smoking weed until I was stoned enough to come to work*, he thought in silent honesty.

"Well, at least you have an excuse this time," Dan muttered, tugging at his belt loops and shuffling his feet. "I'll sign you in at seven thirty. Don't forget to clock out." He turned then, looked around, called out to another worker docking a pallet jack.

"Thanks, boss," Mason said, and headed out to the parking lot. The clerks at the first convenience store knew him, and other employees might be there on lunch break. He drove past that one and the next one, then pulled over at a liquor store. There was a hooded zippered sweatshirt in the back seat amongst old guitar magazines and crumpled fast food bags.

Mason donned the wrinkled sweatshirt and pulled the hood up until he was in the liquor store. Once inside, he put the hood back to avoid looking suspicious, moving quickly until he had gathered a twelve pack of cold beer, a cheap styrofoam cooler and a bag of ice. Placing them on the counter, he had a flash of idiotic genius and returned to the cooler for a plastic bottle of apple juice.

The clerk was a little old man in a faded Hawaiian print collared shirt buttoned to his throat. He sat on a vinyl stool and watched a little television next to the register. Tufts of white hair poked out from under a black baseball cap with a Jack Daniels logo on it. Slow as only an old man can be, he rung up Mason's purchases and counted out his change while precious seconds ticked by in agonizing sobriety.

Cooler in the trunk, half the beer in the cooler and half beside it nestled in a dirty blanket next to the haphazard curves of jumper cables, ice dumped in the cooler over the beer. Mason was behind the wheel, keys in the ignition, when he cursed and slammed his fist on the dashboard. He went back inside for cigarettes and some gum.

Finally, he had made it to the park that day and started guzzling beer. Halfway through the third can, it came up on him, but he caught it in his mouth and swallowed. By the time he had finished it, the numb flush of inebriation had begun to spread across his cheeks, and it was time to get back to work.

Hands steady, he poured the apple juice out on the grass and filled the bottle with a fourth beer for drinking on his way back to work. For the first time since it had happened there was only a dull darkness when he closed his eyes instead of a glob of bloody flesh flattened by glass. Mason had almost smiled.

He had been drunk ever since, three days sneaking drinks at work and chewing gum maniacally between. He went home at night and sat facing a blank television screen, smoking and drinking, drinking and smoking until he passed out to sleep fitfully on the dingy little couch at the foot of his bed. It was too much to take six steps and fall into bed, so he didn't. His guitar sat untouched and unnoticed on its stand night after drunken night.

He was drunk now, staring at the tip of his smoldering cigarette and not seeing it, sitting on the couch and not feeling it, sipping at a beer and not tasting it. And when he closed his eyes, there was an image there, but it was blurred and meaningless and would fade entirely to a dull and empty darkness once he got good and shit-faced.

Mason upended the beer.

CHAPTER 9

"It's time, Paul."

Kris was talking. Paul could hear him, but Brenna was talking too. Eyes closed, he tried to lose himself in her voice.

"Paul." Kris was starting to sound irritated. "I know you're not sleeping."

The effort of blocking out Kris while straining to hear Brenna was too much. Paul opened his eyes and sat up on the edge of the bed, looking at his friend in the doorway.

"I was listening to Brenna," Paul shrugged, unapologetic. He looked Kris up and down, noting the flowing plain brown pullover robe he was wearing. It whispered along the floor when he walked, brushing lightly along the smooth stone of this odd place. He had worn it the whole time they were here, and had taken to the habit of clasping his hands in front of him, obscured in the overlapping sleeves as he walked. Paul had seen others dressed the same way in the hallways and some of the classrooms his friend had dragged him to. Kris seemed to have picked up the affectation from the others; you almost never saw their hands. "Still stuck in the same dream, huh? Nice toga."

Kris shook his head, moving agitatedly, standing in the doorway. The robe swished quietly against the floor. "This isn't a dream, Paul. You have wasted all of your time here trying to listen to Brenna and insisting this is all a dream." The robe swished again as he stepped into the room. His naked hand appeared for a moment to push the door closed, only to vanish again under voluminous sleeves. "This isn't a toga, either; it's a Guide's robe, which I wear because I am a Guide. Your Guide. Which you would know if you had been going to class." Kris did not seem to be trying to keep the irritation out of his voice at all now.

Paul shook his head sadly at his friend. "Yeah, yeah, and I'm a wanderer. It's just a dream, buddy, you're probably not even real. This is all in my head. Quiet, now. I can hear Brenna."

Kris sighed heavily. "You're not a wanderer, you're a Walker, and you don't even know what that is," he complained. "It doesn't matter, though. It's time for us to go."

"Go?" Suddenly he was standing too. "Where are we going?"

"You're going back," Kris replied slowly.

The omission did not escape him. Paul stopped halfway to the door and met his friend's eyes. "Where are you going?"

Kris shrugged and unraveled his hands from the sleeves. Reaching for the door with one hand, he caught Paul's shoulder with the other. "I'll be around," he said, peacefully. As the door opened, sounds poured through along with bright white light that Paul thought must be either God or fluorescents. Then he realized one of the sounds was Brenna's voice, and felt his friend's hand leave his shoulder as he rushed the open doorway. Kris was calling something after him, but he couldn't make sense of it, and he was shifting, falling, turning…

CHAPTER 10

Brenna leaned forward in her chair, one hand clasping Paul's as it lay across his stomach and the other combing his hair back gently again and again with slender fingers. They had talked about living on the beach before, and that's what she was talking about now.

"We'll have a nice big porch, big enough for a swing and a couple of rocking chairs." She spoke softly, watching his face to see if he heard her. "We can sit and watch the ocean, listen to the waves, sip syrah. It will be so calm and still and all we'll have to do for miles is be together and love each other and we'll be happier than we already are, more in love than we have ever been."

Paul's eyes fluttered open. "Windows," he croaked, squeezing Brenna's hand.

Her eyes widened. "Paul? Paul!" Brenna gripped his hand and stood up, leaning over to kiss his forehead and then his cheek, then his forehead again. She fumbled at the rolling tray for the cup of water she had been sipping. Helping him to sit up, she held the water to his lips. Paul smiled a little and lifted his hand to hers, but wrapped his fingers around hers instead of taking the cup from her. Together they tilted the cup back, and Paul drank, slow and deep.

"Windows," Paul said again as she took the cup away with her other hand to clasp his fingers tight. She looked at him confused. He smiled weakly. "We'll need windows on the porch so you don't get cold. The beach can get cold at night."

Brenna leapt on top of him and straddled his hips, burying her face in his chest. All of her worries and fears and anxieties from the past few days poured out in a torrent of tears and quiet sobs of relief. She stayed that way several minutes, wrapped in his arms, saying "you're back" or "everything's going to be okay" every few breaths until her voice became a murmur and her tears subsided. Paul held her even closer then, and she relaxed her whole body and melted into him.

After laying there on top of him in long sweet closeness, her face against the thin gown next to a wet stain of tears and snot, Brenna shifted her weight. She giggled and looked up at Paul, her chin resting on his chest.

"Are you hard?" she asked him, but her hand slid down between them to grasp the answer herself.

"You want to make sure it still works?" He grinned, but Brenna could only conjure up a weary smile. She kept her hand there, though, and felt him grow even harder as she began to gently knead him through the blanket. They were so close the back of her hand was feeling as good to her as the front seemed to be feeling to him. His eyes narrowed as her's widened, never straying from each other but staring with both hunger and love for long delicious moments. Their hearts beat close to each other, fast.

Just as Brenna's breath began to come shallow, faster, just as, *what the hell are we doing?* flitted through her mind, just as her skin began to flush and her nipples stiffen…just then her brother burst into the room. Brenna looked over, face afire and hair askew.

"Brenna, I—" Matt stopped just inside the room and stood there, perplexed. "Paul?"

Paul's arms were suddenly free as Brenna scrambled off him and collapsed onto the chair and set about composing herself. He gave Matt a little wave. "Hey, buddy."

Matt's eyes were huge. "You're awake."

"I am, my friend. And you are a master of the obvious. Is it not also obvious that you are rather rudely interrupting some hot hospital bed action?" Paul seemed giddy after his three days unconscious, oblivious to Matt's dark mien. "I mean, I know she's your sister, but you've got to be used to it by now. Be a good brother and come back in fifteen minutes."

He was looking at Brenna while he was talking to Matt, saw her look at her brother and back at him. She stood and put her hand on Paul's where it lay at his side.

"Paul…" they both said at the same time.

Matt shook his head fiercely and looked at his sister.

"Bren," he murmured. "No, I…"

Brenna looked at Paul.

"It's Kris," she said softly, looking away. "He's…"

In a rush, it all came back to him: the accident, the timeless dream, Kris speaking to him as he rushed through the door toward Brenna's sweet words and soft hands. Paul's hand went to his face, remembering a windshield, but there were no bandages or sore spots, nothing felt out of place.

"Kris is dead," Paul said suddenly.

Brenna touched her necklace, looked up at him from the chair. "No, sweetie, he's not dead. But he's—"

The door swung open again, an aide coming to see what the change in vital signs was all about. "You're awake," she said, in an indistinguishable asian accent. Tiny and dark of hair and eyes, she smiled as she looked from Paul to Brenna. Then her eyes fell on Matt, and her smile fell at his twisted visage.

"No, he's right," Matt sounded like he was trying to keep an explosion of tears from bursting forth as he looked from Paul to Brenna to the floor. His fists clenched and unclenched and his eyes brimmed with tears. "Kris is dead." Then he turned and stalked from the room, letting the door swing shut behind him. The aide slipped out behind him; either to spread the news of Paul's awakening, to escape the uncomfortable situation, or both.

Brenna sat in the chair and stared after him, one hand on Paul's while the other fingered the stone at her throat. When she turned back to Paul, her dark eyes were wide with anguish. Paul knew why, and he brought her fingers to his lips and kissed them softly.

"Go," he nodded. "He needs you. I'll be okay."

She leaned in to kiss him. "You are so good to me." He always gave her whatever latitude she needed to deal with her brother, and Brenna knew it wasn't always the best timing. "I love you more every day," she smiled.

"And I you, my love," Paul responded. He watched her walk away, and it wasn't until the door closed behind her that his smile faded.

"So." Paul spoke aloud to the empty room. "I assume I'm the only one who saw a little red monster with horns on that girl's shoulder, right?" It made his skin crawl to think of it, and it had taken everything he had to casually ignore it, but he had seen it as clearly as he saw every detail of the room around him now. Five or six inches tall, heavily muscled for his height and covered in crimson skin from hoof to horns, the only thing that he wore was what looked like leather shorts that stretched tight across his thighs and sported a bulging codpiece. He had leaned into the girl's ear and whispered in a hateful hiss, ignoring Paul and Brenna and Matt, the few moments she was in the room. *"Stupid!"* he had heard it say, *"How can you be so stupid?!"*

He had heard strange things before the accident; he was seeing strange things now. In the same moment he had seen the little red horned man on her shoulder, he had known that Brenna and Matt didn't see it. Not mentioning it had seemed a kindness to them.

That wasn't all, though. He had also remembered what Kris had said to him as he rushed through the door and into the light and back to Brenna.

"Ignore the demons and they will ignore you," Kris had cried, his voice fading. "Don't forget, ignore the demons."

It hadn't really made sense to him until the aide walked into the room with a miniature monster on her shoulder spitting hate in her ear. The message kind of hit home for him then, and he had ignored the demon as best he could.

All of the sudden, Paul felt too weary to have a mind so full of questions. He didn't feel like he had just gotten three days of sleep, he felt like he had just spent six months in purgatory. He fiddled with the buttons that lined the armrest on the bulky hospital bed until he was lying flat with most of the lights in the room extinguished. It was dark outside, the end of some day he had lost track of in a string of such days, and Paul yawned and closed his eyes. He was still wishing Matt had waited fifteen minutes as he drifted off to sleep.

CHAPTER 11

"Paul? Paul, sweetie, open your eyes and tell the nurse you want to go home." Weak and sleepy, Paul could still tell it was Brenna reaching to him through the tenuous fog of sleep. Brenna knew best, always.

Paul opened his eyes to a room full of bright harsh florescence, then closed them against the glare. "I want to go home," he said flatly. He squeaked one eye open. "Less lights please."

Brenna turned off the overheads and kept moving, gathering Paul's things and packing them efficiently while the nurse asked Paul his name and the year and Brenna's name and where was he and who was President of the United States. He answered the questions dutifully and seriously, knowing that a wisecrack would earn him a harsh look from Brenna and possibly another night under observation. The task was made easier by the two little demons that sat on one of the nurse's shoulders rather amiably and shouted the occasional phrase in the general direction of her ear. Their voices were as small as they were, though, and Paul couldn't make out the words they shouted between listening to her questions and thinking up his careful answers.

It wasn't long before he was on his way, carrying the things Brenna had charged Matt with bringing in the last few days in paper grocery bags with paper handles in both hands to the elevator. There were books and snacks and bottles of water straining one bag, flowers poking awkwardly over the top. The other bag held his iPod and phone charger and Kris' jacket, which Matt had gotten ahold of somehow and insisted they take home with them. There was a tear along one sleeve and a bloodstain on the cuff a few inches away.

"Do you want me to take you home?" Brenna reached out to take his hand after Paul set one of the bags on the elevator floor. She looked up at him with luminous dark eyes. "Or do you want to come home with me?"

They were alone in the descending little room. Paul set the other bag next to the first, put his hands on Brenna's hips and pulled her close to him. Brenna reached her arms up and encircled slender fingers gently around the back of his neck. One hand drifted lovingly to brush softly through his hair as dark eyes gazed up at him invitingly and a little helplessly.

"I missed you," she breathed.

He bent to kiss her lightly. "I missed you." He kissed her again. "Will you stay with me tonight?"

Keeping her eyes locked on his, stroking his hair, she nodded slowly. "I have an early class. Will you set an alarm for me?"

Paul leaned in close to her to brush his lips lightly across hers, then across her cheek. He could smell her, cocoa and cinnamon, as his lips hovered over her ear and her hair tickled his face. "Do you want a custom alarm or a traditional one?" He murmured in her ear quietly.

Melting into him, her arms encircled around his waist, Brenna turned her head, closed her eyes and rested her head on his chest.

"I hate traditional alarms," she said gently, listening to his heart beat through his shirt. "What are my custom alarm options?"

It was their usual sleepover banter, having spent the night together almost every night for two years they had fallen into sweet routine…after her watching over him three days and nights, after his endless moments without her in another world, they both took exquisite comfort from the romance that was their normal life together.

His chin rested gently on top of her head, Paul's eyes closed too, and he breathed in her familiar enticing smell. "Well," he smiled, thinking of waking up to her, "I could kiss you gently, softly, from the top of your pretty little head to your forehead, then to your soft cheeks and your delicious neck. I wouldn't kiss your perfect little ears, though, because your ears are sensitive and that would wake you up. At this point I don't want to wake you."

Brenna giggled softly, and Paul smiled, his eyes still closed. He loved to hear her laugh. He loved to make her laugh. He loved all the different ways she laughed. But that vulnerable little girl giggle…that was all his, and he loved it the most.

"I would kiss your shoulders and your arms, because they are lovely and taste so good, and my soft and slow kisses would not wake you as I covered your slender and sexy hands with them. You would feel them on your skin, though, and your skin would know I love you, and you would feel that love throughout the day putting a little extra spring in your step."

Brenna's eyes were filled with tears again, happy tears that squeezed through her eyelids. Paul didn't see them as he went on murmuring softly to her. "You would probably start to wake up as I kissed your breasts and your stomach, every perfect curve, every delectable square inch feeling the careful eagerness of my lips."

The brief sound of a muffled bell came as the floor stopped moving beneath them. This late at night, the parking garage was deserted, quiet and still but well lighted and not uninviting.

Paper bags swinging at his sides, Paul continued to detail her morning option. "I'll kiss your sexy hips and thighs, down the smooth soft skin of your calves and all over your cute and tiny and impossibly seductive little feet." His voice echoed off the walls, though he spoke quietly, low and slow words riding waves of deep, tremulous echoes. "By the time I am done, your whole body will be covered in tender tokens of my love for you."

Brenna looked up at him as he set the bags down near her car, a little silver Hyundai. She was in his arms again suddenly, arms encircled about his waist possessively. "That sounds wonderful."

Losing himself in her warm embrace and wide dark eyes, Paul smiled down at her. He spoke in the flat quick tone of a radio advertisement disclaimer: "Please don't consider that to be your only option, or think yourself limited to the specific details of the aforementioned option. All options are simply suggestions that you may feel free to modify to suit your needs and specifications so that you may enjoy pleasure, comfort and satisfaction in whatever fashion you may desire."

Her round, firm breasts moved against him when she giggled. She looked up at him the whole time, though, even when she said, "Will you tell me more about the other options on the way?" Breaking the long eye contact with a seductive sideways lingering look, she opened the trunk and slung the bag of clothes she had carried around her shoulder in. Brenna had the car keys in her hand before they were off the elevator, clutched them in one hand while she was embracing Paul. The trunk was as neat as everything else about Brenna, not just empty but vacuumed recently, the only items an umbrella and a backpack. The necessities lay at straight angles that suggested they had not dared move after being placed so carefully. Brenna tossing the duffel was as close as she could ever get to throwing her hands up and collapsing out of exhaustion or despair.

The remote entry key opened both car doors with a chirp, and it took most of the ride for him to detail all the options she might wake up to in the morning. It helped to talk, to have words to focus on when his mind wanted so badly to spin and whirl and twist with questions.

Finally at his apartment, finally up the stairs and down the hallway and behind closed doors together, finally alone, he took her in his arms again. Brenna gave herself over to his embrace completely, and they held each other for a long time there in the middle of the living room. Reminders of Kris surrounded them, his DVD collection dominated by horror flicks, the pair of cheap swords hanging blades crossed on the wall, an old blue hooded sweatshirt he had worn for years tossed over the back of the couch. Paul could smell his friend's unique woodsy scent with every breath he took in the living room of the apartment that had been theirs. Slow and quiet tears rolled unchecked from his eyes and down his cheeks as walls within him melted at the feel of home and Brenna's arms around him.

After a while, Brenna led him to the couch, sat with him and reached out to tangle her fingers in his hair. Whenever they needed each other most, words were few and gentle between them as volumes of communication were spoken by their eyes and embraces and fingertips, soft caresses and quiet smiles.

She pulled his head to her breast, and Paul twisted his body to lie sideways on the couch facing her. Lying there, quiet, face buried in her chest as her slender fingers combed through his hair, he let the tears flow until he could feel her blouse grow damp against his face. He started kissing her skin where soft cotton came to a V above her breasts, gentle slow kisses of gratitude over her beautiful loving heart. Gratitude turned to hunger as her taste filled his mouth, and his kisses grew warmer and wetter on her shoulder and neck. Brenna's mood shifted with his, one hand grasping his hair and pushing his face insistently against her skin while the other gently encircled his upper arm.

Her lips were parted, her breath coming faster, when his mouth found hers. Long and deep, the kiss was as familiar as it was exciting, somehow full of comfort and desperation at the same time. Brenna's hand clenched and unclenched, pulling and squeezing hair and bicep with a firm but gentle grip, sweet soft moans punctuating each release. Her back arched toward him seductively, her breasts flattening against his chest.

Paul got his knees under him on the couch and leaned the weight of his upper body into her. He brought a hand to each side of her face and began to trace the lines of her cheekbones and jaw with his fingertips, straying to run through her hair every few slow strokes.

When they broke the kiss, Paul's hands framed her face while one thumb brushed her cheek lightly in slow rhythm. He looked deep into her big dark eyes while her slender fingers combed lazily through his hair. They were bright with tears and exhaustion and desire, beautiful and vulnerable to him.

He had thought they would maybe talk long into the night like they sometimes did. They had lost Kris; they had lost each other for what had seemed an eternity to both of them; and they loved to share every silly little detail of their time spent apart whenever they came together again. It made them feel like they were somehow together all of the time.

Tonight there were no words between them though, and every touch created a closeness and a hunger for more closeness as more naked skin was revealed and the touches grew more lingering and intimate. Both of them had their shirts off on the couch, and Brenna had pushed him back on the sofa and straddled him. She arched her back and gripped his knees behind her, pressing her naked breasts into his hungry, wet kisses.

Catching his fingers in her dark thick mane, Paul pulled her head back as he filled his mouth with the intoxicating cocoa taste of her soft flesh. Her nipples were hard and wet from his kissing and licking and sucking, slick against his cheeks as he nuzzled and kissed every part of her that his mouth could reach. He gripped the smooth strong curve of her ass with his other hand, feeling firm flesh through her tight jeans.

Swimming upstream thought the cascading waterfall of straight thick dark hair, his hand gripped her hair close to her scalp and pulled back again, harder. Brenna arched her back more deeply and gave a little cry of pained pleasure. He hauled her in forcefully for a kiss, and they moaned in loving harmony as their lips met again. Her hands moved from his knees to his shoulders as both of his slid under her buttocks. His middle fingers met at the seam of her jeans, settling gently in the soft warmth and hint of moisture they found there. The pads of his fingertips traced lazy circles while her legs crossed over his back and her arms entwined about his neck. He held her close with his hands still grasping her tight through her jeans, strong grip kneading her flesh through the denim.

Carrying her easily across the living room, past the door that had been Kris' room, Paul pushed open his bedroom door and let her fall back onto the bed. He leaned over her, licking and kissing her stomach and worrying at the buttons on her jeans while she caressed his shoulders and tousled his hair. Grasping her pants at the end of each leg, he slid them off in one fluid motion and leaned over her again to kiss the smooth soft skin of her thighs as she lay back and spread her legs for his wet kisses. His own jeans were coming off then, and he stood and stepped out of them while he watched Brenna slip out of her little red thong panties.

Gentle and slow again, Paul dipped between her legs for a quick taste of her and then brought his mouth to hers as he slid his hips between her legs and slipped easily inside of her. He watched her eyes open wide and then close slowly as a little shudder went through her body. When she opened them again, there was a touch of satisfied smile at the corners of her full lips, and her hands reached around to grasp his buttocks and drive him deeper inside her. Brenna cried out, and it was bittersweet; she never would have been so loud if Kris had been in the next room.

They made love, slowly and gently at first, Paul propped on his elbows gazing down at her, hands stretched out to cradle her head and tousle her hair. Brenna's arms were around him, tracing long and loving lines down his back from his hairline to his hips and back again. Just being inside her was everything, every subtle movement a delight of sensation, and their bodies writhed slow and hungry against each other.

Hunger grew sharper as their hearts beat faster, and Brenna's hands were in his hair again as she pulled him to her full sensual lips. She bucked her hips against him, then faster, then grabbed his waist and rolled over on top of him. She gripped his hands over his stomach hard as she straddled him, sitting upright and grinding forcefully into him again and again with her firm buttocks. Crying out with each stroke, louder with each stroke, clutching her hands tighter with each stroke, she looked down and into his eyes as her own glazed over beautifully in her pleasure. Then she cried out one last time, long and loud, falling forward with their hands still between them to hover her face a breath away from Paul's. Her eyes were wide and intense, locked still on his, her wet thick lips parted slightly a few inches from his own. He could smell her breath, sweet and young and deliciously scented with the taste he'd had of her earlier.

Brenna spoke then, the first words either of them had said since entering the apartment. Gazing adoringly through lazy eyelids at him, she smiled a seductive half-smile. "What do you want?" she breathed, still grasping his hands now trapped between their bellies.

If he had a dollar for every time she had asked him that, he would be a wealthy man. He couldn't imagine a way for dollars to make him feel the way he did when she asked him, though; and no pile of gold could do to him the things she did when he gave his answers. Those four little words were worthy of the creation of sound itself, as far as Paul was concerned. It had taken awhile to get used to; he had been shy at first to be asked so directly, but now it turned him on as much as Brenna's dark eyes and round breasts and full lips.

Still looking in her eyes, he murmured, "I want to take you from behind while I play with your breasts with one hand and pull your hair with the other. I want you to put your sexy little ass in the air and turn your head and make as much eye contact with me as possible. I want you to come for me again if you can, and I want you to say my name."

Brenna was on all fours on his bed then, looking back over her shoulder and the firm round curve of her ass at him. "Oh, Paul," she cried as he slid smoothly inside of her again and grabbed a handful of hair. Then they were both crying out loudly as he thrust and clawed at her, and he collapsed finally on top of her with all his weight. They lay like that awhile, breathing heavy with Paul's face buried in her hair and him still inside her. He rolled them both over then, holding her from behind and stroking her hair softly while she drifted off to sleep. It was like throwing a switch, and in a few moments her body and breathing relaxed against him in exhausted slumber.

CHAPTER 12

Mason sprawled on the lumpy sofa at the foot of his bed neither lying nor sitting, a can of beer in one hand and a cigarette held between two fingers of the other. Piles of clothes on the floor had turned to mountains, and identifying the type of floor in the living room would have required moving something wrinkled and smelling of beer and cigarettes sweated out and soaked up and gone stale.

An hour and a half ago, he had arrived home from work, grateful it was Friday. An hour ago, he had arrived at a pleasant numb place somewhere between plastered and shit-faced, and he allowed himself a grim lopsided brief smile. The radio station in the city was playing Muse and Alice in Chains and Nickelback, and all he had to do was tune in his receiver and sit back and listen. And drink. And smoke.

Adorning the rickety coffee table was a wooden box, as long and as wide as his hand and stained a deep brown. The lid had a circular symbol in the center, Celtic knotwork carved into the wood and stained in dark shades in its relief. Stubbing out his cigarette and setting the beer on the tabletop, Mason leaned forward to seize the box. His questing hand brushed aside fast food bags empty and crumpled and stained with grease, drunk dented beer cans, and spent packs of Camel Lights impeding its path.

He opened the box on his lap, sitting up a little straighter. Half a dozen joints rolled around inside, along with a mostly empty baggie and a couple packs of rolling papers. He plucked a joint from the box, put it between his lips and placed the box back on the coffee table, closer to him this time. There were lighters everywhere, Mason always made sure of that, and soon the smoky pungent sweet reek of cannabis overpowered the flat odor of stale cigarette smoke. He puffed away until it was a third of the way burnt, ashes falling on his shirt unnoticed as lazy clouds of smoke formed in the air, his eyelids drooping lower over hazel eyes shot with blood.

The Nickelback song was in its last few bars of reassuring him that he was never alone no matter how much it might seem that way when the tapping introduction to AC/DC's *Thunderstruck* mangled and overpowered the final comforting words. Mason stared in dulled confusion for a moment before he realized it was a ringtone. His phone was ringing, humming and vibrating across the coffee table as other instruments joined the sound of Angus Young's Gibson. It was another moment while he decided whether or not to answer, but he finally sighed and reached for the device.

Thunderstruck told him who it was, and Mason was not surprised to hear his own voice thick with drink when he answered. "Hey, Tyler." He spoke slowly, so as not to slur his words. "What's up?"

Amplifier feedback and the thumping of an off-beat bass drum assaulted his ear, and he held the phone away from his head to give it an annoyed look. "Mason? You there, brother?" A voice emerged from the fading cacophony, and Mason moved the phone back to his ear.

"Yeah, yeah, I'm here," he cradled the phone against his shoulder and took a sip of beer, then set the can down with his free hand. He sat up straight and took two quick puffs of the joint and blew smoke across the room. "What's up?"

"What's up? What's up?" Tyler's high and excited tones were full of good-naturedness. "Where have you been? I've been texting you for days. Are you coming tonight, brother?"

Mason had forgotten entirely. He took a last long pull from his joint and held the hit in while he mashed it out in an ashtray. Though the other man couldn't see him, he shook his head doggedly back and forth as a thin stream of white smoke issued from his lips forcefully for several seconds. It speared through lazy drifting clouds to set them swirling as he watched. "I can't make practice tonight," he said, his eyes drifting guiltily toward his guitar where it had sat untouched since it had happened.

"It's not just practice tonight, man. Cal's in town, remember?" His voice was high and fast and alive with drama all of the time, but Tyler was never actually upset.

"I can't make it, buddy. Sorry." Mason heard a burst of drums as he spoke, and hoped that Tyler hadn't noticed that he slurred the word 'sorry' into an unrecognizable garble of sound.

"What?" Tyler shouted amiably. "I didn't hear you."

"I said I can't make it." Mason's response was loud and firm, harsher than he had meant it to come out.

Tyler was unfazed by the rebuke in his tone. "Sure you can. Get in your car, brother, and get over here."

"I can't. I've been drinking." Mason upended the beer and drained the last few swallows, as if to illustrate his point. "I shouldn't be driving." *I could kill someone. Again.*

Tyler hooted as a bass guitar slid smoothly through a scale in the background. "Is that all?" He laughed loudly. "You don't have to drive, I'll come get you. I'll see you in twenty minutes."

"I can't play," Mason slurred desperately into the phone, but his friend had hung up.

Mason sighed and stood up, cursing.

CHAPTER 13

Paul watched her sleep for awhile, finding his peace in the sight of her so peaceful. The contours of her face swam in shadows, her beauty more stark by moonlight. He wouldn't sleep, though, and once he realized it he became restless. Slipping quietly from under the covers, he shrugged into his robe and padded across the room. It wasn't until he had closed the door behind him that he heard the television.

He tensed, moving slowly and quietly up the hallway, past the closed door to Kris' room. He edged along the wall until there was no more wall and he could see around the corner.

Directly opposite Paul was the front door, the television along the same wall flashing light across an otherwise unlighted room. The plain olive green sofa that sat in the center of the room created a separation in its placement, half the space dedicated to the entertainment center before it. The room behind the couch to one side was the living room, the space they lived in. Behind the other side was the breakfast bar that separated the main room from the kitchen, three stools lined neatly along it. The entrance to the kitchen was just beside him as he pressed against the wall between hallway and cook room. On the far wall, past the door to the main bathroom, was the fireplace they were not supposed to use. And above the fireplace were two swords affixed to the wall, long slim curved steel blades crossed at the middle.

Glancing wistfully at the swords, Paul moved quietly toward the closest stool, keeping his eyes on the silhouette of the back of some psycho's head sitting on his couch and casually watching television. The stool would probably do more damage than the blunted edge of a decorative sword, anyway. Before he could lay his hands on the seat, the head turned and grinned at him.

"Hey, Paul."

Paul froze, his heart beating madly in his chest. "Kris?"

"Oh, come on, don't look so shocked. Come. Sit." He patted the couch next to him soundlessly and turned back to the television.

Feeling rather absurd, Paul crossed the room and sat on the couch next to his friend. "You're watching Smallville?" Paul asked, feeling even more absurd.

Kris shrugged. "I figured out how to turn the thing on, but I can't change the channels." He leaned forward and grabbed for the remote control on the coffee table. His hand passed right through it. "It's really not a bad show."

"I know," Paul snapped in playful exasperation. "I've been telling you that for years, while you made fun of me for watching a show about an invincible immortal super-powered teenager full of angst. It's a good show, good acting and writing and special effects."

Kris nodded agreement. "And you're totally in love with Kristen Kruek."

"I'm totally in love with Brenna," he corrected him.

Smiling, Kris said, "Who looks just like Kristen Kruek."

Paul shook his head. "No, Kristen Kruek looks just like Brenna."

"He sure loses his powers a lot."

Paul laughed. "How many episodes have you watched?"

His friend shrugged. "There's been a marathon running ever since..." he trailed off.

They sat and watched for a few minutes in silence. Paul had seen the episode before, but was lost immediately in the colorful action and dialogue.

The programming went to commercial. "Brenna is so fine," Paul said.

They sat through one advertisement, then another; and then Paul spoke again, quietly.

"I cried for you," he said.

Kris didn't answer, and the rest of the episode they watched together without so much as glancing at each other.

When it was over, Kris waved his hand and the television went dark in the same instant the corner lamp came on.

Paul started.

"That poor girl sure gets knocked out an awful lot," Kris mused, smiling a sly smile. "Her little brain can't possibly be functioning properly at this point, that's a lot of head trauma. Maybe that's why she can't make up her mind and ditch Clark."

Paul's eyes were still wide in disbelief. "Did you just...?"

His friend's smile widened, and he waved his hand again. The television came on, showing scenes from previous episodes before starting into the next. "Cool, huh? Being dead has its perks. I still haven't figured out how to change the channel, though." He looked from the screen to Paul and back again. "Should I leave it on so Brenna doesn't hear you out here talking to yourself and think you're crazy?"

"She can't hear you?" Paul watched his friend watch the screen.

"No, just you. And other Walkers. And demons. And angels. And Guides and Watchers." Kris put his chin in his hand and considered. "Strike that. Everyone can see me except humans."

"Because you're dead." Paul's head was spinning. "Am I imagining this? Am I dreaming?" He looked at his friend defenselessly. "Am I crazy?"

Kris gave him a gentle smile. "It is generally not wise to ask a suspected hallucination if they are indeed a hallucination. A figment of your imagination has power over you only so long as you believe it to be real, and is unlikely to reveal its own insubstantial nature. Meanwhile, the genuine article," he gestured to indicate himself, the genuine article in this case, "is likely to be insulted by the dehumanization that accompanies the idea that they exist only in your mind."

Paul raised an eyebrow. "Well, you certainly talk like Kris. Sorry?"

He shrugged. "Don't sweat it. T.V. on or off?"

"Off," Paul responded. "Brenna won't wake up, she sleeps heavier that I do." He looked at the cable box. "It's not even eleven yet. I need a drink." He glanced at Kris. "Let's go get a drink."

Kris slipped one hand into the folds of his robe and withdrew a plain silver flask. Paul hadn't even noticed he was still wearing the thick and heavy folds of cloth. His friend was starting to look natural in it. "This is all I can drink now." He spun the cap off, and it dangled alongside the flask from a sturdy silver chain affixed to the neck. First he held it between them at eye level, as if to toast, then he brought it to his lips and drank. As he took the flask away from his lips, Paul noticed a thin liquid layer of what looked like blue milk before Kris licked it from his lips in apparent enjoyment.

Kris shrugged and held it out to him. "You should be able to touch it if I will it."

Paul frowned, but he reached out. Grasping the flask, it was cool and light. Bringing it to his nose cautiously, he sniffed. He smelled nothing. He tried to taste it, and it was empty. Finally, he upended it. Nothing came out.

"It's empty." Paul handed the item back.

Taking another swallow, obviously drinking something, Kris was smiling as he licked the remaining blue from his lips. "Never empty to me, always empty to others. It's my canteen. All Guides have one."

"It looks like a flask."

Kris shrugged. Somehow his customary gesture seemed more dismissive in the robe. "They call it a canteen. I heard they used to use big clunky canteens of silver, but they realized an endless container didn't need to be big and they changed it. It was last modified when the modern flask was popularized, and now it fits neatly in a pocket." A glint of silver and it was gone, stowed in the folds of his robe somewhere.

Between the kitchen and common bath were the folding slatted French doors for the laundry inset. Paul opened one door and pulled a pair of jeans on under his robe. He buttoned them and doffed the soft blue cotton, bare-chested for a moment while he reached for socks and shirt.

There was a notepad and jar of pens and pencils on the breakfast bar, and Paul made use of them while he asked, "Where did you hear this stuff?" He placed his bluetooth in his ear while grabbing his wallet from the same wire basket that held his keys and phone.

Brenna, he wrote. *Went to grab a drink. Call if you wake up. All my love…Always…Paul.* Leaving the note out in the open, he looked up to find Kris glaring crossly at him.

"I went to class," he said icily, and walked through the front door without opening it.

Paul exited the traditional way, locking the door behind him.

"You're going to see them, you know." Kris seemed to be floating along the hallway more than walking, hands hidden in the sleeves of his robe.

Paul grimaced. "See who?" He knew what his friend meant, though; and he wished he hadn't asked.

A few steps ahead of him in the hallway, Kris stopped and turned. The hem of the robe didn't swish here like it did in that other place. All of his movements were oddly silent. He faced Paul there in the hallway, hands clasped under folds of cloth.

"The demons, Paul," he said flatly. "You're going to see the demons."

CHAPTER 14

A thick rectangular slab of beveled glass supported by a black metal frame was the centerpiece of the room and the center of attention. Half of the coffee table was covered in beer cans and guitar magazines, a simple glass bong a full foot tall, and an ashtray. Somebody had stubbed a cigarette not quite out in the ashtray, and a long thin finger of smoke drifted from the end of the crumpled butt.

The other half of the glass was empty, clean and transparent without so much as a streak on the surface. A half-empty spray bottle of Windex and a wet crumpled wad of paper towels was off to one side. In the center of the clean section was a miniature mountain of white with a half dozen lines cut out on the table beside it. The fluffy white powder was cut haphazardly, the lines crooked and uneven, a short metal straw beside them on the glass.

The apartment was a larger cleaner version of Mason's studio, a two bedroom that Jason and Tyler shared with the drum kit and mixing board and amps that dominated the living room to one side. Two microphones stood on aluminum stands, making the space seem a stage for the couch facing it. The glass coffee table had been Cal's housewarming present to them, and it had looked a little too classy in front of the misshapen faded brown sofa at first. Much abuse and cocaine later, it seemed to fit right in as they huddled around it now.

Mason stood over the table, sizing up the lines. Finally he leaned forward, picked up the metal tube and snorted a short fat line up his left nostril. He glanced up at Cal, who nodded and grinned, and took another up his right nostril. The metal tube clattered on the glass table, and he stood up straight and tilted his bead back. His nose was instantly and pleasantly numb, and soon his throat was as well. The drip that followed seemed well worth the taste.

"Thanks, Cal," Mason nodded at the younger man across the table. Cal was dressed as Mason had seen him dress every time he had come to visit. Black slacks and black leather shoes, a muted silk shirt that buttoned up the front. This one was a deep burgundy, first two buttons open to showcase a tall gold cross at his throat above a bare chest. His dark hair was a slave to the gel, slicked back close to his head and cut short in the back.

He brightened visibly when Mason acknowledged him, standing up straighter and nodding with enthusiasm. "Anytime, Mason, anytime. I'm glad you could make it." Mason watched him gesture to Tyler and then to the table. "Have another, big brother."

Tyler was already rocking back and forth and twirling his beer can in his hand. "You're gonna get me too high, little brother," he complained amiably. He leaned over, though, and when he stood up again a fat line had disappeared. Sniffing repetitively, he thumbed his nose several times with a smile.

"No such thing as too high," Cal grinned. "Hey Mason, did you bring your guitar?"

"Yeah, I did." Mason nodded, but made no move to act. Tyler was already reaching for his guitar. Tyler was the physical opposite of his younger brother, thick around the middle and standing a stooped five foot eight. Cal was only an inch or two taller, but he was thin and angular and stood more erect. Chatty and sociable, Cal would hook his thumbs in his pockets, lean back coolly a little, like he was relaxing into himself, and talk to anyone. The animated drama of Tyler's voice and mannerisms were reserved for his small group of friends.

Behind the smooth wood and fat strings of his bass guitar, Tyler was calm and focused staring past shoulder length chestnut hair at the fingerboard. It was the only place he seemed to feel at ease, the only time the lines on his face relaxed into a focused and satisfied expression of concentration.

Mason sighed. "I don't play so well when I'm drinking," he said. It was a half-hearted protestation, though, and he could see Jason quietly moving behind the drum set. Tyler was strapped in and plugged in, and his amplifier hummed as he threw the switch.

"You don't play so bad when you've been drinking, either," Cal leaned back and smiled as he watched the players set up. Soon Mason had his guitar strapped on as well, and plugged in. He and Tyler began the ritual tuning of their guitars. An occasional thump from the bass drum behind them punctuated the notes they held as they whined higher or swooped lower. When they were done, Mason ran through a couple of scales and played a few relative harmonics to sample the tuning job. Tyler improvised a short riff that used all four strings on his bass and played it over and over, closing his eyes after a few repetitions and listening intently to his own playing. It was sonic mayhem, Jason thumping along in a regular rhythm that did not match either guitar. All three noisemakers tested the sounds of their respective instruments at the same time, heedless of each other or the collective cacophony. Sounds writhed together and clashed against each other, making the likelihood of these instruments and personalities coming together in cooperation seem inconceivable.

Then Mason was palm muting a power chord over and over, saying, "Check, check, check," into the microphone in front of him. Tyler stood at the mixing board, left hand turning knobs while his right rested against the smooth stained wood of his Ibanez and absently plucked at the second fattest string rhythmically. Mason moved to Tyler's mic after he was satisfied, and then ran through a scale front to back and back to front while Jason checked his microphone.

A moment of silence came then, and Mason had time to appreciate the look of anticipation on Cal's face before they launched into their customary first song. The look gave way to a grin as they came together perfectly in the first few bars of *Enter Sandman*, and Cal gave a whoop when Mason started singing.

It seemed a little easier than usual to Mason, playing and singing. His fingers found their way smoothly from one fretted home to another, the pick seemed a part of his hand. Even his voice sounded better than usual, thick and chunky and crisp all at the same time. *Maybe it's the cocaine*, he thought. Then all thought vanished as he lost himself in playing and singing and listening with his whole being.

He was glad he had come.

CHAPTER 15

"So what are they?" Paul asked as he waited for his drink. "The demons, what are they?"

They had found a booth in the back corner of the club, away from the band and the dance floor and the clamor of drunken activity. It was not as crowded as it could have been, made more surprising by the quality top forty covers the band was playing. Paul was glad for the thinner crowd, glad for the music, glad for the table, glad he had brought his wireless earpiece so he didn't draw attention talking to himself. He liked the song, *Call Me Maybe.*

He was also glad for the bottle of Blue Moon the petite blonde with tight black leggings and top brought him. When she leaned over to set the drink on the table, her miniature cleavage hovered in his face a second longer than necessary while pretty green eyes peered at him under short blonde bangs. She made as if to linger, thanking him with a smile that was turning seductive as he handed her a dollar tip from his change.

Paul pointed at his earpiece, smiled briefly and looked away. "Yeah, sweetie, I'm still here," he said to the inert device. When he glanced back, he found himself watching the smooth black clad curve of her compact ass as she walked away.

Habit and a complete lack of interest in any woman but Brenna found him looking again at Kris across the table. His friend was watching the girl walk away, the expression on his face one of longing more than desire.

"What are they?" He asked again.

Kris shrugged and met his eyes. "They're thought-forms made real, like everything you see around you." He gestured absently at the club without taking his gray eyes off Paul, as if he had actually just explained something.

"How exactly does that work?" He probed.

A lock of hair fell over one eye as Kris tilted his head to one side, considering. One hand appeared from the folds of his robe to push the hair from his eyes, only to disappear and reappear holding the shining silver flask. He set it on the table before him silently.

"Everyone has demons," Kris said, fingering the silver surface of the flask absently. "Most people have one primary demon that is bigger and more powerful than any of the others, but even the most powerful demon typically stays pretty small, with little ability to actually influence the person who created it firsthand. Most demons provide a kind of service, preventing their host from going too far in the wrong direction with the subtle emotional weapons of guilt and shame. They also provide a huge disservice, though, in that it is our demons that hold us back from being our best selves. It can be difficult for a person to see greatness in themselves when they are being constantly reminded of some perceived fundamental flaw, and it is even more challenging to become great if you cannot see greatness in yourself."

Out of the corner of his eye Paul could see the people on the floor writhing drunkenly in time with the music. Little red beings decorated their shoulders, miniature men and women with skin that ranged from a red so light it was nearly pink to a deep dark mottled mix of cabernet and coffee. Horns sprouted from their foreheads or the crowns of their heads, poking through the hair of the demons whose skulls were not bald and shiny and red. They all had tails, too, though some were long prehensile serpents that writhed and coiled through the air while others were short and still afterthoughts with pointed tips.

They were as varied as the people whose shoulders they rode, fat and sloppy here and slim and sexy there. Black leather seemed to be the only choice in material they ever made, whether jeans or miniskirt or jacket or leather undergarments were the outfit. Those that were not barefoot wore black leather boots of every variety imaginable, save one stately five inch tall female in leather garter belt, leather bra, leather thong and widely spaced fishnet stockings. Thick straight black hair cascaded down her back to brush her garter belt, fleshy firm buttocks framed by the belt and the thong and the stockings. Her closed-toed leather platform heels added a half inch to her impressive yet diminutive stature. Smooth crimson skin stretched taut over her generous curves, and her every subtle gesture dripped with sexuality.

Paul sipped his beer, doing his best to ignore the people on the dance floor and the demons that danced or sat or stood on their shoulders. "How do you create a demon?" He watched Kris unscrew the cap of his canteen with the absent ease of something done a thousand times.

Tilting the flask, apple in his throat bobbing, Kris wiped his mouth with the back of a voluminous sleeve and set the silver container down again. The little silver cap swung at the end of its chain for a moment, then stilled.

"Fear," Kris said, solemn. "Anger, hate, worry, envy, resentment. That's how you make a demon. Repeat some thought over and over in your mind, charge the thought with some strong negative emotion, and you create a creature whose sole purpose is to remind you of the thing that created it. It will whisper in your ear that you are worthless or stupid or mistreated, whatever your demon was born from, whenever you will listen. It will drive you to do things to prove your own subconscious obsession powerless, and every move you make in that apparent direction will only give it more power and substance. Demons are the product of some negative belief you have about the world based on repetition and powerful emotion that program you to create your own drama. Demons ensure their continued survival by perpetuating that negative belief and feeding off the resulting fear."

Paul was staring blankly at his friend. "What?" he asked, shaking his head to clear it. Taking a long last swallow of beer, he moved the empty bottle to the edge of the table in hopes that a server might notice.

"It's simple," Kris said, a little impatient. "A little girl hears her mother tell her she's stupid when she spills a glass of milk. The echoes of that otherwise insignificant hurt bounce around in her head until she starts to believe it on some level, and she spends the rest of her life doing things that will prove to herself and the world that she is smart. The more desperate her attempts, the more stupid shit she will do, thus feeding the demon. Even succeeding at something will be fraught with little failures; mistakes that would be inconsequential to someone else are devastating when you need to look and feel smart all of the time."

Paul smiled at the girl with the short blonde bangs and pointed at the empty bottle. Looking back at Kris, he said, "Let's see if I get you here. When we get obsessed with some negative thought, we create a demon with it. Then the demon feeds on our obsession while doing everything it can to perpetuate it so it has more negative thoughts to feed on."

"It's more like a belief than a thought," Kris corrected him, but he was nodding as he spoke. "Usually it's not even true at first, some girl calls a boy a pervert when he shows her his instead of showing him hers, the kid spends the day wondering what a pervert is, goes home and looks it up and spends all night wondering if he is one. When his mom catches him masturbating a few years later, the demon is strong enough to influence her to use that word, pervert, in a moment of shock and distaste. She apologizes for it later, but she only confirmed what the young man already suspected about himself, and that's something she can't take back."

Speaking as he usually did, loping through one long sentence after another and expecting him to keep up, Kris went on. "In trying desperately to appear normal, our young man is gentlemanly and courteous to his first girlfriend in high school. Every time he's with her his demon whispers in his ear that she must never learn what a pervert he is and that he would lose her if she ever knew the truth about him and that a pervert like him doesn't even deserve a girlfriend in the first place. The poor kid is filled with backed up adolescent poison because he's terrified of beating off like some 'pervert' and he's scared to death of making the slightest sexual advance for fear of her reaction. His little demon is no longer so little at this point, sitting on his shoulder and gaining power every step of the way. When he ends up alone with her one night at Inspiration Point, she tells him she wants to get in the backseat so she can see what a pervert he is. He hears that dreaded word instead of the sexy invitation, and he lashes out and hits her."

Walking slowly the last few steps to the table, peering at him under short blonde bangs, the waitress approached and set down a fresh bottle of Blue Moon. A little slice of orange was wedged in the narrow round opening.

Paul put his hand to his ear. "Hang on a minute," he said loudly, then smiled at the girl and handed her a twenty dollar bill. He gave her another dollar from the change without looking up and turned back to his dead friend. "Okay, go ahead."

Smiling at the show, Kris continued. "Now he's not just a pervert, he has actual physical violence to feel guilty about, and our example's chances of connecting with anyone other than his demon at this point are slim to none. He is likely to be consumed by thoughts of his own despicable nature until his demon grows bigger than him, takes control and rapes and beats or kills some girl seemingly senselessly and at random."

The beer looked good. Paul set the orange slice aside and took a long, sweet swallow. It tasted good too. "So people don't do bad things, their demons do? Murderers aren't responsible for their actions? Seriously, dude? 'The devil made me do it?'"

Kris shook his head adamantly. "No, devils are completely different than demons." He waved aside Paul's perplexed look and shrugged. "A demon is a part of someone, it's their creation, their thought-form, their negative belief given a shape and a voice. They can't exist away from their host and creator; they begin to lose strength and power as soon as they lose physical contact with them. You are responsible for your thoughts, you are responsible for your demons, and you are responsible for whatever you do to appease or destroy your demons. You are definitely responsible for the actions you take when you let one of your demons consume you." His hand appeared from the sleeves of his robe to bring his canteen to his lips and tilt it back.

"There are as many opportunities in a day for light as there are for darkness," Kris said solemnly, placing the flask carefully on the table again. "Each person gets to choose what they focus on, and that focus either feeds your demons or keeps them at bay. Some say for every demon there is an angel, that one cannot be created without the other, but I've never seen one."

Paul burst out laughing. "Like in the cartoons, there's a devil on one shoulder and an angel on the other, both trying to convince the poor confused head between them?"

"Yeah, I guess," Kris shrugged. "Not devils, Paul. *Demons.* Devils are different."

The crowd was growing, and the dance floor was thick with humans and demons and quite possibly angels that Paul couldn't see any more than his friend could. He pretended to watch the band, slightly elevated above the small drunken mob at the other end of the spacious room. Each demon seemed oblivious to everything but its host, whispering or shouting in their ear, sitting complacent or dancing along on their shoulders.

His eyes fell again on the one in the heels, standing stately and silent on the platforms and glaring balefully at the woman whose shoulder she stood on. The girl was young, pretty, with dark hair and light skin and a serpentine way of moving on the dance floor that made her sensual curves seem to beckon. Three young men had responded and were vying for her attention.

Paul watched as the striking miniature crimson beauty leaned forward purposefully and intently toward the girl's ear. Somehow, across the room and over the din of dancers and music, he heard her whisper fiercely, "*You're a slut,*" into the girl's ear. The girl had been dancing a brief seductive cooch, head down and eyes mostly closed, lost in the drunk and the dance. At the demon's words, she stiffened and looked up and around her. Suddenly still on the dance floor, Paul watched her recoil as each of the three young men brushed against her in turn, still moving to the music and swaying back and forth while she stood rigid and unmoving.

It was as if the doll-sized figure felt him watching then, and she turned slowly toward him. Her cleavage came into view as her thick coarse black hair swung slowly with her.

"Paul!" Kris' loud voice snapped him out of his reverie, and Paul turned in time to watch his hand pass soundlessly through the table as he tried to slam it down loudly. "Don't look them in the eyes," he cautioned. "You'll activate it."

"Just ignore them, right?" Paul glanced back, though, and saw the dark-haired girl retreating to the restroom hastily. The little crimson temptress on her shoulder was leaning forward and whispering in her ear, but Paul couldn't hear the words. He looked back at his friend. "What do you mean, activate it?"

Kris shook his head in exasperation. "You really should have gone to class," he admonished Paul playfully. "Where is your key?"

"My what? My key?" Paul was confused.

"Whatever the guy who turned you into a Walker gave you," Kris explained patiently. "A book, a metal key, a pocket watch—"

"The watch!" Paul remembered suddenly. "The guy in the overcoat gave me something gold and round and flat, an old school pocket watch on a chain."

"Yeah, that," Kris replied dryly. "Where is it?"

"I don't know." It was Paul's turn to shrug. "I haven't seen it since…"

His voice trailed off, and he held his hand in front of him, palm up. In the center of his palm was a gold pocket watch, polished chain coiled about the body. It hadn't been there a moment ago. Simple smooth gold curved around the back, the front shell the same but for an ornate 'W' engraved in curlicue calligraphy in the center. It was topped with a gold winding wheel and a gold clasp that swiveled and held chain to watch. A little gold button sat atop the winding wheel.

Paul looked over the watch to his friend, raised a questioning eyebrow.

"Open it," Kris said.

He depressed the little button with his thumb. A gold half shell swung on its hinge to reveal the shell's innards. The watch face was unusual, numbers on the outside counting to a hundred with another set of numbers within that, roman numerals one through twelve like a normal watch. Five dials stretched forth from the center, two red hands and three black hands of varying lengths. Between the center pin and the set of roman numerals three symbols were evenly spaced, intricately detailed and yet unidentifiable for being so small.

Except one. One symbol was glowing, and whatever was giving it light also lent it detail. It was a demon's head, grotesque and gnarled by the expression of hatred on its face but beautiful in its detail. Luminous with a golden inner light, the picture seemed three dimensional and somehow alive. Details glowed yellow, but the eyes burned red.

Shifting the object in his hand to make the face also visible to Kris across the table, he saw an angle he hadn't seen.

"Look!" Paul said, a chill running up his spine. "My name is engraved on the inside of the cover." It was, too, four bold letters in the same calligraphy used on the front for the 'W'.

Kris was looking at the watch, an alarmed expression on his face. "Do you know what that says?" He leaned forward for a better look.

"Yeah, it says 'Paul'. Cool, huh?" He grinned.

Shaking his head, Kris leaned forward further and snaked one hand from his robe to point at the glowing symbol. "No, that," he said. "How much time do we have here?"

All five hands were a mystery to Paul. He only knew that no matter how he looked at them they didn't seem to tell the time. Staring intently at the watch face failed to bring a revelation.

"The short red hand is on the two and seems to be moving most quickly," Paul said, trying to be helpful. "It looks like its counting backwards."

Kris peered at the watch again. "It's counting down," he said warily, slumping back into his seat. He screwed the cap back on the silver flask, hurriedly, and stowed it again in the folds of his robe.

"To what?" Paul arched his eyebrows, curiosity to match his friend's apparent alarm.

"It's counting down to your first demon encounter," Kris responded flatly. "We have less than two minutes until you have to face your first demon as a Walker. Where's your weapon?"

"My what?" As Paul said the word *what* the red dial passed the roman numeral for two and started moving faster, sweeping over the twelve and then the eleven and then the ten, crossing a marker every five seconds.

CHAPTER 16

"Dude, that was awesome!" Tyler took a couple quick steps, halted suddenly and then took two more quick steps, erratically keeping pace with the others as they strode the sidewalk. Mason felt as lit up as Tyler was acting, even quiet Jason wore the happy hint of a smile. They were all filled with the excitement that lingers after a group of musicians have played well together, and Cal seemed to have been as much a part of it all just being there and listening.

They were all pretty high on cocaine, too.

Mostly it was the music, though; and Tyler had spoken of nothing else since they had shut down the amplifiers around ten o'clock.

Tyler stopped and looked at Mason seriously as he continued his even pace. "I think we're ready for a gig, man. That was awesome!" A few quick strides took him ahead again, and he looked to Mason again as he passed. "What do you think?"

"That was pretty awesome," Mason agreed noncommittally.

Wide enough for three of them to walk abreast, Mason strode coolly between Jason and Cal on the sidewalk. Tyler darted around signposts and thick round streetlight poles, keeping up without ever quite walking alongside the others.

Cal glanced sidelong at Mason. "You sure you don't want to go back to the club?" he asked. "There were a lot of hotties."

Eyes on the path before them, Mason shook his head and took a drag from his cigarette. "I don't like techno." There had been some fine young ladies at the club they had visited, but the hypnotic monotony of the thrumming beats made him uneasy for some reason. "I heard there might be a good band at Mallory's tonight."

"Mallory's it is." Cal grinned.

"What do you think, Mason?" Tyler dashed past them to stand behind a streetlamp as they passed. "Are we ready for a gig?"

Mason flicked his cigarette a few feet ahead of him. It hit the sidewalk in a miniature explosion of fire and ash to lay there smoking until his foot came down on it in passing. "We need a lead singer."

The hyperactive bass player hooted from behind the trio. "It sounded like we had a pretty kick ass lead singer tonight to me."

"You guys did sound great," Cal voiced his agreement while Jason bobbed his head enthusiastically. "You sing just like the dude from Metallica."

They walked in silence for awhile, the four coming to a stop together to wait for a walk signal. Tyler was able to walk next to Cal as they crossed the street, and the brothers exchanged smiling glances. Bug-eyed and grinning, Tyler still kind of skipped along, though now in step with the others. Soon Mallory's came into view. The first indicator was the little crowd of people milling around outside smoking, visible from half a block away. Soon after were the faint sounds of live music, and then they could read the canvas overhang as they approached. White cursive letters a head high on blue background, *Mallory's* across the front face and in smaller letters again on each side where the banner face turned sharply and attached to the building above either side of the entrance.

Taking a few steps into the street to view a better angle, Tyler called out, "The band sounds good. Five dollar cover."

"Tyler!" Mason glanced over, called out suddenly, his voice taut and hoarse and panicked. "Get out of the street!"

Tyler glanced up and down the empty street, shrugged and skipped back onto the sidewalk. As they approached the entrance to the club, they fell neatly into line behind Cal. Smiling, Cal glanced at the sign tacked up next to the doorman announcing a five dollar cover, then leaned in to say something quietly to him.

Broad in the shoulder and big in the belly, the fellow smiled and shook Cal's hand. Smooth as silk, the little baggie that was in Cal's hand when they came together was in the bouncer's hand as it slid away. The big man grinned and waved them inside, stamping each of them on the wrist as they passed. No one was surprised; this was just how it went when Cal was in town.

The bar was cluttered with drinks and crowded with people, every one of the fifteen or so stools occupied. Swaying to the music, more stood in the spaces between stools holding their drinks. They watched the band or the dance floor or talked loudly to each other, the words drowned in the music and the shouted casual conversations around them.

Between the edge of the dance floor and the bar was a normally wide aisle that was now crowded with drunken young bodies clad in clinging short skirts or dark slacks or jeans and printed tee and polo shirts and low-cut blouses. The three musicians melted into the small tight crowd while Cal worked the bar. Jason stood shy and quiet with his hands in his jacket pockets and watched the drummer onstage. Mason tried to divide his attention equally between watching the band, hearing what Tyler was shouting excitedly to him and letting his hands hang casually at his side while a young blonde's ass pressed rhythmically into his crotch in time with the music.

"These guys rock, man!" Tyler looked over the sea of bobbing heads at the band, then up at Mason, then back to the band. "Don't you think?" he shouted.

Mason had to agree. He nodded, glancing down at the thin black material stretched tight across the firm round buttocks now grinding into him. As the girl swayed away again, he shot his friend a wicked grin. When she glanced back suddenly, though, he was coolly watching the band and paying her no notice at all. She turned away quickly but seemed even more determined to press her skirt back forcefully into his jeans. Mason smiled inwardly.

Over his shoulder, he spied Cal coming towards them clutching two bottles of beer in each hand. Mason started toward him, noticing a guy in the back of the bar jump up out of his booth and bolt for the door. Suddenly he felt icy prickles climb his spine and a cold sweat break out across his face. He took an uncertain step towards Cal and saw a look of concern spread across the other man's features. Cal crossed the space between them and proffered him an elbow. "You okay, man?" He was close, but he still had to shout. "You look white as a ghost!"

Clutching the elbow with one hand gratefully, Mason put his other hand on Cal's shoulder and leaned heavily on him. "I need to sit down," he muttered.

"What?!" Cal leaned in close and shouted right in his ear.

Mason winced at the noise and took his hand from the shoulder long enough to point at the empty booth in the back.

"I need to sit down!" he shouted, and this time Cal heard him. By now, Tyler had turned and noticed them and reached out to tug on Jason's sleeve to get his attention. Mason let them half-drag, half-carry him toward the booth, but his legs steadied as they walked until he was able to take the last few steps himself. He collapsed onto the bench and slid over, rubbing his eyes as he bumped unceremoniously into the wall. Shaking his head slowly, eyes closed, he ran his fingers through his hair a couple of times, felt it damp with sweat. He heaved a heavy sigh and opened his eyes.

The others were watching him closely, Tyler next to him on the cushioned bench, Jason across the table from him and Cal next to Jason across from his brother. The four beers sat untouched between them where

Cal had placed them, an empty bottle of Blue Moon off to the side next to another bottle that was half empty.

Mason managed a feeble smile of reassurance. It was a little quieter back here, but he still had to raise his voice to be heard. "I'm alright, you guys." He waved one hand dismissively and snagged the closest bottle of beer with the other. When he motioned the others to do the same, Cal and Jason both grinned and reached for bottles. Tyler hesitated a moment, watching Mason, then shrugged and joined the others in a long cool drink.

When Mason set down his beer he was fighting a smile. "No worries, guys," he said confidently. "I feel awesome." It was the truth, too. He couldn't tell them why, but he felt happy and giddy and like he might start grinning a big goofy happy cocaine grin if he didn't keep this secret inside and play it cool.

The image had haunted him day and night since first imprinting itself on his windshield, a mangled mess of bloodied face staring back at him constantly behind his eyes. He had thought his drinking had made it go away sometimes; but it hadn't, not really. It was gone now though, gone like he had been pinned under a truck that had been suddenly lifted away. There was no image, no feeling of guilt, and no clear thought about the accident at all except that it had happened.

If he wanted to, Mason could make himself think about it, try to recall the image. He didn't want to, though, and he wouldn't make himself. Ever since it had happened he had thought clearly of nothing else for all his fighting to not think of it. Now it was gone, his full attention on the pleasant mixture of chemicals coursing through his veins and having a fun night out with his friends. He had kept the nightmarish image a secret; now his only secret was that the secret was no longer working its crushing dark magick on him.

Watching the band and the crowd past his friends, he felt their continued uncertainty. The next time Tyler glanced to check on him he was met with a glowering reproach that was somehow full of good cheer. "I'm fine," Mason growled happily. "Now get out of my way." He drained his beer, upending the bottle and gulping, hungry for the drink. "I'm gonna go dance with some hotties."

Tyler exchanged a look with the others, bemused, but he slid out of the booth and stood aside. Letting Mason breeze past, he sat again across from the others.

"Since when does Mason dance?" Cal hollered across the table at his brother.

"I've never seen it," Jason piped up, unexpectedly, his voice barely audible.

Tyler shrugged and shook his head, agreeing with Jason. "Since now, I guess."

"Cool." Cal grinned and took a long swallow from his bottle of Budweiser. "It's a party now." With that, he got up and moved toward the thickening mass of bodies writhing to the sounds of a well-rendered Maroon Five tune, dancing more than walking toward the crowded floor.

Watching for just a minute, Jason and Tyler saw Mason's lighthearted rhythmic movements joined by a smiling dark-haired beauty in a dress, a red tube of tight cotton that started three quarters of the way up her thighs and ended at the upper curvature of her breasts, squeezing them together firmly in an impressive show of cleavage. She smiled up at him and moved close enough to brush lightly against him. Mason leaned in and said something and she giggled and covered her mouth with one hand. The other hand reached out and rested for a moment on his chest as she swayed back and forth in front of him.

They saw that Cal had it even better, with a girl dancing on either side of him by the time he hit the edge of the tight little crowd. He pressed through, though, people made way, and the girls followed attentively. Soon he was lost in a sea of bobbing faces.

Jason looked across the table at Tyler and smiled wanly. They sat quietly and watched the band and the swaying young bodies wistfully together, sipping their beers.

CHAPTER 17

"Where's your weapon?" Kris was insistent, gray eyes wide with alarm.

"What weapon?" Paul felt like an idiot broken record. The arm of the watch seemed to be moving faster, but that was likely due to the impending sense of unidentifiable doom that he felt, and the way he couldn't tear his eyes from it.

"Paul? Paul?" He wrenched his gaze from the countdown as it passed fifteen seconds. Kris was watching the door with anxious gray eyes. "Get ready."

Paul clutched the watch before him nervously, searching his friend's face for answers. "For what, Kris? Get ready for what?" Following his gaze, Paul swept his eyes past the dance floor and the throng of swaying bodies toward the exit.

Vigilantly watching the entrance, it took Kris a moment to realize that Paul had locked eyes with a demon that was already in the club. Hands shrouded before him in the sleeves of his robe, Kris looked up at his friend, over at the demon, back at his friend and then down at the watch in Paul's hand.

Paul sat frozen, eyes wide and unblinking. The dial on the watch stood still, the countdown was over. The demonic symbol seemed to be glowing brighter than before, pulsing lightly.

The gruesome little beast was a fearful caricature of a demon. Paul hadn't seen many demons, but they all looked kind of beautiful in a dark, alluring way. This demon was what he may have imagined if he had imagined a demon back when he thought demons were only imagination. His arms and legs were twisted and gnarled limbs of awkwardly bulging sinew and taut skin and strained tendons, and he clung savagely to his host's shoulder with the long warped claws of beastly hands and feet. Most twisted and warped and hateful was the face, the eyes cold black slits of spite above a nose upturned to resemble a pig's snout. A ghastly sneer showed a dozen teeth narrowing to long and thick needles protruding from wet purple gums.

It was the biggest demon he had seen, just over three feet tall if its twisted limbs would allow it to stand up straight. Glaring at him, it hung awkwardly like an overgrown toddler that insists on being carried. The young man it clung to had his back to Paul and seemed to be enjoying the band and the girl dancing in front of him, oblivious to both Paul and the demon.

"What should we do?" Paul couldn't take his eyes off the demon, though he could feel Kris watching him.

"We?" Kris laughed, a little nervously. "I'm just a Guide. You're the Walker."

Paul finally dragged his eyes from the little red monster to look at his friend and frown. "Guide me, then. What do I do?"

Kris shrugged. "Kill it. Separate it from its host and kill it."

Looking at the demon again, Paul felt a feeling of dread come over him. It may have been the size of a child, but it looked like a killing machine, all claw and tooth and muscle and hate. And horns. Sleek jagged spikes sprouted twisting as long as a finger from its lined and leathery forehead. Paul got an image of those teeth furiously gnawing his knee while those twisted little spikes dug into his thigh, and he paled a few shades.

"How do I kill it?" he asked meekly.

"Where's your weapon?" Kris asked again.

Paul looked at Kris, his eyes wide with fear and a little anger. "What weapon?" he snapped.

Before Kris could respond, they both caught the movement and turned.

Snarling and salivating like a mad dog, the demon climbed to the man's shoulder and launched itself toward them recklessly. Kris and Paul sat and watched it hit the floor heavily, only to rise and lope towards them with a clumsy gait and silent snarls.

"I think we better go," Kris said suddenly.

By the time Kris had finished speaking, Paul's hand hit the release bar on the back door. His feet were kicking up gravel when the door slammed shut behind him with a bang, but he didn't look back and he didn't stop running. Reaching the end of the alley, he rounded onto the sidewalk still at a sprint.

Paul dared a glance over his shoulder just as the demon pitched and rolled its way onto the street, apparently unable to turn at a run any more gracefully than it could lunge. When he turned to watch the sidewalk ahead again, Kris was beside him. Keeping up easily with Paul's frantic flight, he seemed more to be floating along rapidly in a cloud of robe than running or even walking.

Paul skidded around another corner, and Kris pointed across the street.

This was their neighborhood, their favorite bar and restaurant and coffee shop and market all within a few blocks of their apartment. Roche's coffee shop was across the street, and Kris pointed at Roche standing in the open doorway puffing away at a cigarette.

Upright, he was even more imposing than when he crowded his little table in the back of the coffee shop. Although he was leaning against the doorjamb casually, the way his girth filled the doorway was almost challenging just for his size. Fedora tilted forward over his eyes, dark shadows pooled his face even as his cigarette glowed bright red.

Roche noticed them, saw Kris pointing and met Paul's eyes across the street. In the same moment, the demon lurched around the corner. It came more slowly this time, its claws scrabbling for purchase as the nightmarish figure stayed upright rounding the turn. It was learning.

Paul looked back at Roche. The big man flicked his smoking cigarette into the street before him and grimaced.

"Hey, Walker!" He called out. "You'll find haven here." Lumbering casually inside, Roche held the door open behind him.

Without a thought, Paul dashed across the street and through the open doorway. Roche shut it hastily behind him, locking the deadbolt with the keys that hung from the lock. Back in its usual place, dangling from a brand new brown weave of string, the round brass bell clanged merrily with all the activity. Roche waved his hands in swoops and swirls in the space between him and the door, crossing his arms resolutely just as the demon flattened itself against the window in a clumsy lunge.

Tumbling backward, the little red ball of hate launched itself again at the door, rocking it in its frame with the impact. Its face pressed against the glass, black loathing eyes glaring at Paul balefully. Clenching its fists, drawing purple spots of blood digging claws into its own palms, the demon backed up for another angry charge.

"Enough," Roche said flatly. Uncrossing his meaty forearms, he waved his hands again in the air. Paul thought he was drawing some symbol, the same thing three times. When he was done he pushed his hands slowly forward, palms out, as if he were slowly but forcefully shoving something unseen away from him. Paul thought he saw a network of red and white sparks and arcs for a moment, like silently crackling electricity. Blinking, he saw nothing again.

The demon stopped its advance suddenly, standing tilted to one side in the street. Looking around, face expressionless, its gaze swept unseeing past the coffee shop entrance. It turned and walked away slowly, stopping to glance left and right every few steps in bewilderment.

Paul and Kris stood and watched it go, staring through the glass in wonder and fading fear. The figure was approaching the last corner it had turned, walking back the way it had come. They both realized Roche was standing behind them and watching them watch the demon in the same moment.

Robe flowing, Kris whirled on Roche. "You can see me." It was an accusation, not a question.

Paul turned as the demon rounded the corner and disappeared from view. "Thank you," he breathed. There was something in the big man's dark eyes Paul hadn't seen before. "You called me Walker," he remembered aloud.

Voice still accusatory, Kris asked, "What are you, Roche?"

He eyed the friends in turn, glanced past them to make sure the street was empty, and raised his hand to lift his fedora. It cleared his skull completely just long enough to reveal two short stubby sharp horns jutting out halfway between the top of his skull and his forehead. He dropped the hat back into its customary place.

Paul backed towards the door slowly, fear rising again in his throat. "You're a demon?"

Watching Roche shake his big round head, he heard Kris say, "No." Kris wasn't backing away, and Paul stopped when he noticed.

"I'm a devil," Roche corrected him in a kindly tone. He turned to Kris. "Didn't he go to class?" He turned back to Paul. "Where's your weapon?"

It was too much. Paul started laughing suddenly, a little hysterically. He looked at Kris in that absurd robe and remembered the impossible horns he had seen jutting from Roche's head. The demon was long gone, but he turned and looked through the clear pane of door at the spot where it had stood glaring at him. He laughed, the image of the hateful little creature still chasing him behind his eyes.

He whirled on them suddenly. "I don't need to go to class. I need to go to therapy. I certainly don't need a weapon."

The other two exchanged a look. Kris shrugged. Roche eyed Paul in a way that was a little too serious, a touch too solemn. Paul started laughing again, a little maniacally.

"You better sit down, kid," Roche said. He turned and strode to the back of the shop, not looking to see if they followed. When Paul glanced at Kris, he just shrugged. Paul followed the lumbering giant and they all sat at a table, close to the office.

"Demons don't have souls," Roche was already talking as they sat down collectively. "Devils have souls, just like humans do. Some say that souls are created in Heaven and others insist they are created in Hell. Angels and devils know that the soul's journey is cyclical, rising and falling throughout the centuries through Heaven and Earth and Hell. Angels fall and become human, then continue to fall and become devils. Then the tide turns and the soul rises again. Devils and angels and humans are all simply souls in different temporary disguises. I was born a devil, the respectable and proper way. Like most everyone, I have memories only from this lifetime. Like most devils and angels and unlike most humans, I am aware of the nature of the soul's journey. It is not for me to try to cause my soul to rise or fall; my only duty is to cherish the journey."

Paul frowned. "Why would anyone think that souls were created in Hell?"

The devil shrugged. "From the individual's perspective, the soul's journey can often appear to be nothing but an interminable exercise in futility. We rise only to fall, only to rise again. It all seems a bit of a cruel experiment, especially to the falling soul. It's easier for most souls to attribute cruelty to the lower realms than to entertain the thought that God is kind of an asshole. Those on the rise tend to see a different picture, viewing the trials of falling souls as a beautiful fire burning away the darkness. Both perspectives are right, and both perspectives are wrong." He shrugged again. "Each view is wrong simply by virtue of being incomplete."

Hands on the table before him, Paul eyed the now strange familiar face closely. "And what is the respectable and proper way for a devil to be born?" he asked cautiously.

Roche nodded, smiled at Kris. "You know what they say about Walkers, don't you?"

Sitting next to Paul, Kris had his hands hidden away in the sleeves of his robe under the table. He nodded. "They call them the jocks of the afterlife."

"Before there were jocks," Roche smiled, "we called them the knights of the afterlife. All they cared about was killing and tending to their horse." His smile faded as his eyes met Paul's again across the table. "Now most of them don't even ride horses."

Kris turned to Paul. "Never call a devil a demon," he cautioned him. "It's like calling a man an animal. It's demeaning."

Spreading his hands, Paul smiled meekly at Roche. "Sorry."

"It's okay, kid, you didn't know," Roche waved it off lightly. "Seriously, though, where is your weapon?"

Paul just frowned, first at Roche and then at Kris.

"Your armor?" Roche ventured. "Your journal?" Paul's frown gave way to a look of bewilderment. "Your key?"

Paul hesitated, glancing at Kris. The guide shrugged, inclined his head. As soon as he thought of it, he could feel the weight of it in his hand. He splayed his fingers and showed Roche the watch, perching on his palm between them. Roche nodded, seemingly satisfied.

"Why did you help us?" Paul asked suddenly. "Aren't we kind of on opposite sides? Do devils not like demons?"

Roche eyed him skeptically, his eyes returning to the gold watch occasionally as he spoke. "Think of all the humans you have met in your entire lifetime, and then tell me this: have any one of them been pure good or pure evil, utter kindness or constant cruelty, unfailing sinner or untarnished saint? Have you ever met a single human being without a shadow of darkness in them, or one without a sliver of light?"

"Well, no," Paul spoke after a moment. "Everyone has demons, everyone has some darkness. Everyone has some redeeming qualities as well, I suppose."

Nodding, Roche said, "Well, it's the same with devils. Some of us are despicable bastards and some of us are kindly folk with horns. Most of us are something in between." He got up and strode toward the espresso island, still speaking as he filled two glasses with water and brought them back to the table. "The main difference is that as a rule we devils embrace our darkness. We understand that light cannot exist without darkness, and we accept it as a part of life and as a part of ourselves. We don't fight or resist our nature. If the pull of life is ebbing, we ebb with it just as happily as we flow with it. Of course, that's made a little easier by the fact that we live for hundreds of years, sometimes thousands. When you've got hundreds of thousands of tomorrows ahead of you, it can be a little easier to bet that one of them will be better than today. A lot can happen in a century of living, so many things that most humans simply couldn't understand or imagine."

Leaning his bulk over the table, Roche set a glass of water before Paul and one before his own chair and settled back down. "You humans spend your whole lives running from death, never realizing that you are really playing a larger game in which death is just an exciting new beginning," he said. "It's really kind of beautiful."

Soundlessly, Kris disengaged his hands from his sleeves and placed them on the table. "I see a Walker, a Guide and a devil," he said flatly. "I don't see any humans."

A tension hung in the air. "Hey, what did you do to that demon?" Paul asked Roche lightly. "Why did it just wander off? Was that devil magick or something?"

Roche smiled thinly at Kris for a moment, and then turned to Paul. "Sure, call it magick. I just gathered up a strong suggestion as a ball of thought or energy and sent it to him. Most demons are like most people. If you hold something out to them, they'll just take it. It works with lots of things." He eyed the gold pocket watch in Paul's hand.

Paul closed his fingers around the watch again. Something about the way the devil kept looking at it made him uneasy. He found himself thinking more than once that Roche was going to reach over and snatch it from him. Cool metal in his hand, he could feel it ticking through the casing. He wondered what the ticking might be counting down to, or up to.

"Could I learn to do that?" he asked.

"You could," Roche said. "Anybody could, with enough time and enough focus. Of course, that's true about anything."

"What you should learn," Kris broke in, "is how to separate a demon from its host and then kill it."

Roche inclined his head in agreement. "First things first," he said, rising from his chair. Walking toward his office, he stopped suddenly and turned, catching the other two exchanging a bewildered look. "Hey, Paul," he said. "What's your surname?"

"My surname?" Paul asked. "My last name? It's Stone. Paul Stone."

Standing in the open doorway, obscuring the office behind him with his girth, Roche seemed to be considering something. Then he chuckled, a low rolling throaty sound, and disappeared into the office. He was back a few moments later carrying what looked like a sturdy wooden walking stick. Nearing the table, he held it out to Paul.

His first instinct was to reach out and take it; but Paul hesitated, remembering what the devil had said. "What is that?" He asked, keeping his hands before him on the table.

Roche smiled, but it was Kris who answered.

"It's a Walker's weapon," he said, raising an eyebrow suspiciously at Roche. "Where did you get that?"

Ignoring the question, Roche had his eyes on Paul. "It's the difference between you hiding from little red monsters in coffee shops and actually doing your job as a Walker." He set the walking stick on the table before Paul.

Paul shook his head. "I never said I wanted to be a Walker," he said.

"A Walker handed you the key, and you took it," Kris sounded like he was reminding him of some agreement he had made. Roche nodded once, solemn.

Settling heavily in his seat across from Paul again, Roche frowned fiercely at him. "This is not a choice to be made; this is a destiny which you must fulfill. You are a Walker, not because you have a Walker's key but because you have a Walker's destiny. Embrace it."

Unconvinced, Paul leaned back in his chair and crossed his arms across his chest. "I don't believe in fate," he said resolutely.

"You don't believe in fate because you're not old enough to have felt what it can do to you," the devil grimaced. "I'm not talking about fate, anyway, I'm talking about destiny. And correct me if I'm wrong, but not long ago you didn't believe in demons either."

Paul had to admit that was true, and he did so with a frown and a slight shrug of his shoulders.

"Let me give you a bit of advice, kid," Roche went on. "Belief in anything will do nothing but limit you and empower whoever's ideas you are putting your belief into. Beliefs aren't formed by the intelligent observation of objective reality. Beliefs are formed by repeated thoughts or words or actions. We program our beliefs into ourselves and then waste an awful lot of energy trying to prove to ourselves and others that our beliefs are true. Beliefs are a waste of time and energy, and the only thing a belief has to do with reality is that its job is to keep you from perceiving it. As a general rule, if the only way to have something in your life is to believe in it, make sure it is something you really want in your life. Make sure you realize that your belief creates it for you and sustains it for you, not the other way around. And never be so arrogant as to think that your belief makes a thing true in anyone's reality but your own."

"What if I believe in the life I had before, what if my belief is that I don't want to chase and kill demons?" Paul bristled.

Roche nodded. "That's a great example of using a belief to deny all of the evidence being presented by reality. That is why most people succumb to fate instead of fulfilling their destiny. You're going to have a little trouble burying your head in the sands of your beliefs now that you've seen what you have seen. You're a Walker now. Embrace it." Leaning forward, the devil pushed the walking stick closer to Paul on the table with two meaty fingers.

It had character, gnarled wood that twisted and curved with such random precision that it made for an overall straight shaft. Without ornament, it was still impressive, lovingly sanded so the surface seemed to gleam with smoothness. Waist high to Paul, the shaft was near as thick as his wrist. Paul had the sudden feeling that this simple piece of wood was older that he could imagine, that perhaps it was the sands of time that had smoothed its luminous length.

Looking from the object on the table before him to his friend beside him and finally to the devil before him, Paul asked, "What am I supposed to do? Beat the demons to death with it?"

Kris sniggered beside him, and Roche rolled his eyes and shook his head.

"Pick it up," Roche growled. Paul looked to Kris, who just nodded agreement.

Paul sighed and stood up, pushing his chair back with the straightening of his legs. Resigned, he reached out and curled his fingers around the thickest end of the shaft. It was not as heavy as it looked, and when he stamped one end lightly on the floor his hand rested easily on top of the final knot. The height of it was perfect, had he needed a walking stick.

"Hold it in front of you like a sword," Kris suggested, turning sideways in his chair to watch.

He did, feeling a little foolish, one hand above the other on the smooth shaft. The other end hovered in the air between them, menacing the two at the table with a blade that wasn't there.

"Think of a sword," Kris continued. "Close your eyes and picture it if it helps. Better yet, put yourself in the picture. Visualize yourself standing there holding a sword."

Closing his eyes, Paul pictured a sword in his hands, a short thick steel broadsword with simple cross guard and a two-handed hilt. He opened his eyes to the reality of a stick of wood.

"It's all about intent," Roche offered helpfully. "Intent and belief. Intend to hold a sword in your hands, believe you do, and act as if it were true."

Paul frowned doubtfully and lowered the stick. "And that's going to change a piece of wood into a piece of steel? Intent and belief?"

"It will that one," Roche's glance indicated the shaft of wood Paul held. "For you." Kris nodded his agreement.

Paul closed his eyes again, holding the walking stick in his hand and the sword in his mind.

"Feel the weight of it in your hands," Kris guided him. "The leather of the hilt, the heaviness of the steel. Know for certain that you are holding a sword."

Straining his imagination, reaching mentally for something he knew wasn't there, Paul opened his eyes again to frown at the stick in his hands.

Without a word, Roche stood suddenly and turned to stride again toward the door of his office. A moment later, he filled the doorway with his fedora in one hand and a long curved wickedly sharp sword in the other. He made for an intimidating sight, pointed horns above his grimace and pointed steel below.

Paul felt suddenly uneasy again. "Well, if you have a sword already, why do I need to try to turn this into one?" His nod indicated the piece of wood in his hands, made much less threatening in the presence of the devil's huge weapon.

Without a reply, Roche began to approach slowly, dropping his fedora and raising the gleaming blade over his shoulder with one hand as if to strike. A wicked grin stretched the skin of his face, and Paul swore his canines had not looked like fangs until just now. He backed slowly away from the threatening advance, holding the gnarled cane before him in what felt more like a helpless gesture than a defensive one.

Not looking behind him, Paul backed into a table, feeling it press into his taut hamstrings as he heard the feet skid across the floor. Off-balance for a moment, he reached behind him with one hand to steady himself on the table. He gripped the walking stick before him with the other, horizontally, at arm's length and eye level.

In that moment the devil rushed him, light on his feet and seeming to glide more than walk to close the gap between them. The huge sword came down in a swooping arc, and Paul shut his eyes instinctively just before it connected with the walking stick. Eyes closed, he heard metal clang on metal and felt the shock of impact run up his arm to rattle his shoulder in its socket. The blade did not cleave wood to split his face, and when he opened his eyes he saw why.

He held a sword in his hand, much like what he had imagined but not quite. The long hilt was wrapped in black leather, one end an orb of steel the size of a golf ball and the other crossed by a stout steel hand guard a finger's length wide in the center to stretch both directions and terminate in squares the size of dice a hand's breadth to either side. Blood pumping with fear, senses heightened, he noticed a "W" engraved deeply into the cross guard. The blade was longer and not as wide as he had imagined, but the blood groove was there, running nearly the entire length from pommel to a few inches from the roundly pointed tip. Neither heavy nor light in his hands, it was the kind of sword to be wielded with either one hand or two comfortably.

"Nice bastard," Roche acknowledged, lowering his weapon. "I thought that might work."

Heart still pounding, Paul held the blade before him, glaring at the devil. He glanced at Kris and was surprised to see that he was trying not to laugh. The Guide had disentangled hands from robe to cover half his face with one. Muffling his voice did not stop his shoulders shaking with silent laughter, however, and Paul felt fear turn into anger towards both of them suddenly.

"You *thought* that might work?" he raged at Roche, taking an angry step toward him and grasping the hilt with both hands as if ready to swing it. "What if it hadn't? You could have killed me!"

Roche looked at Kris, raising thick eyebrows to crinkle lines across his forehead. "He doesn't know anything, does he?"

The Guide just shrugged his shoulders, sobered by Paul's angry outburst.

When he had attacked before, Roche has seemed to move smooth and effortless and incredibly fast. Steel flashed in the space between them now, with speed so blinding it took Paul a moment to realize what had happened. Looking down, he saw that his shirt had been sliced horizontally across his belly, and was stained with blood where the fabric was no longer whole.

From the corner of his eye he caught a glimpse of the tip of Roche's sword, smeared with blood. He felt a momentary twinge of pain, and when he lifted his shirt he saw the flesh knitting itself back together bloodlessly. Less than a second later his stomach was whole and smooth and flat again. The blood around the wound seemed to be drawn into his skin, leaving neither scar nor stain on his muscled abdomen.

Blood still smeared the end of the devil's sword and stained the slice on Paul's shirt as he dropped it back into place in disbelief. He felt silly still holding the sword; the other blade had sliced under his defense before he could even think of reacting. Lowering it with one hand, he felt the other hand stray unconsciously to where he had just been cut. His fingers slipped through the bloody slit in his shirt to reassuringly touch unblemished skin.

"I healed," he stammered, holding his empty hand in front of him in disbelief.

Kris nodded solemnly, hands hidden in the sleeves of his robe. "Only God can kill a Walker," he said, a touch of pride in his voice. "And God never would."

The devil burst out laughing at that, then sneered at Kris. "They tell you that at Guide School, kid? Don't let them get to you. Most Guides are as pompous and ignorant as human energy workers and righteous and arrogant as angels. I've always liked you, but it won't last if you start spouting ignorant platitudes with an air of spiritual superiority. Anything is possible, and ignoring the darkness is no way to prepare for it."

Bristling visibly from the rebuke, Kris seemed to shrink further into the voluminous folds of his robe. Paul tried to think of something to say to break the tension. "There really are angels?" he asked the devil. He noticed that there was a touch of wonder in his voice.

"Of course there are angels," Roche snorted. "All kinds of them, cluttering up the world and clogging the higher frequency airwaves. Bunch of arrogant holier-than-thou bastards too chickenshit to take any decisive action unless there is a real emergency. Otherwise they just float around all aloof and send positive loving energy into what turns out to be their own personal agenda, spouting off about how selfless they are at every opportunity." He swung the sword effortlessly and absently as he spoke, bloodied blade flashing, and Paul took a step backwards and bumped into the table again.

The devil seemed to notice then that he was waving a lethal blood-stained weapon around haphazardly. He turned and made for the open office door, dipping gracefully to retrieve his fedora from the floor as he passed. Moments later, he returned to the table sans sword, fedora firmly planted on his big round skull. Soon they were all seated again, and Paul's blade morphed back into walking stick as he set it on the table between them. Discouraged by Roche's outburst, he was still curious. "Have you ever met an angel?"

"Oh, yeah," the devil waved the question off casually. "Three..." he broke off, considered for a moment, "...two of my best friends are angels. They're not all bad, especially the ones that remember they are on the way down eventually. There are personal angels, too, like there are personal demons. Regular angels with souls call them 'lights', and all you usually glimpse of them is a little light form hovering over someone's shoulder like a firefly. Some say every time a demon is born a light is born as well. One cannot exist without the presence of the other, no matter how small. It makes sense if it is true. It's got the ripe stench of hopeful belief on it, though, and that tripe is for humans and angels." He looked pointedly at Kris. "Walkers and Guides and devils have no need for such nonsense."

"It makes sense from a psychological standpoint," Kris seemed pleased to be acknowledged by the devil. "Every personal issue has pros and cons, positives and negatives, even if the only positive aspect is what you learn from wrestling the issue."

Roche took a breath, and Paul sensed that he was about to go off on a tirade. Instead he looked from Kris to Paul and nodded. "You're in good hands, Walker. Now get out of my shop and come back in a few hours and buy some coffee."

Back at their apartment, Paul crinkled the unread note and tossed it in the trash. He moved toward the coat closet to stash the ancient walking stick, but it disappeared suddenly. He shrugged, his capacity for amazement at its limit for the day. "Watch T.V. if you want," he told Kris. "I'll just tell

Brenna I left it on if she hears it." He heaved a heavy sigh and added, "Until I can explain all of this to her."

The Guide's eyes widened. "Oh, no, you can't do that," he insisted hastily. "Go to sleep, go to class, learn what you can. How much time do we have?"

It was a moment before Paul realized what he was asking. Holding his hand palm upturned before him, he clicked the watch open with his thumb and peered at it. He turned it so Kris could read the face and see the hands and did his best to look like he was trying to puzzle it out.

"We have about thirty-six hours," Kris was visibly relieved. "Get some rest." He settled his weight heavily on the couch and waved his hand at the television. It came on with a flash of light and noise.

Paul looked at the watch face again, but he just saw dials and numbers. Snapping it shut, he felt it disappear before he could slip it in a pocket.

Stepping into the bedroom, his senses were awash in Brenna's presence, her scent, and the sweet smell of their coming together earlier. He stood there for a moment, letting his eyes adjust. Streetlights prevented his bedroom from ever being completely dark. Brenna lay on her side, asleep and breathing deeply, curve of hip and shoulder swathed in the sheet silhouetted by streetlight. He doffed his clothes, piling the bloodied shirt under the rest until he could dispose of it properly. Slipping quietly under the sheets, he slid his body close to hers. She moved closer in her sleep, pressing her back to his chest and her buttocks into his crotch.

Although he wasn't tired, Brenna's warm naked flesh against his relaxed him to his bones. Her measured breathing soon lulled him to sleep.

CHAPTER 18

The club was closed, but the party wasn't over. Music still played, recorded music that served as background noise piped quietly over the sound system. Top forties hits were the soundtrack to the after party, some of the same songs the band had been playing to a packed club not so long ago.

A dozen people sat at tables or at the bar, Mason's friends among them. Mason was at the bar with the lead singer, a thin girl with a straight frame and smooth pale skin, shoulder length straight black hair with bangs cut just above her eyes. She had a cute face, light green eyes that widened all the way for just a moment right after she would blink. Short and petite, her small round breasts and slim hips made her more pixie-like than boyish. Her light and sheer summer dress, patterned with blue and green flowers, had swayed and swished when she was performing; now it clung to her thin frame in a way Mason found quite alluring.

He had complimented her after the last set, genuine compliments that showed he was a musician. Falling into conversation naturally somehow with a genuinely pretty girl was new to him, but he did his best to play it cool. They had been talking about the songs they had played and the ones playing over the speakers now as they came on.

"You don't seem to sing as many songs by female singers as you do songs by guys," Mason was saying. Her name was Sarah, and she fiddled with the straws in her drink more than she actually used them to sip her long island iced tea as he spoke. "You sing them so well, though. You sang 'Firework' just like Katy Perry, and you can sound just like Lady Gaga or Madonna without even trying."

Holding her drink between them with one hand, stirring absently with the other, Sarah perked up noticeably at the compliment. "I do have to try," she released the straws and held her thumb and forefinger a quarter inch apart. "A little. Besides, saying you can sound like Lady Gaga and Madonna is somewhat redundant. Lady Gaga is a younger, more imaginative, more talented version of Madonna. And Katy Perry writes awesome inspiring songs that lift your spirit and make you want to sing along, but she's not some dramatically phenomenal singer. Tell me I sound like Christina Aguilera if you really want to get in my panties."

"You sound just like Christina Aguilera," he said immediately, and they both laughed.

She made a face. "Liar," she said, though she seemed pleased enough.

"That's my point, though," he pressed, strangely as interested in making his point as he was in the play of sheer dress over smooth skin. "I didn't hear you sing any Christina Aguilera. Or Mariah Carey." He thought a moment. "Or Alicia Keyes. You wailed 'Train Kept A Rollin' like you were Steven Tyler with a brand new set of female vocal chords, you sang that Nazareth tune like I never thought it could be sung. Do you have something against great female singers?"

Sarah eyed him thoughtfully over her well stirred cocktail. "That's it, though," she shrugged slightly, her dress rising and falling over her small breasts with the movement. "I can stylize Aerosmith or Nazareth or AC/DC and it's expected because I'm a girl. I can't sound like a dude no matter what, right?"

She waited for an answer. Mason struggled with wanting to ask her about AC/DC while wondering what she was about to say and what her breasts looked like all at once. A little stupefied by his wonderful choices of things to think about, he managed to nod vaguely.

"If I sing an Alanis Morrisette song, though, I should do my best to sound like Alanis Morrisette. You might walk away from a Train song totally impressed with what I did with it because I'm a girl, but you'll probably think I screwed up if I don't sing a Sheryl Crowe song just like Sheryl Crowe." Sarah set her drink resolutely on the bar and turned to face him again. "Am I right?"

"But you can sing just like Sheryl Crowe. I heard it myself."

"Yep," she nodded. "Impressive, huh?"

Mason smiled, as impressed by her confidence as he had been with her performance. "Honestly, I think that if you let yourself play around with women's parts as much as you do men's parts it might be even more impressive."

Giggling, Sarah covered her mouth coyly with the back of her hand while Mason thought back on what he had just said. He flushed.

"Mason," Sarah said, putting a hand on his knee lightly. A thrill climbed his leg from her hand and seemed to light him from within for a moment. "Are you suggesting that I sing more songs by female artists, only in my own style; or are you trying to get me to have a three-way with you and your girlfriend?"

"I don't have a girlfriend," Mason corrected her quickly, on that point anyhow. "And you know what I meant, though if you're going to dangle a threesome in front of me I'm sure I could be talked into it." Before she could reply, he added hastily, "As long as it's not a devil's threesome." He shuddered a little under his warm jacket.

Drink in hand again, Sarah sucked both little straws until the glass was nothing but ice and a fleeting bubbling sound as the last few drops of cocktail were drawn into her mouth. Licking her lips, she set the drink down to turn again towards Mason. This time she rested a hand on each of his knees as she spoke, and he had to make a real effort to not grin.

"A devil's threesome?" she asked pointedly. "Let me guess, is that two guys and one girl?"

Mason shuddered again and made a face. He nodded.

Her expression matched his own. "That's icky," she said. "Men and women are a mix of sensuality and sexuality, most men being more sexual and most women being more sensual while both sexes have some level of both sensuality and sexuality within them. Two girls and one guy seems like it could be beautiful, steeped in sensuality with just the right amount of sexuality. Two guys and one girl is too much sexuality, I think, and the sensuality would end up either taking a back seat to sexuality or being entirely absent from the experience."

"Yeah," Mason nodded. "Two girls and a guy looks like a love-fest, two guys and a girl looks more like a fuck-fest."

"Exactly. How eloquent of you." A slow smile started on her lips, and she glanced at the small stage she had decorated not long ago with her presence. The most cumbersome items had been removed, drum kit and amplifiers and the band's mixing board. Some remained, though, two electric guitars and one acoustic, a few preamps and microphones on stands.

Sarah turned back to Mason and jerked a thumb over her shoulder toward the stage. "Wanna play?"

Sitting up straighter suddenly, he grinned. "You serious?"

"Yeah, sure," her pretty little head bobbed up and down and her smile grew wider. She swiveled her stool and called out across the bar, "Hey, Mikie, can Mason play your guitar?"

One of the men breaking down the set paused in the middle of coiling a microphone cord around his elbow and palm to nod simply and reply, "He'll have to play the acoustic unless you guys want to use my preamp or the house PA."

Behind the bar, an older fellow with graying hair and sweatpants under sweatshirt piped up. "You can use the PA if you keep it kinda quiet." He shot a look at Mason, a doubtful look that wondered if he could actually play guitar or whether he was just trying to pick up on a girl.

"Let's start out acoustic," Mason smiled at her and stood up. "I have something in mind." He held his hand out to her and she took it and stepped in close enough to smell her sweet pale skin. Then she was leading him, her hand clutching his as she strode barefoot and graceful to the stage. At the step up, Mason held her hand until she was onstage and then let go to turn and retrieve a pair of chairs from a nearby table.

Launching himself onto the raised platform with a chair in each hand, he stopped and set them down, facing each other. By the time he had carefully lifted the black sleek Ibanez acoustic six-string from its cradle and turned, Sarah had already sat in one of the chairs. She had a tambourine in one hand and was smiling up at him while she brushed dark straight hair away from her face with the other. Her every move, her every curve, her very personality, seemed to have a softness and a grace to it. Mason found watching her move and smile and speak not just attractive, not just enticing; he found it intoxicating, and he let himself feel happily intoxicated.

Settling comfortably in the chair, he set the guitar lightly on his right thigh and let it rock back against his chest while he wound the strap around his shoulder. He strummed a G chord and a C and a D, then reached up to tighten the high E string and strum again. The harmonics sounded good, especially so on this guitar, and he modified his chording and strumming a bit so it was the first bars of Janis Joplin's 'Me and Bobby McGee.'

Her pale green eyes blinked and widened, luminous for a heartbeat. The tambourine shook once lightly in her hand, then again as she began to sing the first words.

Mason glanced up from his chords, watching her get lost in it. Somehow his fingers danced along the sparse lead notes while still making a wall of strummed sound. He watched both himself and Sarah in wonder for a few bars, failing to notice that he wasn't the only one listening.

All activity and conversation in the club had slowed and quieted and then stilled. As the first chorus approached, every eye in the bar was on the duo.

And Mason stopped playing. He leaned toward the little singer as if to say something. At the same time, they felt eyes on them, and they turned their faces sideways a breath apart to gaze out at the audience they didn't know they had.

"That was awesome," someone said from a table. "Why did you stop?"

"Yeah, Mason, what the fuck?" Cal hollered from the bar. "Keep playing, you guys."

They turned their heads again at the same time, and he gazed into her pale green eyes as she blinked and widened them once, then again. "Yeah, Mason, what the fuck?" she whispered. "Something wrong?"

Mason licked his lips, his mouth suddenly very dry. He could feel his heart pounding in his throat, and he thought that seeing the whites of her eyes every time she blinked was absolutely adorable. Shaking his head, he smiled a little shyly at her. "It sounds great. You sound great. I just wanted to say something."

A couple more shouts erupted from the after party patrons, and Sarah made a moue rather prettily. "Best say it and start playing before the natives get restless."

"It's just…" Now he felt like a jackass, wishing he hadn't stopped. He looked into her eyes, big and wide and questioning. "Don't try to channel Janis Joplin," he said resolutely. "Channel Sarah."

He leaned back again, starting from the beginning, to sparse cheers and applause. Smooth as silk, Sarah's voice moaned her own low pain instead of Janis' raspy darkness. Right from the beginning, she sounded different, her voice fuller and more breathy all at the same time. Mason nodded his approval to the beat of her tambourine.

The club was still then, but for guitar and tambourine and Sarah's haunting sultry voice singing of love and loss and freedom. It was Janis' song, but in those minutes the dark-haired soulful pixie made it her own, and her hurts widened the low notes while her hope spiked the high. Breathless and grinning through the outro, Sarah and Mason's eyes locked on each other again and again as he gently banged out the final bars on the guitar. He watched her eyes close and her lips cry out the final words to end in a heartwrenching cry of primal release.

Guitar and voice fell silent together to one last jangle of tambo bells. And for a moment, the silence was beautiful and huge and Mason looked at Sarah to find her looking at him in a way he found quite inviting. Like he was food. And she was hungry. No, starving.

Then the cheers and applause erupted, and Mason had a moment to think that it was an awful lot of noise for so few people before he had another idea. He started the arpeggio intro to 'Landslide' by Fleetwood Mac. Watching Sarah tilt her head to the side in the cutest way made him certain it was a good choice. When she looked at him he gave her a serious face and whispered fiercely, "Channel Sarah!"

Sad and soulful, her voice thick and low, almost crackling with emotion, Sarah's 'Landslide' was not just love and loss and cocaine; it was real tears streaming down her face and thickening her voice even more. It was the hope in her eyes when she opened them and looked at Mason like she wanted him to take his hands from the strings and put them on her.

Her voice dropping on the last few words, Sarah looked out at the people listening. Tears streamed down her face and glittered in the stage lights someone had turned on mid-song. Her mouth was open, turned down at the corners ever so slightly. She heaved in a full breath and swung her head to meet Mason's eyes and smile softly, seductively, secretly.

Sarah breathed the final word of the song just to him. She closed her eyes and put one hand on her heart and the other on Mason's knee as the noise of approval and appreciation spilled forth again from their small but attentive audience.

As the noise began to subside, Cal dashed to the stage, flushed and breathless. "Plug in, you guys. Let's have a real after party." Then he turned and addressed the room in the way he had, cool and intense all at once. "I'll cut a fat line of pure white for anyone who helps set the equipment back up."

People started moving all at once, until the barkeep in the sweatpants squeezed a noisemaker horn he apparently kept behind the bar. Then they stopped and looked at him. "And what about the club owner?" He glowered at Cal.

Cal just grinned. "And all the fat white lines the club owner wants."

He stood there, drying a glass and losing hair and sporting a sweat suit, then he returned Cal's friendly grin. "Get over here then," he said, wiping off a section of the surface before him. "The bar is glass." He looked around the room. "Am I the only one who wants a fat line? Get busy, people! We've only got all night, and we're about to hear a show."

The stage swarmed then, nobody noticing Mason and Sarah sitting in their chairs at the edge of the stage and talking excitedly. It took a moment for him to realize that he had reached out and taken her hand. He held it, though, not withdrawing, and she squeezed his fingers reassuringly every few moments.

Across the room, Cal was expertly cutting a score of fat lines on the bar surface. When sweat pants came to greedily snort one, Cal leaned over and asked him something. Two steps away and two steps back and he handed Cal an empty CD case. He set it carefully on the bar and manipulated his razor blade until the little white hill he had poured became two long white bars side by side, an equal sign etched out in cocaine. Like a waiter, he carried the CD case at eye level, balanced on his splayed fingertips, across the dance floor and to the stage.

Mason saw him approaching, and disengaged from Sarah a little nervously. Cal went straight to her though, and held the CD case up for her consideration like a humble peasant before a queen. Sarah's eyes widened, and she turned to Mason with a mischievous look on her face. "Are you going to do some?"

Hell yeah, Mason thought to himself.

"Only if you are," he said to her.

Carefully she took the proffered surface and set it on her knee gingerly. Cal held out his steel cylinder, and she seemed to know what to do with it. When she handed the metal straw to Mason, there was only one long white ridge remaining. She didn't move the case, just held it there and leaned back, so he leaned over and snorted the line off the CD case so close to the bare skin of her thigh. The cocaine filled one nostril, her scent filled the other, and he was intoxicated long before he felt numbness dripping down the back of his throat. They both thanked Cal, Sarah with words and Mason with a cool nod, as Jason and Tyler came up behind him.

"Hey, guys, this is Sarah," Mason spoke as they came to stand beside Cal. "Sarah, this is Jason and Cal and Tyler."

"Nice to meet you," she nodded politely to each in turn. "Thanks again, Cal." She turned to Mason. "Is this your band?"

He nodded. "Jason's the drummer and Tyler is the bass player. Cal is Tyler's brother. He's just visiting for the weekend, up from Santa Cruz."

"You guys need any help up there?" Tyler asked excitedly, wide eyes darting back and forth between the two of them.

Over her shoulder, Sarah saw her band setting up and getting ready to play.

Mason shook his head to save Sarah having to say no. "Sorry, guys," he said. "It's their gear and their gig. I doubt they'll even let me play now."

Someone laughed behind them. Mason turned and saw the guitarist unplugging an autotuner from a blue and white Fender Telecaster. He wore jeans over black leather boots, ripped denim and polished leather. His shirt was a concert tee from a Journey tour a thousand years ago, sleeves cut off to show every inch of his thin pasty arms. "I won't let you play the Les Paul because I'll be playing it." He held the Fender out to him lovingly, one hand cupping the smooth painted curved wood of the body while the other gently clasped the neck. "This is more of a lead guitar anyway."

Jimmy Page and Slash and a score of others would disagree with that, but Mason wasn't going to. Every time he had played the Gibson model, he thrilled at the sound while cursing his aching shoulder; it felt more like a boat anchor than a guitar. He was always surprised to find that the skinniest guitar players seemed to gravitate so often toward such a heavy instrument.

"Mikie, right?" Mason reached out and curled his fingers of his left hand around the neck of the proffered guitar. At the same time, he gripped the acoustic he had been cradling in his lap in the same way and held it out to the other man.

Mikie's dark brown hair was just long enough to be unkempt and a little wild, and it flounced and bounced atop his head when he nodded. After they exchanged guitars, they exchanged handshakes. "I'm Mason, thanks for letting me play. You've got some killer gear."

He smiled as he turned away, settling the black acoustic gently in its upright stand. Soon the thick wood of the Les Paul hung heavily before him, and Mason saw a thick pad was a part of the strap, hugging Mikie's shoulder to ease the burden.

When Mason turned around, he was happy to find Sarah leaning forward and talking excitedly with his friends. Tyler was telling her how they had played in different bands around the city, and they had found they knew musicians in common. "The three of us have been rehearsing for about six months now, two or three times a week," he was saying with excitement and pride. "Mason says we just need a singer." Tyler looked pointedly at Mason and then at Sarah as Mason turned to them.

"How much material do you guys have?" Sarah was being polite, Mason suspected. She had told him earlier that her band was booked every weekend for months in advance.

"Tons!" Tyler, always excitable, was beyond excitement. He zinged with cocaine and hope and possibility, his face wide open like a little boy. "It's mostly rock and metal, but we do some top forty and even some original stuff."

"Original instrumental," Mason interjected hastily. "I can sing Metallica, but I can't sing the songs I write."

A wave of sound overtook them then, first the drummer with a snapping short solo. At final crash, the bass guitar came alive in a jazzy sliding snap-and-pop accompanied only by the thumping bass drum. It went straight into a chunky bluesy scale then, and ended dramatically on the G string high up the fretboard as cymbals crashed again and Mikie's Les Paul came tearing onto the scene. He played an unrecognizable guitar riff, all power chords and palm mutes and simple enough. It made for a powerful sound, though, thick and meaty rock and roll made more so by the huge sound of Les Paul married to Marshall Stack and the tight rhythm of drums and bass.

Sarah was already taking her place, used to this ubrupt and powerful beginning. She stood and handed her chair to Cal on the floor, who took it and set it a few feet away before coming back for Mason's. It took him a moment to move, transfixed as he was by their cooperative sound check. He was used to the cacophony that seemed inevitable before a show or rehearsal, everyone checking volumes and tunings separately but simultaneously. This soundcheck was almost a song in itself. Every few simple bars, an instrument would have an opportunity to play alone while the others were silent for a bar of play.

Standing finally, strapping the pretty blue Telecaster round his shoulder lightly, Mason handed Cal his chair as Sarah stepped to the mic. Barefoot and tiny, her big voice started surprisingly low. "Gotta play, gotta play, gotta sing," she crooned. Her voice fell silent with both guitars while drums tattooed a rapid solo before everyone joined in again. This time she sang higher, closer to her speaking voice but flinty and richer. "Gotta play, gotta play, gotta sing." This round, the bass filled the silence with a simple but lively blues scale and a couple well-placed pops before falling back in with the others.

On the next round, Mason joined in, guessing the notes Sarah was moving up to correctly and wailing them along with her. When the break came, the blistering solo that leapt from his fingers surprised even him. He was right back in line with the others when it came around, and he played single sustained notes to match Mikie's power chords, then did the same with higher octave screaming harmonics, then silenced his guitar with the others to give Mikie a go.

Frowning, Mikie palm-muted a blues scale and ended it by sustaining the highest root note he could find without leaving the sanctuary of the first five frets. It sounded a little flat after Mason's dramatic contribution, but Mason grinned at the guy and nodded like he had just played 'Cliffs of Dover'.

He was still watching the other guitar player, playing off his rhythm, when the next silence came. Sarah's voice filled the room low and crackly, scat singing that went high and piercing to end in a huge and powerful high C that she sustained through the next two rounds of play. She held it over the drummer's solo, turning it into a gravelly piercing shriek that ended as the bass solo did. Somehow she had the lungs to keep it up because that impossibly high end of her voice is what she used when she sang, "Gotta play! Gotta play! Gotta sing!" one last time, and she held the word "sing" over Mason's brief solo.

He loved it. His blurred fingers matched the note, then danced around it, then screamed a harmonic an octave higher. Impossibly, she started to go higher, reaching for the note Mason was holding onto so tenaciously. Before she could get there or break her voice trying, the band joined in and Mason went to playing Mikie's part so he could rhythm his solo, and Sarah belted out "Gotta play! Gotta play! Gotta sing!" somewhere more comfortably within the range of human hearing.

After Mikie's final solo, everyone but Mason went smoothly into 'I Got a Feelin'' by Black-Eyed Peas, the bass player rotating his guitar on its straps across his back and appearing suddenly at the keyboard. He was singing, too, and doing a fine job of it. Mikie did a pretty good rap, although white guys no longer have an excuse for sucking at rap now that Marshall Mathers had turned his talent into an almost god-like presence and clarity of voice. Every time Mason saw a white guy rapping, he thought of Eminem and the guy invariably came up wanting. Of course, it wasn't just white dudes. Black guys often had a better groove and a better feel for it, but their words were too muddled and blurred and sometimes just too racially specific for him to understand or relate to what they were saying.

He had three or four minutes to think, there was not much for him to do on this song. A monster guitar solo would demonstrate a monster ego more than it would entertain anyone. He glimpsed the set list taped to the back of the monitor. Smiling, he noted the first song was "Gotta play! Gotta play! Gotta sing!". The second was of course his opportunity to watch Sarah channel Fergie. Next up was Lady Gaga's 'Bad Romance' and after that 'Drops of Jupiter' by Train.

Mason edged away from center stage slowly to make his way to stand beside the keyboard player with the unused bass across his back. When he wasn't singing, Mason leaned in close to his ear but away from his microphone. "Mason!" he shouted simply.

Still pounding keys diligently, the guy turned his head and shouted, "Robert! Rob! Whatever." Then he turned his head to sing counterpoint to Sarah and the drummer, and they locked it down tight.

Mason expected them to launch right into Lady Gaga, and they did. He watched Sarah, her siren's voice, her petite sexuality, her bare feet making her appear seductive instead of hippie in her naturalness. Smooth shaved legs and arms and carefully shaped eyebrows, with fingernails and toenails an aqua blue that complimented her dress, she took care of her body in consideration of both herself and others. He let his eyes and ears drink her in, playing the scant guitar parts of 'Bad Romance' without looking down at the fretboard.

Standing next to Robert, he watched his deft hands blur across the keyboard. He was playing notes usually sung by female background singers and it had the effect of bolstering Sarah's voice the way Lady Gaga's backup singers bolstered hers.

Mason leaned in slowly, so as not to distract the busy keyboarding. "You don't play bass much, do you?" he hollered in his ear.

Ten fingers impressively busy between two levels of keyboards, Rob nodded to his left hand. "That's where I play my bass."

"Can my buddy back you up?" Mason shouted hopefully.

He was just as surprised to see Rob return his hopeful look. "He play bass?" he shouted, then returned his full attention to his hands for a few difficult bars.

When he looked back, Mason was keeping rhythm on guitar and nodding in response. "Yeah, he's great. He loves playing bass. He's good, too."

As they wrapped up the song to a vocally responsive audience, Rob hit a couple stray notes on his keyboard, and all the band members turned to him.

"Sorry to interrupt, guys," he addressed the group, turned away from his microphone. "What's your buddy's name?" he asked Mason, on the other side of the mic.

"Tyler." Mason couldn't help but grin.

"Tyler," Rob said suddenly into the microphone, his voice bigger and mildly distorted with reverb and chorus.

Mason spotted Tyler leaned over the bar and slowly snorting a line of cocaine the size of a small earthworm. At his name, he finished the line hastily and lifted his head, swiveling toward the stage on his bar stool. Thumb and forefinger guarded his nostrils against any escaping powdered euphoria, and when he said 'what?' it sounded more like 'whud?'. He tilted his head back dramatically then, snorting loudly inward with each nostril while covering the other with his thumb. "What?" he said, more loudly and more clearly.

"Would you please take this burden from my shoulder so I might concentrate fully on playing keyboards?" Rob spoke into the microphone, a little too quickly to catch every word as it was processed by the effects.

Tyler seemed to get the message. He rushed the stage like he was imitating Tigger, even somehow tripping on his own nonexistent tail. He climbed the side of the stage clumsily, then crossed it to take the proffered fat-stringed guitar. Rob whispered a few things, Tyler nodding excitedly in either rapt attention or utter oblivion.

Then it started, all at once and all the sudden like all the others, Rob's keyboard sounded like a piano and his voice again deferred to Sarah's. Her voice danced the melody of the Train song's opening line. She glanced at Mason and caught him watching her. Her notes were precise and clear while her voice poured out thick and flinty. It was all he could do to play his guitar part and try to think ahead if this song had a solo. There was, and the band extended it with very little indication that they intended to. Mason felt it in the movement of the music somehow, though, and he tore into the extra time they gave him as forcefully as he could without interrupting the flow of the song. Coming together at the same time, they wrapped the tune up neatly and professionally to the sound of applause.

A lot of applause. Mason hadn't looked out into the club since the lights had come on over the stage, and he had to shield eyes with forearm to do so now. There were thirty or forty people where there had once been a dozen, and they were all drinking and some were starting to dance.

Sweatpants stood at the door, allowing or refusing people entrance, mostly allowing. He looked pleased, probably because he took money from each patron that passed and simply stuffed it into a front pocket. His pockets bulging obscenely, the man looked like he belonged in a low budget porn flick in profile. Still he grinned and wiped his nose with the back of his sweatshirt, stuffing bills in his pockets.

Silence hung in the air onstage, and Mason looked around to see all the other band members looking at him. He didn't know what to do, so he did what came naturally: he started playing an AC/DC song. Fingers a blur on the fretboard, he tapped the intro to 'Thunderstruck' to a hushed room. Guitar and bass and drums joined him to make a wall of sound, and then Sarah started singing. The notes weren't so high, for her, and Brian Johnson's twisted strained sound was only really possible for Brian Johnson. Mason wondered what she would sound like, from the moment she had mentioned that they covered his favorite band until the glorious moment when she opened her mouth and started singing.

It was beautiful and tortured and raunchy and flinted and perfect, tearing out of her throat like a demon escaped from hell. Mason threw his head back in exaltation, listening to her voice with his whole being. His fingers danced across the fretboard effortlessly, and for a long moment he had the deep sense that everything was right with the world. He could feel his guitar, he could feel Sarah, he could feel the people watching and listening. They were witnessing something magickal; and for that sweet forever moment, his guitar in his hands and her voice in his ears, he was happy.

Unseen by Sweatpants, with his bulging pockets and a few flecks of white clinging to his long nostril hairs, an awkward figure entered the club. Limping but moving with more assurance, the short sinewy demon spied Mason onstage almost immediately. It approached the raised floor slowly, hateful eyes fixed on Mason as it climbed and crawled round tables and people.

There was no hue, no cry, no shrieking young ladies. The demon passed unnoticed and unseen through the crowd, and stopped for only a heartbeat before clambering clumsily but quickly onstage. The twisted face watched Mason watching Sarah, features grotesque even when relaxed. Moving his red-skinned and muscled body between them, one hand clawing its way over the other, the demon climbed Mason's leg past his waist to cling awkwardly to his shoulder.

Mason's body shuddered involuntarily, but he kept playing. His shoulders slumped slightly and he leaned forward a little, but the notes were still there, the sound still pristine. Perched on his shoulder, slipping and clambering down his back and clawing back up his shoulder, the demon took turns looking at Mason, looking at Sarah, then looking at the guitar. Mason, then Sarah, then the guitar. Again and again.

CHAPTER 19

"Am I meeting Matt at the coffee shop?" Paul poked his head in the bathroom. Bent at the waist, blow drying her hair upside down turned away from him, Brenna clicked the machine off and straightened slowly. She caught him watching as she glanced over her shoulder at him. He just stared, her ass nearly as captivating to his attention now as it had been when she was bent over.

She gave a seductive little shake for him, dressed only in a thong and a bra and thigh high stockings. Then she turned and stepped into him, setting the blow dryer aside while she wrapped her arms about his waist and pressed her belly to his crotch. Looking up at him, mesmerizing him with those big brown eyes, she smiled softly. "What did you say, lover?"

The forefinger from each of his hands slid up under the thin material on her hips languidly. He slid his hands around her buttocks to grip them firmly and pull her closer. "Am I meeting your brother this morning?"

"No." She shook her head slightly without taking her eyes off his. "He said he's got an appointment. He also said to tell you he's sorry, but he won't be taking that job."

Paul could hear the irritation in her voice, and he wanted to keep the morning light. "Good," he said brightly. "I'll make some coffee and breakfast while you get ready."

Brenna pulled her hair back in a severe ponytail that showed her stark beauty, her full lips and high cheekbones illuminated brightly by the bar of light bulbs that framed the mirror. "It's not good," she frowned prettily, inspecting her perfection closely in the looking glass. She caught his eye for a moment in the reflection. "He's ditching another real job for some half-baked get rich quick scheme. Ever since Mom and Dad died, he's thought money comes in big chunks for free. Working for little chunks of it confounds his tiny brain."

"So..." Paul backed from the doorway, hands spread defensively. "No breakfast?"

Finally, she melted, and she was his Brenna again. Eyes wide, she said, "Breakfast?" like it was a magical once-in-a-lifetime treat, not something he made her two or three times a week. Just as excited, voice full of awe, she asked, "Can I have an omelet?"

Paul nodded solemnly, stepping close again. "With mushrooms and avocado and cheese and onions."

"And hashed browns and toast?" Eyes wide, she looked up at him like he could somehow make the whole world right again just by making her breakfast. How he wished it were so.

CHAPTER 20

Paul stood before the register and watched her busy herself with dishes for a moment before he called out to her quietly. "Hey Jess."

She turned her head and her blue eyes widened at the sight of him. Dashing quickly down the length of the bar, she exited through the swinging waist-high door at the end and rushed the length of the bar again to give him a hug. "Paul!" she exclaimed, wrapping her arms around his waist and burying her face in his chest as she squeezed him fiercely to her. "You're okay!" She stepped back and looked him up and down in amazement.

"Not a scratch on me," Paul confirmed.

Jessica put her hand out to touch his comfortingly. "I am so sorry about Kris."

Paul had seen him when he walked in, sitting at a table swathed in his robes and sipping from his flask and watching Jessica work. At the mention of him, he rose and glided soundlessly to stand beside Paul.

"He always liked you, you know?" Paul had to ignore his friend's glare to keep from laughing.

"He did?" she asked, sounding sweet and sad and a little hopeful. Paul wished he hadn't said anything, but her response seemed to cheer Kris.

"Oh, yeah," he wanted to lighten the mood. Hers, at least. "His ghost has probably been just sitting around watching you work all morning, wishing he had mustered up the courage to ask you out while he was still alive."

Jessica flushed shyly while Kris whirled around and stalked back to the table.

"Are you coming to the service?" he asked her, serious again.

Jessica's pretty blonde head bobbed solemnly up and down, touch of a frown on her pale pink lips. "Roche is shutting down. It's tomorrow, right?"

"Yeah," Paul nodded. "I know it would mean a lot to Kris if you went. Thanks." He fumbled in his pockets for a minute and brought out some folded bills. "Can I get a coffee?" He asked innocently.

"Oh my gosh, I'm sorry." Just as quick, she was behind the bar again and pouring him coffee. She waved away the two dollar bills he proffered, so he dropped them in her tip jar instead.

She talked while she poured. "Have they found the guy that hit you?"

Paul shook his head, lifted the coffee to his lips. It was hot, but it tasted good. He mused for a moment that he could drink a cup of boiling bleach and probably be just fine.

"The guy that hit Kris had a heart attack, apparently at the same time his tire blew out. He was dead before the ambulance arrived. Kris was…" Paul glanced at Kris, who was poring over a leather bound book open on the table before him. He took another sip of coffee. "Kris never woke up, and he was on life support until…" he trailed off again.

"I'm so sorry, Paul." It was all she could really say. Paul took his coffee to sit with Kris. He made a big show of putting his bluetooth in his ear, holding his phone in front of him and staring at it while he sat down and placed his coffee on the table across from the Guide's canteen. "Good morning," he said, pleasantly enough. "What ya reading?"

Kris closed the book resolutely. "Guide books," he shrugged. "They're mostly obviously biased accounts of other Walkers and Guides along with some truly half-baked philosophies and specific but inaccurate prophecies or prophecies so vague you could prove them true hundreds of times a day."

Paul frowned as he made sense of his friend's convoluted manner of speaking. "Why are you reading it?"

Kris shrugged again. "They're good stories, some of them. And I'm your Guide. I'm learning how other Guides do their jobs by reading about them."

Paul was intrigued. "Who writes these books?"

"The Watchers." Kris said the word as if it explained everything. As far as Paul was concerned, it didn't explain anything. He raised an eyebrow and waited. "Every Walker has a Guide and a Watcher," Kris explained. "Walkers exist in an in-between state, neither of the living nor of the dead. Guides are in a different world that co-exists with the world of the living, but we are clearly dead. That's why I can't touch things unless I will it." He frowned. "Really, really will it." He eyed the flask in front of him as if considering taking a drink, then went on. "Watchers exist in a world alongside the world I live in. Some say they live in the world of the angels, but others say that world is even harder to see. I can see Watchers, but I can't see angels."

"Do you see lights?" Paul asked suddenly.

"Personal angels?" Kris smiled. "I've been working on that. Yeah, kind of. Like Roche said, all I see is a speck of light. If I try to look closer it gets harder to see or disappears entirely." Now he did take a drink, tipping his canteen to his lips and setting it on the table again. His hands disappeared into the sleeves of his robe. "I sure see a lot more demons than angels."

Eyeing the leather bound book lying on the table between them, Paul asked, "Can I read it?" Reaching his hand out, he saw his fingers sink through the book to thunk ineffectively on the table. It looked like he had ahold of it for a second, but as he pulled his hand away it remained unmoved. He frowned. He sipped his coffee. Closing his eyes, he imagined reaching across the table and grasping the book easily, then opened them and reached out to touch the table top under the book once again.

When he looked up, he saw that Kris was laughing silently at him, hands folded in the sleeves of his robe while his shoulders shook under a benign smile. Paul glanced about him to make sure no one was watching him reaching for something he couldn't touch and they couldn't see. There were two customers in the shop, each sitting at a table alone and each too engrossed in the electronic world to notice Paul in his two overlapping worlds. Jessica was working behind the bar, somehow always busying herself no matter the lack of customers. In the back, Roche's customary place was empty. The chair and table looked out of place without the big man…no, the big *devil*, sitting in his usual spot.

"Don't I get a book?" he asked, annoyance in his voice.

Kris shrugged. "You should have gotten one with your key."

"Yeah," Paul snapped. "And a weapon and an overcoat and a horse too, right?"

"A horse?" Kris shook his head solemnly. "No, you don't get a horse. You have to find your own ride and empower it. Besides, you're a Walker. You don't need a horse or a car. You walk between worlds."

Burying his face in his hands, elbows on the table before him, Paul sighed heavily. "I don't even know what that means, dude." He took his hands away from his face and put them flat on the table between them. Looking at his friend almost pleadingly, he said, "So someone is watching us?"

"Watchers don't always literally watch," Kris smiled at him patiently. "They watch and record the noteworthy moments of their associated Walker and Guide, but they don't literally have to watch it or write it to record it in here." He tapped the book before him soundlessly with two fingers.

Paul snorted in derision. "Let me guess. They just have to intend it."

Ignoring his sarcasm, the Guide smiled at him triumphantly. "Now you're catching on."

Glancing quickly about the room, Paul leaned forward and whispered across the space between them. "Is he here now? Is it a dude? Is he a she? Is she here now?"

Clearly enjoying himself, Kris looked over his shoulder. "Yeah, he's right behind me," he answered. "If you want to meet him, just hold your key in your hand and…" he trailed off, smiling.

"Intend it?" Paul snapped, holding his hand palm up between them as the pocket watch appeared suddenly. The Guide nodded.

Looking vaguely over Kris's shoulder, he first tried to imagine someone there, then intended instead to see whatever was there. Colors brightened suddenly, a shape hove into view, and bright lights sparkled everywhere in the air about him. It was as if a glitter bomb had exploded silently, each piece of glitter a light source with its own patterns of movement and degree of brightness. It was beautiful, and Paul sat and watched in awe as the light bathed his face.

"Dial it back a bit." A flat male voice cut through his reverie, and when he focused on the man standing behind Kris the lights faded from view. He was an average height, with a bald head and a clean-shaven simple round face. Gold wire-rimmed spectacles perched on the bridge of his thick squat nose, and he held a book that was twin to the one on the table open before him. A white feather the length of his forearm danced in his hand, a quill pen that he was writing furiously with on the pages he held splayed open in his other hand. His eyes shifted, meeting Paul's for a moment, and he nodded a curt acknowledgement. An older man, in his late fifties or early sixties, he had slim shoulders and a paunchy belly and alert brown eyes that seemed to take in everything. "Andre," he said, and looked again at the book in his hands. The quill never stopped moving.

Raising an eyebrow, Paul glanced at Kris. The Guide smiled and shrugged. He looked back at Andre. "Uh, nice to meet you," he said. "Any way you can get me a copy of that?"

Still writing, still looking down at the book in his hands, he said, "Open your key, Walker."

Paul pushed the little button atop the winding wheel. The cover snapped open soundlessly to reveal the mysterious face and confusion of hands. One hand moved noticeably, the others stayed still.

"Push the button again twice," the Watcher still did not look up from his writing.

Paul hesitated. "Do I have to intend something?"

The feather stopped, and Andre's eyes shifted to meet Paul's for a moment. "Just push the button, Walker. Twice." He looked away as the white quill started dancing again.

A little annoyed, Paul pushed the button, looked at Kris, and then pushed it again.

The gold changed to leather, the disc became a rectangle, and the watch was suddenly gone to be replaced by a leather bound book. It looked the same as the other two, except there was a modern digital display set in the front cover, and the leather was sleek black instead of worn brown. The display had what looked like five sets of numbers: five zeros, then a space, three zeros then a space, then a static twenty-three, a static eighteen, and a thirty-seven that became a thirty-six and then a thirty-five as he watched.

Looking abashed, Kris shook his head as he watched the countdown with Paul. "Of course," was all he said.

Paul opened the book, saw the fine gold calligraphy on the inside of the front cover. It read "Walker Paul Stone". He flipped through the pages, looked up at Andre, then at Kris. "They're blank," he said.

"What do you want to read?" Kris asked gently. "Intention, Paul. That book can be anything you want it to be, tell you anything you want to know that has been written by anyone about anything in all the worlds you will walk."

Paul frowned. "I want to know what's being written about me."

Andre chuckled then, a low bemused sound that didn't interrupt his writing. "They say narcissists make the best Walkers."

Ignoring him, Paul opened the book again to the first page and read.

"Paul Stone reached out his hand and accepted the Key from Walker Peter in the instant before the oncoming car lifted him from the pavement with its low front bumper. Andre's van had come to rest against the frame of the bus stop, and as Paul's head hit the windshield of the car Andre died alone in his vehicle. In that moment, Walker and Guide and Watcher were made."

Paul looked up from the book. "You killed Kris?" he asked, his eyes wide.

It was Kris who answered. "He had a heart attack, Paul," he said gently. "It's how these things happen, we all had to die together."

"You didn't die then," Paul frowned.

The Guide gave his customary shrug. "Just because lungs breathe and a heart beats doesn't mean the soul is still attached to the body. Many souls move on long before the final breath of the body. The medical field defines death as poorly as it defines life."

The door to Roche's office opened then, and Paul was surprised to see Matt walk out backwards slowly, laughing. Roche followed, smiling and saying something Paul couldn't hear.

He glanced at Kris, but the Guide only shrugged and watched the pair conversing.

Reaching out, Roche grasped Matt's hand in a firm handshake accompanied by a wide toothy grin. Paul wondered if Matt could see the devil's fangs. Clapping Matt on the back and pumping his hand furiously, the devil laughed again and said, "Kid, you've got a deal."

CHAPTER 21

Every morning since it had happened, he had woke to that image behind his eyes. Every morning a mess of flesh and hair and bone and blood had been there to greet him. Every morning guilt and fear and shame gripped him as the image haunted him, every morning since it had happened.

Mason lay sprawled on his back, arms spread to either side. As he came awake, he saw a round cartoon head flatten momentarily against the windshield in his mind and bounce off harmlessly. Like a beach ball with a painted smile, it hove into view, flattened and widened the happy smile against the glass, and reformed into a perfect unblemished face as it bounced away out of view. For the first time he thought, *I had a green light, I wasn't speeding*, and then, *What was that jackass doing in the middle of the street anyway?*

He never watched the news or read papers, and had avoided them even more lately, since it had happened. Now he slowly came to realize that it wasn't really his fault, he hadn't done anything wrong, and he had nothing to feel guilty about. It was in these same glorious internal moments that he felt the weight of Sarah's head on his right bicep, and he turned his face slightly to see her sleeping peacefully. Turning his head again to gaze at the ceiling, he let himself smile.

And had Paul or Kris or Andre or Roche been there, he would have seen a man lying in bed with sleepy hazel eyes and mussed longish hair. He would have seen the pretty dark-haired girl sleeping next to him on one side and the child-sized grotesquely misshapen demon lying relaxed on the other side of him.

"It's not your fault," he would have heard the demon whispering. *"You didn't do anything wrong. You have nothing to feel bad about. You have nothing to fear. Relax. It is time to take what is yours."*

Mason lay there, feeling upbeat and confident without knowing just why, wondering how on earth he didn't have a massive hangover. Remembering bits of last night, he turned and looked again at Sarah. This time hunger glinted in his hazel eyes, and he rolled over and began kissing her neck and shoulder.

Her arms encircled his shoulders, coming awake without opening her eyes. She smiled softly, murmured "Mason" breathily and pressed her naked body to his. His hand traced her shoulder and her arm slowly, until she grabbed his hand suddenly and put it between her legs as she spread them. "Mason," she breathed again as his hand felt the slickness and the warmth that awaited him. "Mmm, Mason, I'm so wet for you."

Then he was inside her, she was all around him, and Mason got lost in getting lost in her.

Afterward, they lay happily intertwined as they both burrowed more deeply into the blankets and each other. Sarah was right up against him, her breasts sticking to his chest with the slick sheen of sweat from their lovemaking. Looking up at him from under dark bangs and furrowed brow, she asked sweetly, "Will you come to rehearsal today?"

Mason smiled softly. "If they all want me there, yeah."

"They all want you there," she could not have sounded more certain. Her eyes widened and she said, "I want you there. I want you in the band. They will too, you'll see."

Disengaging from her, Mason lay sideways facing her and propped his head on one hand whose elbow dented the mattress. "Why don't you join my band?" he asked. "I can't just ditch Tyler. He's my best friend. And Jason is a great guy and possibly the best drummer in the city. Dude is solid as a rock. Your guy, what's his name, Don?" She nodded. "His timing was off more than once, and he's just not that fast."

Sarah could't deny what he was saying, but she didn't look too happy about it. She rolled over onto her back and stared at the ceiling, frowning. "You don't have to come if you don't want to," she sighed finally.

"No, I'll come, " Mason said tersely. "Would you just keep your mind open to all the possibilities?"

Sarah rolled out from under the covers and stood next to the bed, talking while she hunted for her clothes. "I never said I wasn't," she said, looking everywhere but at him. "I was just hoping you'd come and play with us tonight. No conditions, no strings attached."

Standing on the other side of the bed, he came around and stood before her, naked, as she slipped her dress over her head then shoulders then down round her hips. She tried to sidestep him, but he put his hands firmly on her shoulders and forced her to look him in the eyes.

"That's too bad," he said softly, his own voice unfamiliar with a gentle kindness. "I was hoping to attach all kinds of strings to you. Band member, friend, lover, maybe girlfriend? I was even thinking of moving past that and trying out some ropes once enough strings were attached. I thought—"

Sarah threw herself at him, hugging him tightly and kissing his naked chest over his heart as he gently encircled his arms about her neck. She relaxed her neck so her head was cradled in his forearms, rolling back to look up at him. He saw tears in her eyes, and he leaned over to kiss the smile on her lips. "No worries," he murmered between kisses. "Not for us, no worries…"

CHAPTER 22

Walker and Guide and Watcher surrounded the small table, Paul and Kris watching Roche interacting with Matt while Andre scribbled furiously, appearing oblivious as he recorded.

Finally, Roche glanced around the café, his eyes falling on each of the trio in turn. Matt followed his gaze and waved to Paul and grinned. Disengaging from Roche with another handshake, Matt made his way to the table. Kris had to scramble to get out of the way as Matt pulled his chair out and plopped heavily into it. The guide stood at the head of the table, trying to regain his composure while Andre sniggered almost silently as he wrote it all down.

Roche disappeared into his office for a few moments and then set up at his usual table. Instead of books and ledgers, he opened a laptop computer on the table before him and went to work at the keyboard while his eyes locked on the screen before him.

Matt was all smiles, bursting with something and all the more charismatic for it. "Morning, Paul," he said. "Want another cup? I'm buying."

Resisting the urge to look at Kris directly, Paul smiled and nodded. "Jess, can you bring us a couple coffees please?" he raised his voice.

Her head appeared above the expresso machine and nodded. "Will do," she said. "Morning, Matt."

"Hey, Jess." Matt was watching Paul. "Sorry about the job thing, buddy," he said casually. The last word Paul would ever think to describe his tone was apologetic.

"No big deal," Paul assured him. "You still have time to reconsider, though. Tomorrow's Sunday, and I'm not going back to work until Tuesday. Tomorrow is…"

Matt's face fell, and he nodded. "I know. Kris' service." He hesitated, then asked, "Hey, do you think it would be okay if I…if I said something? You know, about Kris."

It was impossible for Paul not to look at Kris, and the softness and surprise on the Guide's face was worth sneaking the glance. "I think Kris would like that very much," Paul said quietly.

Matt looked at him again, fiercely. "It's funny you say it like that," he mused. "Kris was into all kinds of weird stuff, afterlife and megaphysical and new age type of stuff. If anyone could find a way to stick around or come back, he could. I think I feel him sometimes, too, like he's still here watching over us." He flushed and looked away. "Silly, huh?"

"Metaphysical," Paul heard himself say woodenly, correcting him out of habit. "No buddy, it's not silly at all."

They sat quietly and drank the coffee Jessica brought them, lost in their own thoughts. After a few minutes, Matt stood and smiled down at Paul, his handsome countenance clear and bright again. "I'll see you tomorrow," he said cheerily. "Tell Bren I said 'hi'!" He stopped at the register to trade words and currency with Jessica, and then he jangled his way out the front door to destinations unknown.

Paul glanced back at Roche to see the devil looking pointedly his way. His eyes moved slowly from Paul to Kris to Andre, then back to Paul. He rose, quite deliberately still looking at Paul, turned and walked to his office. The door stood slightly ajar behind him. Paul hesitated for a moment, then found his feet and starting making his way toward the office. He looked back once to make sure the Guide and Watcher were following, tapping his knuckles slightly on the door as he came to stand before it.

Half-growl, half-grumble, the words were still clear. "Come in."

Paul expected to walk into a small office, crowding together with his unlikely companions. The doorway opened instead into a huge spacious room. Desk and chairs dominated one corner, but the rest of the room was huge flatscreens and speakers and floor space enough for the pristine red felted pool table that the recreational universe revolved around. An old-fashioned juke box sat against a wall in perfect condition, the collection of vinyl singles visible through the glass and lit up in reds and greens and whites. Once they were all inside, the devil motioned Paul to close the door and crossed the room swiftly to open another doorway that stood next to the juke box.

Paul glanced at his companions in turn, but they were already moving past him to follow Roche. Another spacious room awaited beyond the second doorway, and Paul stood in the frame between the two rooms for a moment looking confused and mildly alarmed. The other three were already finding their places at the only piece of furniture in the room, a long thick oak table lined with a half-dozen chairs on either side. One end of the table was empty, but the other end boasted an ornate metal chair that could almost be called a throne. The high curved metal that was the back of the chair was taller than any of them when they were standing, arcing ridiculously high over Roche's head as he took the chair. He moved its metallic bulk with ease, and Paul was surprised to see the Guide and the Watcher both reach out and pull their chairs back from the table to sit. He had grown so accustomed to watching Kris pass through solid objects, he just stood there a moment and watched the unlikely trio.

"Uh, Roche," he said finally. "I'm confused. I'm no architect or anything, but..." His eyes wandered the space before him suspiciously as his voice trailed off. Kris and Andre sat calm in their chairs, nonplussed, one smiling softly while the other wrote furiously.

It was Kris the devil spoke to. "Hasn't he learned anything yet?" he snapped. Kris just shrugged and smiled, apparently amused by both Paul's confusion and Roche's impatience.

"It's a different world, isn't it?" Paul said suddenly. "Humans and Guides live in different worlds, devils must too. Right?"

The devil sighed. "You can say different worlds, you can say alternate dimensions, but that's more dancing around the truth than explaining it. It's more like different levels of reality and perception. From a broad enough perspective, it's all one world, really. Each level of reality depends on the existence of all of the other levels even if they seem to exist independently of each other, and anything you do at any level of reality affects all of the other levels. It's all one world, one universe, one song, some souls playing bass notes while others sing soprano while others bang the drums. We each tend to think our song is our own, but we are really all just brief notes in a grand awesome symphony. Humans, Walkers, Guides, devils, angels. Everyone."

Paul frowned. "So this is a different dimension?"

The devil eyed Paul's companions warily. "You guys are gonna need all the help you can get with this one." Paul seemed the only one not amused.

"It's like a transportation grid in a city," Kris said, unfolding his forearms from the sleeves of his robe and placing his palms flat on the table. "Some streets go North to South, some go East to West, some change direction completely or end suddenly. Freeways cut quickly from one area to another, but can't give you local access. Roads and railroads and footpaths are a whole complete world, and humans live in this world mostly oblivious to the network of air travel and subway systems above and below."

Paul was still frowning. "So angels are the airplanes, humans are the cars, and devils are the subways?" He glanced at Roche and raised an eyebrow. "Are we in the subway system?"

Roche wasn't looking at Paul; he was glaring at Kris. "No wonder he's confused. It sounds like he's better off not going to classes if that's where you're getting this nonsense." To Paul, he said, "Yes, according to your Guides's oversimplified, incomplete and inconsistent explanation of the Universe, we are metaphorically in the subway system. What you might call a higher level of Hell or a lower level of Earth, depending on which direction you're headed."

The sudden stillness of the Watcher's busy white feather drew all their attention. "It's like a musical scale," he said calmly, glancing from Walker to Guide to devil as he spoke. "Each note is complete unto itself, but dependent on the existence of every note above and every note below it, for we souls exist as voices in a universe of relativity. Our identity is largely defined by what we relate to and how we relate to it, but our soul can only sing one note at any given moment. We depend on all the other souls of the Universe to raise their voices with all the other notes of possibility just to make our one lonely voice heard in the beautiful symphony Roche spoke so eloquently of earlier."

Roche had nodded several times while Andre spoke, and the last comment curled one side of his mouth into a half-smile.

"You created this place, though, did you not?" The feather still unmoving, Andre addressed Roche directly. "This is more like a semi-tone than a note, is that right?"

The half-smile turned to a grin then, and the devil nodded with pride.

"Nicely done," Andre said, nodded, and went back to writing.

"So we're in another dimension behind or above or below your coffee shop in a conference room. Heaven is not above or below Earth, nor is Hell. Flying and digging don't raise you to Heaven or tunnel you to Hell. Heaven is right here, Earth is right here, Hell is right here, and what I see is determined not by one set reality but by what frequency I tune into." Paul held out his hand, holding up the leather ledger with the digital countdown across the face. "With this. My key."

"Not your key," A male voice, deep and authoritative, came from the shadows. "A Walker's key doesn't belong to anyone. It would be more accurate to say that the Walker belongs to the key until the key tires of the Walker and chooses again."

The man stepped from the shadows as he spoke, and for a moment Paul thought it was the same man who had given him the key. This man was shorter and more broad about the shoulders. His brown leather hat and overcoat and boots were in perfect condition, a sheen on the leather as if it had been freshly oiled. He had a stern square face under the brim pulled down low on his forehead. He acknowledged Roche reluctantly with a nod. "Thanks for setting this up."

Paul turned to Roche. "What did you set up? Who is this guy?"

"Walker Paul," Roche grinned, "Meet Walker John. Your boss."

CHAPTER 23

The half-smoked cigarette hanging from his mouth had gone out several minutes ago, but Mason didn't notice. Nor did he notice the mess that was his apartment or the lingering sweet scents of Sarah and sex. Nor the demon that crouched beside him on the bed, looking up at Mason then down at the papers spread in front of him in approval.

Cross-legged on the bed, the way he held his electric guitar looked almost like a religious pose, and he pored over the pages before him as if they held the secrets of the universe. They had been blank pages this morning, save for the carefully grouped horizontal lines that made a template for sheet music. He had always known how to read music, but never bothered to much. This morning a song had filled his head, and for some reason he had felt compelled to write out the sheet music.

He'd stare at the pages, then play a few bars, then lean forward and make more notations. He didn't even try to sing it, the notes were too high and wouldn't sound right crooning it an octave lower. The electric guitar made very little noise not plugged into an amp, but he could hear what he needed to hear. His mind added volume and effects without plugging in or pressing pedals.

It seemed a lifetime, and he felt he'd been wrung out like a sponge only to expand into an empty exhausted satisfaction. It had taken only a few hours, though, and he plugged the Fender in finally and flipped the switch on the amp. Glancing again at the sheet music, he stood and strapped on the instrument. The first note he played at volume was the first note of the song, and he flowed smoothly from note to note and chord to chord and intro to verse to chorus. He was not playing his guitar, he was playing his feelings, and he felt both vulnerable and invincible as he listened to the sounds of his own soul.

The final note cried out its last fading breath slowly until a pristine kind of silence filled the room. A gentle knock on the door shook him from a reverie so deep he flinched at the sound. Guitar still at his waist, cord trailing behind him, he went to the front door and opened it.

"Sorry, Missus Jasper," he said to the stooped old lady standing in the hallway. "Was I playing too loud?"

Her eyes were old and milky, but Mason knew the mind behind those eyes and under that beehive of blue hair was still sharp. She reached out a withered, blue-veined hand and placed it gently over Mason's where it rested on the body of the guitar.

"Oh, my, no, Mason," she tsked, then looked up at him. "I was hoping you would play that again. It was beautiful."

She tottered into the apartment, brushing lightly past Mason, and sat on the edge of the bed, apparently oblivious to the mess. Settled comfortably, she looked up at him again. "Do you have any tea, dear?" Mason shook his head numbly. "Oh well, no matter. Won't you play that beautiful song for me again? I simply must hear it."

The demon stood between them, more sure of himself but still leaning sideways from his twisted frame. Unseen by both humans, he looked from one to the other in smug satisfaction and stalked through the closed front door. The opening notes of the song followed his limping gait down the hallway, making him smile so wide his face seemed nothing but fangs.

When the song was over again, another rap on the door revealed his next door neighbor, the one who complained the most about Mason's music at night and alarm clock in the morning and smoking through it all. Big and beefy and balding, he wore a handlebar moustache that made him look menacing when Mason passed him wearing his leather biker jacket in the hallway. The effect wasn't the same as he stood there in sweats and a wife-beater holding a six-pack of beer in one hand. He smiled disarmingly, something else Mason had never seen, and held up the beer. "Nice sounds, neighbor. Can I come in?"

Mason had heard many people call him many things in his lifetime, labels that seemed to fit like no others; loner, hermit, fringe dweller, lone wolf, aloof... Suddenly this loner had a hallway full of curious listeners heading toward his apartment and filtering inside. They were all different age groups and had different lifestyles, and they all wanted to hear Mason play. Many brought gifts, and some took to cleaning and straightening his apartment to make places for everyone to sit and stand. A party shaped up around the hermit.

Through it all, he played. Some songs he knew and some he seemed to be able to make up as he thought of them, always coming back to the song he had penned just this morning as people asked for it again and again. People he hardly knew or didn't know at all brought him beers and snacks and then rushed him to eat it or drink it and "play that song again, please."

His phone was on the opposite side of the room. Mason probably wouldn't have heard it ringing even if it were closer. Maybe someone heard it, but no one paid it any mind, and soon it fell silent again. It beeped occasionally after that, but that was even quieter than the ring. He played on, as attentive in his playing as his unlikely audience was rapt in their listening.

Mason began to think he must have played the song twenty times when someone thought to ask, "What's it called, Mason?"

Mason frowned. He had written every note, could hear every part for every instrument, the lyrics, the melody line. But no title.

Then his face broke into a wide grin. "My Demon," he said resolutely. "The song is called 'My Demon'."

There was a quiet as people nodded and murmered assent, and Mason's phone came alive with the ringtone she had set in his phone as hers when she typed her name and number into it. Katy Perry's *Roar* meant Sarah was calling, and he brushed past his guests to answer.

"Hello? Sarah?"

"Hi, Mason." She sounded drained.

"Everything okay?"

"I don't know. Are you still coming tonight? Please tell me you're still coming." Her voice went from tired to pleading.

Mason nodded. "I'm still coming."

"Would you bring Tyler and Jason please?"

There was a silence on the line then, and Mason let it draw out.

"Only if they're playing," he said finally.

"They're playing," she sighed. "Thanks."

"Sarah?" Mason had the sense something was wrong. "What's going on?"

"We'll talk later," she responded brusquely. "Cal can come too if he wants. See you later."

CHAPTER 24

"My boss, huh?" Paul did his best to sound rebellious. "The more I find out about being a Walker the more it just seems like a big pain in the ass. What do I need a boss for?"

The older Walker found a chair and pulled it to the other end of the table, facing Roche in his throne down the length of it. "I'm more of a coordinator," he said. "I make sure all of the Walkers are doing their jobs, the demons are being handled properly, and that two Walkers never meet outside of training. Have you been trained? Has Peter come to you?"

Paul looked up, cocked an eyebrow at the other Walker, decided to answer his question with a question. "What happens if two Walkers meet?"

"Lines of fate get crossed, their devices interact to create rifts and tears in the very fabric of reality, it is catastrophic." Walker John did not seem to have any sense of humor at all. Every word he spoke was weighted with the gravity of his taking himself very seriously. "If you ever see another Walker, do not talk to them or engage them in any other way. Do not look at them. Do not acknowledge them. DO. NOT. TALK. TO. THEM."

Glad he hadn't bothered to sit down, Paul turned and made for the door.

"Where are you going?" Walker John demanded angrily from behind him.

Paul stopped and turned. "You're a Walker," he said blithely. "I am not supposed to talk to you." Reaching the door, he found he couldn't turn the knob to open it. He whirled, but before he could command Roche to let him out of here, the other Walker spoke again.

"Please don't go, Walker Paul." John's voice was gentle and quiet, though somehow still large and authoritative. "We need your help. I need your help. Please sit down."

Roche sat at the head of the table and gaped. "Damn, Walker," he guffawed suddenly. "You didn't beg like that when I took your weapon. I might have given it back if you did."

"You said you would have a use for it someday," Walker John replied mildly. "It was a good lesson for me, and my weapon was replaced." A wooden walking stick appeared in his hand. Walker John looked at it a long moment before he said finally, "It looks like you found a good use for it."

Roche shrugged his beefy shoulders amicably. "I'm sure it's all just coincidence," he smiled. "Don't you think so, Walker Paul…Stone?"

Under the brim of his leather cowboy hat, Walker John went noticeably pale at those words. His eyes widened, and he looked for a moment as though he was thinking of changing the stick to a sword. Then he shook his head side to side and glared at the devil. "This is serious, Roche. I came to ask for your help too. Have you spoken with Peter? I know you two go back."

"Me?" Roche raised his eyebrows, perplexed. "A Walker wants my help?"

"Yes, we need all the help we can get," he said almost pleadingly. "Someone is killing Walkers."

Kris actually laughed at that, nervous laughter that ended as abruptly as it began. "I thought only God could kill a Walker," he sputtered.

Walker John looked at the Guide strangely. "Oh? And what do you see all around you?" He turned his attention again to Roche. "I know we've had our differences, demon, but I was hoping we could put that all behind us."

"Water under the bridge, human," Roche showed him how many teeth he had, in case he had forgotten. "Who is killing Walkers? Besides God, I mean?"

Walker John looked like he might actually smile for a moment, but he frowned instead. "I was hoping you might have heard something. Dead Walkers have been found on Earth, above and below. They have been stripped of their outfits and weapons and keys and journals, but we don't know why. Only a Walker can use Walker tools, everyone knows that. To top it all off, Peter disappeared right after making Paul. No one has heard from him since."

Heaving a massive shrug, Roche said, "Only a Walker can go above *and* below. Sounds like you've got yourself a Walker killing Walkers and taking trophies. It's not Peter. Have you considered that maybe it's the original Walker? Has anyone ever tracked him down?"

"Walker Marcus? Really, Roche?" His tone was clearly demeaning. "Fairy tales? Even if Walker Marcus was real, he was rehumanized and died eons ago. Next you'll suggest that it's the Walker Demon conspiring with the Walker Angel killing the Walkers. Is that what you're going to say next, demon? Should I have brought an army?" He shook his head and stood up suddenly. He seemed more frightened than angry, and Paul wondered why. "I didn't expect you to help," he hissed at Roche. "I thought I might see hope in you," he glared at Paul. "But you've been found wanting for the company and the secrets you keep. Good day, gentlemen."

And he was gone. No sound, no poof of smoke, just one moment there and the next it was just the four of them around the table. Nobody said anything for a while, each lost in his own thoughts while Andre scratched at paper with quill. Finally, Andre set the quill down, closed the book and said flatly, "Well, that guy sure knows how to make friends."

"Uh…" Paul felt a sentence coming but the wheels in his brain seemed slow and syrupy. "Who is Walker Marcus? What is the Walker Demon? The Walker Angel? And why does everybody freak out when they hear my last name?"

"Stone…" Kris murmured quietly, almost to himself. He looked warily at the devil still seated at the head of the table. "You don't think…?"

"That he's the Stone Walker, Scourge of the Demons, the Walker Eternal, come to wage war on demon and devil alike and drive the lot of us back to Hell bleeding and screaming?" Roche looked at Paul the whole time he talked, and the gleam in the devil's eyes brought him as little comfort as when Roche turned finally to Kris and said, "Nah, I don't believe in prophecies."

"Marcus is the story of how Walkers were created." Kris seemed to be answering the easiest of his questions, but Paul still sat at the table across from him and listened intently. "Marcus was a man, a regular human who could somehow see demons and devils. His wife believed him, but she couldn't see them and didn't know what to do about them. The constant sight of personal demons and devils posing as humans began to drive Marcus mad, and every night his wife prayed for a way to help him.

"Lillian…that was his wife's name, right, Roche?" Roche nodded, listening with little interest. "Lillian fell ill," Kris went on, "and the healer that attended her was weighted down by a score of demons. Marcus wouldn't let the man inside, and they actually fought to the death just outside the house where Lillian lay dying. As the healer and Lillian exhaled their last breaths, Marcus exhaled his last breath as a human, and inhaled the first breath of the first Walker. Marcus had been an unnoteworthy footsoldier as a human, but as a Walker he was stronger, faster, and of course invincible. His wife and the healer could see the demons and devils after they died, and the Walker could see the two of them as though they still lived. They looked to Marcus to lead them. The doctor became his Watcher and Lillian became his Guide, and the three of them created and defined the life of a Walker together over the next several centuries."

"Until they realized they just couldn't do it all alone," Roche interjected flatly. "Devils were free to roam the Earth unchallenged back then, and Walker Marcus decided it was his destiny to violently drive them back to Hell. It was also his destiny to rid the world of demons, or so he thought. They hunted and killed demons and devils alike, but they were vastly outnumbered. They saw it as war, and they decided to create an army of Walkers one at a time by killing humans in threes and somehow passing the powers of Walker, Guide and Watcher to each trio. They were organized with over two thousand strong, and they swept the world over and over for hundreds of years like a surgical plague, ruthless and merciless. Some Walkers were good men, and they would drift off to help good people with their demons. Most stayed to grow the army, though, and their collective thirst for blood grew with it."

Kris was nodding, solemn and a little sad as he studied the table before him. "The only rules they lived by were the ones they made for themselves. If a human had more than three demons, or if any one of their demons was any bigger than a squirrel, they just killed the human to save time. Every time they made a Walker, three normal lives had to end, and they chose who would be Walkers, who would be Guides and who would be Watchers."

"And they chose poorly," Andre took up the story, and Paul had a moment to wonder just how much knowledge these three had in common that he was completely ignorant of. "The Guides didn't learn to guide, they acted more as squires. The Watchers monitored battles and reported progress and spied on the enemy. Most everyone was illiterate in those days, and the Watchers they chose were no exception. That's why the stories are muddled and sometimes contradictory, especially toward the end."

"What happened toward the end?" Now that Paul was curious, all three of them were suddenly silent. Kris and Andre took turns looking at each other and Roche, while Roche just stared at the table before him absently, as if remembering something.

The devil noticed the silence, looked up at Paul and smiled a forlorn smile that looked out of place on his fierce face. "Imagine it, a growing army of invincible immortals with no need to eat or sleep and no purpose but to kill, with no one to answer to but a madman and the woman who loved him. If they saw horns, they killed. If they didn't see horns, they killed anyway more often than not. In their eyes, you were either one of them or the enemy. At some point the whole lunatic company seemed to realize en masse that the best way to get rid of demons for good was to stop them from being created in the first place."

Paul shook his head. "That's ridiculous," he said. "That would mean…"

"That," Kris nodded sadly, "would mean killing all those pesky little demon factories. Why go back to a village every five years and deal with a new batch of demons each time when you can just slaughter everyone in the village and be done with it? No more humans would mean no more demons, and Walkers and Guides and Watchers could live in peace." He removed his flask from the folds of his robe and made about opening it and drinking from it, dismissing himself somewhat from continuing.

"And that's where the story really goes a thousand different directions, depending on who you talk to." Roche nodded at Andre. "A Watcher will tell you that the Watchers saw what was happening and spoke with the angels they could see and the devils still surviving on Earth. They found a way, the key, to rehumanize Walkers and pass the powers onto people more suited to the job. Rules were put in place to keep Walkers from ever organizing again, or even interacting, and Watchers were charged with recording every moment of their Walker's performance of duty in their journal. It is then automatically written in three other places; the Walker's journal, the Guide's journal, and the Walker Hall of Records, where all records are read and reviewed by a Council of Angels that decide on the continued appropriateness of each Walker's behavior. They put Walker John in charge of keeping the peace and keeping the Walkers in line, and he is the only one allowed to speak to another Walker outside of training, or to approach the Council of Angels."

"What do the devils say happened?" Paul asked Roche.

"Same thing, pretty much," Roche nodded. "Except it wasn't a Watcher who went to the angels, it was a devil. We went to war and took huge losses, then handed the whole thing over to them once it was under control."

Paul shook his head. "Why would you do that?"

The devil shrugged. "Angels are the bureaucrats of the Universe. You know the old saying, 'If you need it done now and don't care how it gets done, ask a devil. If you want to make sure the right thing gets done in the right way for the right reasons without hurting anyone else, ask an angel.'"

"And wait," murmured Andre.

"And have faith," added Kris.

"And wait some more," Andre chuckled.

Roche laughed. "You have heard the saying! They really are very thorough and disciplined, though. And the system has worked for thousands of years. Well, for the most part. No one could possibly benefit from starting another war." The devil frowned and studied his hands.

Kris spoke suddenly, softly. "I like the story they told us in class."

Roche nodded respectfully. "It honestly makes the most sense."

The Guide looked at him, surprised. Roche just nodded. "It was Lillian, his Guide. She thought something had to be done about the demons, but when she saw where it was all leading she recanted. She begged Walker Marcus to take her above and below and meet with the devils and the angels with her. She met with the original Walker Angel, possibly even the original Walker Devil. Some even say they talked to God and…and…" Kris trailed off, uncertain.

Roche was shaking his head. "Don't say it," he cautioned the Guide, his voice low.

"Anyhow," Kris continued, "together they came up with a solution, put Walker John in charge, the angels contributed the watches and the journals, the devils contributed the armor and the weapons, and the devils waged war on the other Walkers while the angels put the whole system in place. It all came together as they planned, everyone played their part; and like Roche said, the system has worked ever since. For the most part."

"What happened to Walker Marcus and Lillian?" Paul asked, looking from one to the other.

Kris spoke, his voice uncertain. "Most say what Walker John said, Marcus was rehumanized, Lillian crossed over, and Marcus died a human."

Andre just nodded.

Everyone was so full of answers, but every answer Paul got just filled him with more questions. He looked to his friend, changed by his new knowledge and new role. Then to Andre, a dead man existing only to watch him and commit his every move to eternal record.

"Roche," Paul looked to the head of the table. "What is an original angel?"

The devil stood abruptly. "Class is over," he announced brusquely. "Everybody out. I'll see you lot tomorrow."

CHAPTER 25

"What's the address?" Cal sat at a stop sign long enough to look both ways, then pulled his black Acura smoothly into and through the intersection, glancing at the green and white road signs criss-crossed at the corner. They were on Pine Street crossing Sixth Avenue.

Mason sat in the front seat, hazel eyes hidden behind dark sunglasses. He hit the joint he was holding three times in quick succession, and for a moment his head was surrounded by a cloud of white smoke. As the car began moving the smoke escaped through the open window and he held the joint out to Cal. Cal shook his head. Mason knew he would; he was just being polite. Reaching over his shoulder without looking, he held it out until someone in the back seat took it.

"Thanks, Mason." Tyler.

He dug in his pocket for his phone, scrolled to Sarah's text, read the numbers out. He coughed, smoke whooshing out the window as he spoke. "It'll be on the right."

"Will they have drums?" The only time Jason ever had anything to say, it somehow seemed to start or end with drums. "I didn't bring my kit." Jason's distressed voice was mellower than Tyler's most calm voice.

"I'm sure they'll have a kit there," Mason reassured him. "I don't know why else she would ask me to bring everyone."

Cal grinned. "Everyone always wants me around. I'm the life of the fuckin' party."

Mason chuckled, looking out the window at addresses. He felt a tap on his shoulder, and turned around halfway to take the smoking joint from Jason.

"There it is." Cal spoke, and Mason turned to look out the window. Sarah had been right, the address was hardly necessary. The house was a rambler, made L-shaped by the garage that dominated the side facing the street. One of the two roll-up doors was wide open on the garage, and a drum kit and amplifiers and guitars filled the space where one might ordinarily park a vehicle.

A ten year old green Mazda 626 was in the driveway, a powder blue

70's Volkswagon bus was parked on the street in front of the house and a five year old dark blue Honda Accord was parked behind that. Sarah's car. "Park behind the Honda," Mason said unnecessarily, as Cal did just that. The four got out of the car and Cal met Mason at the trunk to get his and Tyler's guitars.

They had all met the night before, and a minute passed shaking hands and remembering names. Sarah was not shy in greeting Mason first, wrapping her arms around his neck and pressing her moist soft lips against his. He flushed, but wrapped the arm not carrying a guitar case around her waist. Barefoot, she looked even more the pixie standing on tiptoes to kiss him.

The group disappeared into the garage, and Mason was left standing alone talking with Sarah. "Thanks for bringing everybody," she said, suddenly shy. Her bare feet did a slow soft-shoe on the driveway between them as she spoke. "Don got into an accident. He won't be able to play for at least a couple of weeks."

"What happened?" All Mason knew was that the guy played drums, and less than perfectly at that. He tried to sound concerned instead of hopeful. "Is he going to be alright?"

Pleased at his concern, she stepped into him and wrapped her arms about his waist. "I hope so, I think so," she said before her words got muffled in his shirt. Mason put an unsure arm around her shoulders, guitar case still dangling at his side from the other hand. Then she looked up at him. "I talked to him twice today. He said his leg is busted up pretty bad."

Mason frowned sympathetically instead of making a wisecrack about just putting him down. "That's a bummer," he said. *For him*, he thought to himself.

Her arms were still wrapped about his waist, and she looked up past her bangs at him seriously. "We have gigs booked two months in advance," she frowned. "We have four shows this week; one of them is in three days."

"Is that why you asked me to bring the band? So you could steal Jason?" His tone was light, but he couldn't help feeling his body stiffen against hers.

Sarah disengaged from him, took the guitar case from his hand and set it down gently. Everyone else had disappeared into the part of the garage not visible from the street, and Mason was glad for it. Sarah took his hands in hers and looked up at him, bare feet flat on the ground.

"I think you and I shared some very special moments on levels very important to both of us," she said with a blend of confidence and hope. "I want you to always trust me, especially when it comes to music. That's why I want to talk to you first."

Suddenly aware that he hadn't really caught much of a buzz sharing that joint on the way over, Mason wondered what the others were doing behind the closed roll-up door.

"Shouldn't we go inside?" he asked. "I don't want to be rude."

Sarah shot him an annoyed glance, but it melted into a smile as she squeezed his hands lightly. "I want to talk to you first," she repeated, more firmly. "I want this to be our decision, not mine."

"What decision?" Mason was finding it hard, but he tried to hold her gaze as calmly as possible. His attempt at a smile was enough to make her continue.

"I want you and Tyler and Jason in the band," she said firmly.

That got his attention. "You do?"

"If that's what you want." She smiled up at him, the shy pixie again.

"Well, yeah," he nodded. "What about Don when he gets better? What about Robert and…Mikie? What do they think?"

Her straight black bangs brushed her eyebrows as she shook her head. "I haven't talked to them." She held his hand tightly then, her face open and vulnerable, tilted back to look up at him. "I want us, Mason. The music, the band, the relationship. I want to make us a priority, and I want to help you get the kind of exposure you deserve. I believe in you, and I believe in us, and please stop me if you think I'm just some heartsick mindless little twit getting way ahead of myself."

Mason stood there, dumbstruck. He felt her hands go a little weak in his, and he squeezed them tight instead of answering right away. He didn't answer because he couldn't talk, and he couldn't talk because he felt like crying. No one had ever talked to him that way before. His heart felt likely to burst or glow or something. He thought of watching her perform, of touching her and tasting her and longing for her with his whole being. Mason still felt a little in awe of this little faerie with the magickal voice. He hadn't stopped to consider that maybe she felt the same way about him.

Letting go her hands, he dipped to wrap his arms around her waist and lift her as he stood straight and nuzzled her breasts through the thin cotton of today's sundress.

He set her down, grinning. "Are you saying you want to be my Stevie Nicks?"

Sarah had to laugh. "Only if you want to be my Lindsay Buckingham. She frowned, then added, "and if we can avoid fucking a bunch of other people."

"Awesome." Mason was still smiling as he picked up his guitar case with one hand and entwined fingers with Sarah with the other. "Let's go inside and do some cocaine, Stevie."

She stuck her tongue out at him playfully, then let him drag her along most willingly.

It was as cool as she had described it inside, nice big two car garage turned into rec room and rehearsal space. Mason saw why the instruments and amplifiers and mixing board seemed a little tight on the one side; every square foot of space was valuable. All in all, besides musical equipment, there was a pool table and a dartboard and a small portable bar that did not look like it had moved in a good long time. Rugs were tastefully placed on the floor, and rock band posters and tapestries adorned the walls. Sarah pointed after he had a few seconds to take it all in, and he saw a foot tall disco ball hanging from the ceiling.

Just as he had suspected, the sweet smell of cannabis smoke greeted him, teasing as he walked past the musical instruments and cloying as he approached the group of young men gathered about the bar. There were two stools at the bar, but Cal was the only one sitting down. The others waited their turn or watched whoever was taking theirs.

Tyler nearly danced to the bar, except no tune with that particular beat could logically exist. A twelve inch square tile mirror sat at the edge of the bar, and a series of white lines were neatly cut out in parallel on it. Tyler took the metal tube from Robert and swooped in awkwardly and elegantly to snort a line. It took a lot more noise and a lot more frantic movement than necessary, but he finally stood up and tilted his head back while he pinched both nostrils with one hand and passed the straw to Cal with the other. He took a hasty step back from the circle, sniffling, and backed noisily into a barstool that stood against the wall.

"Mason! Sarah!" Cal spied them and held the metal straw in their direction. "Juice up! I want to hear this setup."

She let his hand go as he strode forward, but he took the straw from Cal and dropped his head briefly for one long quick sniff.

"We want to talk to you guys," Sarah said behind him as he lifted his head and nodded at Cal. He turned and held the metallic tube up for Sarah's consideration. She shook her head. Mason held it there until she took it. He moved out of her way, and she looked at him expectantly.

Mason sighed. "We don't want to cancel your band's shows," he said. "We want to play them."

There was a hush, and Sarah moved to the bar and quietly took a line. She faced them all around the bar now, with Mason behind her. In turn, she looked at each musician, and even gave Cal a little smile.

Mikie spoke first. "Who's we?"

"All of us," Sarah nodded. "Except Cal, of course. No offense, Cal."

Cal grinned. "None taken." He took the tube from Sarah. "For what it's worth, being the only one here whose opinion doesn't matter at all, I think it's a great idea."

Robert nodded. His long auburn hair drifted with the nod. "Tyler plays a great bass. It would be nice to have a solid bass line all the time. And we were looking for a lead guitar player." He glanced at Mikie, and was silenced by his harsh glare.

"We've talked about looking for a lead guitar player," Mikie snapped. "We've also talked about how lead guitar players try to take control of the band and cause all kinds of conflict." He turned the look on Mason. "Like you're doing now."

Mason shrugged disarmingly. "You're the lead guitar player," he said. "If I'm in the band, I'll just back you up. I know lots of songs."

"You know lots of songs I don't, you mean?" Mikie strode to stand across the bar from Mason, fists clenched, glaring at him.

"No," Mason shook his head slowly. "I mean, I think all of us together can do a lot more than any of us apart. You're a great rapper. I can play Linkin Park Or Black-Eyed Peas songs, but I can't rap the parts. All I can sing are a few Metallica tunes. I can play whatever part you don't feel like playing, and I'll play it my best."

Mikie was staring at the mirror, a slight frown creasing his forehead. Face flushed, the tips of his carefully wild hair shook slightly. He glanced at Cal. "Can I have a line?"

Cal set the metal straw on the bar next to the pane wordlessly. Mikie picked it up, looked from Mason to Sarah, and snorted up a line. He set the straw back where he had picked it up from. "What about money," he sniffed, looking at Mason pointedly. "Split six ways instead of four?"

"Wait a minute." Cal leaned forward. "What if you guys had more gigs?"

"We play two or three nights a week, every week. Sometimes four." Mikie was shaking his head as if he wanted to be convinced. "You can't double book us on the weekends, and weeknights are hard to get paid for."

"I can get you gigs," Cal spoke confidently. "Paying gigs. Two, three weeknights every week."

Mikie leaned forward, suddenly downright amiable. "Where?"

"San Jose. Santa Cruz." Cal stared Mikie down, and Mason felt pride in the way his friend stood up for them. "I know lots of club owners; I know lots of people that like to throw private parties. I even know a few people that like to get married several times a year."

Rising to Cal's challenging stance, Mikie laughed. It was a harsh, raspy sound. "You want to book us to play weddings?"

"Hey, Tyler," Cal kept his eyes on Mikie as he addressed his older brother.

"Yeah, Cal?" Tyler's whole being went into his answer, his body straightening, his hands twitching, and his voice cracking a bit when he said his brother's name.

"Remember that wedding I took you to last summer?" Cal's hands were flat on the bar in front of him, and he stared flatly at Mikie across the surface between them.

"The biker wedding? Yeah, yeah, I remember," Tyler's head bobbed up and down merrily, chestnut hair sweeping his shoulders.

"Who was the band, Tyler?" Cal's voice was so flat his brother was confused for a moment. Then he realized Cal was being a dick to Mikie, not to him, and he smiled.

"It was ZZ Top," Tyler grinned. "It was awesome."

Cal stared Mikie down a moment longer. "Open your mind, brother." He was showing his charisma again. "Stop seeing obstacles where there are only opportunities. Plug in and turn on and see if you want to cancel all your shows this week or make some money and keep your reputation." Cal looked around the bar and grinned. "Am I the only one who doesn't want to hear more of that magick you all played last night? Let's drink and smoke and snort and play first. We'll talk details when you guys take a break. Where's your set lists?"

Finding himself unpacking his guitar and setting up with the others, Mason thought suddenly that Cal had taken the part Sarah had wanted Mason to play. He felt gratitude again towards Cal, and for the first time started thinking it might be nice to have him around a little more often. Plugging into his electronic tuner, he made a few slight adjustments and set up his small pre-amp on the floor in front of him. Attaching his wah pedal to his volume pedal to his pedal board to his pre-amp, all he needed was a microphone. They were everywhere, and he saw that the mixing board had forty-eight channels on it.

Each personality set up their own way, Jason moving immediately to the drum kit and making adjustments, moving something, touching it lightly with a brush stick, moving it a little more, touching it again, moving something else…Tyler strapped on his bass and went straight to the board with it. He leaned in close and popped his thumb against each string separately, stood up smiling. With just a little volume on the mixing board, he fiddled with the long row of knobs above his channel, listening mostly with his eyes closed. When Mason saw he was done, he called to him.

"Hey, Tyler," He looked up suddenly at his name, eyes wide. "Would you mic my pre-amp?"

Tyler's head bobbed agreeably as he grabbed a low-standing microphone and brought it to Mason's Fender pre-amp. "Sure, buddy, sure," he said, taking the cord to the mixing board. "You're channel 27."

"Uh, okay," Mason said dismissively. "Did you turn my amp on?" He strummed a silent cord.

To the amp and back to the mixing board, and Tyler slowly brought the sound of Mason's guitar to an audible but not overwhelming volume. Mason turned the volume knob on his guitar slowly, turning down while Tyler turned up. He strummed a few clear chords, tapped a pedal with his foot and palm-muted a few power chords, tapped another pedal and screamed through a blues scale a couple times. He nodded finally to Tyler and turned the volume knob on his Strat until it would turn no more and the guitar was silent. This was a whole band, no gaps or weak players. The activity around him soothed him, instruments being moved into place and tuned, Sarah and Cal at the bar shuffling through papers and talking. Set lists, schedules, all the responsibilities he had been working towards being burdened by. It was all here, even the girl he sometimes let himself imagine. Sarah was more than he had even allowed in those moments, though…not just pretty but smart and together and wicked talented…

He felt eyes on him, and turned to see Tyler watching him. His luminous lively eyes looked a little sad, his thin frame still. As usual, the bass guitar looked slightly big on him, hanging from the wide leather strap round his shoulder. He had always looked up to Mason for some reason, even idolized him a bit. Mason was suddenly conscious of how he must look, guitar slung at his waist, sunlight behind him through the open rollup door, his eyes on Sarah somehow lighting him from within. What he had been before had been enviable to someone like Tyler. The dream coming true slowly around him seemed unreal even to Mason. He wondered how Tyler was taking it.

Yet when their eyes met, Tyler grinned and shuffled his feet excitedly. He nodded meaningfully towards Sarah and threw Mason a salacious wink. Then he slap-popped a few notes on his bass. It was plugged in but turned off, so there was barely enough sound for Mason to hear the Seinfeld-ish riff. He grinned at his friend.

Setting his Stratocaster gently on a nearby stand, Mason made his way to the bar. The mirror pane had been pushed to the edge of the bar, with papers spread out over every square inch of available surface. Cal stood at the bar, facing Mason's approach; Sarah sat at one of the stools opposite him.

Coming up behind her, Mason slid in to sit on the stool next to her. She was speaking as he approached, "—think we should change it before Thursday, though. We can play a lot more—" she stopped when she saw Mason, turned to him and smiled and nudged closer to him on her stool. "We can play a lot more rock now," she finished, smiling happy up at Mason.

Studying the papers on the bar, Mason looked to Cal and then Sarah. "What did you guys come up with?" His gaze lingered on Sarah, conscious of her thigh against his under the bar, but Cal was the one who answered.

"These guys have a pretty good system," he explained. Mason reluctantly tore his eyes from Sarah's pale green invitations to watch Cal shuffle papers and hold them up for him to see as he talked. "They basically have three set lists for different situations. One is more top forties, one is more rock, one is a combination of the two. Sarah's right, though, they're kind of weak in the rock department." Cal looked at him suddenly. "Has she heard you sing yet?" Mason shook his head. Cal grinned at Sarah. "You're in for a treat," he said to her.

Mason spoke hastily. "I hardly think they have to turn down a lot of Metallica requests, Cal." He looked pointedly at Sarah. "Which is all I bring to the table vocally."

"You'd be surprised," she answered. He couldn't help but think how pretty she was when she smiled at him. "Metallica is popular. Rob can't sing it, Mikie mostly raps. Will you work with me on other stuff besides Metallica?"

Mason smiled. "We'll see," he said noncommittally. "What set list were you guys going to play on Tuesday?"

Cal handed one across the bar to Sarah, who held it for him to see. "Rock," she said. Looking it up and down, she admitted, "light on the rock." Mason nodded as Cal reached out and grabbed the set list back from her. He picked up a sharpie from the assortment of writing utensils they had laid out, and wrote boldly across the top "Enter Sandman". He handed it back to Sarah.

Mason laughed when he saw it. "They already have a good show-starter," he said. "Hell's Bells" was the first song, now second under Cal's neat scrawl. "Besides, what does Sarah do while I sing Metallica?"

"Watch." Sarah grinned. "Come on. Let's play the sound check—"

"Gotta play, gotta play, gotta sing!" Cal chimed in cheerfully.

"—and then the first three or four tunes on the set list," she continued. "Starting with 'Enter Sandman'."

They took their places while Sarah taped up the set list for everyone to see. Mikie and Robert exchanged a glance when they saw it, but neither one said anything. Jason sat still at the drums with Tyler before him and to his left. Instrumentally, they were best friends, and you couldn't ask for a better rhythm section. Mikie was to Tyler's left in front of him a step. Robert's spot mirrored Tyler's, though he was rooted in place by his instrument and the mixing board beside him. Mason took his place opposite Mikie while Sarah took center stage. Her microphone stand was straight and light, hollow aluminum tubing that forked three ways at the bottom to form a light base. A wireless microphone was clipped into the stand, and a red half-tambourine with a padded handle hung from the microphone.

Tambourine in one hand, mic in the other, all Sarah had to do to get ready was flip a switch at the base of the microphone shaft.

All eyes fell on Jason, the only one who hadn't played with the others. He gave a rare grin, locked eyes with Tyler, and started the opening bar to "Gotta play, gotta play, gotta sing" at the same moment the bass guitar came alive. Mason was only a note behind, and for a moment it was Mason's band playing Sarah's warm-up song. Then Mikie and Robert fell in, and when it came around Sarah smiled and growled, "Gotta play, gotta play, gotta sing," about as low as her voice would go into the microphone.

The sound was huge while somehow not being overwhelming in any way. Every instrument could be heard, crisp and clean and individually creating a perfect blend of collective noise. By the time Sarah was scratching at the upper limits of her vocal range, everyone had exchanged a glance or a grin or a nod with everyone else.

Cal sat on a stool just inside the open roll-up door and watched. He could feel it too, the magick of music being made. Still and solemn, he listened with a soft smile on his striking face. The smile turned into a grin as the sound check song exploded into the first bars of 'Enter Sandman'. He watched Sarah clip her microphone into its stand and motion Mason to center stage.

Still holding her tambourine, Sarah came to stand beside Cal and watch the band play without her. Mason tore into the intro, and Cal watched her watch his fingers fly. "You look happy," he said. He didn't say it loudly, the band wasn't deafening. She didn't respond at first, and he wasn't sure if she had heard him. He looked from her to Mason, then at his brother.

Sarah still watched Mason, but she smiled slowly. "It's about time," she murmured, almost too quiet for him to hear. Glancing her way, he wondered if she had even meant to say it aloud.

Then Mason started singing, and she grinned.

CHAPTER 26

Kris stopped on the empty sidewalk in front of the coffee shop after the door closed behind Paul. When he realized it, Paul stopped and turned to him. "What are you doing?"

The Guide shrugged. "Where are you going?"

"Home, I guess. Brenna will be off in a few hours. We're going to get together."

"I'm going to stay here," Kris replied.

"And watch Jessica?" Paul teased.

Kris just shrugged again. "I'm going to stay here and read and watch Jessica while you go home and watch T.V. and wait for Brenna."

"Alright." Paul started to turn, turned back. "Don't forget your funeral is tomorrow. One o'clock. Don't be late, it would be tacky. You're no Elizabeth Taylor." He grinned and turned away, striding quickly up the sidewalk.

"I wouldn't miss it for the world," Kris muttered, unheard. He glided smoothly up the steps and through the glass front doors soundlessly, his passage disturbing neither door nor dust.

At the corner, Paul didn't head the direction that would take him home. He walked instead toward where streets turned to trees a couple blocks away. Before he even quite realized he had changed course, grass padded softly underfoot and the sounds of traffic slowly gave way to the sound of the wind whispering through the trees. The park cut a wide green swath through the city, a vital lifeline of nature that Paul had explored happily throughout his urban lifetime.

This was not the park he remembered, though. He felt the weight of the gold watch in one hand and a wooden walking stick in the other in the same moment he realized it.

A dim form stood beside a nearby tree, cloaked somehow in shadow although it was mostly out in the open on a sunny day. Paul focused his attention on it, and colors grew brighter all around him as the shape's shadows became details.

Battered leather cowboy hat and overcoat and boots, it was the Walker that had passed him the key. Paul realized it in the same moment he realized he was only a stride away, and the stick became a sword in his hands. He had time to wonder when the journal had become the watch again while he took a defensive stance, crossing the blade diagonally in the space between them.

The other regarded him calmly, leaning against the tree heavily with his left shoulder. A walking stick much like Paul's leaned against the tree next to him. He made no move to grab it. He made no move at all. After a few moments, Paul lowered the sword. He kept it between them, but he lowered it.

Finally, the other stepped forward. Although he moved with no hint of a threat, his smooth and easy approach was that of a warrior, and Paul backed up a step nervously. He dropped the sword to his side, then thumped the end of the walking stick into the ground. He was not about to be attacked. He knew that if he was, there would already be little pieces of him strewn about everywhere.

"Walker Paul," the Walker stopped three feet from him and tipped his hat. He had stepped past his walking stick and, without looking, reached behind him absently with his left hand. The stick leapt through the air and into his unseeing grasp.

Show off, thought Paul, then wondered if he could do that too.

"You have a job to do," the Walker intoned gravely. Paul noticed that his outfit was without patch or tear, though it still looked worn. The burnt holes were gone from the hat, too. "I am here to instruct you in some of the basic elements of being a Walker. I see you have acquired a weapon. That is good. I am also here to answer any relevant questions you may have."

He spoke perfectly enunciated, unaccented American English. His tone was formal and brusque, and Paul thought his voice was more suited to the Queen's English or Castilian Spanish. "Where are you from?"

"That's not relevant," he answered. With his walking stick in his left hand, the other Walker stood in mirror image to Paul. "Have you killed a demon yet?"

Paul shook his head. "What's your name? Peter, isn't it?"

Under the brim of his hat, the other Walker frowned. "That's not relevant," he said again. "Do you know how to separate a demon from it's host?"

Again, Paul shook his head in answer. "How old are you, Peter?" Paul asked.

"That's not relevant," the other Walker repeated patiently. He wasn't smiling, but he wasn't frowning anymore. "Have you identified your Guide?"

Paul nodded. "And my Watcher. They both said I shouldn't tell Brenna about any of this." Paul looked at the other Walker's boots, his walking stick, back up at him. "Brenna. That's my girlfriend."

The other Walker was frowning again. "I don't care," he said bluntly. Then he seemed to reconsider. "Heed their counsel. Anything you tell her puts her in danger. Remember, humans can't see demons, but demons can see humans. Knowing about something you can't see can be as bad as seeing something you don't understand. If you want to keep her, never tell her. If you want her to die, or if you want to lose her, tell her. Sit her down and tell her you see demons and devils and angels and dead people and then slip a diamond ring in her champange." Now he smiled, just a little. "See how that goes over."

Paul shook his head. "Brenna's different," he protested, leaning his weight unconsciously on the walking stick. "She could help me."

The Walker considered him a moment, expressionless. "They're all different," he said quietly, his voice ringing with an honest sincerity that surprised Paul. Quiet a moment, he seemed to be thinking of something, of someone. Then his eyes grew hard and so did his voice. "The best way she can help is by giving you a normal life. You don't just walk between worlds. As a Walker, you must live a life in both worlds. A job and a relationship can help ground you in the world you are serving."

"So I should just kill demons in my spare time?" Paul snapped. "Like a secret hobby?"

"Deal with it how you deal with it, Walker," he answered. "But listen to your advisors and keep your worlds separate."

Walker Peter leveled an unwavering gaze at him, and it took a moment before he realized the Walker was looking intently at his shoulder. "Now," he said sternly. "About that demon…" Suddenly his walking stick was a long, slim sword, and its blade was hovering an inch over Paul's right shoulder. Paul turned his head slowly to regard the blade with a little caution and not a little contempt.

"What demon?" Sunlight glinted off the blade, and Paul blinked involuntarily. The world seemed to lurch and darken around him, and he felt the blade brush his shoulder. Paul stepped away one way while the blade swept away the other way, and Paul saw a little red shape tumble to the ground.

It rolled smoothly and stood up, hands on its hips, glaring at the Walker holding the sword. Not even six inches tall, his dark red skin stretched over a well muscled torso and shiny bald head. Paul was glad to see it had pants on, he had seen enough scantily clad male demons to last a lifetime already. The demon's feet were bare, toes clawed like his fingers. A short red tail with a small barb on the end of it thrust through his leather jeans, curling as he dug his toenails into the ground as if to lunge.

"Do you see it now?" Paul could only nod as he watched the other Walker move casually again with blinding speed. His sword became a long staff with a loop of leather about the end.

The seasoned Walker snared the demon round the neck with the loop of leather and twisted the rod several times to wrap the excess material around the shaft, all in a blur that even Paul could barely see. It was like an old-fashioned animal tamer's tool in the hands of an expert. The demon grasped the staff with both hands as the leather tightened its grip around his neck, and his little clawed feet lifted off the ground for a moment.

Ignoring the demon struggling at the end of the staff, the Walker addressed Paul calmly. "Do you see the connection between you?"

Paul looked intently at the demon. "Well, I guess he kind of has my eyes." The demon's eyes glared at him, black where his were white and scarlet where his were blue. He shuddered a little, shook his head. "No, I don't see a connection."

"Between you." The Walker sounded a little irritated. "Look between you. Do you see a connection?" Paul searched the empty air with his eyes, finding it hard to not look at the demon. It kicked its little legs and gnashed its teeth and clawed the air with grasping hands. "Like a cord of light or a rope made of rippling energy or—"

"Like a long tendril of smoke." Paul saw it, a tube of energy between them. It seemed to spiral out of Paul's head and into the demon's heart. Between them, it drifted lazily but unbroken, dancing in the air.

"Like a long tendril of smoke," Walker Peter confirmed. Still ignoring the demon, he held the staff easily with one hand at arm's length, dangling the figure like a puppy. The demon frowned in irritation and gripped the staff with clawed hands, but otherwise stopped struggling. The Walker explained. "That connects the demon to its host. The first thing you always do is sever that connection. As long as that connection is there, the demon will pass its pain onto its host and continue to draw energy from them at the same time. Sever that connection and you can deal with the demon on its own, without harming the host." He slid a hand into a pocket and withdrew a pair of leather gloves, tossed them to Paul. "Put these on."

Paul was quick too. He snatched the gloves from the air, one by one as they came away from each other in flight, his left hand a blur as he leaned casually on his walking stick in his right. "Why?" He put them on, switching his stick to a sword as he moved it to his left hand to don the right glove. At the sight of it, the demon at the end of the staff renewed its struggles, clawing the air with its feet and the staff with its hands. It snarled, and even spit at him. A little puff of smoke exploded silently where spittle struck dark grass.

"They're bite and claw-proof. Demons can hurt you, and it will take longer to heal. That's why we have the armor." The Walker indicated his overcoat with his free hand.

Paul tried to make a show of looking over his own outfit, jeans and a pocket tee. "We don't have armor," he corrected the Walker. "You have armor. I have a tee shirt and some ugly old gloves."

"It's just in case," the Walker replied calmly, lifting the demon off the ground for a moment at the end of the staff and giving it a little shake. He still didn't look at it. "I'll see about getting you some armor next time I talk to the angels," he said in that matter-of-fact tone. Paul didn't think he was joking for some reason.

"Does it come in black?" he quipped.

Walker Peter turned his attention to the ensnared demon, ignoring Paul.

"You're a vicious little bastard, aren't you?" The Walker seemed to enjoy lifting it just high enough that its feet reached the ground but couldn't get any real purchase. Grass and dirt and rocks sprayed out steadily from the churning clawed feet.

"What else is there?" Paul asked.

Still dangling his prize at the end of the stick, the Walker spoke calmly. "There are sad demons and guilt demons and shame demons and envy demons. Most of them pose no threat, although we still stop them from growing to full size so they can't overwhelm the host."

"What happens if a demon overwhelms the host?" Paul didn't think he wanted to know.

Now the Walker looked at him. "They become one and either the demon takes over the body and we kill them both, or the demon takes over the body and kills themselves, often bringing others along in a rampage of violence or poisoning. Once a demon has control, all is lost in this world. You must kill them both. Then you must pursue them to the next life and separate them and kill the demon. The possessed soul is usually knocked off course, and it becomes a lost soul, wandering one or many dimensions with no purpose and little or no soul memory. It's all very messy, that's why we don't let it happen."

Paul was actually beginning to feel a little sorry for the lively little monster fighting to be free. Glancing its way, he asked, "Shouldn't I be dealing with my own demon?"

The staff was suddenly gone, the leather no longer ensnared the demon's sinewy neck. The Walker stepped back and leaned on his walking stick, looking completely harmless.

Red and black eyes darted from one Walker to the other, but the demon's choice was made in less than a hummingbird's heartbeat. Grass and rocks and dirt flew again, but this time they showered out behind the pumping paws and scratching claws as the demon went to all fours and rushed blindly at Paul. With impossible strength, it leapt as it neared him and came hurtling at his neck, clawing and biting the air in anticipation.

Glad for his own speed and strength, Paul dropped his weapon and put both gloved hands before him. He caught it around the torso at arm's length, but the sheer force of the demon's lunge buckled his elbows. For a moment he was face to face with the hate-filled little monster, and he barely pushed it back to arm's length before a swiping clawed hand ripped his nose apart. He felt the wind at his face from the force of the swing, and the rotten smell of sulfur filled his nostrils for a moment.

Holding it at arm's length was not exactly easy or comfortable. Clawing and biting at the gloves, the demon tried to wriggle free as it fought fast and strong and vicious. The claws and teeth still hurt through the gloves, and he kept losing grip on the frantically wriggling form with one hand or another.

Gripping the demon, a deep frown creasing his face, Paul chanced a quick glance at the Walker. He stood watching, leaning casually on his walking stick. Still not smiling, he seemed to be enjoying himself thoroughly nonetheless. Paul turned his full attention to the demon again just as it slipped free of one hand and reached swiping claws past the glove of the hand still clutching him. Three deep gashes marked Paul's forearm from elbow to glove, and blood welled in them as an agonizing burn felt like it was still cutting him. Deeper and deeper the burn went, until the bones in his forearm were on fire.

Crying out, Paul grabbed the monster fiercely about its sinewed little neck, watching the blood on his forearm stop welling up in the wound just before it spilled across his skin. The wounds began to close as the burning subsided, but the pain had galvanized his will. He held the demon out at arm's length, gripping it with such force he thought its scarlet eyes might pop.

He glanced again at the Walker. "A little help?" he asked. When he looked back his flesh was whole and the demon seemed to be struggling to breathe more than it was struggling to attack. Leather wrapped itself about its neck, and Paul moved his hand so the demon could be properly snared again.

Its eyes brightened and it came alive once more, lunging at him against the hand that still gripped its torso. The lunge ended before it began as the demon was torn from his grasp by the leather thong wrapped tight about its neck.

Paul saw the three thin white lines of scar tissue on his forearm turn to healthy pink flesh, and he dropped gloved hands to his sides in exhaustion. The demon struggled before him, clawing at the leather strap about its neck while its legs pumped uselessly at empty air. He could see the cord between them aglow with pulsing energy.

"See the connection?" The Walker was watching him. Paul nodded numbly. "Sever it."

Kneeling to retrieve the walking stick where it had fallen to the ground, Paul stood wearily with sword in hand. For the first time, it felt heavy in his hand. His shoulder tilted to the side with the weight of it. Gripping it with both hands, he swung it through the smoky rope of energy between them. It seemed to fray, and the demon's eyes widened in apparent alarm; but when he looked again, the connection was still there.

"Your intent is as important as your steel," the Walker counseled him calmly. All the while the little crimson monster struggled, more valiantly than ever before and just as uselessly as always before. "See the cord severed, will the separation as you create it." He considered a moment, then added, "It will be easier with other people's demons."

Gathering his last reserves of strength, Paul swung the sword again, this time his resolve as hardened as the steel he wielded. He felt it as the blade connected, a tug against the weight in his hands. Slicing clean through the rope of energy, Paul watched one end disappear into him as the other retracted like an electrical cord into the demon's muscled chest. It seemed to hit the little monster like a blow. The demon stiffened and then sagged, hanging limp from the neck.

Just as suddenly, Paul was himself again. Strength and energy flowed into him, enlivening his limbs until his cells seemed to tingle with it. He hadn't realized how nice it was to never get tired and have superhuman strength until the magickal feeling had ebbed away. Now that it was back, he seemed to notice it for the first time all over again. Holding the long sword in one hand easily, he flexed his left hand before his own face in wonder.

"Good," the elder Walker nodded once. Then he focused his attention on the demon still dangling at the end of the long staff. "Don't ever do this," he said firmly. Then he extended his free arm its full length parallel to the wooden shaft. Hand open, fingers splayed, open palm facing the demon, the Walker narrowed his eyes in concentration. A beam of yellow sunlight leapt from his palm and shot out into the demon, bathing its little red body in an ethereal glow. Already starting to struggle again, the little red creature's strength was reborn, and its claws began to scar the wooden shaft for the first time.

"What are you doing?" Paul asked, backing up a step.

"I'm giving it energy," the Walker said simply. Then, again: "Don't ever do this."

Paul smiled. "How do I do it?"

The Walker didn't answer, just continued to project energy at the demon. Paul watched its skin grow lighter as it began to stretch. Watching the claws lengthen visibly in the space of a heartbeat, he realized it was growing. It was a foot tall suddenly, fully proportioned, the clawed fanged teddy bear from Hell. It kept growing, but it began to grow disproportionately after that. Its legs were long and slim and sinewy, calves too short and squat under thighs unnaturally long and thin. With thick muscled arms that hung well past its knees, its squat torso was nonetheless heavily layered with slabs of muscle. Claws and fangs and the talons that its hands and feet had become were what grew the most, and by the time the Walker stopped feeding it energy it had grown to just over four feet tall.

Its clawed feet hit the ground as the Walker gripped the staff with both hands. The staff had spun little by little in his skilled grip as the demon's neck thickened, but he had to hold it tight with both hands now to keep the monster at bay.

"Did that take energy from you?" The Walker seemed strong as ever, and Paul was still curious. He didn't take his eyes off the squat slavering crimson beast while he asked.

The Walker shook his head, keeping his eyes on the demon as well. "Not if you do it right." He stole a glance at Paul. The demon tried to grab the staff and jerk it from his grasp, but the Walker held fast, eyeing it warily as he answered. "I do it right."

"How do I do that?" Paul asked again.

"Take a Reiki class," the Walker snapped, suddenly impatient. "Get ready."

"For what?" He didn't need to ask, though. The Walker's snaring staff became a walking stick again, the loop of leather disappeared, and the demon was free. It stood there for a moment, uncertain, as if suspecting a trick. It glanced warily from Walker to Walker, then grinned hatefully and sprinted at the one that had been holding the staff. Paul breathed a sigh of relief in the moment it took for the demon to reach the other Walker, and he allowed himself a little smile as Peter's walking stick flashed out and took the creature alongside its grotesquely misshapen head. Its charge veered off to one side as the Walker stepped smoothly to the other; and after two or three rushed unbalanced steps, the demon tumbled into a heap on the ground.

"Why is it all misshapen?" Paul asked as the demon struggled to get its feet under it again. Watching the monster, the Walker seemed to consider the question before answering.

He decided to answer. "That happens when they grow too fast. Demons ususally grow over time, most of them starting in childhood or adolescence and accompanying us to adulthood. Demons get too big too fast when they are able to hook their host's energy full-time. You won't see it very often. When you do, you are dealing with a powerful demon."

The demon had stood again and was glaring at the Walker. He spread his stance and thumped the walking stick into his left palm with a smack. Pivoting, it came at Paul next. He could see long sharp canines jutting between its lips as it grinned malevolently. Leading with arms outstretched, long claws coming at him fast, Paul locked eyes with the demon as his sword flashed suddenly between them. Taking his cue from the other Walker, Paul sidestepped away from the blow and then turned to survey the damage. Blood splashed with the blur, and he saw it on his blade before he saw the demon. It spun away from him and landed on the ground hard, clutching itself in an embrace with its muscled back to the Walker.

"Well, that wasn't very nice." The older Walker's voice came from behind him. Now there was humor in it, and Paul started to turn and ask what was so funny. Then he saw it, laying at his feet. The demon's muscled left arm had been severed just above the elbow, sliced clean through skin and muscle and bone and lying there lifeless dripping dark purple blood onto the dark green grass.

Paul turned to the other Walker. "I think I'm going to be sick," he said.

"Heads up." The brim of his leather hat nodded, a smile starting on his face at last.

Paul turned, and frowned to match the other's smile. The demon stood there clutching its bleeding stump of an arm with the other clawed hand. Long nails dug into its own red skin as it squeezed tightly, uselessly trying to stop the blood that spurted in all directions between its fingers.

More blood dripped from each claw, and the creature's entire left side was drenched in slick purple wetness. The demon eyed them warily, one and then the other.

It came at Paul again. He tried to change the sword to the walking stick and swing it at the same time, but he buried the tip of the sword in its head instead. The blade made a dull wet thud as it punctured skull and buried itself a handsbreath deep in whatever lie beyond, and the demon collapsed into an ungainly pile of thick muscles and crimson skin slick with purple blood.

Paul held the sword loosely, disdainfully, with one gloved hand. Then he felt it quiver and followed the length of the blade with his eyes. Amazingly, sword still buried deep in its skull, the demon was struggling to rise again. Its eyes were open, although one was full of purple blood and stared lifelessly at the ground. The other eye was alive, and it was filled with hate. Tottering with the weight of the sword and possibly impaired motor functions, it rose slowly to its feet and continued glaring balefully at Paul with its one good eye.

"How do you kill these fucking things?" Paul hissed, clutching the sword with both hands at arm's length. The demon clawed at him with its remaining arm, but only succeeded in slicing off one of its own fingers on the sharp blade of Paul's long slim bastard sword. He looked away, disgusted.

The other Walker watched the scene with obvious amusement. Paul wished he hadn't wondered if the man ever smiled. Finally, he answered, as he leaned casually again on his walking stick and watched.

"At last, a good question." He grinned broadly and nodded. "You have to cut off its head," he said and nodded again. Then he twirled his walking stick; and spinning, it became a long thick steel battleaxe. Shaft and blades gleamed as it spun, double heads a foot long of wicked sharp-looking cold metal. The length of the shaft made it nearly as tall as a man, with leather bound about the last two feet of the handle. "The axe works best," he smiled.

Continuing to struggle against the sword in its skull and Paul's strength at the other end, the demon had reduced its attack to standing in place and swiping at him with its remaining hand. Purple blood splotched its skin from head to toe, from thin purple rivulets oozing around the blade in its head to the messy splatter pumping from the severed arm. The ground all around it was churned dirt and shredded grass stained to a dark shadow by the dripping gore. Every time it swung its arm feebly at him, blood flew from the missing finger to spatter the long blade or Paul's tee shirt or his jeans.

Paul looked at the other Walker, coolly holding the battleaxe at an angle in front of him with both hands. His overcoat was still battered but spotless, his cowboy hat perched at a perfect tilt on his head. The shadow of a smile still played about his lips. Looking down at his blood-stained clothes, Paul caught sight of the demon's severed finger on the ground a few inches from his foot. A droplet of purple blood stood beaded on the black leather of his shoe.

He returned his eyes to the older Walker. "Would you please…?"

Now he did smile, stepping forward and swinging the axe back over his shoulder. "I thought you'd never ask," he said, and swung the battleaxe whistling through the air with his next step. There was a wet thunk of a sound as it took the demon from behind, and Paul watched the last two inches of the blade opening its throat cleanly. Then a shower of purple blood arced through space to drench his face as he turned aside. When he looked back, the head was hanging from his sword lifeless and bodiless. Its one good eye stared off into space, the hate extinguished at long last. Bloodstained and motionless, its red and purple body lay in a heap under the hovering head.

Paul didn't feel like focusing. He didn't want to visualize, didn't feel like turning the sword back into a walking stick or prying the head off the point with a blood-stained oxford. Instead, he opened his hand and let sword and head fall together to the ground. Wiping blood from his face with his bloodied shirt, Paul felt something inside him had shifted. He pointed at the mass of gore before him. "What was that?" he asked the Walker.

His eyes narrowed, his smile was gone. "That. was. a. demon," he said it slowly, as if Paul were a stupid child.

"I know that," Paul snapped. "What was its, uh, job? Its purpose? What was its purpose?"

The Walker hesitated a moment, leaning casually again on his walking stick. "It was making you stay angry about being a Walker, about not telling Brenna, about everything changing. Don't you feel better?"

Paul did feel better, but that wasn't the point. "That's not the point," he said. "I have a right to be angry. I should feel bad about lying to the girl I love. And her brother. And everybody else. Now that I'm a Walker I don't get to have a conscience? I don't get to feel?"

Regarding him skeptically, one eyebrow arched, the Walker spoke. "Don't be so dramatic," he said reproachfully. "Of course you get to feel. You just don't get to feel ambivalence about being a Walker. It's quite simply not allowed."

"Like we're not allowed to talk?" Paul asked pointedly. "You sure have a lot of rules for someone who keeps breaking them. Walkers can't do this, Walkers can't do that. What kind of Walker are you? Do you know Walker John is looking for you?"

Now both eyebrows were arched, a look of surprise at Paul's barrage of questions. "I'm not a Walker anymore," he said. "I'm a Hunter." Then he relaxed, closed his eyes…and disappeared.

Paul cursed and kicked at the demon's head still lying lifeless at his feet. He stepped firmly on its ear, dragging the sword from the gaping wound with one gloved hand. At least he'd got to keep the gloves, stained through with demon blood.

Then he was holding a walking stick at his side with one hand and holding a gold pocket watch in the other. Looking at the alien trees and grass around him, the blood red sky above him, he closed his eyes and thought of the park. Green trees, sunny day, a warm breeze on his face, Sutro Tower in the distance…when he heard birds chirping happily, he opened his eyes.

The demon was gone. His clothes were spotless, not a drop of blood on his shoes or his skin. He still wore the gloves, brown oiled leather that showed no hint of the violence they had seen. Paul took them off and shoved them unceremoniously into his back pocket. They didn't disappear like his key and weapon, and they flopped along noisily as he walked swiftly from the park to his apartment. Brimming with optimism, thinking of his love and her beauty, he nearly walked right past a quiet cacaphony that sounded somehow strangely familiar.

"*Shut up,*" Paul's sharp hearing picked up the fierce but faint whisper. "*Shut up shut up shut up shut up…*"

He slowed to glance in the darkened recessed entry with his Walker eyes.

In the same glance, he saw both the homeless man and the demon on his shoulder. They both slouched drunkenly, the demon hissing its hateful barrage of spite in the man's ear just quietly enough that Paul could only make out a few words here and there under the skipping record sound of the man's voice. "*…worthless drunk…all your fault…waste of space…*"

Another stride and he would be past the scene and closer to home, and a few strides later the image would be replaced by a more visually appealing one by his imagination. Then the man's voice changed, he turned to look right at the demon, and he shook his head. "It's not my fault," he said quietly, as if trying to reason with the miniature monster. "I'm a worthless drunk because of it, I'm a waste of space alright, but it wasn't my fault. She just died."

Paul realized he had stopped to stare in the same moment that the homeless man did, and dropped his gaze to the sidewalk for a moment both to show respect and to gird his supernatural sense of smell against the nearly palpable stench wafting from the vestibule.

"Can you see him?" Paul asked pointedly, his eyes on the demon.

Man and demon suddenly sat up straight together, one on the concrete and the other on his shoulder. The demon's head pivoted so it could level a glare and a snarl at him while the man nodded soberly. "I hear him better than I see him," he replied, his voice hoarse but clear. "I see him more when I get my fill." He held up a bottle of mostly emptiness with a candid shrug. The demon shot him a look of irritation.

One moment, the Walker stood still on the sidewalk; the next he was halfway in the vestibule as his sudden sword brushed the demon from the man's shoulder with the same fluid movement that severed the smoky connection and impaled the demon through the belly; the next he and demon faced each other in a vast landscape full of smoke and charred rock and black shadows even his eyes could not penetrate. He tossed the creature unceremoniously into the stinking air and chopped off its head as it dropped, neatly. He was gone before the pieces hit the hot dirt.

He materialized again in front of the vestibule, bladeless. If the man had blinked, it would seem that his demon had simply disappeared. That's just what he was doing, too, blinking rapidly at Paul and then at his vacant shoulder. "What...I...well...," he stammered, then focused on Paul at last. "Thank you, mister. Whatever you did, he's gone. Thank you."

Paul inclined his head slightly and smiled. Then he turned and walked away.

Perhaps he could get used to being a Walker after all.

CHAPTER 27

Mason lay on his back, staring absently at the ceiling. The weight of Sarah's head on his chest was nice, and the smell of her hair splayed across his torso pleased him even more. He could smell the sex they'd had, the perfume she wore, the drinks they had sweated out…and her unique intoxicating scent in all of it. Her head rose and fell with his every breath, and he watched the back of her head bobbing calmly like a buoy in the deep sea. Curled against him, she lay with one arm across his torso and one leg thrown over his. She sighed a sweet mellow wind over his stomach with her every outbreath.

"Are you awake?" she whispered. Not one to startle, Mason felt his heart race in surprise.

"I thought you were sleeping," he whispered back. He chuckled anxiously, quietly, easing the sudden tension in his body.

Sarah turned her head, pale green eyes wide awake. She grinned at him mischievously. "Why are we whispering?" she whispered. A long lock of dark hair fell across her face, the rest fanning out to tickle his belly.

Brushing the hair out of her face, Mason ran his fingers slowly through her hair, chuckling aloud. "I DON'T KNOW," he said, loudly.

Sarah giggled and closed her eyes while he stroked her hair. A soft smile lit her features, and Mason got lost in her beauty for a long precious moment. When she opened her eyes she saw such love shining in his that she felt tears of happiness well up. Her eyes drifted closed again, squeezing a lone tear from one eye. The warm wetness of the tear splashed the skin over Mason's heart, and he smiled and stroked her hair again.

"I want to be with you," she said quietly, still not opening her eyes.

He smiled a half-smile. "You are with me." Her eyes flashed open with a playful ferocity, and his smile widened. "I want to be with you, too," he said. "I love being with you."

Eyelids widening impossibly at the word 'love', Sarah closed pale green eyes again and smiled. "I want to know every part of you," she murmured. "I want to love every part of you."

Mason was silent, torn between the desire in his heart and the fear in his mind. Sarah opened her eyes, and he wondered what she saw.

"Where did you go?" she asked, perching suddenly on her elbow and looking down at him through the lovely waterfall of her hair.

His arm under her, he cupped the back of her head with the length of his hand. His fingers reached around to brush the hair back out of her face. He let his fingers tangle in it lazily as he met her gaze. "I didn't go anywhere," he answered slowly. "I just don't consider all of my parts to be completely loveable."

Leaning forward, eyes closed, she kissed one cheek, then another, then his forehead. Her kisses were soft and moist, and his skin tingled where her lips touched it. When she drew away again, she smiled to see him smiling. "Those are the parts of you that I want you to know you can share with me. Those are the parts of you that need my love the most."

"No matter what?" Mason arced an eyebrow at her, trying to be playful.

She nodded, serious and innocent and wise all at once. "No matter what."

Mason matched her serious look and serious tone. "I should tell you something." He looked away, as if in internal struggle. Looking back, he locked eyes with her and said gravely, "Sarah, I smoke a lot of weed."

Grabbing the pillow from under her elbow, she whumped Mason in the face with it. They both laughed, but she was serious once more as she put the pillow down and planted her elbow on it again. Her head tilted prettily in her hand as she looked down at him. "Now you owe me a secret," she said, eyes sparkling. "A real secret."

Snaking his arm out from under her, Mason put his hands behind his head casually on the pillow and eyed her with playful suspicion. "I do? I thought I just told you one. I think maybe you owe me a secret."

A frown was starting in Sarah's eyes, and Mason frowned too as it moved to her lovely lips. He shook his head best as he could. Then he sat up, and he was looking down at her. The move was sudden and his look grave. Her eyes widened with surprise, with curiosity, with a little fear.

"Fine," Mason said flatly, looking away. "I have a demon."

Sarah nodded earnestly, gazing up at him, ready for anything. "We all have demons, lover," she said softly, reassuringly. "That's what I mean. You can share—"

"No," Mason said abruptly, cutting her off. He leveled his hazel eyes at her. "I have a demon. I see a demon. With red skin and horns and a tail. It used to sit on my shoulder most of the time, but lately it walks with me and stands nearby. It seems to be getting bigger. I talk to it. It talks to me." Sarah was frozen, looking up at him, eyes wide. Mason sighed. "If you ever tell anyone I told you, I'll deny it. If you ever try to help me make it go away, with medication or with magick, I won't let you, and I won't ever speak to you again." He spoke evenly and calmly, his voice flat and emotionless, looking her sternly in the eye. Then he looked away and said, "If you want to leave, I understand. I would think me crazy too."

In one fluid motion, Sarah was on her knees on the mattress beside him. The fingers of one hand fell softly on his shoulder to grip it lovingly while the other rose to touch his cheek, lightly, then his jaw. Their eyes met. "Is that why you play so well?" she asked, blinking, her pale green eyes widening impossibly.

Mason sighed, and it felt like he lost a thousand pounds with the breath. He fell back and let his head hit the pillow. "Yeah," he said, staring at the ceiling. "Yeah, I think so." He couldn't believe her reaction, and he looked to see if she was still there.

She was, smiling tenderly at him. "You know what this means, right?"

He frowned. "What?"

Putting her hand on his chest just over his heart, she leaned over him so her hair brushed his face. "Either your third eye is open a little more than normal, or you're a schizophrenic whose awesome talent comes with terrible hallucinations."

Mason couldn't help but look in her eyes as she hovered over him. "Why are you smiling? Is that good news?"

Her smile widened, and she swooped in gently to brush his lips with her own. "It is for me," she murmured. "Either way, you need me to take care of you." She hovered over him again, still smiling. "And I need you to need me."

Looking in her eyes, he let himself smile a little. "Really?" he asked, disbelief clear in his voice.

Sarah nodded solemnly, and in that moment she looked very serious and very young to him. Leaning back on her elbow again, she said, "Do you want to talk about it?"

Mason shook his head. "We just did," he said. "I never thought I'd tell anybody what I just told you. Can that be enough for now? I'm still a little shocked that you didn't leave."

Tracing a long feathery finger from his throat to his stomach, Sarah gave him an amatory glance. "Are there any other parts of you that need some loving?" she asked, letting the sheet slide off her small round breasts. Leaning forward, her nipples brushed either side of his face as her hand found the hardness beginning between his legs.

Smiling, turning his head, Mason took one of her pink nipples gently but firmly between his teeth. He licked the nub as it hardened in his mouth, then covered her breast with his mouth as he pushed her back onto the bed and grasped her ass with one hand and her hair with the other.

CHAPTER 28

Paul woke slowly, the smell of strong coffee greeting his return to the flesh. Stretching, feeling the aliveness and the strength in his limbs, he lay there for a minute and breathed in the new day. It wasn't just coffee awaiting him; Brenna's scent filled the room and the bed and clung to his skin. He rolled over to bury his face in her pillow, inhaling deeply nothing but her. Rolling over again, he sat up and reached for the coffee just as the bathroom door opened.

Slowly and quietly, Brenna backed through the doorway. Doorknob in one hand, the other held a towel and languidly pushed it back and forth through dark wet hair. Her lean young body was naked but for the towel, and Paul watched her perfect bare buttocks flex as she moved. Dainty bare feet edged their way backward from bathroom tile to bedroom carpet, and she closed the door silently behind her and turned.

Coffee in hand, crosslegged under the blankets, Paul watched her shamelessly. The perfect curve of ass was joined by the perfect curve of her breast as she pivoted slowly, still drying her hair with one hand. Lifting the other hand to help, by the time she saw Paul watching her it looked as though she were striking a pose for him. She stood there for a moment that could not last long enough for him, arms raised over her head so her breasts stood out, perfect and round. Dark nipples stiff with the change in temperature, back arched and legs slightly apart, Paul traced every inch of smooth soft taut skin with his eyes hungrily. When she saw him looking, she arched her back even more, filling her lungs and pulling in her flat stomach. Graceful curves turned to dramatic lines as her ribcage expanded over her slimming waist. One hand fell slowly from the towel, brushing her cheek and then her breast, tracing the concavity of her smooth belly. As her hand dropped lower, she looked at Paul, watching him watch her fingers graze the shaved rise of flesh above her lower lips.

Raising her hand again to the towel, she relaxed her body to its normal level of overwhelming sexiness. "You're awake," she smiled at him.

Paul nodded and held the coffee cup higher. "Thank you," he said, taking a sip. "And thank you for…" he let his eyes drink in her body again slowly, starting at her beautiful perfect dainty little toes and taking in every mountainous curve and every alluring crevasse before falling into her dark eyes again. "...all of that," he concluded. "Come here."

Dropping the towel beside him on the bed, Brenna took the remaining coffee in its cup from his hand. She turned and set it on the nightstand and turned again to him in all her naked glory. Sliding to the edge of the bed, Paul dropped a foot on the floor on either side of hers; and sitting, wrapped his arms about her waist to lean his head on her abdomen. The soft smooth skin of her belly brushed his cheek, and then his nose as he turned to taste her skin. Brenna's hands were in his hair mussing it lovingly as her unique intoxicating flavor filled his mouth. Kissing her, lightly licking her smooth skin, a soft moan escaped her lips and he felt his body start to react. Pulling her closer and moving his mouth to kiss her softly and repeatedly all around dark stiff nipples, she felt it too. One hand fell lightly to his shoulder to trail down his torso and disappear under the covers. He felt her fingers around him and felt himself stiffen almost painfully at her touch.

"Can I have this now?" Brenna squeezed gently, and Paul moaned as he took her nipple in his mouth. Looking up, he saw her glance at the clock on the nightstand. "Or are you going to make me wait?"

Paul eyed the clock, his next moan one of disappointment. "Will you be okay being late to Kris' funeral? If I was late to my best friend's funeral, would you still respect me? Would you still love me?"

He felt her sigh against him. "Probably not," she admitted playfully. "At the very least, I'd never let you live it down." She stepped back and he stood up, and now their heights were reversed. Turning her head, she leaned her cheek against his chest and wrapped her arms around his waist. He was still hard, and she squeezed him tight so his arousal was embraced by her warm smooth belly, captured between them.

"So, who's making who wait?" He ran his fingers through her hair, then grabbed a wet mass and pulled firmly but gently until her head was tilted back and her eyes met with his.

They were a well-oiled machine then, getting ready calmly but swiftly. Passing each other a dozen times between the bathroom and bedroom and closet, their paths never crossed without a touch or a kiss or a smile. Brenna was ready first, choosing Paul's shirt and tie and standing before him smiling and buttoning it up for him.

He was tying the black fabric about his neck when she asked, "Do you want a coffee to go? There's plenty left." Paul nodded and thanked her, and met her coming into the bedroom as he was headed out.

Holding a strong stainless steel mug with the black plastic lid snug in place, Brenna was holding something else in her other hand. "What are these?" she flipped her hand back and forth a little distastefully, and the brown leather gloves flopped noisily in her grasp. When he took the coffee from her hand, her fingers went like a magnet to clutch the gemstone at her chest.

"I found those yesterday, in the park," he said casually. He sipped the coffee. "You ready to go?"

She tossed the gloves where she had found them on the breakfast bar as they passed. Paul thought the gesture as offhanded as the lie he had told about them. He couldn't help but be bothered that he wasn't bothered by lying to Brenna.

It was a small service, in a small rectangular room. Of the fifty chairs crammed in on either side of the center aisle in neat rows, less than thirty were occupied. Paul saw Kris immediately, standing beyond the end of the row behind the coffin. Flowers and pictures and coffin were all done in simple but elegant taste. Paul squeezed Brenna's hand, still watching Kris survey the turnout. "You're awesome," he murmured.

She squeezed his hand back lightly and let go, hanging back to give him room. Paul walked slowly up the carpeted center aisle, his eyes on his friend. Kris saw him, and they met over the smooth closed black lid.

"Thanks for coming," Kris said lightly. He looked young standing behind the ominous wooden box, younger still for the robes he had taken to wearing. He glanced down at the coffin, back up to Paul. "Did Brenna do all this?" Paul realized the Guide was keeping the tone of his voice light because otherwise it would be thick with emotion.

Paul nodded solemnly.

"Tell her that…" Kris looked away, frowned at the floor. He shrugged. "Would you tell her that you know I would have appreciated it?" His eyes met Paul's again. "A lot."

He nodded again, then swept his gaze across the room behind him. There was no one within earshot. "Who are all these people?" Paul asked. More than half the faces were unfamiliar.

Caught between a smile and a frown, tears welled in Kris' gray eyes. "People from my past. I don't know how Brenna found them." He nodded and Paul turned. "See that lady in the flowered dress, sitting by herself?" Paul nodded. "That's my eighth grade English teacher."

Paul smiled. He'd heard stories. "The one that told you that you were the smartest kid in class?"

Eyes again on the coffin, Kris smiled softly. "It wasn't just that. She hounded me about not living up to my potential, like my parents and other teachers. But she was the only one that made me think she really thought I was something special, like I was depriving the world and myself if I didn't become something." The Guide looked up, and Paul saw pride shining through his tears. "Missus Maggie," he said, his voice low, "I wish you could see me now."

Kris had shed his mortal life like a skin that had grown too constricting. Watching him, Paul realized that his friend was not sad; his mood was one of happy melancholy, his own funeral a scene for an almost detached kind of reminiscence. This was a proud new beginning for his friend. Paul had drenched himself in the purple gore of his Walker demon, and still he didn't feel about being a Walker the way Kris seemed to feel about being a Guide.

Brenna came up behind him then, he smelled her before he saw her. Breathing in deep, he looked Kris in the eye and said, "I love you, buddy." Then she was beside him, looking down at the coffin. One hand found Paul's, her fingers intertwining with his, while the other worried at her necklace. He saw the look on his friend's face before he saw the tears on hers. One after another, wet beads streamed silently down her cheeks. As he watched, a tear dripped from her rounded chin to splat on her hand as it clutched the amulet. Paul pulled the thin material from his breast pocket and handed her the little white handkerchief. She let go the gemstone long enough to take it from him, but she didn't wipe her tears. She clutched the necklace again, kerchief in hand, while another tear fell. Not once did her eyes leave the coffin or did her hand loosen its grip on Paul's.

"This would have meant a lot to him," Paul said softly. She nodded slowly, once, twice, still staring at the coffin. "Want to say anything?" he asked, just as quietly. Her hair swung slowly from side to side as she shook her head. "Want to find a seat?" She nodded again, her eyes leaving the coffin to trail the floor as he led her to a couple of empty spots in the front row, nearby. Sitting next to her, he saw that her eyes once again rested warily on the body-laden box as tears slid slowly down both perfect cheeks. She was striking in her grief, her beauty come alive with stark raw emotion. Expressionless, her face yet had the perfect serene look of the surface of a turbulent ocean. Depth showed in her grief, and in her pride in her grief, and Paul found her more beautiful than ever.

He turned just in time to see Roche fill the open doorway, followed closely by Jessica as he came into the room. They were both clothed all in black, a study in opposites otherwise. Roche looked even bigger in a fitted suit, a mountain of devil flesh with a black shirt and tie. Even the triangle of silk jutting from his breast pocket was black. Unfortunately, the black fedora perched atop his head made him look more the dangerous gangster than the grieving mourner, and Paul knew he wasn't about to take it off. The devil entered the room like he owned it, and surveyed the scene as if anticipating battle.

Jessica was slim and youthful, shy and quiet and beautiful. Her long black dress covered shoulders and cleavage and most of her legs, clinging to her slight curves modestly but not unattractively. Blonde hair tied in a tight bun atop her head, the austere lines of her neck and jawline made her appear even more youthful. She entered reserved and cautious behind Roche, eyes on the floor till Roche turned and said something to her. Stopping and tilting her head to hear, shorter than him in low black heels, she looked Paul's way and saw him. Roche followed her eyes and nodded when his eyes met Paul's, then they both moved up the aisle with assurance.

The devil moved to stand before the coffin while Jessica broke off and made her way to sit next to Brenna. Reaching out wordlessly, she put her hand on Brenna's leg. It broke her from her reverie for a moment, and she turned and leaned in her seat to give the girl a hug. Still neither of them said anything, and a few moments later Brenna was holding Jessica's hand on her lap with one hand while the other toyed with her necklace. Both girls stared blankly at the coffin. Jessica seemed caught up in the thick spell of grief Brenna had cast; or maybe the realization that her friend's body lay lifeless just on the other side of some thin painted plywood hit her, and tears welled in her eyes as well. Paul patted Brenna's leg and stood, coming up behind Roche.

The devil moved aside as he approached, and they stood quiet together in front of the coffin. Looking at Kris, Roche spoke low to Paul. "You got a good girl there," he said. "Hold on to her. Don't ever tell her."

Paul was looking at Kris too. "I won't," he said resolutely. Devil and Guide both looked at Paul, surprised.

"Really?" Kris looked at him, gray eyes wide with relief and maybe a little disappointment.

Roche turned again to Kris when he spoke, then echoed the sentiment quietly. "Yeah. Really?" Then the devil rotated his head slowly again, almost ominous in his tilted black fedora. He raised an eyebrow suspiciously as he made a quiet show of looking closely at Paul's shoulders, one by one. "Hey, Guide," he murmured, his eyes coldly locked on Paul's, "notice anything missing?"

Kris looked to the devil and then to the Walker, only to return his attention to Roche. "What?" he asked, giving a signature shrug.

"Look lower," the devil growled.

The Guide's eyes dropped to Paul's chest, then his stomach, then Roche spoke again, quiet but forceful. "Not lower, jackass. Lower." Kris began to reply, then shut his mouth and nodded. Furrowing his youthful brow in concentration, he examined Paul's shoulders as Roche had. Paul felt like a specimen.

"Your demon is gone," Kris said loudly, the only one of the three who didn't need to lower his voice. He looked at Roche. "His demon is gone."

He shot them both an angry look. "You could see it?" he whispered fiercely. "Both of you?"

Roche's eyes were accusing, and Paul's anger withered. "You met your Maker, didn't you?" His tone was accusatory as well.

Paul nodded dumbly.

"Come by the shop after this," Roche growled, looking down at the coffin. "We need to talk." He looked at Kris. "You too." Then he went and sat on the other side of Jessica, hands on his lap, feet flat on the ground, staring and frowning at nothing.

He looked a question at the Guide, but Kris just shrugged. Then Paul saw his eyes widen and focus on something behind him, and he turned. Smiling, he walked up the carpeted aisle swiftly and met the older couple with a handshake and a hug. "Sharon, Doug, so glad you're here." He put his hand on her shoulder, shook his head, remembering. Kris was dead. "I'm so sorry," he said. He led them up the aisle to the front row, her a pear-shaped sloppily dressed woman with short thin lifeless auburn hair and him a slim and good-looking man with dark hair that was once almost black and was now going to gray. He wore a suit that made his sharp features and graying hair look even more distinguished. It fit his lean frame well, black suit and tie with a gray buttoned shirt, and he wore it as casually as Paul did a pair of jeans and a tee shirt.

"Paul," he said, shaking his hand again and smiling warmly. "Where is the young lady that put this all together?" Doug's charismatic warmth conveyed grief and openness and gratitude.

"Yes, yes," Sharon fluttered her hands uselessly in the air. "We need to meet Brenna."

Paul led them past the two chairs with little black on white "RESERVED" signs on them, stiff paper folded over to make an informative tent, closest to the coffin to the left. The third chair was his, empty, and Brenna looked up at his approach. Her eyes seemed to come back into focus, and she wiped her cheeks with the thin scrap of material she held still crumpled in one hand. She stood up, Brenna again, seeming to understand what was going on before it had happened. Looking past Paul, she registered the faces behind him without knowing them, and she brushed quickly again across both cheeks with the kerchief as fresh tears sprang forth.

"Sharon," she smiled. Touching Paul's arm lightly in passing, Brenna embraced the older woman. "I'm so sorry," Paul heard her say. Disengaging from her, she turned to meet Doug's proffered handshake with a hug as well.

"Sharon, Doug, this is Brenna," Paul said uselessly behind them. "Brenna, meet Kris' parents."

"It's so nice to finally meet you both," Brenna gestured to the seats nearest the coffin, then bent to pick up the signs. Sharon sat next to Brenna, leaving a seat open to either side of them. Paul moved to stand next to the older man.

"Paul, how have you been?" Doug clapped him on the back and edged up the aisle, away from the coffin. "Did you know Brenna was flying us out?"

He shook his head. "It doesn't surprise me terribly, she's pretty awesome. She didn't tell me, though."

Doug leaned in close. "She's pretty hot is what she is."

"There's that too," Paul nodded.

They were quiet then, and the older man's eyes came to rest on the coffin. "He never forgave me," he murmured, almost to himself. Glancing at Paul, he asked, "Do you believe in God, Paul?"

Paul followed his gaze to look at the coffin, then at Kris behind it. The Guide did not appear pleased. Arms folded in the sleeves of his robe before him while a frown furrowed his brow, he watched his father coldly over his dead body. Paul sighed heavily. "Doug, I think there is definitely something going on that most folks can't see."

The older man shot him a strange look, then went and sat by his wife, looking subdued. Glad to see that Kris had exchanged his frown for a sly smile, Paul approached the coffin again.

"What's so funny?" he asked quietly.

"He thinks you were talking about Lisa," Paul looked at him, lost, and Kris laughed aloud. "When you said there's something going on most folks don't know about."

Paul felt the color drain from his face, and he shook his head. "That's not what I meant," he said quietly.

"I know," Kris grinned. "That's why it's so funny."

They stood silent over the sealed box, each in his own thoughts. His smile faded, Kris spoke after a moment. "That's your demon, you know."

Paul raised an eyebrow.

"My Dad," Kris explained patiently. "Didn't you see his demon?"

"No," Paul answered quietly. "Ever since I learned to tune them out, I don't see them unless I want to." He turned, opening his eyes in a way they had not been open as he did. He saw the demon at the same time as he saw Doug, and the man's blank stare suddenly made more sense. Sitting slumped forward slightly, palms flat on his lap, he gazed at nothing with a mixture of dullness and consternation. Kneeling beside him, leaning an arm on Doug's shoulder and whispering fiercely in his ear, was the biggest demon Paul had ever seen. As tall as its host, it wore a suit of black leather, with pale crimson flesh at the collar and cuffs. He had a full head of black hair, and rather a handsome face.

The demon continued whispering, its full attention on Doug. As he focused on its words, Paul was able to tune in and hear them as if it spoke into his ear as it did Doug's.

"…a worthless, unfaithful smear of scum," the demon murmured, his voice low and slow and accusing. "You still have the smell of that slut on you. You always do. You have been stained to your very soul by your infidelity. Your son wouldn't even speak to you because of your disgusting ways, and now he's dead. He might still be alive if you had been a better father. So many things might be different. Maybe if you hadn't spent so much time banging the neighbor, you might have kept your job. Hell, you might be the boss by now if you had focused on work like you focused on getting laid."

On and on it went, its voice calm but wicked, quiet but sharp, until Paul tuned it out. Shaking his head, he turned to Kris and was surprised to see a smug look of satisfaction on his face. Something over Paul's shoulder caught Kris' attention. Paul turned again to find Brenna coming up behind him, concern in her eyes.

Sliding an arm around his waist, she asked, "Are you okay, love?"

Paul nodded, encircling his arm about her and pulling her close. "I'm okay," he murmured into her cocoa hair. "All things considered."

She looked up at him, big beautiful soulful dark eyes round and bright and full of love and sadness. "I'm going to get things started."

"Okay, sweetie." He kissed her forehead, lightly. Looking in her eyes, hands on her shoulders, he smiled. "Kris would have really appreciated all this," he said again.

Brenna bit her lower lip attractively. "Even inviting his parents?" she whispered.

"Even inviting his parents." Paul kept his voice low too. "He was angry with his dad for, uh, what was going on; and he was disgusted with his mom for living in denial and letting it just go on so long." Paul glanced at the couple over her shoulder to see them talking, Doug appearing to comfort Sharon. "He would have wanted them here, though. They're good people."

She nodded, stood on her tiptoes and kissed him lightly. "Wish me luck."

"You're perfect," Paul smiled. "You don't need luck." She scowled prettily, and he nodded. "Luck." Just as he settled into his seat, she began to speak behind him. Her voice was low and full and feminine, and she hardly had to raise it to fill the room.

"Thank you all so much for coming," she said, "some of you from very far away. Although we gather today to say goodbye to a very special young man, every one of us here has a bigger heart for having known him before he passed. Every one of us has memories that we hold precious that we wouldn't have if not for knowing him, and many of us are completely different people having been fortunate enough to be close to him."

"We are here today," she continued, her voice smooth and low and thick with her grief, "to say goodbye to a son, a friend, a grandson. We are here to say goodbye to someone who gave a deeper meaning to those words, who lived a deeper meaning of life. Today we say goodbye to Kris Reed, one of the most profoundly thoughtful and intelligent and kind people any of us has ever known."

Brenna glanced at Paul, and he smiled, unable to imagine that she might need reassurance. Her eyes took in the whole room warmly, and she continued.

"Many feel that a religious figure or a justice of the peace should lead something like this. Kris was not a religious person, however, and honestly didn't have much respect for tradition of any kind." A quiet ripple of laughter warmed the room, and Brenna smiled at the assemblage. "Kris didn't tolerate anything that didn't make sense, and I wanted to make sure to express that in the way we chose to say goodbye to him. It will not be some stranger recapping a life he never knew, it will be his friends and loved ones who speak today. We will do our best to put aside our self-indulgent desire to mourn, and we will today celebrate the life that Kris lived instead of the loss we all feel. Several people will say some words, and then anyone else who wants to say something may do so."

"Afterward, we will all go to the cemetery and visit the spot where his ashes will be interred. There will be catering at the wake, and again anyone who would like to will have the opportunity to speak."

She smiled, a lovely sad smile that lit the entire room. "As most of you know, I am Brenna. I first met Kris when I first met my boyfriend Paul about three years ago. Since then I have thought about things I never would have thought about, had adventures I never would have had and felt things I never would have felt." A tear slipped unnoticed down her cheek, but her voice did not waver. "All because this man of much depth and many facets was my boyfriend's best friend. All because I am lucky enough to be able to say I was friends with Kris Reed.

Brenna turned, her eyes coming to rest on the biggest photograph on the table that easily held the few pictures Kris had allowed people to take of him. Some childhood photos were there too, but the centerpiece really was a great picture. Two feet tall, framed in black and matted in dark blue and gray, it showed him from the chest up. Wearing his gray sweatshirt and a green tee shirt, it was the smile above them that was unusual. Kris was grinning unabashedly, his eyes reduced to merry slits crinkled at the corners. The look was a little childlike, with none of his usual shyness or cynicism.

Remembering when Brenna had taken the picture, Paul smiled. They had gone to Six Flags for the day, and she had caught Kris in a candid moment as he and Paul came off a roller coaster. Upset, Kris had patiently explained to Brenna that he did not like his picture taken, especially by surprise. She had listened, apologized, and offered to delete the photo… if he would look at it first. Viewing the picture on the tiny screen, Kris had admitted it was the best photo he had ever seen of himself. Brenna told him how he looked so happy after every ride, flush with wonder and excitement, and she had wanted to capture that magick when she saw it. To Paul's surprise and Brenna's delight, he had told her he would like a copy of the picture, and that she didn't have to delete it. Now here it was, blown up to a life size image of that happy unguarded moment.

"Thank you, Kris," Brenna said softly, her voice nonetheless filling the room. "Thank you for not accepting things the way they were just because they had always been that way. Thank you for being so smart, so considerate, so understanding of those close to you and what they needed. Thank you for criticizing all of the girls that Paul dated before me until he couldn't stand to be around them anymore."

A murmer of laughter filled the room, and Paul nodded. He chanced a glance at Kris. The Guide stood behind the coffin, arms clasped before him in the folds of his robe, watching Brenna talk to the photograph. His face was a mixture of sadness and gratitude, frowning slightly in an attempt to stay the tears that welled in his eyes.

Who knew, Paul thought. *Ghosts can cry too.*

"Somehow I passed all your tests," Brenna was still talking to the image. "And thank you for that too. Most of all, though, thank you for being my friend. I am more for knowing you. I will never say goodbye because you will always be in my heart. I love you."

All grace and beauty, Brenna turned again to address the small crowd. "Kris' mother, Sharon, would like to say a few words, followed by his father and then by Paul." She stepped aside as Sharon stood, taking her seat as the older woman came to stand before them.

The next few minutes were a bit rough, and it was hard not to notice the contrast between her and Brenna. They were a study in opposites, one young and slim, well dressed and spoken; the other aged and frumpy and overweight. Flapping her hands about uselessly, Sharon first spoke in broken sentences that made little or no sense. Then the tears came, incoherent words turned to incoherent sobs, and Doug finally stood and came to her. He put an arm around her shoulders and led her back to her chair.

Returning to the front of the room while Brenna comforted his wife, Doug took in the whole room before he started to speak. "Kris and I had a falling out when he left home." His voice was even, with an edge of anger that rode thick grief. "I was not a very good father, but I always hoped he would forgive me, that we would reconcile one day." He looked to the tall photograph, frowned at Kris' guileless smile. "Now that I know that day will never come, that brings me great sadness. Yet today I also get a glimpse into my son's life like I never had before. I realize that he was not without family as I look at so many sad faces that I don't know. And bigger than my sadness is my pride. My son touched people with love and caring and wisdom, and it's not hard to see how much this family will miss him."

Doug tore his eyes from the photo as he spoke, looking at every face briefly, then looked again at the photo. "I'm sorry, son. I hope that wherever you are, you can forgive me and that you know how much I love you. And how proud I was." His voice trailed off, then came back strong. "I thought we had so much time," he said sadly, shaking his head and seeming to forget that he was not alone with the photo. "Goodbye, son."

Nodding to Paul as he made his way to his seat, Doug took his place while Paul approached the coffin slowly. Glancing at Kris was a mistake; the Guide gave him a goofy lop-sided grin and did an absurd little dance.

This was not for his friend or for him, though, and he put himself in a place of imagining what it would be like if he had really lost Kris.

Standing in front of the room, Paul let himself become keenly aware of the thing everyone had been staring at. There was a corpse in that black box, a body twisted and mangled beyond recognition. It was Kris' body; that was real, even if he knew the Guide stood behind the coffin as he stood before it gathering his thoughts.

"I met Kris my first year of high school," he began, looking over the friends and family and co-workers. "I always felt like I didn't really fit in, and I was disturbed by it. Kris knew he didn't really fit in, and he was proud of it. Right away, he started making me think in ways I never had. We were inseparable from the beginning."

He understood why Brenna had put him up after Doug, her loving manipulation of events always at play on many levels. "Doug spoke of not being a good father, but I have to disagree. I don't know if anyone could live up to all the standards Kris held people to without a little leeway here and there. When I was sixteen, my parents died in a car accident. Doug and Sharon took me in without hesitation. Those two years showed me what great parents both Sharon and Doug were, to Kris and to me. I don't know where I would be right now if not for them, and I don't care to imagine."

He could see both of them a little swelled with pride, and Doug seemed to be ignoring his demon completely.

"What really saved me, though," Paul went on, his voice growing more somber, "was my best friend. I wouldn't be who I am today if Kris had not been there for me then and in the years that followed. He was always like the voice of my higher conscience. Kris could read people and predict scenarios with the kind of accuracy that made people think he was psychic. Being his best friend was a place of high honor for me, and being allowed into his highly guarded inner life a privilege that made me a better man. I can only hope that in some way Kris will always be with me, the best friend and the best guide a man could hope for." He turned to the photo and inclined his head slightly. From the corner of his eye he saw Kris watching him, solemn. "Thank you, my friend, my brother," he said. "I love you."

Exchanging places with Brenna, their hands touching briefly in passing, Paul did his best to ignore the demon at the end of the aisle. When he watched Kris it looked as though his eyes were on the coffin. For the rest of the service that's what he did, watching his friend watching Brenna, then a co-worker, then Jessica. He found himself lost in the Guide's wonder at how people had seen him, how much he had been loved. The voices were sweet tones without words to Paul, his heart so open that his still mind was unable or unwilling to process simple human messages.

It was not until Matt came to stand at the front of the room that the spell was broken for him. The man's face was tense and deeply lined with grief, a fierce frown distorting the features that were made for a carefree smile. Eyes big and round and helpless with dark half circles under them, the skin of his face was slack and lifeless where it wasn't twisted in grief. Matt looked old and tired and unfamiliar to Paul.

Brenna was someone who preferred to move behind the scenes. Organizing the minute details with the big picture in mind, she shunned the center stage as well as she set it. For Kris, she had stepped up and stepped out of her comfort zone to not only organize this event but lead it. Her brother was the one who sought attention. His loud voice and quick smile and expressive body language made him hard to ignore, and his good looks and guileless charm made him even harder to dislike. Like his sister, today he was a different person.

Standing between chairs and coffin, his dark suit and tie and shirt combined with his serious mien gave him a distinguished air. His face had gone from recklessly handsome to a careful austerity with his friend's death, and for a moment he stood there looking much older and wiser than Paul had ever imagined he could. Then he let his eyes wander the room methodically and a little disdainfully, and when his eyes slid over Paul he felt that Matt hadn't even seen him.

After taking in the whole assemblage with that blank and almost resentful look, Matt turned bodily to stand face to face with the tall photograph. Ignoring the gathering, looking from the picture to the floor, Matt spoke in a voice tired from the emotion that thickened it.

"I know you had a best friend," he said, his frown deepening, "but you were my best friend. Most everybody wrote me off a long time ago as a kid that will never grow up, and I've gotten used to expecting people to expect me to have trouble with grown-up things. You always treated me different, different than anyone. If I screwed up or didn't make sense or didn't follow through when I said I would, you were the only one who treated me like an adult on a path to learning instead of a simple fool who would never learn. You made me examine and explain my thinking, not just to you but to myself, and you were always smarter than all the voices in my head combined."

Matt looked from the photo to the floor and back again, completely oblivious to all else. "I never knew how much you affected me, or how much I looked forward to talking to you about whatever was on my mind. I'm so sorry I never told you. I hope somehow you know it now. My life is not the same without you in it, and I don't like it. I miss you, Kris." Heaving a sigh, he dropped his eyes to the floor again. "I will always miss you."

Instead of taking his seat again, Matt turned and strode up the carpeted center aisle to push through the door and let it swing shut behind him. Paul caught a glimpse of his face as he passed, twisted by a fresh paroxysm of grief. Exchanging a concerned look with Brenna, they communicated wordlessly and instantly. He read her concern for both the ceremony and her brother, and she felt him simultaneously encourage her to step up and speak again and reassure her that he would go after Matt. She relaxed visibly and brushed his cheeks with her lips as she stood and turned. Indulging himself for a sweet moment's moment, he watched her buttocks flex and shift gloriously under the dress as she walked away.

Outside, he was just as surprised to find Matt sitting placid on the front steps as he was to see Kris seated quietly next to him. He hadn't noticed the Guide's disappearance from his own funeral. Their backs were to him, but they both turned as the door closed behind him. He came to sit next to Matt, so he would have a friend on either side of him whether he knew it or not.

Matt sat with his hands folded in his lap, feet flat two steps below the one he sat on. Facing forward again, he stared blankly at the walkway extending from the base of the small stairway to the street. Cars lined both sides of the street, among them three long black limousines and a hearse. Soon it would be a caravan of friends and family and one dead body in a box, but for now the cars sat idle.

"I'm going to miss him." Matt murmured quietly, eyes still glazed over and downcast.

Nodding, solemn, Paul was looking straight ahead too.

"He doesn't have to." Kris spoke suddenly, excitedly. Paul turned slowly to look at him, him and the Guide both sitting up straight to meet eyes over Matt's slumped shoulders. "I can't believe I didn't think of this before. It's perfect." His gray eyes were wide and luminous.

Paul looked questions at him, but didn't speak. He could see the wheels turning behind the Guide's eyes.

"Show him your key," Kris said finally, resolutely. Paul narrowed his eyes and shook his head, subtle and silent.

"Show him," Kris insisted.

Frowning, Paul could feel the weight of the watch in his hand as he thought of it. He cleared his throat quietly. "Uh, Matt…"

He didn't turn, didn't move at all. "Yeah?"

"Uh…" he glanced again at Kris, who nodded his encouragement. "I have something I want to show you."

Finally, Matt turned his attention to Paul as he held the gold watch up to glint in the early sunlight. "What's that?" His voice didn't seem interested in the answer to the question his words were asking.

"Ask him what it looks like," Kris interjected before he could respond.

Paul frowned again, glaring at Kris while he asked flatly, "What does it look like, buddy?"

Narrowing his eyes, Matt said, "Well, it looks like a key."

Looking from the watch to the Guide to Matt, Paul wondered aloud. "It does?"

"Well, yeah," Matt looked at the gold disc in Paul's hand and then at Paul, confused. "A gold key on a gold chain, like a necklace. Am I supposed to know what it's for?"

Feeling just as confused as his friend looked, Paul was surprised to see Kris nodding with smug confidence. The Guide stood in one fluid movement and descended the few steps to the cement walkway. He turned, stood before them with hands hidden clasped in the sleeves of his robe, and spoke.

"Tell him to take it," Kris spoke to Paul.

Paul moved the key closer to Matt. "Take it," he said simply. The young man looked at him a long moment, then reached out wordlessly. As Paul watched, his fingers seemed to reach into and through the pocketwatch without disturbing it. Coming away, the fingers clutched a simple gold key on a thick gold chain and left the watch still sitting on Paul's open palm.

"Tell him to put it on," Kris said.

He shot the Guide an irritated glance. "Put it on," he said.

The chain was long and thick, braided gold with a clasp that Matt didn't have to bother with for the length of the chain. He slipped it over his head and let the key fall to his chest. As it did, his eyes widened and he gasped.

"Kris?" He blinked frantically. "Kris, is that you?" He stood suddenly, buoyant, and advanced unbelieving toward the Guide.

Taken by surprise, Kris fumbled his hands from his sleeves to ward off his friend's approaching embrace. "No, Matt, don't. I—" Matt's arms closed around empty air, and he ended with his arms half in and half out of the Guide's form. He stared awkwardly at Kris from just a few inches away, their noses almost touching.

Stepping back, Matt eyed him for a moment and then turned to Paul. "Is it him? Do you see him?" He glanced at Kris. "What are you wearing?"

Paul nodded quietly. He didn't know what to say.

"It's really me," Kris said quietly. At the sound of his voice, Matt turned and stared with round eyes at the spectre. "There's a lot to catch you up on, but Paul needs your help. I need your help. Matt?" He raised his eyebrows and nodded numbly, but otherwise Matt didn't respond. Kris leveled his gaze at him seriously and said, "Matt, would you help Paul and I hunt and kill demons so that good people can live with their inherent shortcomings in relative peace?"

Glancing sharply at the Guide, Paul added, "People like Kris' father, a good man whose demon threatens to consume him."

"Not him," Kris said thinly. "He can go to Hell. He can rot there."

The entrance was suddenly alive behind them, wide double doors open to emit a small but steady stream of mourners. Stepping aside, the trio soon became part of a small group now crowding the small porch, stairs, and walkway. Paul watched Kris trying to avoid having people walk right through him, rather unsuccessfully, and he turned to Matt with a smile to point it out.

When he saw the look on his friend's face, though, his smile fell. Matt stood looking at the people, edging away slowly with a look of mild terror in his round dark eyes. He was seeing the demons, a dozen people and their dozens of red-skinned barbed-tailed sharp-toothed shoulder-riding soul-sucking monsters, for the first time.

Paul swore under his breath and looked for Kris again. The Guide was standing on the grass, away from the clutch of mourners, an annoyed look on his youthful face. Grasping Matt's thick upper arm firmly, he murmured, "Relax. Come on. Just ignore them."

Leading one friend to stand beside the other, Paul released Matt's arm. Out of earshot of the others, he said, "You two get to my car." He handed the keys to Matt and glanced sternly at Kris. "Fill him in, for God's sake. You better be right about this." He frowned and sighed heavily. "Whatever this is."

Back inside, he found Brenna standing near the coffin. Nearly everyone paying their respects would stop and say something, and Paul found himself in a line to see his girlfriend. Edging through as politely as possible, he finally made his way to her side.

She looked up at him, forehead crinkling prettily over dark round eyes brilliant with tears. "Is Matt okay?"

"He will be," Paul nodded and leaned over to kiss her forehead. "He's pretty shook up, but I think he just needs a little time. If we don't make the wake, we'll meet you at my apartment."

Still looking up at him, she smiled a little sadly. "Thank you, Love."

Paul took her hands in his. "Are you okay?"

The sad smile was back as she squeezed his hands lightly. Her eyes strayed to the coffin, and she spoke quietly. "Nothing will ever be the same."

When her eyes found his again, he smiled and gripped her hands a little more tightly. "It will still be you and me, baby. I love you more today than I did yesterday, I will love you more tomorrow than I do today."

She smiled weakly. "I love you too." One hand strayed to her pendant.

CHAPTER 29

The familiar storefront looked strange, paper taped up over all the windows and the glass door. On the door was a sign, hand-written capital letters in thick black marker on thin brown paper stating simply "CLOSED FOR A FUNERAL AND RENOVATIONS. COME BACK TUESDAY."

Paul exchanged a confused glance with his Guide, and Matt chuckled. "You two aren't the only ones who can keep secrets," he said slyly. He was the old Matt again, easy smiles and confidence turning handsomeness into an alluring charisma. "Roche and I have been busy." He rapped loudly on the metal frame of the glass door with his knuckles.

"You and Roche?" Paul asked.

Kris nodded in agreement. "I thought you guys hated each other."

"Nah," Matt waved his hand dismissively, then curled it into a fist and knocked loudly again. "We just like to give each other a hard time."

The Guide and the Walker exchanged a look. Kris shrugged. "Listen, Matt," Paul started, looking to Kris for guidance. He shrugged again. "There's something you should know about Roche."

A shadow loomed on the paper before them then, the lock clicked and clacked as it turned in its housing, and Roche stood blocking the doorway with his formidable bulk.

"Ah, I see." The devil crossed his arms in front of him and stood blocking the doorway. He looked at each of them in turn, his gaze settling balefully on the Guide. "This your idea?"

Kris nodded, a slow half-smile tugging at one corner of his mouth. "I think it's brilliant."

Roche frowned. "We'll see about that. Interfering with the natural flow of someone else's life is very seldom a benevolent or unselfish gesture. Just because you're dead doesn't automatically stop you having short-sighted human stupidity." Despite his harsh words and tone, the devil stepped aside and held the door open for the trio.

"Think about it, man," Matt was talking before he was through the doorway. "I can distract people while Paul deals with their demons, I can help kill the demons, I can help with Brenna. Kris is right, it is brilliant. Just because it was his idea doesn't mean he can't say it's brilliant if it happens to be brilliant."

The door was closed and locked again before the realization struck Matt. "Wait a minute," he said, turning to eye Roche suspiciously. "You can see him. Why can you see him? Are you a…a Walker's Agent too?"

His laughter was a cold sharp bark, and the devil lifted the fedora from his head as he shook it slowly in negation.

Matt took an instinctive step back when the small horns hove into view; but when he saw the Guide and Walker calm and nonchalant, he paused his retreat. "You're a demon?"

"He's a devil," Paul corrected him hastily. "He has a soul, and a lot of wisdom. He's one of the good guys, buddy."

Instead of taking comfort in the Walker's words, Matt's eyes widened suddenly in alarm. "Wait," he said quietly. "I made a deal with you. I made a deal with the devil."

"Alright, enough." Surprisingly, Kris took charge. "Roche, put your horns away. Matt, calm down. He's not *The Devil*, he's a devil, and Paul's right. He is one of the good guys. I'll fill you in later. What's this deal, you guys?"

"Fill him in now," Roche said abruptly, letting his fedora fall into place again. "The Walker and I need to talk." He strode between tables toward the door in the back. After looking to his Guide and receiving only a shrug as counsel, Paul followed.

He caught himself marveling at the size of the room again as he approached the long table and began to pull out a chair. The devil stood stiff and erect just a few steps into the room, though, and Paul left the chair alone to turn and address him.

"What's up, Roche?" he asked casually. Paul was tall enough that he rarely looked up at anyone, but standing this close he had to tilt his head back to meet the devil's eyes.

Placing his hands on his hips, Roche looked down at Paul. "I need your help, Walker," he frowned. "I need to talk to the Walker Council."

"The…who?" Paul furrowed his brow, then remembered suddenly. "The angels? You want to talk to angels? Sorry, buddy, I don't know any angels." He paused and allowed himself a dreamy smile. "Except Brenna," he added.

Roche growled, his demeanor an odd one for someone seeking a favor. Paul felt the Walker more than ever, however, and the devil couldn't scare him.

"I don't need your social connections, jackass." The devil's attitude remained less than supplicating. "I need your key. And you. With your key, I can show you how to find the Council."

Surprise lifted his eyebrows. "I can go that…high?"

Finally, the devil smiled. "You really don't know anything, do you, Walker? Will you help?"

Taking a moment to think, Paul finally asked the obvious. "Why?"

Frowning again, the devil took his own careful pause before answering the question his question had provoked. "I think I know who is killing Walkers," he said at last, his frown deepening. "I need to find out what the angels know, then go get something from the devils, then bring an end to this."

"Why?" Paul had to ask again. "Why you?"

Crossing beefy arms across his barrel chest, Roche huffed a plume of smoke from one flared nostril. "It has to be me, Walker, and it has to be you. Where is your key?"

Hesitating only a moment, Paul extended his arm toward Roche, hand palm up. The gold watch was light and cool to the touch.

Moving away from the key, the devil came to stand beside Paul and put his hand on his shoulder. "You know how to rise, right?" He glanced sidelong at the Walker.

"I've got a better idea," Paul shook his head. "I'll take you to meet the angels if you'll take me to meet the devils."

Roche's eyes narrowed to slits and a frown darkened his entire face, but his heavy hand remained on Paul's shoulder. "Fine, Walker," he snarled. "You want to go to Hell? Let's go to Hell. Hang on, jackass."

There was no hanging on, though, nothing to hang on to. Paul felt a sudden lurch, a doomed falling sensation, but it was happening both within him and all around him. Dark scenes blurred by him like he was in a glass-walled elevator moving at sickening speeds. He could make out nothing but flashes of light and darkness, and soon even the light seemed to be made of darkness. For the first time since battling his own demon, he felt weak and unsteady and disoriented.

To his surprise, it was the devil that saved him. Through the miasma of visual cacophony and emotional upheaval, Roche's voice eased into his dark reverie, a lighthouse in a storm. "Relax, Walker, breathe." His tone was calm and soothing. "Just go with it. It will get easier. Let go of your tensions and breathe. Relax, Walker. Relax…"

Paul clung to the sound, listened and breathed along with the only constant in a swiftly changing environment. Soon he realized that the outer world seemed to be shifting and sliding more and more slowly, until at last an eerie stillness surrounded them.

Vaguely familiar, the world was deep red and purple and black rock jagged and hard underfoot, punctuated dangerously with both sharp edges and deep crevasses. Black and gray plumes of smoke rose from a thousand distant unseen fires to gather overhead in great dark clouds alive with blue arcs of electricity. Paul couldn't tell if there was sky above or if the smoke clung so close to the earth below because there was earth above as well. The dark and the rock and the generally foreboding feel of the environment certainly felt subterranean.

He turned to Roche, full of questions, but the devil hushed him with a fierce wave of his hand. The rocks seemed to come alive around them suddenly. In a heartbeat they were surrounded by a dozen threatening forms, devils stepping from the shadows into the strange shadowy light.

The Walker went into a half-crouch, brandishing his sudden sword before him in position to pounce or defend.

"We heard you were keeping company with a Walker, demon," one devil growled throatily, stepping forward but staying out of reach of Paul's gleaming blade. He was shorter than the Walker, but thick and wide to rival Roche's great mass. Black leather pants hung loosely about his legs to just below his knees, where they were frayed and torn and burnt. Bulging calves covered in deep crimson skin stretched tight over muscle led to dirty clawed bare feet mottled in red and black and purple. His wide chest and fat red belly strained at the buttons of a leather vest that did nothing to hide the mountains of muscle that were his arms. With no neck to speak of, his thick shoulders bulged around a big bald head. Horns the size of plantains jutted from his wide forehead.

The other devils hung back. Paul watched them peripherally, sizing them up. He didn't see any weapons, just claws and fangs and horns and a lot of leather. One devil puffed busily on a cigar, and Paul found himself wondering what they smoked in Hell. Keeping his attention on the apparent leader wasn't hard, he was the biggest and closest by half. Paul risked a glance at Roche.

Standing with his hands on his hips, the familiar devil was looking at the other almost disdainfully. There was a touch of compassion in his expression that was tainted with faint disgust. It was the look a teacher might give a student upon discovering him masturbating between classes, understanding but nonetheless creeped out a bit. Roche spat on the ground between them, and the spittle sizzled and smoked when it hit black rock.

"Take me to your Master, you insignificant piece of Helltrash," Roche said flatly, baring his teeth. Unable to turn and get a good look at him,

Paul couldn't tell if the devil's teeth were longer than he remembered or if it was just the strange dark light in this place. Although his stance remained casual, his twisted snarl and grating voice were threatening enough for Paul to tighten his grip on the bastard sword's leathered pommel.

"Hear that, boys? This one's so old he's gone senile." The fat devil laughed uneasily and took a miniscule step back, eyeing his companions as if to warn them. "He came to ask me to take him to the boss." Another chuckle started deep in his throat, only to turn to a strangled squeal as Roche dashed forward and somehow found the devil's throat in the mounds of fat and muscle with his huge clawed hand. Lifting the devil bodily at arm's length before him, Roche tilted his head back and let the fedora fall to the ground.

Roche's horns grew, long and sharp and wicked, and his body began to follow. His muscles rippled and flexed, stretching and growing, until a different being stood there holding the devil by the throat. Grown to eleven feet tall, his body had gone from stout and bellied to muscled and statuesque. His red skin seemed lighted from within by a golden glow, his face youthful and serene and beautific. The only thing that seemed the same were his eyes, ancient blackness that coldly watched the dangling devil gasp for breath.

When he spoke, his voice was changed as well. The grating tones were gone, replaced with a deep honeyed voice that was almost musical. "If any of them move, Walker, cut off their heads." The words and the voice were still the devil's, no matter the change.

Paul nodded, watching the circle of devils around them with a wary eye. None of them looked like they were considering moving as an option. The one with the cigar stood stock still with the fat brown smoking stub jutting from the corner of his mouth. Glancing at Roche's heavily muscled, long back, the Walker was suddenly not at all concerned with numbers. He smiled inwardly.

"I think you misheard me, pigshit," Roche's thick honeyed voice addressed the devil whose attention and larynx he held firmly. The devil seemed much smaller than he had a few moments ago. As he scratched and kicked far off the ground he reminded Paul of his Walker Demon. "I didn't ask you to take me to your Master. I told you to. Now let's try this again, and try not to let your feeble-minded incompetence and hugely inflated overconfidence get you and your pathetic little buddies killed."

Roche let go as suddenly as he had snatched the devil up, and his fat form crumpled into a helpless heap at Roche's feet. "Take me to your

Master, you insignificant piece of Helltrash," Roche said once more; and then he was Roche again, his voice changing to a graveled bark by the end of the sentence. In a flash of liquid gold light, the grumpy stocky old devil was back again and kneeling to retrieve his hat where it had fallen.

Standing slowly, dusting his fedora with the hand not holding it, the devil gave Paul a long look while the schooled Helltrash staggered to his feet. Looking into Roche's dark fathomless eyes, Paul was awash in the Infinite, seeing the perfect beauty of the soul beyond while viewing the stocky bulky body of the devil at the same time. He felt euphoric, giddy even, and on the brink of some soul-shaking epiphany.

A long grunt from Roche broke the spell, and he turned to follow the bested devil as he trudged away slowly, not looking back. Paul fell in behind them, noting that the rest of the devils had slunk away as quickly and quietly as they had appeared. The devil led Paul and Roche through rock and smoke to the mouth of a cave that opened at the base of a tall twisted rock hill. It looked to be one tall jagged and cracked rock rising so high the peak was lost in black and gray clouds. Peering into the tunnel, Paul could see only inky black. In a flash of brilliance, he imagined his sword a flashlight, and was disappointed a moment later to still be staring at the long blade in his hands. He tried again, closing his eyes this time to better engage his imaginal mind.

When he opened his eyes, he noticed that the devils were both watching him. The devil he knew wore an expression of bemused curiosity, the devil he didn't looked both irritated and fearful. Roche smiled. "What are you doing, Walker?" he asked.

Nodding toward the blade, Paul answered. "I'm trying to turn my weapon into a flashlight."

The other devil started laughing then, only to be abruptly silenced by a casual backhand from Roche that lifted him off his feet and sent him through the air to land heavily on his back. Roche did not even deign to glance his way, either to hit him or to watch him fall.

"Good thinking," Roche nodded to Paul, the picture of patience. "Think harder, though, Walker. Your weapon is ancient, from a time when human historians mistakenly assume swords and axes and such did not exist. It has many possibilities, but the possibilities are limited to the imagination of those who forged your weapon at the time it was forged."

Paul raised an eyebrow. "Before there were flashlights," he said flatly, disappointed. Then he brightened, and the sword melted and re-formed in an instant into a torch, reeds dried around three feet of bundled wood.

The end was burnt black, but dark and cold. He glanced at Roche. "How do I light it?"

"With the spark of your imagination, Walker," Roche grinned, obviously proud. "Or like this," he shrugged, then snapped his fingers. The tip of his thumb was a lighter then, yellow and orange flame dancing harmlessly over his deep red skin. He touched it to the end of the torch and it blazed suddenly into bright hot light. The dark mouth of the cave became the gaping entrance to a dim tunnel, twisting slightly left and then abruptly in the other direction out of sight.

The fat devil led the way into what turned out to be a network of subterranean passageways, choosing without hesitating at one fork after another. Paul tried to keep track: right, right, right, left, right, but soon gave up and was content to hold the light aloft and watch his step. The thought came to him that he was willingly following two devils deeper and deeper into Hell, but he quickly dismissed it.

Occasionally they passed a door or a series of them, heavy stone slabs with iron hinges and handles. Finally their trek ended at such a door, this one at the end of a wide hallway dedicated to it. The hallway leading to it was more inviting than the others they had traversed, with a long patterned rug in every dark shade of red imaginable. Iron wall sconces were spaced at regular intervals along both walls, and in each simple metal cup a black candle guttered and popped and burned dark red flame.

Paul was wondering how one might knock on a stone door when their escort leaned his shoulder into it and pushed it open. Apparently devils weren't real big on manners. The room beyond was a study in contrast to everything he had seen in this place. Surely the walls and floor and high ceiling were stone, but it was impossible to tell. Wide and tall and grand, the thickly carpeted floor and artfully adorned walls made Paul feel like he was stepping into a castle.

Two golden suits of plate mail armor stood on either side of the entrance just inside the door, holding swords of glinting platinum before them. A trio of wrought iron chandeliers were spirals of candleholders hanging from thick cables affixed to the ceiling high above them. Each finely twisted spiral held hundreds of candles. The weight of the heavy metal and the black wax drippings covering them strained enormously at the cables they hung from.

Changing his torch back to walking stick, Paul thunked one end on the thick carpet and leaned on it a little. Curious, he peered into the narrow eye slit on the visor of the suit of armor closest to him. The shadows within the helm gave way to two burning red eyes with black pupils that were inky vertical slits in a sea of scarlet. Paul jerked hastily away, glancing at the two devils walking before him to see if they had noticed.

Their attention was on an ornate couch in the center of the room. Paul had glanced at it, deep red and black leather and silk like the other sparse furnishings in the room. He had looked more carefully at the seat behind it, a high-backed throne that looked as though twin dragons had been bronzed in the midst of combat. Long sinewy smoothly scaled necks arced to nearly describe a heart, serpentine heads almost meeting high above the floor in an eternally shared snarl. Their slim bodies intertwined violently to form both lethal embrace and a nice smooth sitting surface with arms too widely spaced for anyone less than twenty feet tall to use both at once. Each arm was the rounded golden tail of a dragon, and the whole thing was supported only by taloned dragon feet bracing against its enemy and the floor. The only thing that even really gave it away as a throne were the black and crimson silk pillows propped neatly against the dragons on the seat.

Paul had looked at the throne first, imagining a huge deadly demon all teeth and claws and violent tendencies. In his certain search for an ugly monster, he had missed the small beautiful monster lounging on the couch between him and the dragon throne.

Half-lying and half-sitting, one elbow propped beneath her while the opposite hand held a bejeweled stone chalice, the devil held a pose that would have appeared slovenly if she wasn't so breathtaking. She was the pattern the room had been designed around, her skin and clothes the palette of colors that painted everything in sight. Smooth and scarlet and luminous, her flesh was covered only by a flowing silk teddy that seemed to move with a life of its own. The thin black material flowed over her firm round breasts, showing curve above and cleavage between and the hint of nipples beneath without ever giving up a glimpse. Although it covered her flat belly, it showed all the contours of her wide ribcage and slim waist, then hiked up over one well-rounded hip to puddle seductively between her thighs. It was below as it was above, showing enough flesh to make Paul feel as if he was seeing too much. He could tell that she was not wearing any underwear, and that she was smooth and hairless where it counted most, but every time the silk shifted the inviting view never quite became an open invitation.

Her legs were bare, rounded hips and buttocks curving to strong but slim thighs, smooth scarlet skin a rippling puddle of sexuality from the dangerous curves of hip to the dainty turn of her ankles. Tiny feet with talons filed to toenails and painted black lent an air of femininity to her overt sexuality, and Paul saw that her fingernails had undergone a similar treatment. Her fingers looked long and slender, but only because her hands were small like her feet.

Trying not to look in her eyes had drawn his attention to every other part of her, and when he finally focused on her face his breath caught for a moment. She was stunning, her wide round face framed by flowing curling hair of every dark shade of red and orange known to devils. Like flames, her hair seemed alive and illumined, dancing about her shoulders and breasts in beautiful animation. Wide and full and thick, her lips gleamed with a lipstick the color of demon blood, the only true purple in the room. Her nose was slim and straight, narrow and perfect.

Paul's eyes found hers, big round dark orbs with irises aflame. A crimson slit cut through the orange, her pupils like a cat's, an almost pink line framing the irises in a stark color contrast. The orange flames of her eyes were flecked with gold and scarlet. His gaze locked on hers, Paul felt that he was getting a more intimate view of her than had she moved aside the flowing silk and spread her thighs. Her eyes burned with hunger and sex and fire, the heat of a desire unquenched for centuries. Inviting and aggressive, she seemed to slip inside him through his eyes, drawing him in somehow so that he felt surrounded by her essence and at the same time permeated by it. A scent filled his nostrils, a potpourri of dried flowers and burnt sage and a touch of sulfur, cloying and thick but not unpleasant. Breathing it in, he felt he was breathing her in; and as his breath came more shallow and swift he felt his heartbeat begin to race with desire. Although she was three long strides from him, he felt her hands on his flesh, her wide full lips on his, he tasted the flavor of the smell in his nose on his tongue.

Tearing his eyes from hers, he still could not stop looking at her. His gaze rode the cascade of hair that fell between her breasts, and he could see that a sheen of sweat had appeared in the crimson valley, and that she was breathing shallow and ragged and hungry breaths just like he was. Watching her round grapefruit-sized breasts heaving under the black silk, he could see her firm nipples standing erect under the thin material.

It was a long flushed moment before he realized that the other two devils were watching him watch her in apparent amusement. He had somehow forgotten them entirely, along with everything else in existence but red hair and scarlet skin and eyes of flame. And that smell, still clinging to the inside of his nostrils to taint his every inhalation with sweet sexy death…

Head swimming, heart pounding, Paul closed his eyes and breathed in deep, and behind closed lids he saw Brenna. Shadow of dark hair falling across her face, eyes big and round and dark, looking up at him full of love. His next breath was long and smooth and deep, scented with leather and dirt and smoke, and his mind was his own again.

When he opened his eyes he watched her rise gracefully from the cushions, holding the stone chalice aloft with one steady hand while the other ran slender fingers slowly through the tangled fiery curls of her hair. She seemed to have composed herself as well, but her round colorful slitted eyes watched him with wonder and curiosity.

As she stood, their devil escort dropped to one knee across the room from her and bowed his horned head. Red and orange fire floated about her head and sparked in her eyes as she flashed a glance at Roche, acknowledging him for the first time and perhaps expecting him to bend his knee as well. The devil didn't move, and her eyes were back on the Walker again almost before they left him. Bare feet sinking into the thick carpet with every step, she approached Paul with long languid strides, peering at him with a curious ancient intelligence. She was close enough for him to smell her breath before she stopped, rising to her toes to bring her eyes even with his mouth, and sage and sulfur tickled his nostrils again. Paul felt his heart quicken, her breasts brushing lightly against his stomach as she rose to gaze even more closely at him. Looking down at her, Paul took shallow breaths and kept his mind on his Earthly love while her otherworldly beauty and intoxicating scent sought to overwhelm him again.

Still looking at him, her eyes wide and alive and brilliant, she spoke at last. "Leave us," she said, and her voice was as beautiful and strange as the rest of her. Soft and throaty and feminine, her sultry tones were flecked with flint as her eyes were flecked with gold. At her words, their escort stood and scurried out gratefully, followed by the two suddenly animated suits of golden plate. Paul noticed long red prehensile tails with dark forked tips trailing behind them as they left, holes cut in the armor to accommodate.

"You bring a Walker to my house, demon?" She turned on her heel abruptly and walked to the dragon throne like a woman who wanted to be watched. Her tail was short and slender, swishing languidly behind her to hint at the dark curves underneath where her rounded buttocks met. She sat on the throne, crossing one leg over the other demurely, and watched Roche coolly. With a wave of her hand, she indicated the couch before her, which turned out to have a mirror image of itself facing the throne. The devil approached the throne but did not sit, and Paul followed suit.

"Trying to start another war, old friend?" Even with her tone flat and calm and unfriendly, her voice was a melodious sultry song.

Roche was surprisingly respectful, shaking his head solemnly while removing his fedora to hold it before him. "No, I'm trying to prevent one," he said quietly. "Someone has been killing Walkers."

Amusement played at the corners of her mouth, and she took a slow sip from the carved stone cup. When she drew the chalice away, her tongue slid between her lips. It was a deep purple and forked, sliding slow wetness over her thick lips. It was only a moment, but the moment was long and Paul's imagination was off. He felt his heart start to race again.

"Not my doing," she answered Roche, "and not my concern. Although you tempt me, bringing a demon killer into my home. Without even an introduction. Why is it that demons have no manners? Bloodlust I understand, carnage and warcraft and power wielded and gained are beautiful and poetic things. Possessing the body or heart or soul of another or of many others is a hunger both sublime and terrible. But a lack of manners is just plain inexcusable. You've got a place in the hierarchy, demon, undeserved though it may be, and you should act like it."

She didn't wait for a response, but rose and glided toward Paul, extending the hand not encumbered by the chalice. "It is a pleasure to meet you, Stone Walker. I've read all the prophecies, you might say I'm a big fan. I am Lilia."

When she said her name, it rolled off her forked tongue like she was speaking another language for the space of one word, a blend of Russian and Spanish that made the simple syllables sound regal. There was a pregnant pause after, and Roche seemed to remember his manners.

"Lilia," he said boldly, his voice curling strangely around the name as hers had. "Keeper of the Nine Gates, Queen of the Dark Fallen, Forger of the Key, I bring you Walker Paul." He glanced at Paul. "He hasn't done much yet."

"Oh please," she purred, her voice flinted sugar. "Don't be so modest. He is the Stone Walker, Scourge of Demon and Devil alike, here to bring anyone with horns and a tail to a fatal and final end with stone heart and dry eyes and bloody steel. Unless we bend the knee, of course." She looked at Paul, her eyes aflame. "Should I kill you now, Walker, or give in to my fate and plead my fealty?" Her hand dropped.

Paul turned to Roche, utterly confused. Roche frowned deeply and looked down at the sexy little devil. "You don't really buy all that, Lil," Roche said gently. "You know our old prophecies get interpreted to fit every possible point of view, and when that doesn't work they just edit it to fit whatever happens. The only book that has been tampered with and changed more than our book is the human's Bible. Everybody knows that." Roche crossed his beefy arms in front of him, tapping his hat absently against his hip.

"Uh, I didn't know that," Paul admitted, glancing curiously at Roche. "Who tampered with the Bible?"

"The past has already happened," Roche said resolutely, ignoring Paul. "The future is yet to be determined. Please don't judge our new Walker on what others say he may do. That is how prophecies fulfill themselves."

The scarlet lady sighed, then smiled up at Paul a little helplessly. Her scent climbed inside him again, and he had to resist the urge to take her in his arms, to thrust his hands into her fiery mane, to kiss those soft full glistening lips, to pull her body close to him…into him…

"What do you want of me?" she breathed, lovingly invading Paul's eyes with her own.

Opening his mouth to answer, Paul was glad Roche spoke first. "We need a key," he said. That was not even close to what Paul had been about to say. The devil's graveled voice broke the spell, though; and Paul's thoughts were his own again. That didn't stop him from watching her walk back to the throne, thin black silk sliding smooth and seductive over firm flexing rounded buttocks.

Perching at the edge of the throne, knees together and feet apart on the floor, she leaned forward and leaned one elbow on her knee. Her ample bosom strained against fabric as she leaned forward. Her upper body was as overt as her lower body was innocent, knees primly locked together. She watched him watch her, clearly enjoying the attention.

"What's wrong with his key?" Paul was getting used to her looking at him while addressing his companion. He thought it best to keep quiet until he felt himself again.

Roche was shaking his head doggedly. "It won't go everywhere we need to go."

Now she did look at Roche, and the fire in her eyes were flames of anger. "You're going to have to do better than that, demon."

The big devil hesitated. "We need a key," he said slowly, "that will give us access to personal portals."

She threw her head back and laughed then, a wordless melody with a hint of danger. "And who will hold this key?"

"I will," Roche answered.

"And you will return that which you have taken from me?" Her eyes narrowed, and all signs of humor left her flawless countenance.

Roche sighed heavily. "You know I can't do that, Lilia." Her eyes flashed angry fire, but he spoke again quickly. "I will do what you asked me for… before. That is all I can offer."

Thoughts churned behind those beautiful otherworldly eyes, trained warily on Roche. Then she turned them on Paul, fires turned passion once more as her cloying scent came to him again like a jolt of pleasant electricity. "Come here, Stone Walker. Show me your key."

He looked to Roche for guidance. The devil did not look pleased, but nodded nonetheless. Paul approached her slowly, holding the glint of gold before him on his upraised palm. She leaned forward further, giving him an even better vantage point to see the swells of her breasts and the dark valley between. When she placed her small scarlet hand over his, it covered the watch but only half of his larger hand.

And then her flesh touched his for the first time, and the electricity he had felt before was an insignificant little zap next to this sudden intense current. He was a cool flowing river, she boiling molten lava. They flowed into each other and through each other, creating a new liquid energy that cooled her heat and warmed his chill, and he knew her secrets and he knew her soul. She was there inside him too, every door thrown open to her. He wanted her, he needed her, his body ached to follow his soul into her.

The key caught fire between their hands then, and white and orange and green flames engulfed them to their wrists. Intense heat seared his hand. Paul wondered if his flesh was burning away and reforming itself, but he did not pull away. The heat rode the river of their shared energy, and soon his every cell burned with it. It was painful and pleasant all at the same time, like a deep stretch or a workout made infinitely more intense. Somehow it felt like the pain was good for him, and he neither flinched nor wavered but stood his ground and let it consume him.

When it was too much, when the fire within became his whole world and all thought of all else burned away by the intensity of it, the flames between their hands guttered out suddenly and she drew her perfect slender fingers away from his. The pain was gone, but Paul felt different for having endured it. Stronger, more sure of himself, a thousand doubtful voices in his head that he hadn't known were there before were gone. His eyes met Lilia's over the key, and he thought she looked changed by the experience as well. They gazed at each other in stark amazement, eyes wide, completely invincible through utter vulnerability. The glint of metal shifted his attention.

"It changed," he said, bringing the key closer both to inspect it curiously and re-establish his personal identity. Everything about the watch was the same except the color. "It's silver," he said, happily enough. He had always preferred silver to gold.

"No," she purred, "it's platinum."

Paul grinned. "I got an upgrade," he said lightly, pivoting to show it to Roche and to look at something other than breasts and lips and hair.

Her low flinted voice behind him corrected him again. "You got *the* upgrade, Stone Walker," he turned to watch her lips sound the words. "Do not take it lightly. And be very careful with your Agents. This power must not fall into the wrong hands." She looked pointedly at Roche as she said the last, and her message seemed clear enough. Still she added, "Especially his."

The devil's customary frown deepened, and he clenched his fists at his sides, crumpling the forgotten fedora in his anger as his face reddened. "Let's go," he grunted between clenched teeth. Lilia waved her hand in negation, though.

"Not so fast, demon," she murmured. "You owe me, and so does your pet Walker."

"I owe you," Roche acknowledged with a nod. "The Walker does not. Stay away from him. If you truly do not want to see those prophecies you speak of come to pass, leave him be."

"I will leave him be." She was still close enough to Paul for him to smell her delightfully invasive scent. "He will come to me."

Roche put his hand on Paul's shoulder heavily, and the Walker grasped his key tight and thought of the smells and sights and textures that were the devil's playground. The world went to black and then they stood in Roche's rec room between the pool table and the big screen.

"That was easy," Paul mused.

The devil grunted, hand still heavy on Paul's shoulder. "A little too easy," he said. "You got yourself one Hell of an upgrade. Now up, Walker. Time to hold up your end of the deal."

"Hang on," he frowned. "I've got some questions for you. Lots of them, actually."

The huge meaty hand on his shoulder squeezed painfully, and Paul felt sharp claws pressing through his shirt and into his flesh. "That wasn't part of the deal, Walker. I take you down, you take me up. Find your own answers."

"Well, maybe we should let Kris and Matt know what we are up to." Still a bit shaken, Paul thought he could use his Guide's grounding presence. "We were gone at least an hour."

Roche indicated the clock on the wall with a nod. "Time passes slowly above and below, more slowly the further up or down you go. In the queen's chambers, one might say you have all the time in the world."

His glance at the simple round hanging timepiece confirmed it; only two or three short minutes had passed in what had seemed hours to his mind and centuries to his soul.

"Now let's go, Walker." The words were a growl, his impatience palpable.

Looking into the devil's fathomless dark eyes, Paul remembered the side of Roche he had seen in Hell. And although he had a newfound confidence, although he felt the ache of great power in his bones, he thought it best to stay on the devil's good side.

He smiled wanly. "Going up." As he closed his eyes and thought of what he should think of, he felt the devil loosen his grip.

And then the world went white.

CHAPTER 30

His body was the wind, a cool calm breeze directed by his thought and contained by nothing. And then he was a raging gust, an elemental delighting in its own dramatic existence. It seemed strange that there might be a hand squeezing his shoulder, since he didn't have a shoulder. He was the wind…

"You really need to learn to ground yourself," A deep grating voice cut through his captivating reverie, and Paul remembered that he had eyes and he opened them. Looking down, he saw that he had a body as well. Still, though…he was the wind. His feet stood on what looked like clouds or liquid light or a polished sunbeam, he couldn't tell as it shifted pleasantly without disturbing his stance. There was no sensation underfoot, no sensation in his entire body save the feelings of lightness and spaciousness and awe.

The sky around them, if indeed it was the sky, was white and gold and blue bands of light, glorious and alive with subdued intensity. Even the devil was not immune, gazing about with eyes wide and slack face, arms hanging limp at his sides. Paul noticed that the fedora was not just in place on his head, not just looking fine despite recently being crumpled; it looked brand new. There was no fraying of the band, no faded colors. Roche looked younger too, worried angry lines of his face smoothed into wonder.

"Where is the Council?" Paul asked quietly, not wanting to raise his voice in this place. Even his voice was the wind, whispering a soft melody of words. All he had to do was ask, apparently. A looming light structure hove into view, a grand ancient castle as clean and flawless as if it had been built yesterday. It floated firmly anchored in the same clouded liquid light they stood on.

No moat ringed the castle, no guards flanked the open front entrance, arced bluish grayish light hewn to look like flowing stone. Apparently there was nothing to fear here, and his instincts told Paul the same. This seemed a place where even thinking of anything going wrong was utter ridiculousness. All was well and right with the world, and the Walker strode happy and whole into the brilliant hall.

The walls were aglow, the floor seemed to shine with love for the high light ceiling, which seemed to reflect the warm ambiance back tenfold. Paul looked about with wonder, furnishings and ornamentation alike was flowing colored light. When he glanced back, he saw his devil companion hesitating at the light arc, then tracing his finger swiftly and carefully through the air as he had when warding off Paul's first demon. When he was done, he removed his hat respectfully and stepped through the entrance.

Paul turned again and did a double-take, surprised by the sudden appearance of a proper reception desk piloted by a tall indistinct being of white and violet and golden light. When he looked closer, a figure coelesced into view: now he could tell it was female, he could see that she was blonde and slim and pretty enough, pale blue eyes the color of shifting clouds. Her garment was pure white, woven light, a robe much like the one Kris wore.

She didn't have a halo, or wings, much to the Walker's disappointment. There was a luminous smoky band of white light framing her, but Paul could see that around humans on Earth when he tried. He counted himself fortunate that there were no flashes of breast or inner thigh to distract him, and that her eyes were open and warm instead of alluring and invasive.

"May I help you?" she asked, her voice light and airy but melodic. Paul realized people's voices were going to be a real disappointment when he resumed life on Earth. She gave him a pleasant smile, and the Walker thought it funny that it looked a little fake. Maybe some folks can't even be happy in Heaven.

"Oh, yeah," he smiled warmly at her. "We're here to see the Walker Council."

Her fake smile fell, and she glanced disapproving over his shoulder at his horned companion. Roche stepped forward in haste, nodding his head respectfully at the robed receptionist. "Devil Roche and Walker Paul to see Angel Stephan, please."

The receptionist neither acknowledged nor ignored the devil. "Do you have an appointment?"

Roche shrugged. "Probably. It's hard to surprise an angel."

Nonplussed, she flipped open a thick appointment book that hadn't been there a moment ago. She ran her finger down the page and then stopped. "Demon Roche and The Stone Walker?"

The Devil gritted his teeth and smiled. "Close enough," he said pleasantly.

"You're late," she told Paul abruptly. "He's waiting for you. Follow the light."

A golden orb the size of a golf ball appeared suddenly before him, floating in thin air at eye level. It began to drift away, but paused when the

Walker did not follow.

"Excuse me," he said politely, addressing the receptionist. She returned her attention to him reluctantly, pale blue eyes no longer hiding her irritation. "Are you an angel?" he asked.

He could see Roche stiffen beside him, but the question was asked. The girl shook her head plaintively. "I'm a light," she said simply.

"You came from Earth?" She nodded. "Do you...do you like it here?" he asked.

She smiled wanly and stole a look over her shoulder before she answered. "You know what they say."

"No," Paul shook his head. "What do they say?"

"Even Heaven isn't always Heaven." Her voice was still musical, but it was a sad song.

"You're a light?" he said, his voice full of wonder. "I've never met a light before. Does that mean you don't have a soul?"

Roche coughed loudly beside him then, and Paul realized the girl was staring coldly at him. "Follow the light please, sir. Good day."

"Wait," Paul stammered. "I'm sorry. I—" The devil's meaty paw grasped his upper arm firmly, and he let himself be dragged away from the awkward exchange.

They followed the light, and Paul didn't try to talk to the hovering orb even though he sensed intelligence in its warm glow. It led them shortly to a door, or rather a rectangle of liquid light darker than the wall of liquid light it swam in. Rather than opening, the opaque surface simply disappeared when the hovering orb touched it, and the light winked out with it, leaving an open light doorframe.

Without hesitation, Roche strode though the entrance with his fedora respectfully held over his belly. Paul was not halfway into the room before a booming happy voice and a swirl of bright multi-colored light lifted the devil off the floor. "Roche! Roche, you old devil! Good to see you, friend, good to see you!"

Eyes round with wonder, Paul watched the devil hover a foot off the liquid light floor in a spiraling updraft of every happy bright color known to angels. Roche chuckled low and steady under his breath, slightly uncontrollably, like a baby delighted with the adult making the same silly face over and over. Finally he drifted slowly to rest on the strange solid light footing, and the tornado of light became a river of light that flowed to a spot between the Walker and the devil and slowly formed into the shape of a man.

Standing with his back to Paul, the Walker could only see the angel's countenance in the change it had brought to Roche's. The devil's eyes were bright and happy, a guileless smile turned the corners of his mouth up and his cheeks into little round fleshy orbs of joy. Paul thought he looked a little like Santa Claus in all his jolly fatness, and he wondered if his belly was jiggling under his dark pressed suit.

When he turned, all the thoughts in Paul's mind were washed away by a crystal clarity pregnant with impossible optimism as their eyes met. He tried to find his voice, to say something, anything, but he just smiled dreamily at the angel.

He looked very much the ordinary man in one respect, shorter than Paul and wider, though not as wide as Roche. His stout body was covered by a long flowing white robe, made of a finer light substance than the receptionist's. With a round and boyish face and a fluff of thin auburn hair, his happy grin and luminous dark eyes were his only exceptional physical qualities. It was the big bright soul shining through them that made it so; and Paul felt not just at ease, but at home with an old old friend.

"Excuse my companion, he learned his manners in Hell." The Walker heard Roche's words, knew he was still staring dreamily at the angel, but somehow he couldn't find his voice anywhere in the ocean of happy stillness his brain was swimming in. He just stood there, staring into the angel's luminous brown eyes, smiling a stupid happy smile.

"Your first angel?" His voice was big and deep and sonorous, and its kind musical tones almost brought tears to his eyes.

He nodded dumbly, still at a loss for words.

"Angel Stephan," Roche said formally, "meet Walker Paul. Walker Paul, stand in awe. I present you Angel Stephan, Master Weaver of the Loom of Light, the Watcher's Watcher, the—"

"Enough, friend," Stephan cut him off kindly. "The past is the past. Let us delight in the present. I have gifts for you." He didn't move to fetch anything, but suddenly he held a wide thick deep white box in each hand, banded about by a ribbon of silky white. Presenting one to Paul and the other to Roche, he grinned a happy boyish grin under sparkling brown eyes.

The devil had his box in his hands and had removed the ribbon to flip open the lid before Paul finally found his voice. "Thank you," Paul stammered, not reaching for the gift. "I mean, I can't…I didn't bring you anything."

"Nonsense," the angel boomed heartily, thrusting the box at Paul with both hands. "You brought me two of my favorite things. An old friend and a new friend. Take it. Open it. Delight in it." His grin widened when Paul took the package, and they both turned to see Roche holding up his gift.

It was beautiful, a long heavy chain of woven light of every color imaginable, dancing and flowing playfully through the thick links. It was wrapped in long delicate white feathers, the liquid light glowing through the thin almost translucent quills. Beautiful and artful and otherworldly, it took a minute looking at it before Paul realized it was a set of very lovely looking manacles.

It was a long quiet moment before Roche lowered the long thick links of light and feather back into the box. Closing the lid and holding his beefy paw over it as if the chain might try to escape, the devil leveled a serious gaze at the angel.

"So you know," Roche said quietly.

"I suspected," the angel responded kindly. "Do you know?"

The devil looked down at the box, and his veined taloned fleshy hand. "Not for sure. But I suspect." He sighed heavily. "And I've got a feeling."

"Intuition is the devil's logic," the angel mused, as if he were quoting an ancient adage.

With an angel to his left and a devil on his right, the Walker could do nothing but stand between them holding the box, looking back and forth between them uncomprehending.

"Does the Council know?" Roche arced an eyebrow at the angel, concerned.

"What do you think?" Stephan's sonorous voice sounded suddenly weary. "The Council doesn't know anything until they have investigated, discussed, held a dozen trivial votes on a dozen trivial issues, discussed some more, filed papers on their findings and conclusions only to discuss things one last time before voting on a final decision. They tell me they don't meddle in the affairs of man because free will is a precious gift. I think mortals just don't live long enough for them to reach a final decision on how they should meddle, no matter how slowly time passes here. Bunch of self-righteous self-serving haloed beaurecrats."

Now the angel was the grumpy one and the devil wore the happy smile. He nudged Paul roughly with his elbow, chuckling. "Told ya."

Stephan brightened, turning to Paul and clapping his hands like a child. "Open your gift, Stone Walker. Open it."

He wasn't sure he liked that name as much as all his new acquaintances seemed to. Still, Stephan was an angel and Paul was about to open a gift from the angel in Heaven. Things could be worse. The silk ribbon of light slipped easily aside, and he lifted the lid and let it fall to the floor when he saw what was inside. The lid hit the floor and was absorbed in a muted flash of light, Heaven's perfect recycling system.

A black leather cowboy hat, new and oiled and with a narrow brim, sat atop thick folds of black leather. Then Paul was the little boy, and it was Christmas morning. He put the hat on, pulling the brim down low on his brow and marveling at the perfect fit. Grasping the thick soft overcoat by the collar, he let the box drop to the floor before he realized it wasn't empty. Another muted flash of light, and the box was gone, leaving a pair of black leather boots to stand invitingly empty at his feet. Well, one was empty. After he shouldered his way into the armor, the Walker kicked off his shoes and tried to stick his left foot in the left boot.

Pulling his foot out, he reached in with his hand and removed a beautiful sheathed dagger and held it before him. He pulled the simple leather and iron sheath away from the spiraled silver hilt crossed with a sturdy handguard spiraling either direction perpendicular to hilt and blade. The naked blade was flowing platinum light, and the glow of Heaven glinted playfully on its lethal sharpness.

"He already has a weapon," Roche told the angel.

Stephan smiled benevolently. "They say the Stone Walker wields two weapons."

"And a platinum key," Roche grumbled while Paul pulled the boots on for another perfect fit. If the devil was in the details, an angel must have put him there. "You'll never guess what he got in Hell," the devil said dryly.

"Now all he needs is a dragon," the angel quipped merrily, nodding at the weapon in Paul's hand. "Try it," he urged. "It's the latest model."

Remembering their recent sojourn below, Paul thought of a flashlight. A heavy long black mag light, like human police carried, appeared heavily in his hand. He clicked it on and grinned, although the bright beam was relatively dim in this place made of light.

The devil was clearly not as impressed with the light source as Paul was. He turned to Stephan. "Will they meet with us?"

Watching the Walker discover a pair of black leather gloves folded neatly in a pocket and pull them on, the angel shrugged. "They'll see you. Are you sure you're ready to be seen?"

Roche grunted unhappily. "Might as well make it sooner rather than later." He glanced at Paul, covered in leather head to toe but for his bare happy face. One hand gripped his weapon of choice, the bastard sword that had come to feel so familiar in his hand. The other held a broad short sword, thick and sturdy platinum blade dancing with light as though fresh from the forge.

"Now you look the proper Walker, Walker," Roche showed his teeth in a devilish grin.

Smacking the flat of his new blade against the deceptively soft armor, Paul felt almost no sensation transferred through the magick material. "This is awesome," he grinned. "Thank you, Stephan." The angel nodded, pleased.

"Hey, Roche," Paul spread his arms wide to make his torso vulnerable between the blades. "Hit me. I bet I won't even—"

He had forgotten how fast the devil was. His big meaty fist took him full in the stomach, gracefully flashing between the Walker's swords. Paul was lifted bodily off the luminescent floor by the blow. He flew across the room to bounce violently but harmlessly off the far liquid light wall and unceremoniously to the floor.

Still gripping his weapons, Paul leapt to his feet and grinned triumphantly. "Didn't feel a thing," he pronounced smugly.

The devil wasn't done with him. His hands were dancing though the air as Paul had seen him do before, furiously drawing some symbol or spell. When his hands stilled, an orange and red fireball erupted from his open palm and blazed across the room toward Paul. It started out the size of a softball but grew as it came, and the last thing he saw before he covered his bare face with armored forearms was a beach ball inferno set to engulf him. He was thrown against the wall again to fall to the yielding floor, again.

Paul stood uncertainly. Smoke was rising off his armor, choking and blinding him. Blinking rapidly, he could see that his right forearm was aflame, as was the bastard sword. There was a thin jellied substance coating arm and sword, and that's what was burning, some kind of napalm from Hell.

Thinking on his feet, Paul imagined his new weapon a fire extinguisher. Nothing happened, so he patted the fire on his forearm out with the flat of the broadsword's thick blade. The sticky burning jelly stuck to the blade instead of being extinguished by it; and for a long composed moment he stood there, grinning at Roche with a flaming sword in each hand.

"Didn't hurt." Paul beamed.

"You're hat's on fire, Walker," the devil said calmly, then turned to Stephan and began to address him in hushed tones.

The Walker frowned. He could feel the heat on his head, no warmer than a heating pad, but still confirmation that his hat was indeed aflame. Staring at the flaming swords, he wondered if changing them would just give him a couple flaming walking sticks. In a burst of insight, he thrust the blade of the longer sword into the yielding liquid light floor. When he drew the sword aloft again, it was clean and brilliant and most importantly no longer on fire. He thought it gone, and it was.

Reaching his free right hand to lift the new hat from his head, he could tell from the sudden warmth that he had plunged his gloved hand right into the fire. Unperturbed, he held the flaming short sword and hat before him and imagined them whole and unburnt, the fire gone. Whole and unburnt, the items still danced with flames.

Paul closed his eyes, envisioning the hat cool black leather sans flames, did the same with the sword. When he opened his eyes he could see that the flames were finally dying down, but that could just be the Hellish napalm burning off at last. He didn't want to catch himself imagining that his imagination was somehow more powerful than it was. The last of the flames guttered out under his fierce uncertain gaze.

He thrust the sword into the soft light floor and imagined it gone, placed the hat back on his head still smoking but no longer on fire.

Stephan and Roche were both looking at him, quietly amused. "You ready, Walker?" Roche spoke through his smile.

"Ready?" Paul adjusted his hat so the leather brim was low over his eyes. His hand came away trailing a thin tendril of smoke. "Ready for what?"

"To meet the Council," Stephan answered melodiously, giving Paul a benign smile.

"More angels?" he asked excitedly. "Hell yeah."

Seeing Stephan's pained expression, Paul winced. "Sorry."

CHAPTER 31

The Walker Council was both impressive and disappointing for Paul. There were nine of them, Stephan one of the nine. All of them were aglow with brilliance and beauty, but the dazzling effect wore off by the time the third angel was being announced. Every one of them was King of this or Prince of that, with a long list of vague titles that sounded impressive enough but completely failed to inform.

"…Directly Appointed Arbiter of Walker Justice, Keeper of the High Secrets, King of the Last Walker Tribe, Walker Angel Luther."

Fighting the urge to yawn, Paul bowed his head respectfully when the name was finally pronounced, as he had seen Roche do twice before. Then Stephan began the long monologue that would introduce the fourth of the nine angels, and Paul said a silent prayer of thanks that he was no longer aging and that time passed slower here. Surely God could hear his prayers in Heaven.

At long last, he had heard all their names and titles without hearing much at all, when Stephan hesitated and looked at Roche. The devil shrugged and nodded for him to go on. "Walker Council of Angels, I present you the Exiled Demon King, Walker Exterminator, Bane of the Wicked Walker," (Roche winced at that one) "Warlord of Walker Hell, again exiled, Devil Friend to Angels and Verified Son of God, Original Walker Demon Roche."

The Council bowed politely as one, Paul apparently the only one surprised by the announcement. He whirled on the devil, wary eyes wide. "What—"

The devil's heavy hand fell on his shoulder and he hissed, "Later." Stephan began to announce Paul as he slid out from under the unwelcome weight of the devil's paw.

"May I present New Walker Paul." Stephan's booming voice seemed to finish the short introduction before it began.

Paul frowned fiercely and stepped forward. "May I present myself, The Stone Walker, Scourge of Demon and Devil alike, destined to bring any being with horns and a tail to their final end or to their knee with stone heart and bloody steel, Platinum Walker, Wielder of Two Weapons…" He trailed off, trying to remember everything he had heard people say about him. "…The Dragonslayer, The Walker Eternal, Walker Paul."

No one in the room seemed pleased with his pronouncement but Stephan, whose eyes and grin grew simultaneously larger as Paul dragged out the introduction. When he finished, the angel looked as if he was resisting the urge to applaud.

"How can we help you, Stone Walker?" One of the angels spoke, his voice a crisp melodious song of ice. Somehow his simple woven light robe was whiter than the others, and the hard handsome ageless face did not seem at all interested in helping.

Roche began to speak, to step forward, but Paul stepped roughly in front of him and talked loudly over him. "Ladies and…" Looking around, Paul realized all the angels were male, dour-looking faces illumined by the ethereal all-pervading light of this place.

He cleared his throat, started again. "Gentlemen of the Walker Council of Angels, someone is killing Walkers."

A few of the angels exchanged looks, but none of them spoke. This was no news to them. "We need to stop them. Roche might know who it is. He might know how to stop them." He trailed off, realizing that he really had no idea what they were doing here. He stepped aside and addressed him without looking at him. "Roche?"

All eyes were on the devil then, save Paul's. He let his vision be delighted by the warm glow of the liquid light of Heaven while listening intently to the devil's every word. The Walker was tired of being caught off guard.

"I have my suspicions," Roche said carefully. "I do not wish to convey certainty regarding any of my suspicions considering a lack of concrete evidence. Yet I am an interested party, and prefer to see Walker issues resolved with as much compassion and as little violence as necessary."

"This from the King of Walker Hell." Another angel spoke, crossing his arms over his chest under an austere pinched face.

"Exiled," Roche reminded him. "Exiled for working with this very council to free righteous Walker souls. Remember, Andal?"

Eight luminous pairs of eyes turned to one angel, whose dark skin and dark hair were matched by eyes of swirling dark chocolate. He leaned forward with a soft beautific smile and spoke in a lilting voice of quiet authority. "Stephan forgot the titles I gave you so long ago, Demon Angel, Heaven's Heart in Hell. Do you remember what I told you then, friend? The only danger in saving the world is that the world will always forget.

Let the world save itself."

The beautiful angel relaxed back into his high seat and was quiet again, as he seemed to tune the room out to lose himself in some blissful internal reverie. Paul wished he could do the same, although he sensed the dark angel would not miss a word of what was said.

"There are places I can go that…others can't," Roche went on, treading carefully. "I can gather information; I can chase a suspect to Hell to bring them to you for questioning. I can be of great use to the Council in bringing this issue to a swift compassionate conclusion."

The one who had spoken to Paul addressed Roche now in icy tones. "Are these things you propose to do freely, from the kindness of your heart? Or are you proposing a deal, devil? What do you want of us?"

"Only to know what you have found, and who you suspect. Only what I need to help you." Roche could apparently be supplicating when he wanted to.

"We must discuss this amongst ourselves," the angel answered coolly. "We must put it to a vote. We must—"

Andal spoke again then, and although his voice was quiet it overwhelmed the other angel's, like a CB transmitter with a stronger signal easily walking over a weaker one. "We have found eight Walkers dead, three above, three on Earth and two below. All of the bodies were stripped of weapon and armor and key, and have been brought here awaiting location of their souls. Possible suspects include Walker Peter, Walker John, Walker Paul, Queen Lilia and Devil Roche."

"In what order were the bodies found?" Roche asked as Paul and another angel spoke at the same time.

"I'm a suspect?" Paul sputtered.

"This is highly irregular," a stout bald angel with a wide plain face raised his voice.

The angel with the luminous tunic and the cold voice spoke to Paul. "Stone Walker, have you not had unauthorized dealings with Walker Peter as well as the Original Walker Demon? Did you not dispose of a demon with no prompt from your key in a realm off limits to you? Did you not take an unauthorized trip to Hell actually accompanied by the Original Walker Demon? Did you not in Hell have dealings with the Dragon Queen herself? Did you not kill the demon meant to keep you humble in your new power?"

"Well," Paul jumped in at the angel's first pause, "when you put it that way, it sounds bad. What about Walker Marcus?"

Roche and Andal spoke the same words without hesitation, a devil and angel duo. "Walker Marcus is dead." They exchanged a look that made Paul instantly suspicious.

"Where is his soul?" he asked carefully.

When Andal leveled his gaze at Paul, the Walker remembered what he had seen of Roche's power. He didn't want to know what an angel might be capable of, properly pissed off. The angel turned his attention again to Roche and spoke as if they were the only two present. "One above, then one on Earth, then one below. Then above, Earth, below, then above and then Earth. Obviously, we presume the next will be taken below. Although what business Walkers suddenly have in Hell remains a mystery."

More than one suspicious pair of angel eyes moved to Paul. He stared at the liquid light floor, pretending to be suddenly captivated by the play of black leather soles on woven luminescence.

"Should you take any unauthorized action, be assured there will be consequences," the angel with the icy tone said coldly.

"Yes, King Roche," Andal spoke in a sonorous tone of respectful kindness. "Should you save the world yet again, be prepared to take the blame." He stood abruptly, apparently signaling the end of the meeting.

The devil reached his hand to Paul's shoulder, but Paul sidestepped it and imagined himself in the gutted coffee shop with his Guide and his Agent. "Find your own way down, demon," he muttered as the scene around him shifted and blurred.

Paul appeared between them, not unhappy with their collective reaction. They both blanched, turning quickly away and stepping back defensively. Matt looked ready to come at him, while Kris hovered uncertain and studied him. It must have been an impressive sight, him flashing into existence between them all in black oiled leather, hat pulled low over his eyes. The boots added an inch or two to his height, and surely the low cowboy hat made him look taller as well. He thought about flashing his twin blades, but he didn't want to appear unnecessarily showy.

"It's me, you guys," he growled. His voice sounded flat and low, and the lights and colors around him felt subdued and two-dimensional. "We have to get out of here. Come here."

Recognition came to both of them at the same time, and they stepped toward him. The Guide looked concerned, Matt excited, and they both tried to ask questions at the same time.

Paul put a hand on each of their shoulders, willing his hand to fall on the Guide's shoulder instead of through it. He didn't hear either one of them, and when he said, "Hang on," the first word came out in the devil's coffee shop and the second one in the living room of Paul's apartment. The Walker let his arms drop to his sides and doffed the overcoat, letting it fall to the floor. He let the hat fall on top of the crumpled overcoat and perched on the arm of the couch to remove the boots.

"Oh shit," he said, remembering. "I forgot my shoes in Heaven."

CHAPTER 32

The Walker gathered the armor, boots, hat and overcoat and thrust the bundle at Matt. "Put this on," he insisted, then turned to the Guide. "Roche is the Original Walker Demon. How do we guard against demons?"

"You don't," the Guide shook his head. "Guarding against the devil is the same as engraving an invitation. Everything you do to keep out the demons just makes more space for them. The walls we build against them are the weapons they wield against us."

Frowning fiercely, Paul demanded, "And what if the devil is banging down your door?"

"Philosophies diverge slightly on that point." The Guide seemed immune to the contagion of Paul's panic, standing serene with his hands buried in the sleeves of his robe. "If you are human, it's simple. Don't invite him in. Find a quiet place and ask yourself frankly just what you did to bring the devil to your door."

"And if you're a Walker?" Paul snapped.

Kris shrugged. "Also simple. Open the door and cut off its head."

A light rapping on the door caused all three of them to jump, and the Walker leaned back against the weight of the familiar bastard sword as it appeared in his hand.

"Cool," Matt breathed at the sight.

The Guide glided between them to put his eye to the peephole.

"Careful," Paul hissed.

"Of what?" Kris whispered over his shoulder with a wry half smile. "I'm dead." His shoulders relaxed and then tensed again as he looked out.

"It's Roche," he said, still looking through the distorted lens. Paul tightened his grip on the bastard sword and glanced at Matt.

The black leather overcoat fit him well, but the hat was too big. It perched widely on his ears, bending them a little with the weight of the oiled leather. The brim would have completely hidden his eyes if he hadn't had his head tilted back, a little comically, to gaze with wide eyes at Paul's weapon.

"And Brenna." Kris stepped away from the door just as she knocked again, a little louder this time.

Paul hesitated, but only for a moment. He closed his eyes, took a deep breath, and opened them to a room with neither weapon nor armor. "Cool," Matt said again as the Walker stepped forward and disengaged the deadbolt to swing the door inward.

"Hey baby," he forced an easy smile, opening the arm not holding the door invitingly to her. Still sedately stunning in her black mourning garb, she stepped into his embrace.

"Look who I ran into on the way here," she said, encircling her arms about his waist and pulling her body close to his. "He said you left your shoes at his place." She glanced down at his shoeless feet and then up at him, curious.

"Yeah," Paul laughed uneasily. "Roche has an awesome rec room behind the coffee shop. The pool table is on a really nice rug, though, so if you want to play pool you have to take off your shoes."

"You were playing pool?" Brenna's tone was not quite disbelieving.

"Well, yeah," he stepped aside so she could see her brother behind him. "Roche thought having a couple drinks and shooting a little pool with friends might cheer Matt up a little." When he saw her eyes soften at the sight of Matt standing behind him, he knew her heart was melting at the thought of him caring for her brother.

Brenna laid her head on his chest, squeezed him lovingly about the waist. He glared at the devil over her head and spoke cheerfully. "Then I realized what time it was, and I rushed out of there and forgot to grab my shoes. Matt and I were halfway here by the time I realized it, but I knew you were coming and didn't want to keep you waiting."

The Walker smiled, pleased with himself. The lies weren't just coming easily, they were making him a better boyfriend in her eyes.

"Thanks, Roche," he said, reaching the arm not encircled protectively around Brenna to take the shoes. "Thanks for everything."

His voice had an edge of sarcasm to it that was not lost on Brenna. Hand going reflexively to her necklace, her beautiful dark eyes gazed up at him, trusting, curious. "Aren't you going to invite him in?"

A sweeping glance at the Guide and Agent won him only a shrug as counsel. "Roche, you old devil," he said grandly. "Won't you come in?" Standing aside, he swung the door closed behind him, not bothering to lock it.

Trying to make the three guests with earthly desires comfortable while ignoring the Guide for Brenna's sake, Paul seated his girl as far away from the devil as possible, with Matt between them. "Drinks?" he asked when everyone was seated, Brenna on the couch closest the kitchen, with an empty cushion between her and her brother on the other end. Roche sat in an easy chair to Matt's left.

Grasping his hand, Brenna pulled him to the couch beside her.

"I'll get it," she said, rising gracefully. "What does everyone want?"

Smiling up at her gratefully, Paul said, "Would you open that bottle of syrah on the counter?"

Her luminous eyes brightened more at the word. "Absolutely. Roche?"

The devil smiled at her. "Scotch."

Paul glanced at Brenna. "I think there's some kind of whiskey in there, behind the Patron."

"I'll take a beer," Matt chimed in unnecessarily.

As soon as she was out of earshot, the devil leaned in and growled, "Your manners are worse in Heaven than they are in Hell, Walker."

"My manners?" Paul hissed, ignoring the questioning glance Kris exchanged with Matt. "You lied to me."

"No," Roche shook his head. "I didn't tell you everything. For your protection." He spoke in hushed tones, then let the volume of his voice rise as he said, "Like you do with Brenna."

"What's that, Roche?" She heard her name from the kitchen.

The devil raised his voice even more. "Just telling Paul how important it is to have a support system at a time like this. That he's very lucky to have you."

"How sweet," she came into the room to hand Roche his whiskey and Matt his beer, then turned to head into the kitchen again. Paul watched her walk away, entranced as always by her rounded flexing buttocks.

"You've got the wrong idea, Walker. You need me. You're in danger." The damned devil was whispering in his ear again. "Give me a chance to explain."

There was no chance now, though, not even opportunity for Paul to respond as Brenna swept gracefully into the room holding two wide crystal wine glasses. She handed one to him as she came to sit beside him, half full of dark red deliciousness. The cloying scent of sage and sulfur filled his mind for a moment, but the Walker dragged his thoughts out of Hell and smiled at his girlfriend.

"Mmm," he murmured, putting his nose in the glass and filling his senses with red grapes fermented ten years ago. He held up his glass and glanced at the Guide. Apparently not wanting to be left out of the drinking circle, Kris stood to the devil's left with his uncorked canteen in hand. Paul raised his glass.

"To Kris," he said.

"To Kris," the room echoed, and even the Guide drank the toast.

"Can I tell them now?" Matt was looking earnestly at the devil, who grinned broadly and nodded. He turned to his sister and Paul, excitement lighting his unlined face. "Do you guys remember, about a year ago, I bought stock in that internet startup company?"

Brenna leaned forward, one hand on Paul's knee beside her. "The one whose technology you knew nothing about being started by some kid who couldn't get his patents together or get his business out of his parent's basement?" Paul stiffened uncomfortably at her tone.

"Yeah, that one," Matt grinned, unfazed. "He got his patents together, I guess. He sent me a letter thanking me for my support. And a check." His eyes twinkled merrily. "For thirty thousand dollars, dividends or something he said. He also said to watch for more for at least the next three quarters." He glanced at his sister. "That's every three months, right?"

"One of your investments is paying off?" Surely Brenna didn't mean to sound quite so dumbfounded. "Well, good for you, little brother." She smiled her beautiful smile and began to raise her glass.

"Wait, there's more," Matt grinned, glancing again at Roche. The devil sipped his whiskey. "We're going into business together. We're going to turn the coffee shop into a nightclub. The cool thing is, we can lock up the booze and still have it be a coffee shop during the day."

Brenna spun her wine glass in one hand and lifted the other from Paul's knee to worry at the gemstone about her neck.

"That's actually not a bad idea," Paul mused, raising an eyebrow at Brenna. "It's a good neighborhood for it, Mallory's is close but not too close, there's lots of parking nearby. That's rare in the city."

"What about the liquor license? And the additional labor and management and all the renovations required?" Brenna was always good at playing the devil's advocate.

"All taken care of, little lady," Roche nodded. "I know some people. Turns out your brother does too. Grand opening Tuesday night. You two better show, we'll be having a memorial for Kris and a hot new band."

Brenna smiled beautifully at the devil. "That's great, you guys. We'll be there." She raised her glass tentatively. "What are you going to call it?"

The devil nodded. "She's right. We should change the name. What do you name a night club?" He rubbed his chin thoughtfully.

"And a coffee shop," Matt reminded him.

"Tell you what," Paul said slowly, looking from one face to the other as his thought crystallized. "I'll make up some labels for the beer I just bottled. It's perfect, it has a little bit of coffee but it's smooth and drinkable. You can give away a free beer to the first fifty customers who walk through the door."

"Better yet," Roche responded. "We'll buy it from you and sell it for twice as much. Do you have fifty bottles?"

Paul looked up and to the left, remembering. "I have forty-six." He eyed the bottle in Matt's hand. "Forty-five."

Leaning forward suddenly, Roche snatched the brown glass bottle from Matt's hand. "This is it?" Paul nodded. The devil tilted the unlabeled bottle for a long swallow. He handed it back, wiping his mouth with his sleeve. "We'll take it. That one too. Figure up a price and start brewing up a new batch."

Paul smiled. "I already started a new batch. And seriously, you guys can have it. My contribution."

"Start a bigger batch," Roche insisted. "And figure up a price. Your contribution is going to be a bigger part of this business than that. We need a big picture guy. We want you to manage the place. The beer is your first great idea. We'll brew our own beer. We'll blend our own coffee too, add some out of this world beans. God knows we have the space for everything."

Paul saw a confused look pass over Brenna's pretty features, and he smiled lamely. "Roche's place is a lot bigger than it looks from the outside."

"There's a basement," Roche rushed to explain.

Paul shook his head. "I don't know anything about managing a bar or a coffee shop."

"Sweetie," Brenna's hand was on his leg again. "Five years ago you didn't know anything about central office equipment installation, and now you're bored with it. This might be just the change you've been looking for."

"I still don't know anything about central equipment blah blah blah, and I'm his best friend, and I'm already bored with it." Matt pretended not to notice Kris glaring at him.

Everyone had to pretend not to notice when the Guide said, "Well, that didn't take long, you sonofabitch."

"I don't know," Paul's eyes searched Brenna's for guidance. "I make good money."

Roche waved his hand dismissively. "You'll make more here," he promised. "I'll top your salary and work out a percentage so when you do your job well you get paid well. You can keep your job for the first couple of weeks if you're not sure, be as busy as your pretty little angel there." The devil inclined his head toward Brenna, and she flushed prettily.

"What do we call it?" Matt asked, and Paul was glad Brenna could not see the evil gleam in his eye as he looked at the trio of supernaturals.

"The Devil's Brew." Paul smiled. "The beer, the bar, the coffee shop. Roche's special blend. All of it. We call it 'The Devil's Brew.'"

Roche jumped to his feet, whiskey sloshing in the low glass. Remembering how fast he had seen the devil move, Paul leaned forward to angle his body protectively in front of Brenna. He needn't have bothered. The devil raised his glass, and Paul relaxed.

"To 'The Devil's Brew,'" he roared; then, as Paul raised his glass, "and to the new manager, Wa—" the devil stopped himself, eyes widening in alarm. "Paul. To Paul." He upended his glass and drained it to Matt and Brenna's echo.

The Walker caught his Guide's eye as he tilted his silver flask, and Kris just shrugged and took another long swallow.

Paul drank, tasting a hint of sulfur in the thick crimson liquid that hadn't been there before.

CHAPTER 33

Paul lay quietly, listening to her deep even breathing. They always slept close together. They teased each other in their waking hours about who was the more earnest cuddler, but by night they clung shamelessly to one another. One arm under her pillow, her head pleasantly crushing his bicep, the other curled around her lovely nude torso to cup a handful of bosom.

Back pressed against his stomach, her ass arched into his loins, sexy even in sleep. He could smell her hair, cascading across the pillow to tickle his face. And their sex, the sweet scent of their togetherness, on the sheets, on her pillow, on his face, in her hair. This was home, this was where he was himself, pressed against her and filling his senses with her.

He wanted to wake her, to tell her everything. Not because he felt bad about lying to her, but because he wanted her a part of everything, and this was becoming such a big part of him. Never before had he kept anything from her, as much for himself as for the relationship. Sharing everything was a cathartic and intimate experience for him, wanting to know her thoughts on his every thought.

Lying still, he knew he would not wake her. Telling her meant losing her...

His Walker's body crackled with aliveness and strength, but Paul felt weary deeper than his untiring bones. Holding her, breathing her in, he didn't notice he had drifted off until there was a loud knock on the door.

When he sat up, he was alone; not with Brenna in his apartment, but in that other place. Alone, surrounded by yesterday's yesterdays, by dreams dreamt and those yet to be dreamed.

The knocking came again, more insistent. Paul went to the door and threw it open, itching for a fight. "Andre? Kris? What...?"

For once the Watcher didn't have his nose buried in his book; and though his hands were at his sides he may well have been towing Kris along by the ear, the way the Guide looked. Hands hidden in his sleeves, Kris appeared more sullen than somber, shoulders slumped and eyes downcast.

"Come with us, Walker," Andre said in a crisp tone, turning on his heel and starting up the long hall. Kris followed, wordless.

"Now hang on," Paul roared, standing stubborn in the doorway. "I'm sick of being a pawn in everyone else's game. Tell me where we're going, tell me what it's about, and I'll decide if I feel like coming along or not."

The Watcher stopped, but didn't turn as Kris did. "Telling you will take too long, I am taking you to a place where I can show you. It's about you, and your misguided Guide, and what's going to happen if you abuse your power and position the way he wants you to. Come, Walker."

Too tired to argue anymore, Paul fell into step beside Kris. "What's going on?" The Guide only shrugged, so he pressed another issue. "What's an Original Demon?"

The Guide glanced sidelong at him, shrugged again. "There are two types of devils, most are made the traditional way."

"You mean sex?" Paul arched an eyebrow.

Andre chuckled quietly, but he said nothing and did not turn as he led them down the long hallway.

"Devils tend to be, ah, violent in the bedroom. And when two devils have finished their bloody kinky coming together, one or both of them are often mortally wounded. It's no big deal, they're not going anywhere but Hell. But when they both breathe out their dying breath at the same time, expiring together in a pool of their mingled sex and gore, something magickal happens." Kris was his excited self again, explaining the mysteries of the Universe if anyone cared to listen.

"Sounds disgusting," Paul cut in.

Kris shrugged. "You should see how some humans look having sex."

Andre chuckled again, and this time he did turn briefly to eye the Guide suspiciously. "Is that what you've been doing since you died? Spying on people having sex?"

"No," Paul laughed. "He's been watching Jessica all day."

Kris looked at him suddenly. "Do you know that she never leaves? She went to the funeral with Roche, but I've never seen her walk out of the coffee shop after they close."

"Huh." Paul frowned. "She probably rents a room from him or something. The place is huge, who knows what else is back there."

Frowning, the Guide lowered his voice. "You don't think they're…"

"Together?" Paul laughed again. "Roche and Jessica? Seriously? No."

"Do you watch her when she uses the restroom?" Andre teased over his shoulder.

"No," Kris snapped. "It's not…I'm not like that. She's just a very sweet girl." He grimaced, eager to change the subject. "Anyway, when the timing is right, something magickal happens. A lost soul is pulled from its confused limbo to be born a devil on its way up."

"In Hell?" Paul frowned.

"Well, yeah," the Guide shrugged. "That's where devils are born, Paul."

"What about its parents?" The Walker asked.

"What about them?" Kris responded. "Devils are left to fend for themselves in Hell, unless they are born to royals. Devils are not exactly known to be great nurturers."

"Doesn't sound very magickal to me," Paul sniffed.

"I guess it's all a matter of perspective," the Guide shrugged.

"So what's an Original Demon?"

"Here we are." Andre stopped in front of a plain doorway like all the others that lined these endless halls.

"No." Paul clenched his jaw so hard he could feel his teeth grinding, even in this place. "I am going to ask this question one last time, and someone is going to have to give me a straight answer. What. is. an. Original. Demon."

The two dead men exchanged a glance, and Andre nodded for Kris to answer him.

"Well," Kris began. "You know how demons and lights are made, the two sides of every issue that is important to the individual. Two voices with opposing perspectives that ideally teach the human to find a healthy balance. When your demons and angels dance in step with each other, a human can find peace."

The Guide stood tall and proud and wise and went on. "When God has an idea, however, It does not tolerate anything but the stillness of Eternity in It's mind once the thought is formed and its subsequent creation manifested."

"It?" Paul frowned. "Did you just call God an 'it'?"

"Of course not," Kris spoke to the taller man. "God is *the* It, God is *everything that is*. What would you like me to call It? He? She? Quebon of Zorbon? The Great Bright Light? Pick one, I don't care. God sure as hell doesn't."

Paul shrugged, abashed. "Let's go with 'He'."

"Chauvinist," Andre chuckled.

"And what if I said 'She'?" Paul growled. He was starting to sound like Roche when he was angry.

The Watcher smiled amiably. "Then I would have called you a feminist. Or a pussy. Relax, Walker. We're all friends here. I was raised Catholic. You think I like to walk around listening to this schmuck call Him 'It'?"

"So God is real." Paul smiled at the thought.

"Sure," the Watcher nodded. "She's everywhere."

He turned back to the Guide as he began speaking again. "When God has an idea, or an idea is born that affects God somehow, HE does not abide voices in HIS head for long."

"So God has a head? Is it male or female?" Paul was having trouble letting this go.

Kris rolled his eyes. "I was speaking metaphorically. Anyway, God is his own Walker, and separates himself from his demons and angels as soon as they are fully formed."

"Trouble is," Andre broke in, "God's demons and angels have souls. They are literally created by God, and all God's children have souls."

"So?" Paul was perplexed. "What's the trouble?"

"All souls are on the move, always either headed up or down." Kris answered. "A soul will rise from devil to human to angel over a long series of lifetimes, only to fall again. Each lifetime is mostly or completely forgotten as a new lifetime is begun, and a soul can have years or lifetimes in which things seem to take a downward cant or an upward swell; but the progress of the soul is not measured in years or lifetimes or what seems to be, and a soul rises or falls heedless of outer circumstance or appearance."

The Walker crossed his arm skeptically. "Are you talking about reincarnation?"

"No," Kris shook his head. "Reincarnation is an earthly concept as you understand it, and earthly concepts invariably exclude two thirds of the picture. I'm talking about soul continuity. Everyone is either headed up or headed down, and all paths lead to God."

"All paths are God," Andre chimed in wisely, but not very helpfully.

"An Original Demon is different, though," Kris explained. "Original Demons stay devils, no matter where their souls are or which way they're headed. Same with Original Angels, they can have the darkest stained soul and still appear to be angels, with all of an angel's powers." He sighed. "And they don't forget. Their bodies change, some, but they never change bodies. They never start a new lifetime."

Andre nodded. "Some say it drives them mad. I say they're mad to begin with. A soul coupled with single-minded purpose is dangerous in any realm, no matter which direction the soul is headed."

"But Roche could be a sheep in wolf's clothing," Paul countered. "He could be an angelic soul with nothing but good intentions in a devil's ill-mannered body. Right?"

Kris started to nod, but Andre was suddenly shouting at Paul. "You're idiots! Both of you! Jessica is Roche's prisoner, Kris! Roche is a devil, Walker! How obvious do you need obvious to make itself for it to be obvious to you?"

The Guide's hands were at his sides, clenched into fists as he glared at Andre. "His prisoner?"

Andre frowned, regaining his composure. "More like a willing hostage," he said blithely. "It's an arrangement between families. Keeping her on Earth keeps the peace in Hell, somehow. It's complicated."

"Wait," Kris relaxed his hands at his sides. "So what does that make Jessica?"

"A pawn, from the sounds of it," Paul growled angrily. "Just like the rest of us."

Andre stepped away hastily. "Enough. You two need to see this." He opened the door he had brought them to, letting it swing inward toward the scene that drew both Guide and Walker in immediately.

Doug stood in what looked like a hotel bathroom, cramped and small but clean. He peered at his own reflection in the mirror, twisted and tear-stained. There was a knife in his hand.

"Dad?" Kris stepped forward in alarm. "Dad?"

"He can't hear you," the Watcher's voice came behind them.

The demon stood on the other side of the beaten man, his voice strong and loud as he stood tall. "The only good thing you ever did is gone," he said, in a casual conversational tone. "Everything you touch goes to shit. You are worthless. You are beyond worthless. You have deficit value. Even if you spent the rest of your life as a saint you couldn't drag yourself to the lofty status of worthless."

Doug stared at the grief and the guilt in the mirror, mumbling under his breath. "Worthless," he murmured. "Everything I touch...deficit value... no redemption. No forgiveness. Not ever."

The demon grew suddenly, almost imperceptibly, and grinned wickedly. It stepped forward and dissolved into Doug's body. He stiffened, then looked down at the short sharp pocket knife he was holding as if seeing it for the first time. Without hesitating, he plunged the blade into the wrist of his opposite arm and sliced quickly upward. Blood spewed over his arm and his face, and he grunted mindlessly with the pain he had inflicted on himself.

"Dad!" Kris screamed, dashing forward. His insubstantial hands swept through the man and the knife alike as his father passed the blade to the bleeding arm. Paul was just as helpless, learning suddenly how his friend felt all of the time as his hand passed unnoticed though Doug's shoulder.

It was one of those forever moments; and when his mind should have been fully consumed with the alarm he felt, a part of it broke off and mused calmly in reminisce. He remembered Kris telling him one time that suicides who cut diagonally across their wrists often have difficulty with slitting both wrists. If the first slash is too deep it can sever the tendons necessary to grip the blade for the second cut. In his helplessness, staring at the long open gash along the straining tendons as the bloody hand gripped the handle, Paul wondered if his father had told him that.

In a fresh cascade of slippery red wetness, Doug opened the other wrist and collapsed to the floor, sobbing. "So sorry, son, so. so. sorry." His blood was everywhere, his clothes dripping with it, his face smeared with it, his hair matted with it. He was a writhing dripping mass of self-pity dying at their feet, and they couldn't even speak to him. The knife lay where he had dropped it, painted in blood from handle to blade.

Paul stood watching, helpless and in shock, as Kris fell to his knees and sobbed, reaching again and again for his father. "Dad…no…please, Dad…no…" He saw a bloody hand twitch, the nearby gash giving up one last weak spurt of blood.

Kris stood and whirled on Andre.

"This is what you wanted me to see?" He shrieked, tears streaming down his face. "You wanted me to watch my dad kill himself? While I can't do anything? While Paul can't do anything? Why, Andre? Why even show us?"

The Watcher, unfazed by the outburst, answered as calm as if Kris had asked him for the time. "If I had told you, you wouldn't have listened. This doorway showed you not what is happening but what is about to happen. You needed to learn that your personal feelings must never get in the way of the job you have to do."

Now Paul whirled on the Watcher. "This hasn't happened yet?"

Andre shook his head. "It's about to."

He willed his hand to fall on the Guide's shoulder, and he shook him. "Kris."

"What?" the Guide was still glaring at Andre.

"Come on," Paul spun him around and held up the platinum key. "We've got a demon to kill."

Catching sight of the Watcher's look of smug satisfaction as the room faded from view, Paul called out to him. "You know what, Andre? You're an asshole."

The last thing he saw was the Watcher's fading face crumple into a frown, and the last place he expected to find himself was back in Brenna's arms. Extricating himself carefully from the warm cuddle, he thought of his armor as he slipped out the door. He greeted the robed Guide waiting in the living room in leather duster, hat and boots.

"Are you naked under there?" Kris made a face.

Paul's hand fell on the Guide's shoulder. "Let's go."

CHAPTER 34

Paul was a ghost again. This time it was by his choice, by his Walker will, and he was no helpless bystander. Walker and Guide stood before a closed light green door like all the other light green doors in the hallway save the identifying room number. Room 216, the door his intent had collaborated with his key to bring him to.

Unnoticed, they moved through the closed door and into the room beyond. It was a hotel room, nothing special about it: a bed and a television and a small sofa next to the wall by an even smaller desk.

The couple was in bed, Sharon under the covers on her back, snoring lightly while Doug lounged on top of the covers watching television. With all of the lamps extinguished, the play of light from the television illuminated the room eerily. The man was bathed in a wash of colors, the shifting scenes on the screen lighting his face in one moment only to plunge it into darkness in the next.

Mark Harmon was on the screen, talking guardedly to a pretty older lady while he sanded a boat too large to be removed from the basement they were in. Doug stared blankly at the screen while the demon beside the bed murmured its endless cruel monologue into his ear, oblivious to everything but his message and its victim.

Moving quietly, slowly, so as to not disturb his slumbering wife, Doug rose from the bed to stand beside it. He waved the remote control absently in the general direction of the television, muting it but leaving the light shifting and flashing across the room.

Paul noticed that he was wearing the same thing he had been in the vision, pajama bottoms and a tank top whose light colors drank up the silent cold fireworks show from the television. Listening to the demon's low rant, the only sound in the room now, he was reminded of the bloodied dripping state of those clothes every time the screen went dark.

Staring sadly down at his plain partner, Doug drank in the words he didn't know he could hear. "*...ruined your life, ruined her life, ruined your son's life, you even ruined Lisa's life. If you weren't around, maybe the little slut would have found a decent guy instead of wasting her time on a piece of shit* *like you. If you weren't around, maybe everyone would be better off."*

The Walker tuned out the hateful words. He didn't need to pry into details to kill the demon, no matter how available they may be to him. Thinking of his sword, he glared at the monster and willed it to see him. It continued talking, heedless of his intent, its full attention on Doug as he collected his pocket knife from the nightstand and ambled mindlessly toward the bathroom door. A sly slow smile of triumph curled one edge of the creature's mouth as it followed.

The demon didn't notice him until the Walker stuck a gloved hand into its horned face and shoved violently. Losing its balance, breaking off its hateful monologue, the demon's eyes widened with fear as it stumbled backward and finally registered the danger. Watching the thick rope of flowing smoky connection between man and demon, Paul's fierce intent seemed to cleave it in two the instant before the upswing of his flashing sword took it.

Still falling backward, helplessly off balance, the demon watched the two ends of the energetic bond disappear into it and its host. Its face went slack in alarm while the upswing of the Walker's sword became the downswing of his snaring staff and settled neatly around its shoulders. Paul spun the shaft once or twice more than he needed to, delighting darkly in watching the black and scarlet eyeballs pop out of the demon's hellish face. Bringing up a clear image of the open park setting where he had battled his Walker demon, he turned and let his free hand drop to the Guide's robed shoulder. The last thing they saw as the room faded from view was Doug dreamily returning to bed. Setting the pocketknife on the dresser and climbing under the sheets, he leaned over to kiss his wife on the cheek. A happy, silly, sleepy smile lit his face as he picked up the remote again to turn off the television.

Then the world was a wooded glade, darkened more than illumined by the distant alpenglow. The Walker thought them upward, and the world brightened around them. The man-sized demon struggled mightily at its tether, its supernatural strength held in check easily by the Walker's single gloved hand.

Wondering what the new weapon's battleaxe might look like, Paul was pleased to see a tall light metal pole with a slim long single curved blade appear in his hand. He proffered it to the Guide.

"It's your Dad's demon," he said. "You want to do the honors?"

Kris frowned in distaste and stepped away. "I don't think I'd have the stomach for it," he responded. "No offense to the Walker's duty, I know it has to be done." Looking at the captive monster, his face hardened. "I'm glad it's you, Paul. I'm glad you're the one who's going to save Dad. Give him Hell, Walker."

Then the axe and the snare were gone and the Walker faced the demon with nothing between them but the tall blades of grass and the pine-scented air. Paul wished that he still smoked, now would be the perfect time to casually light a cigarette for dramatic effect. He'd have to remember to pick up a pack, now that he didn't have to worry about his Walker's lungs.

For a moment he thought it was going to run, it stood there so long eyeing him warily. Bigger than the demons he had faced before, it was also more thoughtful, more deliberate. Then it curled its hands into clawed talons and came at him in a crimson blur. Paul tried to catch it with a powerful roundhouse and step away to the other side; but as the punch landed with a sickening crack, the demon wrapped an arm about him and dug long claws into his duster. They went down together, the demon rolling on top of him with the force of the Walker's own blow. Its bulk bearing down on him, Paul jabbed his fist explosively at the demon's torso as it struggled to rise.

Then rise it did, flying bodily through the pleasantly scented evening air in an arc that took it a dozen feet high to land twenty feet from the Walker with a muffled thump.

On his feet, dusting leaves and grass absently from his supple armor, Paul advanced threateningly on the demon as it gained its feet. Breathing heavy, its eyes wide in fear and anger, the demon's jaw canted to the side at an unnatural angle. It spread its arms as if to roar in fury, but the Walker dashed forward at the speed of thought and punched his gloved fist into the red muscled belly.

He remembered a friend he went to school with telling him about his karate lessons, of how he was learning to aim his punches behind the head instead of at the face. Paul had imagined the grotesque image of a man's face exploding in blood and flesh fireworks as a fist found its way to its target.

Much to his chagrin, that's very much like what happened here. Instead of sending the monster flying in another glorious arc, Paul's gloved fist punched through the demon's flesh like a huge hard bullet. Up to his elbow in demon flesh, Paul felt wet warm purple blood on his face. The demon rained heavy blows on his back and head, clawing and punching frantically in a blind animal panic. Paul tried to wrest his arm free, but succeeded only in circling round and round the demon in a macabre bloody dance.

Panicking a bit himself, Paul imagined his new short sword in the hand not using the monster as a bloody anchor. He stabbed at the demon's muscled torso again and again like an evil red pincushion while blows rained down on his hunkered head and shoulders.

Then his hat was knocked off suddenly, and Paul felt the next blow full across his face as sharp claws opened chin and cheek and forehead in painful searing gashes. The Walker cried out, his face aflame with pain, his thoughts on fire. When the next blow rained down, his blade flashed and a bloody stump bounced harmlessly off his shoulder. Thick purple wetness stained the black leather in a spurting spray of gore as the demon drew it away in a howl of pain.

Bringing his knee to his chest and planting his left boot firmly on the demon's torso, Paul shoved and pulled at the same time and finally succeeded in yanking his arm free. He watched the demon warily as it tumbled backward and crumpled to the ground, disappearing his weapon and bending to pick up his hat. It was covered in blood, he was covered in blood, his body layered first in leather then in sticky purple wetness. His face felt fine, healed, as he removed a dripping glove to touch his blood-drenched visage tenderly after planting the hat firmly back on his head.

The lifeless bloody heap began to stir as Paul pulled the glove back on and thought of the light sleek modern axe he had proffered to the Guide. Holding the long shaft diagonally before him with both hands, he looked around him curiously. "Kris?" he called out.

Silence answered from the quiet little forest around them. The Guide was nowhere in sight. Paul shrugged, ready to put an end to this. He advanced on the demon as it rose, the last dying sunlight shining through the openworked pattern of gaping wounds on the monster's torso.

Raising the gleaming platinum blade over his shoulder, the Walker rushed the demon. As he brought the axe down in a deadly arc, the world went white around him and Paul was suddenly fighting for breath and for purchase in a liquid white cloud of lethal love.

Weaponless, mindless, floating and falling at the same time, the Walker felt his weapon torn from his weakening grasp. He swung his bloodied fists at nothing in particular, each punch passing through overwhelming brightness weaker and slower than the last. One arm dropped to his side, then the other, then his consciousness left him like a few fanned tendrils of smoke rising from a dying ember.

CHAPTER 35

A sweet melodic voice soothed him awake, whispering away his fear, his muscles relaxing until they felt like to puddle to the angel's feet. For she was an angel, there was no mistaking it: she towered over him in sublime luminous garb with the feathered wings arcing tall behind her and the glowing golden halo above her head and the whole bit.

Her face was sweet perfect beautiful kindness, and to look in her eyes was to gaze at the sky and fall in love simultaneously. Paul stared in stark shameless wonder, his own blue eyes wide with awe as they begged her to keep drinking from him and pouring herself into him. She was everything, awesome and powerful and all around him while standing still before him. Her melodious voice sang a sweet song his heart longed to follow.

"Too many Walkers," she was saying, "too many and too powerful. And too violent," she looked at his bloodstained clothes with sweet disdain. "Far too violent." She returned her eyes to his, ravaging his mind with a stark lovely stillness. And his duster and gloves were clean and new again, not a trace of purple blood in this bright beautiful place that was her, that was life, that was everything.

"You carry the platinum key, Walker." It was not a question, but Paul nodded dumbly in awed agreement. "You shouldn't have that. No Walker should have that kind of power. Walkers wield the powers of immortals with the minds of men. Men are meant to live the lives of men, with vague ignorance of the worlds above and the worlds below."

The Walker just nodded, helpless in his own love for her. Of course she was right, she was so right, in every way right could be conceived.

"Give me your key." Her musical lilting tones ended its mad angelic song with an order. For a sweet forever moment the Walker continued to nod agreement and stare searching into her eyes. Then something sparked inside of him, some infinitesimal part of his identity that had slumbered while he spent a century in her eyes.

His world would end if he refused her, her love for him would cease and all he knew would be gone. Musing over the possibility of telling her 'no' was considering pushing a button that would end the world. Yet he fanned that spark of defiance deep within him until he began to remember who he was.

"No." His voice was a whisper, a breeze lost in her sweet still tornado. Paul was suddenly aware of his hand, and he clenched the cool platinum disc that was in it.

"No," he said, more loudly. He felt his eyes harden, his thoughts becoming his again. He thought himself *up*, but felt no rise within. Thinking *down* fiercely, he floated still helpless in her liquid light cloud. Then Paul saw it, a shimmer behind her, a doorway in the light prison walls. He had to get to that, if he could only get past her…

Watching the shimmering portal, Paul's eyes widened as a figure stepped though it. Then there was Roche, the devil holding the feathered manacles he had been gifted in Heaven. "Don't give her your key, Walker," the devil growled, his voice a grating cacophony after the angel's sweet deadly song.

"I wasn't going to," Paul spoke slowly, the only multi-syllable words he had spoken in what felt like a sweet euphoric eternity. As the angel took her eyes from Paul to turn and face the devil, her beautiful countenance twisted into a mad snarl of rage. Her eyes flashed burning crimson, and Paul thought for a moment that horns might sprout from her skull to knock askew her shimmering halo.

No horns appeared, and as she turned her back to Paul her shoulders slumped and she stepped toward Roche a normal woman. Her halo and wings winked suddenly out of existence, and she stood looking up at the devil in a plain white robe and a beautiful but ordinary human body.

"Roche," she breathed, his name a familiar song to her heavenly voice. It was a sacred beautiful word when she spoke it, a word of the cant lilted with that accent he was growing so fond of hearing.

Her name had that same otherworldly sound as it rolled off the devil's forked tongue, and it took Paul a moment to sound it out in flat English in his head before it came to him. "Ehcor," he had said, murmuring it like an ancient secret kept for eons. The Walker realized it was the devil's name backwards; or perhaps Roche was the angel's name backwards. Either way, it was a beautiful simple thing, an idea so simple and elegant it could only be a child's or God's.

She approached the devil slowly, trudging forward to collapse into him. Catching her as she fell, Roche pulled her close and held her tight against him. Weeping into his beefy shoulder, her words rode waves of sobs to Paul's ears.

"It's…it's all wrong." she moaned, letting the devil's embrace support the weight of her body sagging against him. "…like you said before…too many Walkers. Too many wicked Walkers."

"Shhh, it's going to be alright, everything's going to be alright now," Roche murmured softly to her, stroking her long light hair soothingly. "Just tell me where the Walkers are."

She shook her head slowly, sadly, back and forth. "They're dead, Roche," her voice suddenly sang clear again. "They're only the first, too. Don't you remember what you said? The Walkers need to die. *All of them*. It's not right, what they do. And it's not right how they do it." She spoke into the devil's soft shoulder.

Paul couldn't see the angel's face, and he couldn't be more grateful. No longer swimming in the sublime detached notion of his own demise, the only light he could see from those eyes of sky was the luminous reflection on the devil's face. In itself, that was almost too much.

Paul watched his eyes, soft and sad, as he looked down at her. "I was mad when I said that, my angel."

"No," she folded her arms between them and looked up at him, still encircled in his embrace. "You were right. I was mad, blinded by bliss. Like you are now. I didn't want it to end; I didn't want me to end."

The devil's hands went to her shoulders, as if he meant to shake some sense into her. Instead he clasped them tenderly and spoke gently down to her. "Tell me where the Walkers are. Give me their keys."

"No." She said it again, and this time a ball of brilliant liquid light erupted between them to send Roche sailing violently away from her. While still aloft, the devil began to change and the angel rippled into her full height. By the time Roche hit the wall of light he had come through, both had transformed into beautiful terrible monsters. The Walker couldn't decide which was more disturbing, the breathtaking luminous murderous psychopath or the saintly creature with the pointed horns a foot tall.

Roche bounced harmlessly off the wall and rolled gracefully to his feet. For a long glorious moment he stood there before them, tall and muscled and thoroughly otherworldly, with no idea what was happening behind him. The Walker and the angel stared past him, watching as a door opened in the liquid light wall where the devil had struck it. Devils began to step through the door: one, two, three, six of them. By the time Roche thought to look behind him, there were over a dozen devils crowding the light space with more streaming in behind them. The luminescent walls expanded suddenly, and the doorway turned into a wide arching entrance.

The devils poured in, Paul losing count at a hundred and eyeing the wide entrance. He meant to use it as an exit, and he glanced at Roche to see if he meant to do the same. His eyes still familiar, the great being nodded at the portal. "Get out, Walker. Go."

Paul hesitated, watching the devils line up in loose but orderly ranks. These were not the spineless urchin they had met in Hell; these devils were armed with long curved swords and heavy battleaxes, garbed in chain mail or light plate armor over their leather clothes. More than one of them held flaming long manacles that dripped fire to fizzle out on the liquid light floor.

"Yeah, Walker, get out," one devil jeered across the light space between them. Then the wide entrance winked out of existence, and the devil laughed and shook the manacles in his hands. "Or stay. I always wanted me a pet Walker."

Another devil stepped forward, plate armor clanking as he rose a long curved blade over his head. "Bind the demon and the angel!" he called out, apparently in charge. "Kill the Walker!" He charged forward to close what had become a wide gap between them as the magickal space had expanded from intimate room to a wide luminous battlefield. The devil horde moved as one, charging and calling out, "Kill the Walker!" over and over.

Two sides of the same supernatural coin, angel and devil both reacted at the same time. Ehcor was a beautiful sight, rising from the liquid light floor gracefully and throwing out a long liquid light rope that twirled neatly about the torso of the leading devil. Slashing at the light fruitlessly with his sword as he was lifted from the ground, it flashed through empty air time and again to leave the light rope unscathed. Then a brilliant pulse of light traveled from the angel's outstretched hand as it held the energetic noose, and the devil was transformed into a perfect ash sculpture of itself.

The light rope disappeared, and the ashes scattered to dissolve as they drifted to the light floor. The lead advancing devils saw it, and slowed their approach almost imperceptibly as Roche tore through their ranks.

As fast as the angel was graceful, Roche was a beautiful crimson blur cutting a wet purple trail through the small army diagonally. One devil's head disappeared, near one edge of the horde, to be replaced by a spewing fountain of blood. And before his body could drop lifeless to the cloudy floor, four other spewing fountains dotted the crowd.

"You okay, Walker?" Roche was beside him, leaning over to tower over him slightly less. The curved swords that he held in each hand looked much smaller than they did when the tall muscled devil warriors were waving them around. Both blades were smeared in thick purple blood.

Paul nodded firmly, then thought how quickly he would like to move and moved at the speed of thought. He took the horde from the other side, sudden swords in each hand. The first devil saw him coming, impossibly, and swung desperately but haphazardly at the approaching black blur that he had become.

Without slowing, floating more that he was running, the Walker knocked the blade aside with one sword while slicing its head off cleanly with the other. He danced among the monsters as if they were frozen in time, slashing and running to behead one, then another, then one more at the far edge of the armored mob.

Two seconds hadn't passed since he had left the devil's side, and he counted the bodies as they fell. Damn, one less than Roche. "I'm fine, devil. You okay?" He looked up at the statuesque monster in mock concern. He was getting used to seeing him this way.

Roche grinned, his handsome eternal face made wicked by his long sharp fangs and pointed horns. "Let's do this." Then they were set upon by devils, a puddle of crimson flesh and flashing steel that poured in like a wave to drown them.

They weren't there to overwhelm, though, Walker and devil flashing black and red in opposite directions to boomerang again through the mob. The devils were fast; but they were faster, and blade met neck more often than steel as they blurred through the armed crowd again and again. More than once a curved blade sliced at Paul, but he pushed aside the slow motion attack with a blade or simple sidestep easily. On his third pass through, a blade caught him on the shoulder and bounced harmlessly off his duster as he slowed to finish off a devil with a wide smile across his throat leaking copious amounts of blood but still knitting itself back together.

Was that his kill, or Roche's? He had been trying to keep a count, but had lost track by the time he flashed as far away from the battlefield as the liquid light walls would allow. As soon as he was standing still and alone, the devil stood beside him again.

"Try to find the door," Roche said, watching the devil horde milling about in aimless paranoia without an enemy to focus on. The angel floated high above them, vaporizing any devil that came near her and politely ignoring those who stayed away. The remaining army organized reluctantly, about thirty devils closing a wide circle around her, four swinging flaming chains.

Paul frowned, confused. A sudden crimson flash of light, and the devil showed him what he was trying to tell him. Roche blurred a red arc twice around the circle of devils closing in on Ehcor, this time picking up devils as he passed and throwing them against the far walls with impossible strength to match his incredible speed.

Remembering how Roche bouncing off the wall had let the devils in, Paul joined in the ghastly game of devil's toss. Dashing forward and grasping a devil from the edge of the horde by its free wrist, he spun twice like a discus thrower and let go. Dodging a slashing blade, he watched the devil hit the wall at the same time as the sword he had been clutching a moment ago. His muscled mailed body exploded in a gory purple splash that dripped down the wall for a short second and then disappeared. The sword vanished harmlessly when it hit the wall. No doors opened.

Another slash came at him, the same brave devil trying to make a name for himself. Paul caught the wide blade in both gloved hands and pulled, hard and fast. The devil tumbled forward, off balance; and Paul pulled again, wrenching the sword from his grasp and tossing it aside.

The Walker grasped the devil firmly by the wrist and flung, watching as it arced gracefully to bounce harmlessly off the wall. He noticed Roche swinging his arms smoothly in a huge glorious muscled blur that propelled one devil after another in a straight line at the wall. They exploded in disgusting purple and scarlet displays at regular intervals at precisely the same height, systematically moving along the wall one exploding dripping disappearing smear after another. Paul felt a little inadequate at only six foot tall, no matter his incredible strength.

He imagined his walking stick and swung it like a bat with both hands as he blurred up behind a devil. A spray of blood erupted from its torso as the rounded wood cut the devil in half with a blow that nearly took the walking stick from his hands.

Paul dashed into an open area to survey the scene and collect his thoughts. Most of the monsters were gone, their heads chopped off or their bodies incinerated by the violent new game of devil's toss or the angel's disintegrative love. The dwinding remainder was busy trying to get as far from both Roche and Ehcor as possible. They still held swords and manacles, but they held them up defensively, backing away warily. Their brothers exploded against the wall at regular intervals as the crimson giant blurred through the thinning mob.

It was all so surreal, the angel floating oblivious while the devil painted the light walls in splotches of purple blood. Paul thought back to his childhood, watching his favorite cartoon. He imagined a giant wooden club in his hand, with a handle he could grasp that widened to a stout rounded shaft as tall as he was and twice as big around. Disappointed that a walking stick dripping purple blood was still in his hand, the caveman battle cry died on his lips.

Then Roche went down, a devil got lucky as the blur rushed him and tossed his flaming chain to tangle Roche's legs. Three armored devils went down with him, his blurred advance suddenly a stilled heap of crimson bodies. Paul watched three curved blades rise from the entwined mass, and he moved. A bastard sword in one hand and a short sword in the other, he blocked two curved blades swinging at the huge devil struggling with the flaming chains. The third blade struck Paul in the side of the face with a sickening thunk and buried itself a half inch deep diagonally across his nose and right cheek. He pulled away violently, the skin and muscle of his face knitting together the moment the blade broke loose.

Paul spun, a blurred pinwheel lethal at waist height. Knocking aside swords and lopping off heads, he took care of the three before they could completely regain their feet. The whirling blades passed harmlessly over Roche as he lay there engulfed in flames from knees to ankles.

Disappearing the short sword, Paul plunged his hand into the flames and grasped the hot thick chain. It seemed to fight him, like it had a life of its own, and he wrenched free one end just as he realized what Roche was doing. Entangled about his thighs, the devil scissored his ankles back and forth, kicking the chain away as an open manacle lunged forward again and again like a cobra, trying to snare him. It did have a life of its own, a flaming hot single purpose.

Just as he realized it, the manacle at the end he had just pulled free clamped down on his wrist, hot through the sleeve of his duster.

"Hang on, Roche," he cried, then dashed off as fast as his thought could carry him. Just as he'd imagined, the huge devil spun three times in the air and landed gracefully on his feet while Paul arced a blazing comet orbit around the levitating angel.

"Roche! Down!" Paul cried, swinging the long chain round and round his head in a flaming blur. He moved as he saw Roche drop, zigzagging among the remaining devils with the whirling chain and taking off their heads easily in a burst of flame and blood. When he stopped a ways off from Roche, Paul let the long flaming chain run out its momentum in slow lazy circles until coming to rest on the luminous clouded flooring.

The manacle about his wrist clicked and opened, setting his arm free. His gloved hand still grasped the flaming chain.

Roche was Roche again, and he sauntered casually to Paul's side. There was not a scratch on either of them.

"New toy?" The devil nodded at the flaming set of chains. "Master of the Manacle," the devil teased.

"Reigning Champion of Devil's Toss," Paul replied, grinning.

Roche nodded, "Scourge of Demon and Devil alike," he chuckled. There were two devils still remaining, as far away from the Walker and the Original Demon as they could get. They looked terrified, banging on the walls frantically and stealing furtive glances over a shoulder periodically to see if death was approaching with cowboy hat or pointed horns.

"The Devil's Angel," Paul said, thoughtfully. He looked around. "Hey Roche, where did the angel go?"

"She disappeared when I went down," he answered. "The angels sent the damned devils for her, and they almost got me instead."

Paul arced an eyebrow. "You think the council sent the devils?"

Taking long careful strides, Roche was kicking his feet along the liquid light floor. Soon he held aloft two sets of flaming manacles in one beefy paw and the feathered liquid light chain in the other. "I know they did. They used this." He shook the light chain.

The Walker frowned, the picture of seriousness. "Is there a tracking device in it or something?"

Roche gave him a long hard look. "I think I have a new title for you, Walker," he said, smiling. "'Stupid Brilliant'. Yeah, the angels used heavenly technology to plant an interdimensional tracking device in the manacles." He chuckled, but it sounded more like an amused growl. "Or something like that."

The devil held his arm out before him, dangling the liquid light chain to the liquid light floor. "Sever it," he growled.

Paul thought it over for a minute. Then he shrugged, and his sudden sword flashed between them. He was surprised to feel just a slight tug as the blade slashed through a thick beautiful link. There was a burst of light, and then it was gone.

Nodding, Roche slung the flaming manacles over his shoulder and nodded at the set Paul still clutched in his gloved hand.

"You going to keep that?" he asked.

He looked down at the flaming chain. He thought it gone, the same way he did his key and his weapon. To his surprise, it worked.

"Yeah," he said, spreading his now empty hands. "I think I will."

Roche burst out laughing. "See? Stupid brilliant. I love it. How about a ride home?"

"Can we leave?" Paul looked around at the liquid light walls. They appeared as seamless as ever.

"Oh yeah," the devil waved his free hand dismissively. "She can't keep us here unless she's here to keep us here."

Paul glanced at the remaining devils. "What about them?"

"Leave them." He chuckled evilly. "They'll find a way out eventually. Maybe." He glanced at Paul. "Unless you want to kill them."

Shaking his head, Paul let his hand fall on the devil's beefy shoulder.

"Hey," Roche said as liquid light became shapes and colors, "where's your Guide?"

CHAPTER 36

"It's the same thing I tried to do," Roche moaned, sitting slumped forward in his chair. He had fetched a bottle of scotch when they sat, proffering Paul a drink from it before unceremoniously upending it. Now it sat on the table before him, half full.

"What?" Paul sat on the edge of his seat, tense and nervous. He had refused the drink. "What's the same thing you tried to do?"

The devil spread both hands flat on the table on either side of the bottle, staring at the brown liquid. "I tried to create an ancient spell."

That didn't sound quite right. Paul frowned. "How do you create an ancient spell? Isn't that like a brand new antique?"

"Most ancient spells are ancient by virtue of being old, indeed," the devil smiled, one thumb absently spinning the upright bottle in place on the table between his meaty paws. "They draw their power from either being used by many or being closely guarded by a few. Either way, intention and belief are the only two actual ingredients necessary for any magick to work. Most folks just need props to define their intention or refine their beliefs. They call them tools, but they're the real tool."

"Roche," Paul gritted as patiently as possible between clenched teeth. "What is the other way to make an ancient spell?"

The bottle stopped spinning long enough for the devil to take a healthy pull. "Be ancient," he grinned, setting the bottle back down to start it spinning again. "Be ancient and have very strong intent."

The Walker nodded. "All Walkers must die."

"It's nothing personal," Roche said in earnest. "It's a principle. For me it was seeing how some Walkers used their powers, even after the council was put in place. A complete lack of supervision coupled with extraordinary abilities in an essentially human mind is a recipe for some pretty ugly scenarios. The good being done by Walkers was overshadowed by the evil they got away with; and even their results were often stained by their wicked means of attaining them."

Paul smiled. "Bane of the Wicked Walker." He was impatient for action, but the more he learned of Roche the more sympathy he had for the devil.

"I got this idea," Roche murmured, spinning the bottle, "based on the power of the three. A way to end all Walkers."

Paul gulped uneasily. "The power of the three?"

"Yeah, you know," the devil shrugged lightly. "All creation comes in threes. It is said that you cannot have up without down, and that is true. It is incomplete, however, in that it leaves out the place from which up is being perceived as being up and down is being perceived as being down. Up cannot exist without down, but it also cannot exist except in relation to a fixed point of perception. Most people, and indeed most philosophies, assume the point of perception to be a given. It is their viewpoint, and is thus rarely considered as a variable. Yet it is perhaps the most important variable. Climbing a ladder makes what used to be up become down. An angel's nightlight would blind a human in its brilliance. A human's scalding hot water is a devil's lukewarm bath. Then there are all the trinities in creation, both holy and unholy."

Roche glanced from the spinning bottle to meet the Walker's eyes. Paul did his best to look solemn and wise. He wished Kris were here, to flesh out the devil's ancient perspective.

"Mother and father create the child, but the child creates the mother and father aspect in the individuals, which completes a trinity within each of them. The Father, the Son, and the Holy Ghost, of course; Heaven and Hell and Earth. Creation is rooted in the power of the three when it comes to both perceiving and manifesting. Often the perceiver neglects to acknowledge that they are creating an entirely different reality simply by perceiving it in their own unique way. Subsequent attempts at manifestation are usually efforts made to change the outer world so that reality will mirror or express that perception. Yet the outer world is already perfect. Reality is not there to be shaped to meet our needs, reality waits for us to perceive it in a way that no longer creates inner conflict. When we see that reality is not the problem, that reality simply embodies the problems our perception creates, we are free to live a reality that is no longer inherently problematic."

The devil took a long drink from the bottle and smiled. "Peace is not won by murdering everyone who has a gun," he said quietly. "Peace is a personal choice, to be cultivated within. If you want peace on Earth, cultivate it inside. If you want to force others to live the way you think they should, both the concept and the experience of peace will forever elude you. When we realize that peace cannot exist without conflict, we can choose peace and allow others to choose conflict and be at peace with both our decision and their freedom to choose differently. Our perception does not create objective reality, but it does define our subjective reality; it is in acting from that standpoint that we manifest the very evidence we often find disturbing."

"So there was a time," Paul replied slowly, "when you perceived Walkers to be fundamentally flawed in concept and practice. And looking for it, you saw it everywhere."

The devil nodded. "The way Ehcor sees it now."

"And you decided to kill all Walkers?" Paul tried to keep his voice from sounding accusatory.

"No," Roche responded firmly. "That was the sticking point for me. Not all Walkers were wicked, even I could see that. I had to find a way to strip them all of their Walker status and re-humanize them. There was no system in place for me to do that alone, no existing ancient spell that would draw all Walkers to one place and sever their relationships to their keys. Walker John and the council had control of the keys and the rehumanizing secret, and they weren't about to share it with a mad devil."

The Walker frowned. "So you made one up. You made up an ancient spell."

"It's ancient now, if it makes you feel any better," the devil shrugged. "Everything you know was made up by someone. What most people accept as truth is usually more of a common agreement over an idea than it is the truth. That's why there are so many versions of it."

Paul looked at the devil doubtfully, but he didn't argue.

"I took elements of devil magick, angel magick, and man magick and made up an ancient spell. According to the spell, I had to kill nine Walkers, three above, three on Earth, three below."

"Wait a minute." Now Paul needed to argue. "According to the spell you made up, right?"

Roche frowned. "I didn't make up magick, Walker. I just created a new pathway of possibility within what already existed. I wasn't looking to re-invent the wheel, I was trying to un-invent the Walker." He took a long last pull off the bottle, draining the vessel. "Besides, I didn't have the understanding then that I have now. I thought that the laws of the Universe were fixed, like most souls do. And so they were for me."

"So you killed nine wicked Walkers?"

Chuckling, the devil shook his head. "No, Walker. I found them exceedingly difficult to kill. I chased the first Walker through more landscapes on more levels than I knew existed. Every time I killed him he would just reappear on another level, unscathed. Even when I finally figured out how to kill him, his soul kept trying to reanimate the body. So I imprisoned his soul in a space only I could enter or leave and went after my next wicked Walker. It was easier the second time, I had the first Walker's key and weapon. And soon I had a small collection of wicked Walker souls and keys and weapons. The spell was working, I could feel it gaining momentum with every death."

"How many Walkers did you kill?"

"Four," the devil replied uneasily. "It was a messy business, too. These were the most terrible humans I had ever encountered, warriors that had been battling demons and devils for centuries. They wielded the power of angels with souls that had lost all humanity in a wide river of purple blood."

"Then they organized," Roche went on. "Walker John pulled together an army of Walkers and devils to hunt me down and take me out."

"Walker John tried to kill you?"

"Oh yeah, firsthand even. It was a glorious fight, but once I got his weapon he flitted away and walked between worlds so swiftly I couldn't follow." Roche grimaced. "Besides, I had my hands full with the army waiting to descend upon me if he failed. I tried to fight them, but I could not kill any of the Walkers. John had chosen his army carefully. They were all good men, souls on their way up, compassionate killers who viewed their prey with respect."

The Walker arched an eyebrow. "So you couldn't kill then in good conscience?"

"No, no, nothing like that," Roche waved a meaty paw dismissively. "I was a devil on my way down, I had no qualms about killing them. It would have violated the spell, and either sent its momentum in a different direction or sent me back to square one. The Walkers didn't hold back their attack as I did mine, and it was beginning to look like the only possible outcome was an army of Walkers killing God's Walker Demon. And for a moment I considered that that was the outcome I had hoped for all along. I didn't care if Walkers existed or not, I just wanted to end my miserable fall."

"What about the devils?" Paul asked.

"Oh, them I killed," the devil shrugged. "It was down to me and forty or fifty righteous Walkers by the time I accepted my fate."

"Then what happened?" Paul urged.

Roche smiled, remembering. "Ehcor saved me. She swept in and gathered me up and took me so high even the righteous Walkers couldn't follow. She imprisoned me there until my soul hit bottom and began to rise."

The Walker frowned. "She *imprisoned* you? For how long?"

"A couple hundred years," he replied casually. "It was the only way. I owe her a great debt. A debt it is time to repay." He sighed heavily and looked long and hard at the empty bottle.

"Roche," Paul said carefully. "What happened to the Guides? The Walkers' Guides?"

"I killed them," Roche replied. "I killed them all."

Paul gulped. "Do you think Kris is dead?"

"I don't know, Walker. She's had to alter the spell in some ways. Walker John struck a deal with the devils to enlist their aid in hunting me, promising that Walkers would leave devils alone on Earth. Ehcor herself pointed out the flaw in the system, that none of this would have happened if all Walkers were souls on their way up. They called all Walkers and rehumanized them again, returning keys only to the rising. Only souls on their way up are appointed Walkers and Guides and Watchers now. There are no more wicked Walkers to kill, no more devil hunters. Besides, I didn't need to kill the Guides to complete the spell. I would kill the Guide first to shake the Walker's confidence while also eliminating a helpful companion. It was a double win for me, not a hard call to make. She's doing it differently. Your Guide could still be alive. We need to get to her before the devils find her again, or before Walker John pulls together another army. If they kill her, the souls she imprisoned could be lost for an eternity. Including Kris."

"Well?" Paul stood suddenly. "What are we waiting for?"

The devil took one long last look at the empty bottle and stood slowly. He looked weary down to his rising soul, memories of a thousand past battles sucking the excitement from the battle to come. When he came to stand next to the Walker, Paul looked him hard in the eye. His hand fell on his shoulder, but for a time the world did not shift around them.

"Hey Roche," he said quietly, seriously. "Thank you." He felt a fraction of the world the devil carried on his shoulders, and it was an overwhelming burden. He wondered if anyone had ever thanked him for all that he was, for all that he had done. "On behalf of all Walkers, on behalf of the world, thank you. The world is better for you being in it."

The life came back into the devil's eyes, and he grinned. "Screw the Walkers, screw the world. You're alright, Stone Walker. And you're welcome. Now let's go make us some history so everyone can forget it."

Paul thought of the angel. It wasn't hard; it was honestly the most sublime experience in his lifetime's storehouse of memories. She was love, she was light, she was beauty, she was completion…and as he felt the light shining on his face, his skin glowing with her love, he couldn't help but smile softly.

Paul opened his eyes, slowly.

CHAPTER 37

There were Walkers everywhere. Eight stood in a protective circle around the angel as she hovered just off the liquid light floor. They were in a space similar to the one they had battled the devils in, but the walls were woven light of many colors instead of shades of bright.

At least fifty others encircled the Walkers that guarded the angel. They seemed hesitant to attack their brothers, some circling the phalanx slowly while most just stood there looking armed and dangerous and confused. Paul spotted Walker John as he raised his longsword over his head and cried, "Attack!"

A wave of Walkers converged on the angel from all sides. Although they obeyed immediately, it was still half-hearted. The ring of eight staved them off. Steel flashed and clanged impressively, but no blood was shed. The angel's protectors fought with a righteous passion, their eyes glazed over in blissful surrender while their blades flashed quicksilver thought. It was a blurred and bloodless standstill, fantastic and boring at the same time.

Paul glanced at Walker John, watching the battle from afar. His arms were crossed, his weapon disappeared, and a fierce frown strained his stern face. Looking at him, Paul felt himself suddenly full of fury at him.

"Hey Roche," he growled. "How exactly do you kill a Walker, anyway?"

The devil surprised him, not hesitating at all before responding. "Separate him from his key and his head at the same time. The best way I found was to cut off the arm not holding the weapon while cutting off the head at the same time. It's a gruesome art, but it's all about the timing."

"Thanks," Paul responded. "Be right back."

Then he was a blur of black leather and sudden swords, rushing the ancient Walker at the speed of thought. Walker John was quick, too. His blade appeared and flashed a wide arc of defense as Paul closed in. The force of the swinging steel nearly knocked Paul off his feet as it met his short sword, and he skidded to a halt just before Walker John. He thrust and slashed madly at him, but the older Walker parried every blow neatly with his single blade.

Paul's strength and speed made him appear the great swordsman usually, devils and demons falling at his feet like practice dummies. He felt like a kid swinging two sticks in the backyard and pretending at swordplay against this Walker. Trained in fencing when blades won wars, Walker John fended off his blinding sure swings again and again and again. For all the fighting going on, even Paul could not penetrate the Walker's expert defenses to draw blood. Just when he began to think this might have been a stupid and possibly suicidal idea, he thought of Roche.

His short sword became a long light axe mid-swing, and he thought *stupid brilliant* as the blade sliced a long gash in Walker John's right cheek. Both Walkers paused in disbelief as the wound knitted itself together neatly and bloodlessly. Then Paul moved, swinging the bastard sword at the Walker's free hand and the axe at his exposed neck.

Walker John drew back just in time, his face going white as both blades bit flesh in passing. His exposed wrist and neck wore short shallow red dashes for a moment before healing rapidly. It was enough to both frighten the veteran Walker and enliven the new one.

Paul's eyes narrowed as he advanced, while Walker John's widened in fear as he backed away. Still watching Paul warily, he cried out suddenly. "Walkers! Now!"

Then Paul was swimming in a sea of leather and steel. Rotating slowly in place, he spun and swung two swords again, high and fast, to protect his exposed head. Blows rained on his armored torso, but every Walker that came close enough got as good as they gave. More than one leathered form exploded from the mob to land healed some distance away. His sword slowed once as he beheaded one Walker, catching on his thick spine. It was whirring and blurring again before the body hit the liquid light floor, and Paul didn't have the chance to see how the Walker healed. A few moments later the same face hove into view behind a long gleaming double-headed heavy battleaxe.

The fraction of a fraction of a second he had lost beheading the Walker put Paul just that far behind the battle he fought. One arm was suddenly still in its blurred path of destruction as a large quick gloved hand clamped about his wrist like a vice. Paul swung his free arm, short sword set to take off his opponent's arm at the exposed wrist. Two sets of strong grasping hands suddenly clutched his swinging arm, Walkers appearing at his side in a blur.

Paul felt a feeling of smug satisfaction as the short sword bit into the flesh of one of the Walker's faces as he appeared. It stuck there, an inch deep in his head from chin to cranium. His ear was cut neatly in half by the buried platinum blade, and Paul wondered how his brain could be working right with an inch of metal in his skull. The Walker held on, though, gripping Paul as fiercely as Paul gripped his weapons.

Immobilized, Paul watched the Walker whose head he had so neatly removed coming at him with a grimace and an axe. A quick glance confirmed what he had feared, that his supernatural ally was similarly predisposed. A crowd of Walkers surrounded the beautiful monster as he fought valiantly with all his awesome power. The devil was swinging a curved sword the size of a helicopter blade at blinding speeds, walking a rotating slow circle through his own sea of death. His long wide blade occasionally disarmed or beheaded a Walker, but he mostly just swept them violently aside.

Turning for a better view, Paul saw that Roche dragged behind him three sturdy Walkers clutching a long feathered chain of liquid light terminating in a manacle clamped about his thick wrist. The devil needed his help as much as Paul needed his.

In the moment the re-headed Walker planted his foot and started his swing, Paul leapt. With all his strength and all his might and fully intending to fly like a bird, the Walker launched straight up like a rocket, three brothers in tow.

Two of the Walkers held on tight, not startled by their sudden flight enough to let their grips lax. The big dark fiercely strong one did, though, holding on just long enough to rise with his brothers before Paul felt his clamped hands relax on his wrist.

They were a rising cloud of violence then. Paul wrenched his sword arm free to swing the long blade at the two clutching his arm. The swift arc of gleaming steel presented them the simple choice of letting go or losing their heads. They let go, and the short sword was pulled from one of their skulls to join in the dance of danger.

It was a little awkward cutting and slashing in mid-air; Paul hadn't realized how much the strength and skill of swordplay depended on having your feet firmly on the ground. Every weak blurring slash hit home, the three were so close to him; and in the long moment before their weapons appeared the only sound was his swords hitting leather with a muffled thump or flesh with a quiet clean squish.

Just as weapons began to flash into existence in their hands, Paul got the hang of suspended swordplay. He knocked aside the big Walker's sword easily and slashed through neck and wrist simultaneously with a wide blinding double arc. Two swords came at him then, the blows weak and uncertain either because they were rising through the air or because of their brother's lifeless body floating beside them. The force of the blows had sent both head and hand flying away in opposite directions; but the rest of him rose along with them, spraying blood in all directions as he floated lifelessly still clutching his weapon.

The three Walkers battled as their ascent slowed, metal clanging on metal and thudding against leather. None of their hats were still on, and one black and one brown cowboy hat floated in the cloud of blood and leather and steel. A cheek or a forehead would open in a gash that would close itself swiftly here and there, but Paul could not find another fatal opening.

The fighting drove them apart as they fell, and soon swords were unable to touch in the widening gaps. For two long seconds they dropped, helpless to do anything but fall. They hit hard in a tight mob of Walkers, and Paul was pinned by a dozen impossibly strong hands before he had a chance to rise. Struggling frantically, he caught sight of the big Walker's head as it hit the ground nearby and rolled on the liquid light surface. Two warriors raised heavy battleaxes, in time, tall Walkers Paul had not come face to face with before. Their eyes were sharp and luminous and distant all at once, round with awed ecstasy.

He realized they were two of the angel's guard, two of the eight dead Walkers somehow alive in this place and under her spell. Paul heard her voice singing sweetly from far off, and wondered if it would be the last sound he heard. She was calling to her Walkers, telling them to bring her the key and the devil.

The twin swing stopped before it could start as a bright white light erupted through a far wall to spew forth a brown leather blur. Four eyes went from luminous to lifeless as Paul watched, and two weapons hit the liquid light floor in time with two heads. He heard the angel scream in beautiful tormented anguish as heads and hands littered the ground around him, watching her dead Walkers disappear when they landed. The other bodies weren't vanishing, however; and Paul was soon buried in bodies and covered in blood.

No one held him down anymore, and he disappeared his weapons to push away the pile of headless one-handed corpses. Rising shakily, he saw Roche standing alone in a similar heap of gore. They exchanged tired breathless grins, then turned at the same time to see what the other two survivors were up to.

The angel flapped her wings frantically, held in place mid-air by a long flaming manacle clamped about her ankle. A lone Walker held the other end in his bare hands, dripping blood and flesh and flame to the liquid light floor. His hat was gone, his hair blasted flat by the downdraft from the angel's wings. His brown oiled leather duster flapped in the gusts, and when he turned his head Paul recognized him.

From the moment he had laid eyes on him that first time in the street, Paul's life had changed in more ways than he thought possible. He was the first domino in this insane constant free-fall that was his life now, and Paul gripped his key hard in his gloved hand as he thought of it.

Then he rushed forward, arriving at the Walker's side just after the devil. He'd had to stop to pick something up. They hauled the angel in together until she realized what was happening and rushed them. She hit the trio in a blinding burst of explosive light, and the three of them flew in all directions like shrapnel. None of them went far, though, as each snapped taut at the end of the length of chain they held.

Paul thought he was pretty clever, stopping to pick up a feathered liquid light restraint before joining the capture. He was both pleased and disappointed to see that Roche had done the same. The damned devil was somehow faster than him. Now they had her, Roche holding tight a flaming chain clamped around one of her wrists while Paul's cool strong feathered chain held the other. The other Walker still held his flaming chain, his face grim with determination.

Ehcor stood with her chin on her chest, her posture statuesque but sad. Shrinking into her beautiful womanly form, her face was still too perfect to be anything but angelic. A handful of keys, ancient thick keys of forged metal, spilled from the hand held taut by Paul's chain. She raised her eyes, bright blue flecks of love and endless sky, to meet Paul's.

"Call them to you, First Walker," she said. Even in this form, her lilting tones made him want to sigh in abandon and do her bidding forever. He remembered Brenna.

Paul narrowed his eyes, holding tight the chain. "What do you mean?" He glanced at the others. "What does she mean?"

They came together before the angel, Paul switching chains with his maker wordlessly. The immortal breathed in deep, his first breath clear of the reek of burning flesh since the capture had begun. Ehcor seemed beaten, letting the slack in the chains created by their coming together allow her hands to clasp each other before her meekly.

"Paul," Roche said, "this is First Walker Marcus." When he said one Walker's name he was eleven feet tall, a breathtaking monster towering over them with horns a foot long. By the time he said the other's he was by all appearances a man again, save the two pointed nubs on his head. The other

Walker seemed as unperturbed by the transformation as Paul was.

"Wait a minute," Paul frowned. "I thought your name was Peter."

The Walker shrugged. "I never said that."

"All Walkers were rehumanized after the war," Roche explained. "Only those who fit certain criteria and who swore obedience to Walker John and the Council of Angels were made Walkers again. It wasn't until the whole ceremony ended that Walker John was told the story of the first Walker, and he declared that Marcus had obviously been rehumanized and had slunk away."

Walker Marcus took up the story. "When we were all called together, I was able to watch without being seen. I had never even met Walker John, and I didn't know if I could explain to a new Walker how time can change you. I had just begun to rise and to see the good I could do. My key was called, and I watched it fly to Walker John with all the others. My abilities were a part of me, however, and I thought myself to the other side of the world. I earned my way as a mercenary and built a quiet comfortable isolated life for myself and my immortal companions." He held the chain in his hand loosely, recalling ancient memory.

"Imagine my surprise," he said, his austere face hinting at a smile that would never come, "when a Walker came to me one day and told me I was perfect for a very special job. I didn't know whether to laugh in his face or suspect a trap. Instead I agreed, and introduced him to my Guide and Watcher, who by then were able to fool anyone but God into thinking they were normal living breathing people."

"We had had to move around a lot and live quietly on one dimension for a long time. It was refreshing to think of not having to hide from everyone anymore. The arrangements were made, much less sloppy than our first transition, or yours," he nodded at Paul. "Sorry about that."

Paul shrugged it off, the flaming metal in his gloved hands clanking gently with the dismissive gesture.

"I became Walker Peter, and enough time had passed that no one that I ever encountered recognized me as anyone else," Marcus went on. "I made sure to never call the attention of the Walker Council or demons or angels to my activities, and Walker John and I had never met face to face. I was made to swear to obey, as all new Walkers were; and there was never a reason not to until recently."

"Walker John," the angel raised her head suddenly in alarm. "You have to find him. He—"

A blur with a battle cry exploded from the shifting tones of the liquid light floor then, Walker John's brown leather duster streaming in the wake of his advance. In one swift movement, Paul tossed his flaming chain at Roche and dashed between the oncoming Walker and the angel. They collided at full speed to go down in a tumble of leather and sudden swords. They rose as one, slashing at each other repeatedly and uselessly. Then Paul brought his sword down in a wide arc while stabbing forward with his short blade. Walker John parried the stab skillfully and brought his own blade up to sweep aside the bastard sword.

Paul let the force of the parry turn to a boomerang arc as he willed the sword to turn to a snare. As his bastard blade was knocked aside, the noose fell about the Walker's neck to settle loosely on his shoulders. When he realized what was happening, John tried to drop to his knees and raise his arms in an attempt to dislodge the snare. Paul jerked hard with one hand and slashed fury with the other, and Walker John fell forward face first as his hand and sword bounced away harmlessly. He sprouted a new hand immediately, but the weapon still lay on the liquid light floor. Paul disappeared one weapon and spun the other, snaring the sprawled Walker painfully and lifting him to his feet before the others.

He looked past one captive to the other. "Ehcor, you were saying?" The name sounded flat and bland when he said it. He'd have to learn the accent of the ancient cant. The angel smiled at him nonetheless, and the smile melted his heart.

"He found out who Marcus really was, and that Paul had his key. He came to me to convince me to help him become Walker King, and to rule at his side. He said he would do anything I asked if I helped him capture the new First Walker." The angel's eyes went fierce as they fell on Walker John. "Then he gathered a Walker army to kill us all."

"You were going to kill us all." Walker John spat, struggling awkwardly at the end of the long pole. "All the Walkers, Roche, yourself. Why?"

To Paul's surprise, the angel looked to Walker Marcus for guidance. He shook his head, solemn.

"That is not for you to know," she fixed her attention again on Walker John. "If I kill you it may complete the spell I no longer wish to cast. We made a bargain. I captured the Stone Walker for you, now you must do as I ask." She smiled sweetly at him. "Please kill yourself."

Marcus spoke up. "Call his key to you, First Walker. You're the only one who can."

When Paul freed one hand to reach out to Marcus, Walker John tried to struggle but Paul held firm. "Here," he said, proffering the platinum watch to its rightful owner. "I don't know how." When he tried to take it, however, the metal melted and dissolved into Paul's gloved palm. He frowned, but Marcus actually laughed.

"Not everyone gets to choose their path," he said, solemn again. "Call the key home to you."

"I don't—" Paul began, but he broke off as Walker John jerked backward and pulled the snare from his grip. He seized the shaft again immediately, but the snare was empty and the veteran Walker was diving to the liquid light floor to roll and rise bearing two long swords. Marcus made to move, but Paul's hand fell on his shoulder.

"No," he said fiercely, frowning. "He's mine." His lightening fast advance was met by Walker John's mid-dash, and they circled each other in a whirlwind of clanging metal that seemed to swirl the dancing liquid light they stepped in. His mind planned stabs and swings and parries with the smooth quicksilver thoughts he was growing so used to. They seemed hopelessly evenly matched, to Paul's pleasant surprise. He had to think of something, though; something other than an eternal wicked fast melee just waiting for one of them to slip.

Slicing and slashing and ducking and stabbing, Paul thought of Roche and how he seemed just a touch faster than any of the others except Marcus. Was their ancient status responsible, were their thoughts just a little faster for having thought so many more of them over the centuries?

Swinging one blade and blocking with the other, it dawned on him. He was in one blade, in the other, he was in his body, he was in his mind as much as ever despite the violent swordplay. His thoughts were quicksilver, but they were quicksilver exploding in a dozen directions. The other Walker showed the same complex play of thought and emotion on his sneering face as he slashed and parried Paul's blows.

Taking a sudden step back, the Stone Walker closed his eyes and stilled his mind. Instead of being in a dozen different places, he was nowhere; and Walker John's flashing blades slashed at suddenly empty air. When Paul reappeared behind him, he acted faster than thought, his mind still as both blades arced with seeming life of their own to remove the veteran Walker's head and hand as he turned. Paul sliced off the second hand for good measure as the body fell and his thoughts came back to him. Then he disappeared his weapons and thought his bloody duster clean and new again.

Walker Paul closed his eyes and imagined a small gentle cloud of keys floating at him. He opened his eyes and caught them in flight, nine thick ancient wrought keys that disappeared as they touched his hands.

Rejoining the others, Paul grinned at Roche. "Stupid, huh?"

The devil grinned back and shrugged his beefy shoulders, the chains in his hands clanking with the rise and fall. "Stupid brilliant."

A bigger cloud of keys floated gently their way, rising from the bodies of some fifty fallen Walkers. These Paul grasped sadly, one by one, thinking of all the brothers he had lost today. Before the last one could disappear, he proffered it to Marcus. "Walker Marcus," he said solemnly, "I have a job you would be perfect for."

He shook his head, making no move to accept the key. "It's just Marcus now. I've been on the rise for a long time, I have other interests to pursue, a calling louder than killing demons. Surely our paths will cross again in this perfect place we call life."

Devil and Walker exchanged confused glances, but the angel just smiled in satisfaction and withdrew something from the folds of her robe. She held it out with the hand whose wrist was manacled by a flaming chain, and the dancing fire played off the carved liquid light horn. A simple curved hunk of what could have been ivory if not for its flowing aliveness, the horn was a little over a foot long and open at both ends. The angel looked at Paul. "Take it, Walker King. Call all the Walkers here and make them swear their obedience to you."

He started to protest, but Marcus laid his free hand on Paul's arm. "It's the only way," he said solemnly. "This is only the beginning, and you're the only one."

Sighing heavily, Paul reached out his free hand and imagined the horn in it. It leapt neatly through the air to land in his grasp and he smiled, pleased with himself. Then his smile fell, and he looked at the angel. "Do I blow it?"

Roche guffawed loudly, but Ehcor just gave him a kindly smile and shook her head. "Call them here in your mind, all of them," she said in the beautiful lilting musical voice. "Speak to them through that."

Paul closed his eyes and imagined himself surrounded by all the Walkers in the world. Reality overwhelmed his imaginings when he opened his eyes, though. He had expected a few hundred male faces under hats over dusters, a sea of leather. Instead there were thousands, men and women, and kimonos and tribal armor and katanas far outnumbered cowboy hats and longswords.

"Call their keys to you," the angel called out over the sudden din of thousands of Walkers turning their way. A cloud of objects rose from the crowd and floated at him, keys and watches and long sharp bone fragments or teeth. Paul disappeared them before they engulfed his group and raised the horn to his lips.

"You all knew Walker John," he spoke into the horn. His voice carried to forever in every language, and the stirring crowd stilled to listen. "Walker John conspired to kill the Original Walker Demon and the Original Walker Angel and become Walker King. He was responsible for the deaths of over sixty immortal Walkers in his mad quest for power. He is dead now."

He watched the reaction ripple through the crowd, spoke into the horn again. "I killed him, let that be known. Our ranks were falling apart due to his rules and silly superstitions, and the Walker phenomenon has created consequences through our individual efforts that must be met with the iron fist of combined intent. Join me. Follow me. Walk with me."

"Or what?" cried a lone loud voice from the crowd. Heads nodded in curious agreement.

"Or go home human," Paul answered simply into the mouthpiece. "I won't kill you unless you attack me, but all Walkers will be my Walkers from this day forward."

"And who are you?" Another voice cried, and the crowd bristled restlessly in agreement.

This time Paul answered in thoughtless action, appearing beside the speaker to collar him and re-appear in the same instant holding him helplessly aloft by the neck before the immortal gathering. He dropped him, and he and his weapon fell to the floor. The man made as if to rise, but Paul glared at him and spoke into the horn. "On your knees!" he commanded him fiercely. "On your knees before the First Walker, the Stone Walker, scourge of Demon and Devil and Walker alike, Wielder of Two Weapons, Walker King and Friend to Devils and Angels, Walker Paul. Kneel before your king or go home human."

If anyone slunk away, he neither saw them nor knew how they got home. It took some time to exchange a man's obedience for a key one at a time, and the Original Walker trio took their leave quietly in the long impromptu ceremony. It seemed hours before he imagined the army home and this battlefield closed to all but himself and God.

He found Roche and Marcus drinking quietly in the devil's den. "Where's the angel?" he asked, placing his hat on the table as he sat.

They exchanged a glance, but neither responded.

"Where's Kris?" he asked suddenly.

Roche eyed him over a glass half full of brown liquid. "She had the Guides. She let them go."

"Your Guide wasn't there," Marcus said simply.

Paul frowned. "Where the hell is Kris?"

CHAPTER 38

Kris found himself in the coffee shop, not knowing he wanted to come here until he materialized himself seated at a table alone. The havoc of the remodel was all around him, the shop dark but for a lone work light glaring from a distant corner. The bright but lonely glow cast more shadows than light.

He was shaken by having witnessed his friend hacking and stabbing at his father's demon, and he had had to get away. Paul would be fine, the Walker seemed like he could handle himself. What good was a ghost in a fight anyway? It was possible to get a little high on the endless milky liquid in his canteen, and that's what he set out to do.

Then Jessica came out of Roche's office, heading straight for the lone table in the midst of the tidy chaos. She pulled out a chair and sat across from him after setting a small flowered cloth bag on the table. Seated, she began to unpack the contents of the bag, a nail file and bottle of polish remover, a bottle of color, nail and cuticle cutters. Kris watched her with the same fascination and adoration he always did, feeling a little guilty watching but not enough to stop. Jessica began to do her nails in the spare light from the lone work lamp.

"It's funny," he murmured out loud. "I never really confided in anyone but Paul until he met Brenna. Then Matt was someone I could talk to about some things, but not like I could Paul. Now they're the only friends I have who can see me and they're both too wrapped up in everything to do anything but ask me questions from time to time."

He chuckled, tilting his flask to his lips. "Now the only person who listens to me can't even hear me." He wiped his mouth with the heavy cloth sleeve of his robe. "Good thing, too," he smiled. "Since I tell you everything."

Jessica filed and buffed her nails as he spoke, eyes on the task in the near dark room. "When I was a kid," Kris said, "my mom would do her nails. The chemical smell would always give me a headache as soon as I smelled it, but I would hang out anyway. Now that I'm dead it doesn't bother me anymore. Funny, I would have given just about anything to sit and talk to you and watch you do your nails while I was alive, headache or no. I guess being dead has its perks."

He watched her work for a while in silence, shamelessly adoring the tiny little crinkle that formed vertically between her eyebrows when she concentrated hard for a moment.

"I planned to ask you out every day," he said quietly after a time. "I would always find an excuse not to, and trying would seem harder each day." Kris heard voices on the other side of the closed office door, muffled and indistinct. He didn't know what kind of company the devil kept late at night, and he didn't think it any of his business. The sounds faded and didn't come back, and the Guide went on telling her what she hadn't heard a dozen times before.

"I wanted to get to know you so badly I never got to know you," he smiled sadly. The milky liquid was starting to make him feel light-headed and mildly euphoric. He took another long drink. "I saw Paul kill my dad's demon tonight, the one that's been eating away at him and ruling his life at the same time." He took another drink, considering. "No, I saw Paul mutilate it. I assume he killed it. It was disgusting, mostly because Paul seemed to enjoy how disgusting it was. He couldn't just kill it. He had to hack it to pieces first."

Kris set the bottomless canteen on the table before him and leaned forward, remembering something. "Jessica," he said seriously. He slurred the name a bit, his tongue tied up on nervousness or drunkenness. "Andre said something curious to Paul and me. He said something about you being Roche's prisoner or hostage or something." His voice was clear, but he felt sheepish saying it. The Watcher was probably just messing with them. Paul was right, the guy was an asshole.

"I want you to know something," he forged on while she layered the nails of her left hand in a sweet light pink. "If you can't hear me, I guess it doesn't matter what I say. If you can, I want to say this. If you're in any kind of trouble, now or ever, and if there's any way I can help, let me know. I totally understand why you would pretend to not hear me all the times I've come here and talked to you. Just so you know, if you can hear me, I would do just about anything for you. Making you smile would be a happy full-time job for me if I could have it, but I would help you as a friend if…if you didn't feel those same feelings." He trailed off awkwardly and watched her pack her little bag up slowly and with great care. "Just so you know," he added, lamely.

She stood, the little flowered bag in her hand. Blonde hair flowed loosely about her shoulders as she removed the rubber band from her ponytail and shook her head. It was sexy and sweet at the same time, strands brushing over the curve of her breasts under the penguin pattern pajamas. Her hand trailed lazily down her shoulder to undo the top button of the modest top. Kris looked at her curiously for a moment, then looked away as the next button came open.

"Uh," he said awkwardly, averting his gaze. "I have to assume from your lack of response that you think you are alone in whatever you are doing." A quick glance showed her bare skin from throat to midriff without being open enough to show her breasts. As one side of the top fell aside, he looked away again quickly. "Much as I might like to see what's coming, I, uh," he cleared his throat. "I need to take my leave."

She giggled then, a sweet innocent musical sound, and he snapped his head around to catch her looking right at him and refastening the buttons she had undone carefully with one hand.

"Don't go," she smiled. "I'm sorry. It's just hard to believe you're as decent a guy as you are. You don't follow me home or into the bathroom or anything."

The Guide's face went from shock to shame, and he grimaced. "It must be nice to have a stalker so respectful of your privacy."

Jessica giggled again, clutching the small flowered bag with both hands almost nervously. "You're not a stalker," she said, looking away. "You're the closest thing I've ever had to a boyfriend. You're the closest I've come to even having a friend up here."

The Guide shook his head, unbelieving. "You could hear me this whole time?"

Jessica nodded, biting her lip guiltily. "I'm so sorry. I just...oh, I shouldn't have told you I could see you. You're going to hate me."

"Why can you see me?" The Guide was curious suddenly. "Are you really Roche's hostage?"

"Oh, no, Uncle Roche is my guardian. My mother acts like I'm her property." She frowned a pretty frown. "So he plays along and says I belong to him now. This is where I need to be." She paused. "This is where I want to be," she said firmly. Her seriousness made her seem more the sweet little girl than ever.

Kris smiled, pleased. "So who is your mother?"

Jessica bit her lip again, glancing to the floor and back at him. "This is the part where you start hating me," she murmured.

"That could never happen," the Guide said slowly, with such sincerity that the girl sighed and nodded. Hope lit her beautiful blue eyes.

"Okay," she said, "help me move this table."

The Guide held his hands up. "I can't," he said. "The best I can do is turn stuff on or off, lights or electronics."

Circling the table to stand beside him, so close he could smell fresh flowers and clean shampoo on her soft honeyed hair, she put her hands on the edge of the table.

"Here," she said, "put your hand on mine."

Kris put his hand right where hers was. Larger than hers, his superimposed hand made hers vanish at the wrist. He felt a tingle in his fingers. "Sorry," he said, pulling back to hover his hand over hers.

Jessica smiled. "No, do that," she said. "Feel my hand from the inside."

Letting his hand superimpose itself over hers, he felt the tingle coalesce into sensation. "Hey!" He grinned. "I can feel it! Like when I was alive!" He turned his head to thank her, still grinning. She turned to him at the same time, her mouth open to speak.

Suddenly their mouths were overlapping like their hands, the sensation in his lips overwhelming and delicious and delightful.

The both pulled away, mirror images of shy awkwardness.

"Sorry," Kris said again.

"No. Don't be. I mean, I'm not." She glanced shyly at him. "Just...I just have to show you something first. Help me move the table."

His hands went through the surface, and he frowned.

"You sit on chairs and benches, right?" Jessica nodded at the chair he had occupied. Kris shrugged, wordless, nodded.

"Do you know why?" she asked. The Guide just shrugged again. "You assume you can," she said slowly. "You can feel the seat beneath you because you know you will. Now feel the edge of the table because you assume you can. Don't focus on doing it, proceed with the knowledge that you will feel it."

For the next several minutes she coached him, and soon he was picking things up and moving them around like he could when he was alive. Without even thinking about it, he moved the table easily out of the way. When he turned to face her she was unbuttoning her top again.

"Jess, I—" he began, averting his gaze.

"Oh, just turn your back," she said. "It's probably better that way anyway." He turned away as she continued speaking. "I just don't want to ruin my pajamas."

Then there was a soft clink, a small metal object landing on wood, and her voice came again. It was different somehow, lower and lovelier and thicker. "Okay," she said quietly. "You can turn around. Please don't scream."

The Guide turned slowly, his eyes widening as his mouth fell open a bit in dumbfounded awe. A long sinewed serpentine creature crouched before him, twenty feet long from the tip of its forked tail to the end of its narrow nostrils. Smooth luminous scales covered every flowing muscle, dark red beautiful armor. Wings were folded at its back; and as he watched they opened, thin delicate membrane covered in flexing shifting scales. The long serpentine neck stretched until he was face to snout with it, long teeth inches from his nose as he looked in its eyes. They were ringed red and blue and black, and luminous, a crimson slit in the center like a cat's eyes.

"Jessica?" Kris murmured, his voice full of wonder. The giant serpentine head rose and fell in wordless affirmation. "You're a dragon?" Again the head rose and fell, the bright eyes watching him closely.

"You're...you're beautiful," he whispered. "Can I...can I touch you?" When the head rose and fell again, her eyes closed and a tear slid down each of her scaled cheeks.

The Guide reached a careful hand out to lay it on her long sinewed neck. He stroked the smooth scales slowly, delighting in the sensation as much as the moment. Her eyes were still closed, but tears flowed freely down her cheeks as he touched her jaw lightly with the other hand.

"You're breathtaking," he murmured, seeing her serpentine lips curl into a slight smile. It exposed more of her long pointed canines.

"I thought you were the most beautiful girl in the world from the moment I laid eyes on you," he whispered, stroking her shoulders lovingly, lightly. "But this..." he wrapped his robed arms around her thick scaled neck where it met her shoulders, laying his face against her smooth cool skin. "...you are amazing."

Then she changed, right there in his arms, and her young naked body clung to his through his robe. She put her face to his chest and cried happily, looking up at him time and again, her eyes wide and vulnerable. They swam beautifully with red and black and blue, shifting from her dragon eyes to her normal eyes and back again with compelling fluidity. He held her, arms around her shoulders while hers tightly encircled his waist.

They both felt his very human reaction at the same time, and she started giggling through her tears. "Let's go to my chambers," she said, her voice thick with happy emotion. She stepped away reluctantly and stood in front of him for a moment, nude in the sparing light. This time he didn't look away, because she didn't want him to. Her body was perfect, thin and smooth and shapely just as he had imagined, light pink nipples and blonde tuft of a landing strip just as he had hoped. He smiled. Just as he had told her. He felt himself flush, happy and guilty.

Jessica slipped quickly into her pajamas again, pointing at something on the floor near Kris. "Would you hand me that?"

He recognized it as he picked it up. "Your toe ring," he smiled. "I've never seen you not wearing it. When I could see your toes."

"It helps me maintain this form without having to think about it," she said, kneeling to slip the simple silver band onto her toe. "You know, like Uncle Roche with his hat."

The girl held her hand out to him, palm up. Kris put his hand around hers and let her lead him to the door in the back of the shop. As they approached, they could hear muffled voices on the other side of the door. Without hesitation, Jessica reached out and turned the knob, pushing the door inward.

When he heard the next words, they were clear and the voice recognizable.

"Where the hell is Kris?" he heard Paul ask.

The Guide stepped into the room quietly. "I'm right here," he said.

Paul whirled and grinned. "You're alright." His eyes fell on Jessica and the smile was gone. "What's going on?"

Roche was there with him, and so was another man Kris didn't recognize. The Guide shrugged, noncommittal. "You tell me." He still held Jessica's hand, and he felt her edge closer.

"I'm Marcus," the stranger said, stepping forward and extending his hand. The Guide released Jessica's hand to step forward and shake, and the man said, "Kris, Jessica, a pleasure. Please excuse me, I was just leaving."

Marcus turned to Paul, putting his back to the Guide and the girl. "You should see the Council soon," he advised. "I am on my way there now. Would you like me to pass on any messages?"

The Guide could see his friend's face, and he was surprised to see it twist into an angry mask of rebellion. "Yes," Paul said firmly, fiercely. "Tell them the Walker King will be organizing the Walkers and allowing them to communicate and assist each other in their duties. Tell them I have over fifty keys to find Walkers for, and that I am going to find them. I am going to change the way things are done in the Walker world, and once I decide just what I'm going to do I will let them know how they can facilitate my reign."

"Tell them," he growled, "that if they send anyone after me, angel or devil, I will kill first and ask questions later. I expect them to have found and punished any angels involved in the death of over fifty Walkers, thousands of devils and nearly an Original Angel and Demon. If they have not been found or punished to my satisfaction, I will find them. I will avenge every one of my brother's deaths a thousand times over, I will chase those bastard souls to Hell. Tell them that."

His back still to Kris, Marcus shrugged out of his overcoat. "Is that all?" His voice was calm and formal, cool in the heat of Paul's anger.

"For them," Paul nodded. He still looked angry. "Now you tell me where the angel is."

With one hand, Marcus held out his duster to Paul. With the other, he removed his hat and set it on the table next to him. Paul took the overcoat, anger turned confusion on his face.

"What's this?" he demanded.

The Guide watched Marcus shrug his shoulders, heard his emotionless voice reply. "It's grown too heavy. Until next time, Stone Walker."

And then he was gone. No flash of light, no fancy fireworks, just an empty space where he had just stood.

"Well, sonofabitch," Paul swore. He turned to Roche. "Answers, demon. Now!" He slammed his fist on the table.

The devil smiled wanly and shook his head. "Another time. It's been a long day. We all need rest." He bared his teeth a little then, a reminder that he was not to be trifled with.

Paul turned to Kris, a frown still creasing his brow. "Let's go home, Kris," he said stiffly. The Guide felt Jessica's hand in his again, clasping firmly and almost possessively. He squeezed her hand gently.

"No," Kris shook his head. "I'm staying here with Jess." He nodded at the devil. "If it's okay with Uncle Roche," he added.

The devil grimaced, but this time he did so playfully. "As long as you don't call me that. I've been telling the girl to talk to you since you died. I think you'll make the cutest couple. Of course you have my blessing." They blushed shyly and smiled together.

"As for you," Roche turned to Paul, all gruff business again. "You got room in your pocket for a few more keys?" He held up a keyring. "It's your lucky day, Walker. You saved the Walker world, you became King of the Walkers, you killed the last of the Wicked Walkers and best of all..." the devil grinned suddenly, baring his wicked sharp canines. "...tomorrow is payday!"

The Walker hesitated, then shrugged and took the keys. Gathering the duster and hat Marcus had left in his arms, he regarded each of them in turn with cold curiosity.

And then he disappeared.

CHAPTER 39

Paul didn't go home right away, materializing instead in the park that was his only battle site on Earth. It was dark and still, his Walker eyes seeing the world in shades of luminous moonlight. All he had to do was focus on a shadow, no matter how dark or distant, and his supernatural eyes revealed its depths to him.

Now was not the time to focus on the darkness all around, if ever there was one. He felt as though he was still covered in layers of Walker and devil blood, no matter how intensely he thought his armor clean and spotless and new. Walking the trail slowly, he let his thoughts churn noisily in his mind. He would walk all night if he had to; he would not bring this foul mood to bed with Brenna.

There was a part of his mind that never stopped thinking about her, that always reached for her mentally with a sweet combination of love and need. He had felt that throughout his interminable day, had reached inside for that solid ground to survive in that world where days passed in minutes or to die with dignity and real love in him. When the Walkers had knelt before him one by one, she had come into his mind again and again. He wanted her by his side, either supporting and encouraging as his queen or just running off together and living the typical fringe dwelling Walker's life in their bubble of bliss.

Suddenly it was obvious to him, and he stopped in his tracks to smile peacefully at his own thoughts. Turning, he walked quickly back the way he had come, resolved. He would tell her. He would tell her everything, then he would show her to prove he wasn't crazy. Maybe kill a demon or take her to Heaven for a little vacation. They could spend a week there and not even be missed but for a few minutes.

Walking was suddenly too slow for the Walker. He would tell her in the morning; his rush was to hold her, to smell her, to breathe in his sweet love knowing everything was going to be all right. Everything was going to be all right because they were going to come first, always, like before. There would be no more secrets.

With a thought he was standing outside the bedroom door, disappearing his outfit to enter the room naked and soundless. It was dark, shadows shades of moonlight describing the flowing lines of her seductive slumber. Sliding under the sheet silently, he came up behind her to press his chest against her back. Her body relaxed into his with a sigh as his arm lay across her evenly rising and falling ribcage. The taut fleshy curve of her ass ground almost forcefully into him for a moment as she came closer in her sleep.

Tracing the slight curve of her belly, he let his fingers curl around her breast lightly. He held the handful of firm softness a long moment, then flattened his hand against her chest to feel her beating heart beneath. Funny, usually he tangled his fingers in her necklace when he did that. Paul let his light touch drift to her neck, curious.

Her necklace was gone. Paul had never seen her without the gemstone secured about her neck, and it wasn't there. In the same moment he encircled his hand around her throat and realized the amulet was missing, a different smell wove its way into the complexity of Brenna's earthy seductive scent.

Brimstone, he thought, then wondered how he could know what brimstone might smell like.

Brenna turned in his arms, eyes wide and black on scarlet. She hissed, baring long canines as she stretched the crimson skin around her lips into a savage snarl. There was fury in her eyes and a long curved dagger in her hand. Paul rolled away to stand naked next to the bed, gaping at her.

"Brenna?" he said, dumbfounded.

She perched on the mattress, nude and beautiful and coiled to strike. "Walker," she hissed hatefully, Brenna's voice gone to hell; then she sprung at him, the long sharp blade flashing in the moonlight.

Dear Reader,

You deserve an apology. Cliffhangers can annoy me as much as anyone; however, I do have both an explanation and some good news when it comes to this one.

This is not a short story, as you may have guessed. Even picking up here in the modern day like we did, a lot of worlds and even more lives were touched by this particular series of events. Now that you have gotten to know some of the key players, it's time for everything to take a bit of a turn.

From the beginning, this was planned out as a trilogy. I had to pick a good stopping point for the first book, and it made the most sense to end it on this dramatic shift. Back then, I had to assure readers I was working diligently on the next one, and would get to the final book immediately after that. Now, I can tell you something way better.

First of all, the whole trilogy is complete. The story picks up right where we left off here in 'Rise of the Walker King', with a fresh perspective and a promise of continuity. The series then comes to a satisfying and epic conclusion in 'Fall of the Walker King'.

I hope you loved reading this book as much as I loved writing it, and that you continue on with the next two books in the trilogy. After that, you might want to know a little more about some of these characters…and if you do, I'll have some good news for you then as well.

Meanwhile, please take a few minutes to check me out at jaynorry.com so we might get to know each other a little better. I write books about the deeper meaning, in many genres; and I post blogs and short stories from time to time as well. While you're there, you can sign up for 'The Secret Society of Deeper Meaning' to get updates from me and special offers for members only.

You never did get that apology, did you?

Sorry about that.

Thanks for reading!

All the best,
Jay